TIME & TIDE

After the death of her mother in 1813 seventeen-year-old Anna Mason assumes many of her mother's tasks in running the household of Hawkshead Manor. Jonathan Wetherby, a business colleague of her father's, is entranced by Anna but she doesn't feel she is able to return his affections while her father remains so devastated by his wife's death. However, whilst Anna's father, John Mason, is an outwardly respectable merchant in Whitby, he is also the brains behind a leading smuggling operation in the district, a fact which may have serious repercussions for Anna's future when she stumbles on the truth.

TIME & TIDE

TIME & TIDE

by

Jessica Blair

Magna Large Print Books
Long Preston, North Yorkshire,
BD23 4ND, England.

British Library Cataloguing in Publication Data.

Blair, Jessica
    Time & tide.

        A catalogue record of this book is
        available from the British Library

        ISBN   0-7505-2027-2

First published in Great Britain 2002
by Judy Piatkus (Publishers) Ltd.

Cover illustration © Angelo Rinaldi by arrangement with
Artist Partners

The moral right of the author has been asserted

Published in Large Print 2003 by arrangement with
Piatkus Books Ltd.

Magna Large Print is an imprint of Library Magna Books Ltd.

Printed and bound in Great Britain by
T.J. (International) Ltd., Cornwall, PL28 8RW

All the characters in this book are fictitious and any resemblance to real persons, living or dead, is purely coincidental.

For

the one who inspired me,

and
for

all my readers

Acknowledgements

I am grateful to my twin daughters Geraldine and Judith for reading my manuscript with a critical eye and for their suggestions for the development of the story.

I thank my grandson, Dominic Hudson, for sailing information.

As always I must thank my editor Lynn Curtis whose expertise is ever appreciated.

My thanks also go to everyone at my publisher, Piatkus Books, for their continued support.

Visit the Jessica Blair website at: www.jessica-blair.co.uk

Prologue

Anna sat by the open glass doors that led to the balcony on the south side of her turret bedroom. The cool breeze was refreshing after the heat of the day, caressing the trees with a lover's touch. The plantations around the house were suffused with the late-evening light which brought out the subtle differences between greens, painting a delicate tapestry of colour. They rustled, the wind drawing the changing notes of God's music from them. This was His world, only His sounds drifted across the peaceful valley, no man marred its tranquillity.

But Anna knew there were other times when the peace of this old house was cruelly disturbed. At such times the wind howled in fury and the forces of nature, wind and rain as allies, pounded the trees and bent them with a lashing force as if to tear them from the ground. The trees groaned in torment and creaked with an unearthly note foreign to this valley. At such times the house tried to hide itself from view, clouds and mist sweeping down the hillside to shroud it.

Furies had stalked this house, but now Anna sat transfixed by its beauty and peace, far from the madness she had known here and which she hoped would be laid to rest once and for all within the next hour.

He would come. Nothing was more certain.

Then the last act, the exorcism, would be played out and the house and she would be free from the turbulent past, released from its uncertainties and ready to face their future. Her investigations and planning, since that fateful day had led her into realms she would never have thought possible. Now she awaited their fruition.

She laid her head against the chairback and closed her eyes. She listened, and in her mind the sound of breaking waves mingled with the sighing wind, and the sounds stirred her memory.

Chapter One

The insistent thrumming of a horse's hooves brought Anna's head up sharply from the 'The Lady of the Lake'. She was sitting on the window-seat of her bedroom in Hawkshead Manor. The urgency of the sound sent a shiver of foreboding down her spine, blighted the bright sunshine of this almost perfect day in the summer of 1813.

She looked out of the open window oblivious to the well-kept lawns that sloped gently away from the house to the valley below where oak, Scots pine, beech, ash and larch clothed the landscape. The view that usually soothed and reassured her did nothing to quell her mounting sense of unease today.

Anna focused on the rider who was bent on reaching the Manor as quickly as possible. Jack Crane, the undergroom! He had accompanied her mother on her morning ride. Though Elizabeth Mason was a competent rider, her husband John always insisted that one of the grooms accompany her in case of accident. Anna knew her mother considered this to be namby-pamby but she made no objection nor criticism of her husband's concern, for she knew it arose from his deep love for her. Now Jack was returning alone!

For a moment Anna sat transfixed, too stunned to contemplate why Jack was unaccompanied.

15

Then she leaped from the window-seat, cast her book to one side and ran from the room. She was along the landing in a flash and raced down the stairs as fast as she had ever done in all her seventeen years. The black and white chequer-board of the marble floor was a mere blur beneath her flying feet in her haste to reach the front door. She flung it open and ran into the sun-filled air, feeling no joy in it today. Her steps faltered as she stood undecided what to do next.

'Father!'

How he came to be there she never did find out. Had he too felt alarm on hearing the rapidly approaching horse or had word come to him after an observant servant had recognised the rider? The queries remained unspoken. It didn't matter. He was there and Anna felt some consolation in his presence. But she sensed his inner tension as his arm came round her shoulders seeking comfort as much as giving it to a seventeen year old facing imminent tragedy.

She heard footsteps behind them and knew, without turning, that they belonged to Charles, her brother, two years older than herself. He came to stand beside his father.

Anxiety heightened in the little group when they saw the rider's face drawn tight, not only by the exertion of the ride but also by the news he reluctantly carried.

He pulled the panting horse to a halt at the foot of the terrace steps. 'It's the mistress, sir,' he gasped. 'She's been thrown.'

John Mason's immediate question, one he did not want to voice in front of his children, was in

16

his eyes. He knew Jack had read it correctly when an almost imperceptible nod came in return. It struck him like a blow from a heavy hammer. He felt numb yet his mind roared, pleading for this not to be true. Although he felt frozen in this moment when happiness became a stranger, he was already bursting into action.

'Get me a horse, quick!' he called to Jack who was already anticipating the order by turning his mount towards the stables. 'Wait here,' he said to Anna and Charles. 'I'll be back as soon as possible.'

'I'll come with you, Father.' Charles started towards the steps.

'No, stay with Anna!' John called over his shoulder as he ran from the terrace.

She moved closer to Charles and took his hand in hers, drawing strength from his touch. Later, that moment would remain vivid in her mind as the time when she left her girlhood behind and assumed the responsibilities that had been her mother's.

In a few minutes their father and the groom appeared, setting their horses to an urgent gallop. Anna and Charles watched them race across the countryside until they were lost to sight.

Silently, brother and sister leaned heavily on the stone balustrade, hardly daring to move, as if their remaining still would prevent the unthinkable happening.

The rumble of iron-shod wheels penetrated their shocked minds. A horse and trap appeared driven by the head groom. He had harnessed it quickly after being given the news. Moving clear

17

of the house, he put the horse into a brisk trot.

Anna glanced at her brother. 'Oh, Charles, is ...' There was no need to say any more. Her tear-dimmed eyes and the catch in her voice completed the question.

He moved closer to her and put a comforting arm around her shoulders. 'We can only wait,' he said with quiet resignation, and then added with an attempt at reassurance, 'It may not be as bad as we expect.'

Half an hour later the small cortège came into sight. Brother and sister stared at it anxiously. The trap, driven slowly, was followed by their father, his shoulders slumped, his head bowed. Jack had taken up the rear, slightly to one side of his master but in close attendance.

Anna and Charles had sensed from the aura around the small procession that their worst fears were realised. They came down the steps from the terrace as the trap stopped. Anna had been watching her father anxiously. She saw the pain of tremendous loss etched on his face. The impact of tragedy was there for all to see. Her heart went out to him. This should not be happening to a man of forty-three who had always brought joy in his wake. Now he swung from the saddle as if he was carrying a heavy load, his expression frozen in a mixture of disbelief and resigned acceptance of what had happened, knowing there was nothing he could do to reverse the tragedy. He should be swinging from his horse with all the gay abandon she had seen in him so many times, mischievous laughter on his face as he came to help his vivacious wife from her mount. Anna could almost see them coming up the steps, arms around each other, laughter on their lips and in their eyes, two people joyously in love and not embarrassed to let anyone see it.

Now her father moved ponderously from his horse. He seemed to see his children for the first time. Anna caught his expression and it brought tears streaming down her cheeks as she rushed to him. She flung herself at him, her arms encircling his waist as if she could impel comfort into a body racked with pain. His arms came round her but they carried none of the warmth that she knew so well. Then Charles was beside them, his arms round them both, trying to be strong for them all but knowing he was failing pitiably. They stood clinging together in their shattered world.

'I must see to things.' John's voice was scarcely above a whisper. He eased himself from them and they had to let him go. He went to the trap, stood there for a moment. The head groom and Jack were already waiting, their faces solemn. He nodded to them. They knew what they had to do. Slowly they eased their mistress's body from the trap and carried it with reverence up the steps and into the house. John and his children followed. Word had spread quickly through the house and Mrs Denston the housekeeper, Mrs Fenton the cook, three maids and two footmen, were standing at the foot of the stairs, their faces grave and tearful for they knew they had lost not only a charming and thoughtful employer but a friend as well.

The head groom and Jack laid the body

carefully on the bed and then retreated quietly, leaving the family alone.

Anna stared at her mother, hardly able to believe that she would not wake up, turn her head, smile and speak, for at this moment Elizabeth appeared to be in a tranquil sleep. There was no mark on her face, nothing to show that she had been fatally injured.

The three of them stood beside the bed, silent, each feeling a loss they had never expected. A world had collapsed around them, a world that but an hour ago was normal, filled with life, in which an unsullied future stretched before them. Now the atmosphere in this room was heavy with grief. A darkness had descended upon it in spite of the brightness of the day beyond the windows.

A bewildered Anna, standing between her father and brother, needed comfort. She let her hands slip slowly into theirs. For a moment there was no response, then she felt their fingers tighten on hers as if that would give her strength to understand what had happened. A few moments later she sensed a slight tremor in her father's hand. She glanced sideways at him, fearing something terrible was happening to him. She saw silent tears streaming down his face. She could never describe the shock she felt at that particular moment. Her father crying! She had never seen him do so. She had not thought it in his nature even though she knew him to be a sensitive man in many ways. The enormity of seeing a man of forty-three crying impinged on her mind with a force that made her heart go out to him, wanting to ease the pain he must be feeling. Her own seemed trivial in comparison.

Throughout her life she had witnessed the love that these two spirited people had shared, a love that had enveloped her and her brother in a cocoon of reassurance and safety, one that had spilled beyond the immediacy of their own needs to be shared with others too. Now so much had gone with that silent figure on the bed. Tears came to Anna's eyes and flowed down her cheeks. No sobs racked her body and in that there was all the more torture, for the depths of her feelings were all confined to silent suffering. Concern for Charles caused her to steal a glance at him. Through blurred eyes she saw that he shed no outward tears but from his grim, shocked look of incomprehension she knew he cried inwardly for the mother they had both adored.

Elizabeth had brought light and laughter to Hawkshead Manor. Her marriage in 1793 to the eligible twenty-three-year-old John Mason when she was twenty-one had been the wedding of the year in Whitby. How others had envied her the young man who had inherited his father's merchant business at twenty-one, who was handsome with sparkling blue eyes that missed nothing, could tease and be serious, and whose tall figure was slim and athletic. He had a sharp mind that was matched by hers and together they had built on the goodwill and enterprise the elder Mason had created. They had expanded and taken a second ship to trade with the Continent. Anna knew how much her mother was involved in the business and ready with advice, even though she kept in the background. She knew her father had counted himself more than lucky to have married such a clever woman but also one who made any man's head turn, for Elizabeth was regarded as a beauty in Whitby and the surrounding area. Anna had heard people say that it was a match made in heaven and as she grew older hoped that one day people would say that about her own marriage, when and wherever it happened.

But now what did the future hold? How would her father cope without his beloved Elizabeth? Overwhelmed by his tears, sensing the devastation he was feeling and seeing the slump in his body, she knew he faced a bleak future sunk in the darkness of utter and irredeemable loss.

Anna's eyes were fixed on the face as pale as the pillow on which it lay. Her tears stopped. They would flow again she had no doubt but not at the moment. It was as if her mother had told her she would always be there for her and that she wanted her to be strong in order to fulfil a new role, for the sake of her father. Anna felt a strength she did not know she had. She hoped it would be with her through the trying months ahead.

High on the cliff at Whitby, where a gentle summer breeze played with the grasses, Elizabeth was laid to rest. Her grave lay amongst those of sailors who had perished when the sea had raised itself in anger. The old parish church was full to overflowing. The sorrowful atmosphere at the graveside had filled the vistas of land, sea and sky as people watched the coffin lowered into the ground and then expressed their sympathy to John and his children as they left them to their final grief at the edge of the open grave.

The carriage came to a halt in front of the main entrance to Hawkshead Manor. The old house seemed to hold a sorrow of its own at the loss of the spirited woman who had once walked its corridors and filled its rooms with life. At the same time it seemed to Anna that it wanted to help, to ease the pain of the man, his son and daughter who had been at one with the lady it had lost. Anna resolved that she must gain the assistance of the house that had so much character of its own and had returned the love John and Elizabeth had given it. Anna felt she had gained an ally and with it came renewed confidence to face the future.

The door of the carriage was opened by a groom and Charles stepped to the ground. He turned to help his sister and then they both stood to await their father. He moved wearily out of the carriage, his eyes cast down. He did not speak. His movements were slow and heavy as he climbed the four steps on to the flagged terrace that stretched the full length of the house. Anna and Charles followed.

The glass door was opened by one of the maids who had stayed behind so that they would be in attendance when the master returned. They took his coat and those of Charles and Anna and informed them that some refreshments had been put in the dining room though they knew little would be wanted as something had already been arranged for the mourners at the Angel Inn in Whitby. That interlude had been a trial for Anna and Charles for they had seen how much their father was suffering, having to receive so many sympathetic words and glowing tributes to his wife. Thankfully they would now have a quiet time to themselves.

John sighed the deep sorrowful sigh of one bowing to the inevitable. He started towards his study.

'Some refreshments, Father?' said Charles.

He shook his head but did not utter a word.

'You should have something,' Anna pleaded. 'You had nothing at the Angel.'

He did not reply, but opened the door to the study, stepped inside and closed it behind him.

She started after him but Charles laid a restraining hand on her arm. 'Not now,' he said. 'Let him have some time to himself.'

'But...' Anna started to protest, her face showing deep concern for her father.

'He's grieving, Anna. Let him alone,' her brother advised.

'But I'm worried for him. Will he ever get over this loss?'

'He must. He still has a life to live. It will be hard but he has us and we must do all we can to help ease the pain for him.'

Anna nodded. She knew Charles was right, but that it would not be easy for either of them. They had their own suffering to deal with.

Charles took her by the elbow to the dining room. 'Something to eat applies to you as well.'

They found a tray of cold ham, pickles and bread arranged at one end of the long oak dining table. As she took the first mouthful Anna realised how hungry she was. The rigours of the funeral must have held her hunger at bay but now the past had gone and the present imposed itself. Surely her father must be feeling the same? He had had nothing at breakfast and had refused every offering at the Angel. She must see that he had something before long.

When they had finished their meal Charles bowed to her suggestion that they take something to John. She put some ham and bread on a plate and they went to the study.

They found him slumped in his chair behind his large mahogany desk, staring vacantly at its surface. He did not look up when they entered the room and made no acknowledgement when they placed the tray in front of him.

'Father,' Anna said quietly, 'do try and eat something.'

He shook his head. His eyes were lifeless. Anna was horrified by what had replaced the lively brightness she had always known. 'Please try.' Her plea carried the tone she had used as a child, one which always melted her father's heart so that he never refused her wish. But now there was no reaction. She glanced at her brother, seeking help.

Charles stepped beside his father and rested his hand on his shoulder. 'Do try.'

John shook his head.

'You should.'

'I'm not hungry.'

'Very well,' put in Anna quickly. At the same time she signalled to Charles that they should go. 'We'll leave it here in case you feel like having something later.' She turned for the door and was followed by Charles.

'I don't think he'll touch it,' he said as the door closed behind them.

'I know,' replied Anna. 'But we made progress in there.'

'Progress?' Charles was puzzled.

'Yes. Don't you realise that, apart from the brief words he used when he accepted condolences, those were the first words he has spoken all day. In fact, they were the first words he has spoken to us since...'

'You're right.' Charles's doubtful expression lightened when he realised the truth of her words.

'So it's a start. Hopefully we can build on it. In fact, we must.'

'From his attitude at the moment it will be hard.'

'I know. Mother is lost to us too.' A catch came to her voice. 'But she wants us to rise above it and take care of Father. We must, for her sake. I'll go and see Mrs Denston and together we'll have a word with Mrs Fenton to plan something tempting for Father at the evening meal.'

Charles watched his sister walk away. She seemed so much more grown-up. A new maturity had come over her from the moment her mother's body had been laid on the bed. Though he had taken care of the funeral arrangements to relieve his father of the disagreeable task, he had found reassurance in having a sister to consult, one who was ready with suggestions. A new role had been thrust upon her and she was not one to shirk responsibilities. Charles was thankful for the new woman who had emerged from the tragedy without the loss of the younger sister he loved.

Anna left the domestic quarters half an hour later satisfied with her interview with Mrs Denston. The kindly lady whom she had known since she was six had always run the household with understated efficiency that held the respect of the other staff and had, with the minimum of consultation, left her employer free to devote herself to helping her husband's mercantile business. Anna had indicated that she wanted Mrs Denston to carry on with her duties as she had always done and said she hoped they could work together as amiably as the housekeeper and her mother had.

Mrs Denston's attitude had been reassuring, for over the years she had come to regard the generous Mason family as her own. She had watched this girl grow towards a fine young woman and had seen in her in the last week a full blossoming that she admired. She knew that Anna, though her heart would be hurting for many a day yet, would cope with the new responsibility that had come to her early in life.

Anna crossed the hall towards the stairs. She paused and glanced at the study door. She felt a welter of feelings for her father. She wanted to run to him and cry with him but, knowing that would only add to his misery, ran quickly up the stairs to her own room where she flung herself on the bed and let the tears of exorcism flow. As they subsided, she started in surprise. She twisted over, eyes wide, ears alert. A voice? Her mother's? It couldn't have been. Just the sighing of the wind, surely.

Again?

'Don't weep for me. Don't weep for yourself. Live your life.'

'Mother?'

Anna sat up in bed. Her eyes looked round quickly, searching but knowing no tangible form would fit the voice whose words and meaning were clear in her mind.

It was seven o'clock in the evening when Charles tentatively pushed open the door of his father's study. He found John still seated in his chair, still staring at the desk in front of him.

Charles's heart was heavy. His own mourning had been spent sitting on the terrace looking out across the lawns that fell away to the natural beauty of the valley his mother had loved so much. He knew he would always find communion with her there, a place where nature's sounds enhanced its appeal and the distant murmur of the sea sent out a special call of its own. He remembered how he used to admire the way she handled a horse and the patience she had had when she was teaching him and Anna to ride. Such a skilful horsewoman – how had she come to be killed doing something she loved? He had thrust the question from his mind and allowed the vision of a beautiful lady with laughter on her lips to replace it. That was how he wanted to remember her.

Now he wished his father could do the same.

'Father, our meal is ready,' he said as he crossed the floor.

His father did not seem to hear him. Charles was filled with anxiety. What could he do? 'Father?'

He looked up at his son and nodded.

Charles's heart raced. A response. He must handle this carefully. 'The meal is ready.'

'Very well.' John stood up somewhat reluctantly, but, though he wanted to be left alone in his study, deep down he knew that it would hurt his son and daughter if he did not respond to their solicitude. He straightened his coat, and stepped from behind his desk.

'Hello, Father.' Anna's effort at brightness belied the anxiety she'd felt when he and Charles entered the dining room. Her hopes that her father had thrown off some of the demons that she knew must have haunted his mind ever since her mother's accident were dashed when she saw his drawn, solemn face. It bore no resemblance to the man who but seven days ago took life with joy and exuberance, viewing each day as a new adventure to be shared with his beloved Elizabeth.

She shot her brother a questioning glance and received in return a grimace that told her he saw no change in his father though his appearance in the dining room might be taken as a step forward.

29

That it was not soon became obvious. John merely picked at his food and stared most of the time at his plate with unseeing eyes. Anna's and Charles's attempts at promoting some sort of conversation were met with silence. It seemed he did not hear their words. Halfway through the meal he laid his napkin on the table, stood up and left without speaking.

Concern was etched on Anna's face and her eyes filled with pity. She shot a cry for help at her brother and received a look which said, 'Say nothing. Let him go.' The silence that hung between them charged the room with helplessness until they heard the door of their father's study close.

'Charles, what can we do?' Anna's plea came from the heart.

'I don't know,' he replied with a sad shake of his head. 'I wish I did.'

'We can't go on like this. He's spending all his time in the study. He leaves most of the meals that Mrs Denston sees are taken there untouched. I thought we had achieved something when you got him to come to the dining room this evening, but you saw what happened.'

'I was hopeful too. Something will have to be done. There's the business to see to also.'

'Has he never mentioned it?'

'No.'

'Thank goodness he took you into it when you were seventeen.'

'Yes, I can help run it, though Gideon Wells is a capable manager and after fifteen years with father knows our affairs inside out. He can't make deals, though. Father always did that. There are some contracts coming up for renewal in three weeks and I don't know whether he will want to renew them. He must get back to work.'

'Then we will tackle him about it. But first we must find the right time to do so.'

That opportunity did not come for two weeks. In the intervening days an air of depression hung over Hawkshead Manor. John Mason spent most of his time in his study. He rarely came out, and meals taken there were merely picked at. He never ventured to the dining room again though each mealtime Charles came to fetch him. Brother and sister dined alone.

Each day Charles's concern for Anna grew as he saw the weight of the situation begin to take its toll on her. Her healthy colour was disappearing for she wouldn't leave the house in case her father suddenly needed her. Night only brought a heightening of her worry. Her father would waste away physically and mentally if something was not done. Those thoughts brought tears. If he wasn't aware of his own needs, wasn't he at least solicitous of hers? She had lost a mother with whom she was close. Now more than ever she needed a parent's love and support to mend a broken heart. She could not go on like this much longer.

Charles did get a break from the heavy atmosphere when he went to Whitby about business matters, but that also brought problems as the day for renegotiating several contracts grew nearer.

He came home late one afternoon to find Anna desperate and determined. He could tell something was wrong the moment he came in the front door for she appeared immediately and hurried across the hall to him. 'Charles, a word. Now!' she said in a voice that would brook no refusal. She led the way to the drawing room.

She swung round to face him as soon as he had closed the door. He saw her agitation bordered on anger. He had never seen his good-natured sister like this. 'What's wrong?' he asked.

'We've got to do something about Father,' she said with such force that he knew there had been trouble.

'What's happened?' he asked in a calming tone.

'Mrs Denston tells me that Father has become insulting to the maids who take his meals to the study. They go to a lot of trouble, do it quietly, and now he is telling them to make less noise, and that if they don't they can leave. Apparently he rails at them in foul language if they offer to draw back the curtains. They have been complaining to Mrs Denston who has tried to keep things on an even keel but today the maids said they would all leave. They used to be happy here but now... If they do go we'll get no one else. Word will soon get around about their reason for leaving. Desperate times need desperate measures. I'm going to tackle him, but I want your support, Charles.'

'You have it.'

'Right. Come on.'

She flung open the door of her father's study, breaking the habit of a lifetime – she did not knock first. Without altering her pace, without a glance at her father, she stormed across the room and drew back the curtains with a vigorous swish.

'Do the others, Charles!' she ordered tersely.

He was already on his way to another window.

Light flooded into the room.

Anna swung round to see her father sitting behind his desk. Papers he had been flicking through by the light of an oil lamp were strewn across his desk and littering the floor.

'Open a window and get the smell of this lamp out of here,' she called to her brother. She went to the desk and blew the lamp out. 'This has got to stop. Father. We cannot go on like this.' As much as the sight of the broken man disturbed her she was determined not to hold back and summoned all her resolve to go on. She stood firmly before him. Her heart was full of pity. The man she'd once idolised had vanished in the space of a few weeks. But somewhere beneath that drawn, pale face and haggard look she believed the person who'd once filled the house with joy and laughter was still there. That person needed rescuing. She had entered the room full of resolution to do that even though she knew it might be a formidable task. But she took heart from what she saw might be a chink in the armour he had drawn around himself. Though his hair was long he was clean-shaven. There must be a little pride left for him to accomplish that task on the occasions he briefly left his room.

His sunken eyes moved to meet her gaze. She wanted to rush round the desk and take him into the comfort of her arms, but knew that was not the way.

'We can't go on like this,' she repeated firmly. 'There are other people living in this house who have lives to lead. They cannot have them wrecked by your stubborn and inconsiderate attitude. You cannot shut yourself away from life. All of us – Charles, me, Mrs Denston, Mrs Fenton, all the servants – feel the loss of Mother deeply, but we have to go on. So have you. Death is a part of life, we cannot alter that. No matter what we do, or how we mourn, we cannot bring Mother back.' Even though she was hurting him, she lashed out these last words. She saw him flinch. It made her pause.

Charles seized the moment to take up the initiative his sister had gained. 'Life does not stop because you have lost a wife and we a mother. There are things to be done, Father, things that need your attention.'

'You and Gideon Wells are quite capable.' John's words came weakly, as if he did not want to be bothered with speaking.

'Father, Charles needs you. So do I.' Anna took up the initiative again. 'The household will disintegrate because of what you are doing. The maids are threatening to leave. They say it is not the happy place it once was.'

'How can it be?' her father snapped.

'I've tried my best but even though you spend all your time in this room it is creating an atmosphere throughout the house. Your discourtesies to the servants are worsening. That must stop. This house must return to a normal routine.'

'How can it?'

'By all of us, including you, making an effort. I know it can never be exactly the same but we are doing a disservice to Mother's memory if we don't try. The atmosphere you are creating is destroying it. I don't want that to happen. I won't let that happen.'

A catch came to Anna's voice. Tears streamed down her face. She turned and hurried from the room.

Charles shot a quick look at his father but could gain no impression of his reaction. He hurried after his sister. When he came into the hall he saw her leaning against the rail at the bottom of the stairs. He crossed quickly to her and put his arms round her sagging shoulders.

She turned to him, thankful of the support and comfort. 'Oh, Charles, did I say too much? Did I hurt him?'

'No. What you said was right. It must be making him think. All we can do is wait.'

Charles was already in the dining room when Anna came in for dinner that night. She had hoped that her father might be there and felt an almost overwhelming surge of disappointment when he was not.

'It appears we weren't successful,' she commented wearily as she sat down.

'Don't give up hope,' replied Charles, patting her hand comfortingly.

'If we can't drag him out of his apathy, I don't know what we will do.'

'Give him time to consider what you said.

Remember the shock he received at losing Mother.'

'Didn't we all?'

'I know, but it would be different for him, in a way we cannot understand.'

Mrs Denston accompanied the maid who brought in the soup. 'I'm sorry to intrude, miss, but I thought you should know that I have spoken again with the servants. None of them really wants to leave and they have agreed to do nothing for another week.'

'Thank you, Mrs Denston. I am grateful for what you have done. Both Charles and I...' She stopped and stared in the direction of the door which was opening.

Her father walked in slowly with an apologetic air, as if intruding where he thought he should not. He stopped. No one spoke then he said quietly, 'Mrs Denston, please see that a place at table is set for me.'

'Yes, sir.' Her delight at his request was obvious. She gave Anna a reassuring smile and hurried away.

As the door closed behind the housekeeper, Anna and Charles jumped to their feet and rushed to their father. Anna flung her arms round him and Charles grasped him by the hand.

'Welcome back, Father.'

'I love you dearly,' cried Anna. 'I'm sorry if I said anything to hurt you.'

John smiled wanly. 'You made me think. Let's sit down.'

A maid came in and quickly set a place for him at the table. She was followed by another with some soup.

Not a word was spoken. Anna and Charles were pleased to see that their father had discarded his rumpled suit and dirty shirt, and that he had tidied his hair. Anna felt that her words must have had some effect.

As he laid down his spoon, John said, 'I am sorry for the disruption I have caused.'

'Don't apologise, Father, it was the result of shock,' said Charles.

'That's as may be but I have hurt you both and I don't want that, so this is what I propose. Charles, you run the business along with Gideon. We'll talk about that in my study later. You, Anna, will run this house and do whatever you like with your time. But leave me to myself. If I want to live with my memories of your mother, then that is my affair and mine alone. Not yours, nor Charles's, nor anyone else's. I will not receive people. I will not visit. The memories of any associations I shared with your mother would be too painful.'

'But you cannot cut yourself off from the world,' protested Anna.

'I can and I will if I desire it. That does not preclude your inviting people to the house but you will let me know first so that I can retreat to my room. Oh, and no parties.'

'In other words, you want to be a recluse in your own home even though there will be other people around?'

He nodded. 'That just about sums it up.'

Objections sprang to Anna's lips but she saw a warning light in her brother's eyes – make no fuss, we have progressed to here and this situation is far better than the one we had.

'Very well, if that's the way you want it,' she agreed meekly.

'It is.' John glanced at his son.

'Very well, Father.'

'Good. We have an understanding. You and I will talk about the business in my study after dinner.'

Chapter Two

John settled himself in his chair while his son took one on the opposite side of the desk.

Charles was pleased to see that, during the course of the meal, Mrs Denston had organised a quick cleaning and tidying of the study, something she had been unable to do during her employer's self-incarceration. The smell of polish hung in the air.

His father made no comment but plunged into the matter he had mentioned at table. 'As I said, Charles, you will take over the running of the business.'

Though his voice was firm so that there would be no misunderstanding the implication, Charles saw no light of enthusiasm for the topic in his eyes. Whenever discussions about trading had arisen before this John Mason had been eager and involved. Now that was missing. It was if he had lost any personal interest in the business.

Charles felt he must try to counteract that. His father must have something to occupy his mind, to prevent him dwelling too much on his loss. 'I thank you for your trust, but do you think I'm experienced enough to take on such a huge responsibility?'

'No one ever has enough experience or knows sufficient. We learn all the time. You are capable of doing so. You have a sharp mind and learn quickly. You'll manage well enough with Gideon beside you. He knows the business inside out, having been with me for fifteen years, but he would never presume to instigate new deals. He would not relish the responsibility in case they went wrong, but he'll see that they are carried out efficiently and to the firm's advantage. So it will be up to you to negotiate new business and renew existing contracts.'

'I thank you for your confidence. You know I will do my best.'

Charles was delighted that his father had shaken off his almost-overwhelming apathy this far at least. His voice was stronger and his brain obviously alert. Charles took these as encouraging signs. He saw in them hope that before long his father would resume a normal and full life and throw off the shackles of despair.

But that hope received an immediate setback when his father continued, 'I meant what I said. I want no part of it.'

'But what about the negotiations that will have to be completed soon?'

'I told you, you deal with them.'

'But I need to know...' Charles's protest was cut short by a sharp retort.

'You see to them. The business will be yours and Anna's one day so you may as well get used to it now. I have no interest in being consulted. I want to lead my life as I indicated.'

'But you can't cut yourself off.'

'I can and I will. I won't shut myself away as I was doing, Anna made me see that was wrong, but otherwise I will do what I said.'

'What about the smuggling? Do you want me to continue with that?'

'That is up to you. It brings in a sizeable income. We've built up some good connections. Local people look to us to provide cheaper goods and regard us as freetraders. We've got the ships and the cover of our legitimate trading, but you've still got to be wary of the law and there'll always be Preventive Men out to catch you. You've got a good lieutenant in Edwin Bennet. He knows what's required, where to recruit the right men when necessary, and is absolutely loyal. If you do decide to continue I must insist that, just as we kept our smuggling a secret from your mother and Anna, it must still be kept secret from your sister. She must never be placed in a compromising position through knowing of our illegal activities.'

'She'll hear nothing from me.' Charles paused and then added, 'I believe that you had some contacts on the Continent you never disclosed even to me.'

'I'll not do so now. Nothing was ever formalised. They could have been very dangerous and, for your part, are best forgotten. Concentrate on the connections you already have.'

'Very well. One other thing, Father. Your collection of art works – do you want me to look out for more items as you did whenever you were away on business?'

For a moment Charles noticed distress on his father's face and wished he had not brought the subject to his notice, but then he saw John master his immediate feelings.

'No, I shall not bother with that any more.'

'Don't lose your interest.' There was a touch of pleading in Charles's voice.

John gave a wan smile. 'There's no incentive now.' A catch came to his voice. 'I bought every piece for your mother. She loved them so much and I came to appreciate art through her. Now...' He spread his hands in a gesture of resignation.

'But you'll keep the collection?'

'Of course.'

'Good.' Charles was pleased. He hoped that one day the carved ivories, miniature paintings, exquisitely crafted silver necklaces, jewelled rings and pendants, illuminated manuscripts and caskets, would bring back happy memories instead of the hurt they were causing now.

'Have you any further questions?'

Charles thought for a moment and then said, 'I don't think so.'

'Then, we have an understanding?'

'If that is the way you want it.'

'It is.'

'So long as you also realise that if at any time you want to take back control, you must do so.'

'I don't think I will do that. I just want to be left in peace with my memories.'

When Charles related to Anna what had passed between him and their father regarding their legitimate business she listened carefully, hoping to find some clue as to how they should approach their altered lives.

'I would say, now he has got over the initial shock and apathy, he has come to terms with the situation,' said Charles in conclusion. 'You are the one who brought that about. Of course, life will never be the same for him but I think, in knowing that, he has chosen a path for himself and feels that he can manage that way. It's important we respect his decision and abide by his wishes.'

'Do you believe he'll show an interest in the business again one day?'

'I think there is every possibility. My only fear is that by spending so much time on his own, without contact with other people, he may brood too much and never look forward.'

'We can't force people on him.'

'That could prove fatal. We must guard against that even if we offend.'

'What worries me is how he is going to occupy his time, after so much of his life was taken up with the firm and his visits to the Continent?'

Charles gave a little shrug of his shoulders. 'I don't know. We'll have to keep alert to what he is doing, but I'm not going to be around here all the time now that I have the responsibility of the business.'

'You mustn't neglect that.' Anna gave him her understanding. 'I'll be here. I'll keep my eye on Father.'

'Mr Charles!' Gideon Wells jumped to his feet when the young man walked into the office of Mason and Son, Merchants, on Whitby's Church Street. Its position gave it a view of the quays on the opposite side of the road that stretched along the east bank of the River Esk. Relief showed in his eyes. 'I'm pleased to see you. How is your father?'

'Recovering, but slowly,' replied Charles as he sat down and indicated to Gideon to do the same. 'When he will return to work, I don't know. He says that he wants me to look after the business. With your invaluable help, of course.'

'You always have that, Mr Charles. Your father has been good to me since he gave me my first job. I'm glad you have come this morning because there are several contracts coming up for renewal, as you are probably aware.'

'Yes, I had them in mind but could not act before I knew what Father wanted to do.'

'Quite so, Mr Charles, quite so.' Gideon stood up and crossed the room to a plain chest. He was a tall slim man who wore his clothes well. His face was fine-boned with high cheekbones over which the skin was drawn tight. This gave him rather a pinched look but that was deceiving as all those who made his acquaintance were quick to realise. His eyes reflected good humour and friendliness and his voice was warm. His mind was sharp, too, as anyone who tried to outsmart him soon found. John Mason had been quick to recognise his valuable qualities and at the same time assessed Gideon as a man who would never try to usurp the responsibilities of his employer or superiors, though he was ready with advice when asked. He was ready now when he placed in front of Charles several sheets of paper that he had taken from a drawer.

Charles turned the sheets over one at a time, running his eyes quickly over each in turn. The nine pages referred to three contracts. He pursed his lips and nodded thoughtfully. 'All worth renewing,' he commented, after a moment's hesitation.

'Do I detect a little reluctance about one of them?' Gideon asked.

'The wine we ship for Harding's. I think we could charge more. He raised the price to his customers on the last shipment and will make a tidy extra profit. I think we should have some of that this time.'

'I think you're right,' Gideon agreed, but added a caution. 'You don't think he'll look elsewhere?'

Charles gave a little smile. 'Not him. He knows we make fast voyages and are willing to put in an extra one quickly if he requires it. He also knows we arrange our sailings so that we always have a ship available if required. I'll go to see him later. Has anything else happened while my father and I have been absent?'

'Nothing extraordinary,' came the reply. 'Sailings have been normal. The *Grace* made good time on her last voyage from Spain with a full cargo of wine and lace. Captain Wilson out-ran a French frigate. He handles his crew well. They all signed on again for her next voyage. She leaves tomorrow for Spain again, calling at London with farm produce and will pick up a cargo of cloth there.'

'Good. I'll pay the *Grace* and Captain Wilson a visit later today. What of the *Gull*?'

'Due in from the Baltic with timber tomorrow, all being well. Before she sailed Captain Morris indicated that he would retire after her next voyage.'

45

'Early retirement? I rather thought that might be the case with his wife not well. I'll have a word with him when the *Gull* docks. A good man. We'll be sorry to lose him. Have you any idea about a replacement?'

'I think there are several who would jump at the chance to serve your father. All of them are in employment at the moment but I believe when word gets around about Captain Morris, you won't be short of applicants.'

'Of those who would you select?'

'Captain Joseph Walford. He's an able man, though some say he's unbending and despatches heavy punishment if anyone crosses him.'

Charles nodded. He had heard of Captain Walford's reputation and also knew that Whitby sailors respected him because he was fair-minded and only punished if it was deserved. 'Would he take on the responsibility of finding a return cargo if necessary?'

'Aye, I believe he would.'

'Next time he's in port, arrange for him to see me.'

'I'll not forget.'

They continued to discuss the state of trading for a while. Though he made no comment Gideon admired Charles's grasp of the merchant trade. He had learned quickly and thoroughly from his father. As they talked he sensed that the circumstances had brought a new bond of understanding between them. He was pleased that Charles would include him in making any future decisions but relieved that the young man would take the ultimate responsibility. He had always got

46

on well with him and could recall the first day Mr Mason had brought his five-year-old son to the office. The boy had had a lively curiosity and from then on took every opportunity to accompany his father, for he loved to be amongst the activity on the quays and in the ships. Gideon had watched him grow through his school years into a well-built young man, six foot tall and with dark brown hair. His hazel eyes held a concentrated gaze that gave the impression that his attention was riveted on the person to whom he was speaking, but Gideon knew that was false and that even in the course of conversation or discussion the young man was fully aware of other people and all that was going on around him.

When Charles left the office he paused on the doorstep and cast his eyes over the bustling port that always set his pulse racing. True, he loved the peace of Hawkshead Manor but the heartbeat of Whitby along the banks of the river always enthralled him.

Dockers swarmed up and down the gangplanks of ships tied up at the quays along the east bank, loading and unloading the goods that brought economic prosperity to this Yorkshire port. Denied easy access to the hinterland, its highway was the sea. Because of this his father had made a fortune. Charles would see that the family continued to do so.

He crossed the road to reach the quayside, dodging horses and riders, trundling carts and the mêlée of those on foot. He paused a moment, listening to Whitby sounds: commands roared by overseers, mates cajoling sailors to greater efforts so that ships would be ready to sail on the evening tide, suggestions shouted to passing girls, chattering of friends and acquaintances, yelling of youngsters in chase, the creak of ropes, the groan of timbers, the lap of water, and over it all the screech of seagulls gliding lazily overhead, alert for any titbit to devour.

Charles breathed deeply, taking in the smell of rope, timber, smoke, fish, seaweed, and the salt brought in on the tide to mingle with the fresh water of the river between the cliffs that formed the backdrop to Whitby's red roofs.

This was the breath of life to him and he wanted to be a part of it and instrumental in the future growth of the port. To this end he was determined to use every ounce of the responsibility thrust upon him by his father.

He turned along Church Street in the direction of the *Grace* lying upstream. He did not rush, for after his absence from Whitby since the death of his mother he wanted to absorb its atmosphere again. He exchanged passing greetings with all manner of people pleased to see 'Young Mr Mason' among them again.

His gaze drifted over the ship, a stout vessel that had a purposeful air about her. She had been constructed on the other side of the river at the yards of the Fishburn family, renowned for the strength of their ships that plied their trade all over the world. Charles recalled the day his father had taken possession of his second vessel and named her Grace. Hard work, endeavour and a shrewd mind had brought him to this logical point of expansion.

Charles walked up the gangplank and was greeted by Captain Wilson who had been keeping a watchful eye on the loading of local produce bound for London. He was a broad, weather-beaten man with a dark moustache and trim beard just beginning to show tinges of grey. They hid a craggy, determined jaw but could not hide the resolution that emanated from his steel-blue eyes and the set of his body.

'Good day, Mr Charles. It's good to see you about again.'

'I'm delighted to be back among all this activity.'

'How is your father?'

'Recovering slowly though I fear it has hit him hard.'

'No doubt he'll be pleased to have his mind occupied with work again.'

'I don't know when you will see him in Whitby, or indeed in the office.'

Captain Wilson raised an eyebrow in surprise.

'In the meantime,' Charles continued, 'he has left me in charge, along with Gideon.'

'No doubt you'll cope, Mr Charles.' Captain Wilson's voice had the ring of certainty about it. Over the years he had seen Charles grow into a likeable young man with a sharp mind and a willingness to learn. He'd always thought that he would have liked a son like Charles, though he wouldn't exchange any of his four daughters.

'I mean to, Captain Wilson. I don't want to let my father down. Is everything in hand for tomor-row's sailing?'

'Aye, it is. A good crew.'

'Gideon tells me they all signed up again for this voyage.'

'Aye, they have that.' The captain gave a little smile. 'They know if they sign up with me they'll not come under the eye of the press gang. I'll stand no interference from that lot.'

Charles nodded his approval of the captain's attitude. 'Have a good voyage.' He knew there was no need to ask about the cargo the *Grace* would pick up in London. Captain Wilson would have that in hand and Gideon would have seen that the clerks had recorded it in one of their many ledgers. He started towards the gangplank with the captain's smile still wide and the words of reassurance spoken after him.

'We will that. Regards to your father.'

Charles left the ship satisfied that, in the absence of his father and himself, the trading business of Mason and Son, Merchants, had been in capable hands. Now he must verify the state of the other enterprise favoured by his father, a secret from Anna as it had been from their mother, a business that sheltered behind the front of a respectable family and the legitimate business conducted from their offices in Church Street. In his legitimate trading John had made many useful connections on the Continent. When the importing of French goods was prohibited during the conflict with Napoleon, he covertly arranged shipments of brandy, lace, silks, glass, perfumes and tea. There was a ready market among the local gentry and professional classes and his second business had prospered.

John Mason had realised from the outset that

successful landings of contraband and its subsequent disposal would need considerable organisation so he set about finding a man whom he could trust. A man who, apart from working alongside John, could also take full responsibility for the arrangements when a landing was pending. He had found such a man in Edwin Bennet.

Born and bred in Whitby, he had the sea in his blood. From an early age he had sailed the North Sea with his father and three brothers on all manner of expeditions so long as there was money at the end of them. On one such venture their ship foundered and Edwin's father and brothers were all drowned. He counted himself lucky to have been too ill to sail with them that day. Edwin determined to keep their memory alive by continuing to sail the same waters. He knew the Yorkshire coast like the back of his hand, and had an uncanny ability to assess quickly any unfamiliar stretch of coastline. An ability to devise the best landing places, as the situation demanded when contraband was due, and a knowledge of which local folk could be trusted, were other important assets. Edwin was responsible for getting the required number of men, horses and carts to the chosen landing spot, and overseeing the transportation and storage of the contraband before it was covertly delivered. For these heavy responsibilities John offered him one-quarter of the profits.

Now Charles made his way quickly to the small house in Tin Ghaut, a short narrow street close to the bridge that ran from Church Street to the river. His knock on the door was answered by Edwin who showed some relief at seeing him. He ushered Charles inside and took him into a modest room, comfortably but sparsely furnished. Edwin saw no need for elaboration in this house, for his plans were to move into more salubrious surroundings once he had made enough money, a resolve he had made when down on his luck and one he now saw as achievable thanks to Mr Mason's smuggling enterprise.

'I'm that pleased to see you, Mr Charles. I hope you have a message from your father. How is he?'

'He's very down but he's managing,' replied Charles. 'Until he returns to take an active part in our business, we are to carry on. Before my mother's death he'd made arrangements for another consignment, due in four days. I'm going to see Nick and Ralph to make sure everything is in hand. You'll see that Tod's Barn is clear?'

'Aye. In your absence I made the usual distribution.'

'Good.' Charles nodded and smiled with approval.

Tod's Barn stood on the cliffs, three miles along the coast, close to the tiny village of Sandsend. The building and some adjoining land had been bought by his father to serve as an initial hiding place for contraband. People had no interest in a derelict barn awaiting John Mason's decision to repair it and use it as shelter for cattle he would run nearby. What few folk knew, and they were only the trusted ones, was that there was a passage from the shore to a cave in the cliff, and beyond that another passage which came up into an old storage room in the barn, the legacy of smugglers from a hundred years before. The hiding place had long fallen out of use and out of mind, until John, accompanied by Charles, had accidentally discovered it when walking on the cliffs. It had sparked off the idea that smuggling could form a lucrative adjunct to his legitimate business.

Charles was aware that his step was a little quicker as he walked along Church Street in the direction of the White Horse where he knew he would find the two men he wanted to see, for they were always there at this time every day when not at sea. His quickened pace was an automatic reaction to the knowledge that he was engaged in an illicit pursuit that attracted danger.

Entering the inn, he went straight to the bar and ordered a tankard of ale. Though no one would have noticed, his gaze had swept the room and he knew from a forefinger that brushed across a man's forehead that his arrival had been noticed. It was a method of communication they always used to signify that a meeting was imminent at the usual place. He took his drink to a table and sat so that he could see the room. He leaned back against the panelled wall, the epitome of a young man at ease, taking a few moments from his work to enjoy a drink.

The two men rose from their table and, with a nod to the barman, left the White Horse. A few minutes later Charles finished his drink, exchanged a word with the man behind the bar and walked casually from the inn. He paused outside and glanced both ways along Church

Street which was teeming with people busy about their everyday lives, hurrying to destinations known only to themselves: sailors heading for ship or inn, wives doing their daily shopping, other idling their time away in window-gazing, coveting the goods on display, or chatting to friends they had just met, all adding to the cacophony of sound reverberating from the walls of the buildings that lined the street.

Charles stepped into the dust of the roadway and headed into Bridge Street. He went with the flow of people crossing the bridge to the west bank. He turned along St Ann's Staith and made his way to the small jetty that marked the end of Haggersgate. Here two fifty-ton sloops were tied up side by side. He climbed over the rail and ducked his head on entering a small cabin. The two men who had left the White Horse before him were seated at the table which occupied the centre of the small space.

'G'day, Mr Charles. Sorry about your mother.' The taller man's tone was sympathetic, the other man agreeing with a nod as he fixed his eyes on the new arrival.

'Nick, Ralph.' Charles's voice was crisp. He acknowledged their commiserations as he slid on to the seat next to Nick.

Nicholas Laven was over six foot and broad with it. He seemed to fill the cabin. His square-jawed, angular face was tanned by the sun and burnt by the wind from a life in the open. His ginger hair was cut short but still frizzed out of control. His broad hands, fingers misshapen by accidents at sea, rested on the table. Dark brown eyes extended a welcome to Charles, who knew they could flare angrily if provoked. Behind them was the nimble brain of a man who could make decisions which were rarely wrong – a valuable attribute in the trade of smuggling on behalf of the Masons, who of course looked upon themselves and these two men as freetraders. At the same time all three men sitting at this table knew that there were others who did not regard their enterprise with such latitude. They all recognised the need for caution in the risk-running world in which they moved.

Nicholas Laven and Ralph Myers, independent fishermen, first came to John Mason's notice when they had lost their vessels, driven on to the cliffs below the abbey when running for the harbour in a storm. They had been lucky to escape with their lives but had lost their livelihood. When John approached them with the proposition that he would provide the money for two fifty-ton sloops to run contraband goods to the Yorkshire coast, they'd had no hesitation in accepting in spite of the dangers. It meant poverty would no longer stare them in the face and they saw the possibility of making more money than they had done by fishing. They knew John Mason as a man considerate to his employees but he was raised even higher in their estimation when he proposed that they would each receive an eighth share of all profits from their ventures.

'How is your father?' asked Ralph. His gravelly voice had the ring of genuine concern.

'Still badly, I'm afraid. He won't be taking an

active part in the business for a while, but wants us to carry it on. I've just seen Edwin and he's ready for the next consignment.'

'That's the one arranged by your father?' Nick asked.

'Yes.'

'We're ready to sail. We'll take the *Hunter*.'

The manoeuvrability of the sloops enabled them to run close in shore and use creeks and inlets without the risk of being trapped by changing winds. Nick and Ralph handled them skilfully.

'The usual contacts on the Dutch coast always have goods ready and will be on the look out for our signal.'

'Good. We'll expect you in four days. What time?'

'The tide will be right at eleven.'

'We'll be ready. A prosperous voyage, gentlemen – for all of us.'

Chapter Three

Charles enjoyed the ride back to Hawkshead Manor. He took the cliff path past the ruined abbey which gave breathtaking views of the coastline and tranquil sea, today reflecting the blue of the cloudless sky. Only the shadow of his recent tragedy marred the satisfaction of a good morning's work which had assured him that all was well with the Mason enterprises. He wished his father had been with him to participate in the decisions he had made and hoped Anna's day at home had not been trying.

He was pleased when he saw her sitting on the terrace enjoying the afternoon sunshine. She laid her book on her lap when she heard the approach of hooves. He swung himself gracefully from the saddle, patted his horse's neck and came up the four steps to flop into a chair beside his sister.

'How was your day?' she asked.

'It went well. Gideon has looked after things. The *Grace* is leaving today and the *Gull* is due in tomorrow. Captain Morris wants to retire after the next voyage.'

'Because his wife is unwell?'

'Yes.'

'I must make a point of calling on her next time I am in Whitby.'

'I'm sure Captain Morris would appreciate that. How's Father been?'

'He went riding this morning, returning only in time for the midday meal. He said very little, and what he did was of no consequence. We finished our meal and he went into his study and has been there ever since.'

'On a fine day like this? I know he's been out all morning but why shut himself away now? He could have had your company out here.'

'Exactly. It seems he wants to cut himself off from everyone; even seeing his family is to be kept to the minimum. It worries me, Charles. What might it do to him eventually?'

'It may be that we remind him too much of Mother.'

'That may be so but I would have thought memories of her are precious. I know they are to me, and sharing them with others is important too.'

'Will he be at dinner?'

'I expect so. He gave no indication one way or the other.'

'I'll see what I can do this evening.' Charles pushed himself from his chair. 'I must go and change.' He went back to his horse and led it to the stables where he handed it over to the groom.

When Anna and Charles walked into the dining room that night they were glad to find their father already at the table.

'Hello, Father.'

He nodded but did not speak.

Anna and Charles glanced at each other and went to their places. Both had noticed that their father was smartly dressed and were thankful that he still took a pride in his appearance. He had always been particular about his clothes, even when visiting the office or out riding. They took heart from the fact that he still cared for his appearance.

'Did you have a good ride this morning, Father?' asked Charles as the door opened and a maid walked in with a tray on which stood a soup tureen.

'I did indeed,' came the reply. John's voice was tinged by a note of regret, 'but someone was missing.'

Neither Anna nor Charles spoke in reply, not wanting to add to the pain their father was feeling. Anna turned her attention to the tureen that the maid had placed in front of her. She took the serving ladle and poured some of the broth into a soup plate. She handed the plate to the maid who was standing beside her waiting to serve the two men. When she had done so she left the room.

'Was it busy in Whitby?' Anna asked with a glance at her brother, knowing he would realise that a change of subject was desirable.

'It was, as usual.'

Their father made no comment. His head was slightly bowed as if he had to concentrate on taking his soup.

'A lot of people asked after you, Father,' Charles added brightly. 'They hoped they would soon see you back in Whitby.'

His father glanced up. 'They'll have a long wait.'

'Father, do you think that is wise?' Anna asked.

'It's what I want,' he replied firmly.

'But...'

Her sentence was cut off before it really started. 'I thought you understood from what I said before that I don't want to see people? Your mother and I mixed so much that meeting any of them now would revive hurtful memories.'

'But you can't avoid every association you and Mother shared.'

'I can – if I choose.' John's expression became sombre. 'Now that's enough,' he added sternly.

'All right, Father,' put in Charles, recognising that they should drop the subject, at least for the time being. 'But that does not preclude your taking an interest in the business. You can do that from here. You wouldn't have to meet anyone, if that's the way you want it.'

John laid down his spoon. He placed his hands firmly on the table and looked at each of his children in turn before delivering his reply. 'I built that business up for your mother, and of course you two when you came along. Your mother had a big influence on what I did. She was interested in the business and played an important role in it with her encouragement and advice. If I take an active part now I will miss her influence and that will be painful. Please, just leave me with my memories. You two are capable, we brought you up that way. Anna, run the house. Charles, look after the business. Let that be an end to it.' He picked up his spoon again as if dismissing any further discussion.

'I hope some day Mother will tell you to take up your rightful role again,' said Anna, quietly but resolutely.

Her father met her gaze but did not reply.

Little was said during the rest of the meal and when it was over John declined a chance to share the rest of the evening with Anna and Charles.

Over the next three days life at Hawkshead Manor seemed to settle into an unexceptional routine. John went riding every morning. He never said where. Anna and Charles did not ask but they guessed he visited the wood where the accident had taken place. He spent the afternoons in his study, at mealtimes said very little, and only spent a few minutes in the drawing room after dinner with Anna and Charles.

On the fourth day the pattern changed when Charles announced that he would be going into Whitby again that evening.

'What on earth for?' asked Anna.

'Business.'

'Can't you get it done during the day?'

'This man could only see me tonight, and business is business. I can't miss an opportunity to advance it. Remember, Father sometimes had to do this.' He glanced at John and recognised from the look in his eyes that he knew what his son would be about. Charles was encouraged by this unmistakable stirring of interest although outwardly his father showed none. 'I may stay in Whitby the night. It depends how long the meeting takes.'

'As you wish,' said Anna.

Charles left immediately their meal was finished. As they walked from the dining room, John took his daughter's hand. 'You'll have no one to sit with you this evening, would you like me to?'

'Father, I'd like nothing better,' returned Anna with delight. Maybe this was an opportunity to breach the wall her father had built around himself. 'I'm sorry Charles has had to return to Whitby this evening.'

'There are some aspects of negotiations that are better conducted over a glass of wine or tankard of ale.'

'Don't you think he could do with you beside him?'

For a moment John stiffened but then he relaxed and said quietly in a tone that indicated he would not discuss the matter further, 'He can manage perfectly well.'

Anna knew it was wise to say no more, but her comment had set her father's mind into a reflective mood. He realised Charles had gone to Whitby because of the expected run of contraband. The thought set his blood racing as he recalled the inherent danger that spiced the business. He had always enjoyed the challenge of getting contraband ashore safely and outwitting the authorities. He hoped his son would be as successful tonight.

When he went to his bedroom he drew back the heavy velvet curtains and stared into the night. Clouds drifted slowly across the moon, allowing it now and then to bathe the fields and trees with a silvery sheen. A smuggler's moon. On such a night, with his pulse's beat heightened by the thrill, he would gallop home to the arms of his beloved Elizabeth. His natural sensuality, intensified by danger, enticed from her the same passion that marked their unbounded love for each other. Now, with his mind immersed in memories, he sighed and turned away from the window to his lonely bed.

Three miles beyond Whitby, Charles slowed his horse to a walking pace when he reached the tiny hamlet of Sandsend. Cottages that seemed bent on hiding themselves from prying eyes huddled beside the stream that ran through a gully, forming a natural route from the shore.

Although the occupants kept up an innocent face, smuggling was second nature to this small community as John had found out after his discovery of the cave. They knew how to keep their mouths shut. Smuggling supplemented their meagre income from fishing, but they appreciated that their legitimate trade had brought them their knowledge of the sea and its ways. They had used it and combated it from their cobles, seaworthy boats of a unique construction that enabled them to be launched from open beaches and to deal with the heavy seas likely to be encountered off the Yorkshire coast. This made them ideal boats for smuggling as well as their primary purpose of fishing, for they could rendezvous with larger smuggling ships at sea and run the contraband quickly ashore.

Charles glanced seaward. The water lay almost still, glimmering in the pale moonlight like pewter. He was thankful. The *Hunter* and the cobles should not be hampered by the sea tonight. Silence hung like a protective cloak over the hamlet but Charles knew that Edwin would have primed its inhabitants to be ready for the intense activity that would take place before the night was out. He reckoned that, as much as his father might try to eliminate reminders of the past from his mind, his thoughts tonight would be on the beach at Sandsend. Charles gave a wry smile as he wondered what Anna would think if she knew he was engaged in an illicit enterprise instead of a meeting in Whitby.

He halted his horse in front of a cottage, swung from the saddle and gave three knocks followed by two sharp raps on the door. A moment later it was opened by Edwin. Not a word was spoken as Charles stepped inside. The door closed, cutting off the light that had betrayed their activity.

'Everything ready?' he asked automatically though he knew with Edwin's efficiency it would be.

'Aye,' came the reply. He indicated a tankard and a jug on the small wooden table that stood in the centre of the sparsely furnished room. The only light came from a single oil lamp suspended from a central beam.

Charles poured himself some ale, holding up the jug to Edwin who nodded to affirm that Charles could top up his tankard for him.

'You couldn't persuade your father?' he asked as he sat down at the table.

Charles shook his head. 'Tonight wasn't discussed, but no doubt he knew something was afoot when I said I had to return to Whitby.'

Conversation drifted and became spasmodic. Both men recognised the tension that was mounting in the other. Edwin's examination of his watch became more frequent until finally he slipped it into his waistcoat pocket, stood up and drained his tankard. As he wiped the back of his hand across his mouth, he nodded to his companion.

When they left the cottage Charles took a spyglass from his saddlebag. Without a word the two men climbed the hill behind the row of cottages to a position that gave them an uninterrupted view out to sea, the stark cliffs rising away to their left. To their right the beach was backed by low-lying land before it too rose to higher ground nearer Whitby.

They settled themselves in a tiny hollow. Charles swept the scene with his glass, dwelling on the land to the right. Edwin produced his own spyglass from the deep pocket of his coat and concentrated his gaze on the sea.

As the minutes ticked away Charles could feel his tension deepening. It must be time for the prearranged signal. What was causing the delay? Trouble in Holland? A search by a Revenue cutter? An accident? All manner of reasons began to storm his impatient mind. He became so full of doubts that he was startled when he felt a tap on his arm. He turned to see Edwin, still holding his glass to one eye, pointing out to sea with his other hand. Charles turned his gaze in that direction. A light. It disappeared. Another flash followed by two more. He waited until Edwin judged the moment right for them to move.

'Let's go!'

Each knew his role in the events to come. They

ran down the hillside. Edwin stepped deftly on each stepping-stone to cross the stream, then gave four sharp knocks on certain cottage doors.

Charles did the same on the other side of the stream. No word was passed as men and women emerged from their cottages. Men made their way to the cobles on the beach. Women alerted neighbours to be ready to receive contraband and hide it until such time as they were instructed what to do with it. Four men had run to a stone shed that acted as a stable on these occasions. There, horses had already been hitched to two carts. By the time Charles and Edwin had completed their tasks those carts were on their way to the beach and the whole shore operation, as planned by Edwin, was in motion.

Charles headed for the five cobles which were being pushed into the sea. As soon as they were buoyant six men scrambled into each vessel, put out the oars and held the cobles steady. Charles was at the water's edge with his spyglass trained on the spot where they had first seen the light. Darkness. He held his breath. Nothing must go wrong now. A light! Nearer. The *Hunter* was coming closer to the shore. Four quick flashes. The sloop was in position. He waved his arms at the men watching from the cobles. They dipped their oars and the five cobles moved away.

Though still tense, Charles felt a sense of elation now that the operation was underway, but he knew that vigilance could not be relaxed. He turned and saw what he expected to see: Edwin's organisation in full flow. Twenty men and women were moving silently across the sand towards the gently lapping waves, to be in position for the returning cobles. He knew that five men would be making their way to the cave in the cliffs and that there would be two others in strategic positions from which they would be able to detect any movement that might indicate that Preventive Men or troops were about. The two carts, axels well-greased to prevent any undue noise, moved quietly past him towards the water.

It seemed an interminable age before the first coble, moving strongly towards the shore, was sighted. Then it was there, aground on the beach. Immediately the shore was a hive of activity. Men and women ignored the water as they moved beside the boat. Bladders of brandy were passed to the women who hitched them to a broad belt beneath their skirts and set off for their walk to Whitby, knowing no decent Preventive Man would dare ask them to raise their skirts. Men heaved small barrels of gin on to their shoulders and hurried up the beach to the cottages where the contraband would be hidden by others waiting to play their part in the operation. Large barrels were raised carefully from the coble to the carts that had come close. Once the last item had been unloaded eager hands helped to get the coble floating again and away to the sloop for the next load. The second boat was already at the beach and being unloaded even as the third was approaching. There was no let up until a coble arrived and it occupants announced they had the last load.

When that was dealt with the smugglers began

to disperse, some to their Sandsend cottages, others to dwellings a mile or two from the shore. Some followed the path taken by those women already on their way to their homes in Whitby. Charles and Edwin hurried towards the cave. As they neared it the two carts emerged, having disposed of their loads. Inside the cave, dimly lit by shielded lamps, men were transferring containers of tea, bales of fabric, barrels of brandy and gin, through the passage to the hidden recesses in Tod's Barn.

Edwin and Charles cast a supervisory gaze over the whole scene. When the last barrel had left the cave they looked around to make sure that no incriminating evidence had been inadvertently left behind, then made their way through the passage to the barn. They helped stow the remaining goods, but Charles kept one barrel back. Edwin removed a stone from the wall and from the cavity behind took out some small pewter beakers. Charles filled them and each man took one. Not a word was spoken as Charles raised his in appreciation of a job well done. They all drank and silently left the barn, each knowing, as did those who had left from the beach, that they would be suitably paid for their night's work.

Satisfied that there was nothing to indicate how the barn was being used, Charles and Edwin made their way down to the cottage. Silence hung over Sandsend as if the night's activity had never happened.

Edwin mounted his horse and the two men, alert for anyone in authority who might block their path, rode steadily in the direction of Whitby. They met no one. The clouds had thickened by the time they reached the town. They kept their horses to a walking pace as they followed the steep path to the river and crossed the bridge. Ships creaked beside the quays, ropes rubbed as they fought the flow of the river bent on taking the boats downstream. Buildings were dark, alleyways darker still. In these early hours of the morning only the watchman was aware of their progress but he kept to the shadows and ignored them. Charles Mason and Edwin Bennet together at this time of night meant one thing. He had already noted several women returning to the town but an hour ago. He had not challenged them, nor would he approach the two riders. He did not want to lose the brandy that would come his way for turning in the other direction.

They reached the end of Bridge Street where it met Church Street and drew their horses to a halt. The only sound was the scurrying of rats.

'We'll let our usual customers know that the cow has calved,' said Charles.

Edwin acknowledged the words that signalled an arrival of contraband.

'Immediately?' he asked.

'Yes. May as well get some money in, and the sooner this lot's moved the sooner we can handle another batch.'

'Right. I'll be away.' Edwin tipped his hat with his forefinger and turned his horse towards the White Horse where he had permanent stabling.

Charles turned in the opposite direction. As he

rode beside the quays he felt a deep sense of satisfaction that his first smuggling operation without his father's supervision had gone well. He turned into Green Lane which took him to the top of the cliff near the abbey. The clouds had thinned again and the moonlight sent shadows moving eerily around the ancient stones. Charles put his horse into a gentle trot to Hawkshead Manor.

'You were very late back last night, or rather it was this morning,' said Anna as her brother, a little bleary-eyed, came into the dining room the following morning.

'I'm sorry if I disturbed you,' he replied apologetically. 'I nearly stayed in Whitby but it was a pleasant night for a ride.'

'It must have been serious business to have taken so long.'

'It was. It concerned some goods I want to import from Holland and it needed careful negotiation.' Though there was no reference to the smuggling in his words, they were not altogether a lie. There was a contract connected with the Masons' legitimate business that needed his attention and during his ride he had given it some thought. After he had spread the word that the cow had calved he would devote his immediate attention to Mason and Son, Merchants. 'It means,' he went on, 'that I might have to be away a few days. Certainly I will have to go to Hull and maybe to Holland.'

'Holland?' Alarm came into Anna's voice.

'Yes.'

'When?'

'Next week.'

'But isn't that dangerous? Europe is far from settled. Who knows what Napoleon will dream up next?'

'He's reeling after his unsuccessful campaign to take Moscow, and Wellington is driving the French out of Spain. The war will soon be over.'

'There may be no fighting in Holland now but if Napoleon is desperate who knows where the next upheaval might be?'

'I can't sit around like some mollycoddled child. I can take care of myself. Besides, the people I want to see will look after me.'

Anna shrugged her shoulders in resignation. 'I hope you know what you are doing. Do be careful. These are dangerous times.'

The matter was dropped when the door opened and their father, dressed for riding, walked in. 'Good morning to you both,' he said. He kissed his daughter and, as he went to his place at the head of the table, caught the gleam of success in Charles's eyes and smiled to himself.

He waited to broach the subject until they had left the dining room. Anna went to the kitchen to consult Mrs Denston and the cook. John picked up his coat and hat and made for the terrace. Charles followed quickly.

'All went well last night,' he said.

If he expected his father to be enthusiastic and offer him congratulations, he was disappointed.

'I thought I told you I did not want anything to do with our businesses? I hoped you would respect my wish.' John's tone was harsh, his

71

expression withering.

Charles shrugged his shoulders in irritation. 'I just thought you'd like to know,' he muttered.

But John had said all he was going to say. He swung on his heel and left the terrace for the stables.

Hurt, Charles waited and a few minutes later watched his father appear on horseback and put the animal into a fast gallop as if the pounding hooves and rush of the wind could drive his recollections from him. But Charles knew that was not the intention. Father was heading for a rendezvous with his memories in the wood in which his wife had been killed. That gallop was a signal to him that his father had meant what he said and intended to have his wishes respected. Anger that his son had chosen to disobey him spurred the ride.

Charles sighed and tightened his lips with annoyance. He had hoped he might have sparked some interest in his father and so opened the possibility of his returning to the business again. He walked slowly back into the house. Anna was just coming from the kitchen.

Knowing her brother's moods, she asked, 'Something annoyed you?'

'Father!' He grunted with disgust. 'I mentioned the business, tried to get him to talk about it, but he rounded on me in no uncertain terms.'

'Did you tell him about going to Holland?'

'I didn't get a chance.'

Anna grimaced at the thought of her father's lack of interest. It was so unlike him. Before his wife's accident he had been full of enthusiasm for any project concerning the business or the estate.

'All we can do is chip away at his stubbornness while trying to understand his feelings. Are you going to Whitby today?'

'Yes.'

'When will you be back?'

'Not until this evening.'

'I'll try and get Father into a better humour by then. Do you want me to tell him you are going to Holland?'

Charles gave a half-laugh 'Please yourself, but if you do he'll more than likely bite your head off.'

After Charles had gone, Anna went to her room, deep in thought. She stood for a few minutes staring out of the window without taking any notice of the scene before her. Then, a decision made, she swung round from the window, strode to the mahogany wardrobe, flung open the double doors and pulled out her riding habit. She changed quickly, leaving her day clothes scattered on the bed. If she stayed to put them away neatly her determined mood might vanish.

She took the stairs almost at a run and in a few minutes was requesting Jack to saddle her horse. She waited impatiently, keeping her thoughts concentrated lest she allow pity to soften her attitude.

Once in the saddle she set her horse into a gallop. The exhilaration of the ride helped to heighten her determination. Nearing the wood that clothed the valley with oak, birch and pine, she slowed her mount to a walking pace. Reaching the trees, she slipped from the saddle and tied her horse to a branch. She started through the wood, following the path she surmised her father would have taken. Her movements quietened after half a mile for she wanted to observe him before making her presence known.

She stopped when she caught her first glimpse of him, then edged forward a few more steps until she had a better view. He was sitting on a fallen tree, elbows on his knees, chin cupped in his hands, staring at small open piece of ground a few yards in front of him. His shoulders were bent as if oppressed by a weight he could not lift. Her determination almost evaporated in the sympathy that threatened to overwhelm her. This was her father and he was suffering. It needed a strong will not to give way to the feelings that began to flood into her mind. But what she was going to do would be done from love for the dejected man sitting a few yards away. She moved silently to the tree. He started as she sat down beside him. For the briefest of moments there was a flash of annoyance at being disturbed, but it vanished when he felt her fingers take his hand.

'Father.' Compassion took over. In her tone there was sorrow for intruding, and desolation at her own loss. 'Do you come here every day?'

He nodded.

She rallied her resolve. This cauterising of the soul in the place where his wife was killed was not healthy. It could overwhelm and destroy any mind.

'Is that wise?'

'Where was the wisdom in your mother's death?'

74

'No one can answer that but God.'

'Is there a God?'

'Yes,' she answered firmly. 'Sometimes He works in ways we don't understand, but who are we to question them?'

He didn't answer. It was as if he did not want to try to fathom an explanation.

'Mother wouldn't want you to be like this.'

'With her gone my life means nothing.'

'Ridiculous!' Anna's tone became harsh. 'That's being disloyal to her and all that you and she did together. To abandon it now, as you are doing, undermines everything she ever did.'

He shook his head. 'You don't understand.'

'I know I can't on your level, but I can on mine. Charles and I lost a mother whom we dearly loved, with whom we shared so much. We feel the loss deeply but we know, I certainly do, that she would want us to go on living and developing in the way she had visualised. Not to do so, or at least try to do so, would be disloyal to her and to her memory. Life has to go on.'

'You are young,' he replied lamely.

In his tone she detected a slight weakening of his attitude and that her words were making him think. She must be careful and not let hostility creep into her argument. 'You aren't old.'

'I feel it.'

'That will pass, unless you let your present attitude take over and blind you to what is right and what you should do. Don't you think I need you, and Charles too, especially to help with the responsibilities you have thrust upon him? To carry on with as near normal a life as possible will need strength. I believe you have it, and with Mother's help you will cope with the years ahead.'

She felt him stiffen and knew instantly she should not have talked of her mother's help from beyond the grave. But the words had been said and she could not retract them.

'Don't talk nonsense,' John snapped. 'How can she help?'

'I believe she can and will. We'll never understand how but I know she is watching over us.' Anna stood up. She had said enough. Words can linger in the mind and she was sure these would in his, hopefully for his good. She walked away. She felt him watching her but he did not call out or make any move to join her.

Her emotions ran high as she walked through the wood. Her love for her father was deep. It tore at her heart to see a hurt so intense that it blinded him to reason. The pity and the sorrow she felt for him brought tears to her eyes. When she reached her horse she could do nothing but give way. She laid her head against the saddle and wept for him, for herself and for her mother.

Eventually she straightened, took a handkerchief from her sleeve and wiped her eyes. A deep sigh helped to fight the oppressive burden she felt beginning to weigh heavily upon her too. She must not give way. She must be strong. Their future lives were at stake.

Anna swung into the saddle and rode home at a gentle pace, giving herself time to regain her composure before handing her horse over to Jack. She went to her room, changed, tidied her clothes and sat looking out of the window. The clouds that had billowed did not mar the blue sky but enhanced it. Two gardeners tended the colourful flowerbeds beside the well-trimmed lawn. Trees across the parkland were content to be caressed by the gentle breeze. The scene was one of peace and tranquillity. She wished it was so in her father's mind. With that desire came a determination not to be defeated.

An hour later she saw him return. He rode his horse slowly but did not look around him, observing the appearance of the house and the gardens, noting what needed attention as he would once have done. Was it because his lack of interest continued or was he deep in thought about what she had said?

She heard him go to his room and a short while afterwards return downstairs. She knew he would be in his study. When she came down for the midday meal she did not call on him but went straight to the dining room. She had ordered a simple meal of soup, cold ham and cheese, as they would be dining more lavishly in the evening when Charles was there.

The maid had brought the tureen of soup and Anna had started to ladle some into a bowl when her father walked in. He said nothing but sat down and took the bowl she offered him. She left him to open a conversation but his only word throughout the meal was 'thank you'. As soon as he had finished he left the dining room. She watched him go, sadness in her heart.

It was still there when, in the late afternoon, she

rose from her chair in the drawing room on hearing Charles's return. She had sat with the door to the hall open so that she would not miss him. She wanted to acquaint him with the facts of her meeting with their father in the wood. She did so quickly and with some concern.

'This is all we can do, Anna, keep trying to make him think and see that his attitude is wrong.'

'I did not mention your coming visit to Holland.'

'Very well. I'll do so during the meal.'

From the moment that their father joined them in the dining room the conversation was light and inconsequential. Anna drew some hope from the fact that he joined in.

They were well into their main course of goose when Charles looked at her and said, 'Next Tuesday I will be going to Holland. I must see about our contract with the de Klerks. Will you be all right, Anna?'

'Of course,' she replied.

He looked directly at his father. 'You'll look after her?'

'She is my daughter and my responsibility,' John replied a little testily as if there was no need for Charles to have posed such a question.

'I just thought I would mention it as you shut yourself out of our lives so much.'

Anna sensed her father bristle at this inference. His eyes flashed angrily but she breathed more easily as the storm subsided. 'Anna will be perfectly secure. She is capable of looking after herself, but I will see that she is not alone.'

Both Anna and Charles felt that another breach in the wall had been made. It seemed to widen when their father asked with interest, 'Will you sail directly from Whitby?'

'No. I will go from Hull as I must see Mr Heatherington. I think I might be able to make a shipment for them from Holland so that the *Grace* will be a full ship on her return.'

John nodded and Charles took it for approval of his plan. He exchanged a quick glance with his sister and each realised that the other thought they had made even more progress. Their father had at last shown some interest in the business.

But later Anna was forced to wonder just how much they had made.

Chapter Four

'Oh, damn! I'm off!' John's words shattered the tranquillity he was sharing with Anna.

The weather had settled into a fine spell and today was even better than the previous four. John had taken his usual ride in the morning. He always returned in time for the midday meal but Anna had noted that he had been absent from the house longer these last three days. She surmised he was spending more time at the place where her mother had been killed, and this worried her, but she deemed it wise to make no comment, at least until she judged the time was right. In the afternoon father and daughter took advantage of the pleasant weather to relax on the terrace.

Anna looked up from the book she was reading to see what had caused her father's remarks.

He was already on his feet and striding into the house. 'I'm not at home!' he called emphatically, and disappeared.

Anna's gaze turned to the driveway which ended at the front of the house. She had no trouble in recognising the gig that was trundling its way towards her. The bright blue paintwork identified it as Mrs Belinda Blenkinsop's. Only she dared display her uninhibited eccentricity this way. She wanted people to recognise her instantly. Even without the noticeable colour Anna would have identified her from her imperious posture as she sat full-bosomed beneath a flamboyant wide-brimmed hat, its large feather swaying with the movement of the carriage.

Anna sighed. Really her father shouldn't have fled like that. He wouldn't have done so before his wife died. He would have observed the niceties of etiquette and tolerated the drivelling chatter of this overbearing woman. Now Anna would have to cope with her on her own even though Mrs Blenkinsop had her daughter, Cara, with her. She would hardly dare open her mouth in her mother's presence even if she got the chance, which was unlikely. Anna laid down her book on the low table beside her chair. She stood up and moved slowly to the steps leading from the terrace.

'Hello, my dear,' Belinda Blenkinsop called heartily, raising her left hand in greeting while keeping her right hand on the reins and bringing the horse to a halt.

'Good day to you, Mrs Blenkinsop,' returned Anna. 'Hello, Cara.'

Cara's weak smile in return told Anna that she wished she was here without her mother's overbearing, though well-meant, presence.

'Come, Cara, help your mother down,' said Belinda with an impatient snap in her voice.

Cara, who was the same age as Anna and had shared private tuition with her, scrambled down from the gig and turned to assist her mother. Belinda's bulk did not make her effort to leave the conveyance easy but she managed it with due comment on Cara's inadequacy, though the poor girl could do no more than give her support. With feet firmly on the ground, Belinda quickly smoothed her dress and straightened her hat.

'My dear, it is so nice to see you. So uplifting to be visiting Hawkshead Manor again.' Her smile was beaming as she took Anna's hands in hers and offered her cheek to be kissed.

'And it is nice to see you, Mrs Blenkinsop. You are most welcome.' As Anna made her kiss she caught Cara's look which signified the unspoken comment from her friend: 'You're a liar for the sake of etiquette.' Anna smiled and winked at her. 'Come, do sit down. I'll order you some lemonade. It will have been a warm ride.'

'Thank you, my dear. Most kind of you.' Mrs Blenkinsop took Anna's arm as they went up the steps, only releasing her grip as she lowered herself into the chair vacated by John a few minutes ago.

'I'm sorry my father is not at home. Pull up another chair, Cara. I'll order the lemonade,' said Anna as she went into the house.

A few moments later she reappeared to join the guests. Mrs Blenkinsop had removed her hat and placed it on another chair she had instructed her daughter to bring. She was patting her sand-coloured hair into place. 'This is such a pleasant aspect,' she commented with a sweep of her hand as if she was putting the finishing touches to the landscape. 'Your great-grandfather certainly knew how to pick a wonderful position. Now tell me,' she leaned a little closer to Anna and lowered her voice as if seeking a confidence, 'how is your father? Getting over his terrible loss, I hope?'

'Slowly.'

Belinda pursed her lips and gave an understanding nod. 'It will take time, I know, but the sooner he can get back to work and mixing with people again, the easier it will be.'

'Yes, I want him...'

'And you, my dear. How...'

'Ah, the lemonade.'

The arrival of the maid, with three glasses and a full jug of lemonade made from fresh lemons, momentarily halted the flow of words, but only momentarily for, as soon as the maid was out of earshot, Mrs Blenkinsop continued with her question. 'How are you managing to deal with the loss? I know just how you are feeling. After all, I too suffered the same bereavement earlier this year, as you will remember.'

'It was hardly the same, Mama. Grandma was so much older than Anna's mother, and it was a blessing in her case.'

Mrs Blenkinsop looked sharply at her daughter. She did not like to be corrected but she knew Cara was right. 'Quite so. Mother was eighty-nine after all, and she was suffering.' She turned back to Anna. 'I'm sorry, my dear, you must be feeling terrible after losing a mother so young and vivacious and full of life...'

'Mother!' Cara's tone was sharp as she dared to interrupt in apology for her mother's faux-pas.

Not realising how inappropriate her last three words had been, Belinda looked askance at her daughter.

'I can't imagine why you're interrupting,' she snapped in irritation, but did not wait for an answer. She turned back to Anna. 'I was pleased to see that your father has ventured back into Whitby again.' This information confounded Anna but she hid her surprise. 'Well, not exactly in the town. I saw him visiting your mother's grave yesterday, and the day before when I was putting flowers on my mother's grave.'

Anna grasped at this news. So that was why her father had been absent longer than usual. 'He did not tell me that he had seen you.'

'I don't know whether he did or not. Oh, he can't have done. The two graves are on opposite sides of the cemetery. He would have come and had a word with me if he had, but he was leaving as I arrived.'

Anna had no doubt that her father had wanted no contact with Mrs Blenkinsop just as he had no desire to meet her today.

'Was there anyone else about?' she asked tentatively.

'No.'

Because of his desire not to meet people, Anna was surprised that he had visited the cemetery. She imagined he would make his approach with caution, even waiting until there was no one about and hastening away if anyone should appear once he was there. Her thoughts were interrupted by Mrs Blenkinsop's voice again.

'Your father and my husband are such good friends, I'm sure Henry will be only too glad to help John through this trying time. I'll tell him to come and bring your father up-to-date with what is happening in Whitby and get him interested in things again. Bereavements are hard but we have to cope with them and get on with life. Now, my dear, why don't you think of having one of the parties that the Masons of Hawkshead Manor are famous for? I'm sure that it would help to ease the shock and make you realise there is still a life to be lived. You know, they were the talk of the district once. They could be again.' She gave a slight pause and, realising that she had over-stepped the mark of etiquette, added quickly, 'Of course, it would have to be after your period of mourning has ended.'

Anna shuddered to think of her father's reaction should she suggest such a proposal. Thank goodness he had escaped from this talkative and insensitive woman. Did Belinda Blenkinsop not realise that her mother had been a vital part of those parties, that she was at their very heart and without her they would not be the same?

'Of course, my dear, you would have an important role to play as the hostess, a part once ably filled by your mother. Oh, I can see her now, coming down that wonderful stairway into your hall, making her entrance like the queen she was. The Queen of Hawkshead Manor. So radiant in whatever she wore. You have her beauty, my dear, I'm sure you could do it.'

The words, bringing back vivid memories, drummed in Anna's mind with an ever-increasing beat. She wanted to scream at this woman to stop talking but instead allowed her to go on reviving precious scenes. As a little girl she would sneak from her bedroom on to the landing and watch the guests arriving. Everyone was so elegant, the ladies in their colourful evening gowns, the gentlemen in their white shirts, black ties and frock coats. The evenings were so joyful as guests, greeted by their host, assembled in the hall with their drinks, and awaited the appearance of her mother. In spite of her concentration on the scene below Anna was half-listening for the sound of Elizabeth's door opening. When she heard it she would scramble hastily into the shadows, hidden, so she thought, from her mother's sight, and study with breathless admiration the dress she had chosen for this particular party. Whatever it was it always enhanced her natural beauty and stunned the guests into silence when they caught their first glimpse of her, pausing at the top of the stair before making her way down in the charged silence. When she was halfway a ripple of clapping would start and then, mingled with gasps of admiration, it would break into a crescendo.

Anna had watched such an event many times until this year when she was seventeen and had accompanied her mother down the stairs to be presented to all the guests. It was then that she realised the entrance her mother made was not an invitation to flattery but was her way of welcoming her guests. The memory would always be special to Anna, for three weeks later her beautiful mother lay dead.

Now she shuddered at the thought of doing this without her but, unknown to Anna at the time, Mrs Blenkinsop had sown a seed that was to have a profound effect on the future.

'Oh, those certainly were joyful times. Others tried but no one could match the parties at Hawkshead Manor. Do think about reviving them, my dear.'

Anna nodded. 'Maybe.'

'Cara, you must try to persuade her. When she comes out of mourning, of course.'

'Yes, Mama. How is Charles, Anna?' Cara had squirmed during her mother's insensitive chatter and wanted to try to get the subject away from that which she could see was causing her friend pain.

'He's very well, thank you, Cara. He's working again now. He's in Whitby today and is talking about going to Holland next week.'

'Holland! Isn't that rather foolhardy with political and military developments so unstable on the Continent?' Mrs Blenkinsop was away again, having taken the opportunity of her daughter's question to take a reviving sip of her lemonade. 'You never know what will happen there. I know Napoleon seems to have made some blunders but he's not a man to under-estimate. He would dearly love to bring us to our knees and might do anything to achieve that, even to embroiling Europe in a yet more damaging war. It doesn't bear thinking about! If your Charles has to go, do tell him to be most careful and exercise the utmost caution.'

'I'm sure he will,' replied Anna.

'Business, I suppose?'

'I expect so.' Anna knew Mrs Blenkinsop was fishing for information, so added, 'Though I know not what.' She said it in such a way as to imply that she did but was not going to tell anyone. She saw Cara give a little smile at the way she had 'slapped her mother's wrist' as she would put it. Anna was pleased that she had given her friend some amusement.

'Ah, well,' Belinda sighed. 'Men do like to have their little secrets, though I must say Henry has none from me.'

The two girls exchanged glances as Mrs Blenkinsop reached for her glass again. Cara raised an eyebrow by which Anna realised she knew more than her mother, who was naive in thinking she knew everything about her husband. No doubt Cara also knew, as Anna did, that Mr Blenkinsop sought escape from his wife's constant chattering by visiting known disreputable houses in Whitby and its neighbourhood.

'The next time you come into Whitby you must... Did you know that Cara has heard from Sophie – tell her, Cara...' But before Cara could say a word her mother had launched into the tale herself. The words flowed unceasingly for another half hour when, to Anna's relief, Mrs Blenkinsop stopped in mid-flow and said, 'Cara, we must be going.'

She knew that this was a signal that her mother wanted helping from the chair and was on her feet immediately. With her daughter's assistance, and Anna standing by, Belinda struggled to stand upright.

'This has been a thoroughly enjoyable visit, my dear. Thank you for your hospitality.' She took hold of Anna's arm and started for the steps. Cara picked up her mother's hat and followed. Reaching the gig, Belinda turned to Anna, 'Do pay us a visit and bring your father along. I'll do as I promised and send Henry to see him. And do remember what I said about reviving the famous parties. It would be good for your father, and of course for you and Charles.' She squeezed Anna's hand, expecting the gesture to give reassurance to the young woman.

Cara and Anna helped her into the driver's seat. Cara handed her the hat and while her mother was adjusting it to her liking, the two friends embraced.

'I'm sorry about all the chatter,' whispered Cara.

Anna gave a little chuckle of understanding. 'Take care, and good luck.'

Farewells were called again as Mrs Blenkinsop got the horse under control and turned the gig away from the house.

Anna strolled slowly up the steps, paused on the terrace to watch the departing guests for a few moments, and then flopped on to her chair with a sigh of relief. Peace descended over the scene again. She picked up her book.

Ten minutes later her father appeared. 'Gone?' he said as he sat down, then added with a teasing twinkle in his eye, 'I hope you had a very enjoyable time?'

'Oh, wonderful,' returned Anna, mockery in her tone. Her expression changed to a more serious aspect. 'I suppose she means well and has kindness in her heart, but she chatters without thinking what she is saying and that can be embarrassing and sometimes distressing for the listener. She sends her regards and intends that her husband shall visit you with all the latest news from Whitby.'

John cast a helpless look skywards. 'Poor old Henry, he'll have to do as he's told. But remember, Anna, I won't meet anyone with whom your mother and I were friends.'

'But, Father, you can't cut yourself off forever.'

'I can if I want to. I suppose Mrs Blenkinsop told you she had seen me at your mother's grave?'

'She did.'

'Old gossip! But I avoided her.'

'She wasn't sure whether you had seen her or not. She thought you probably hadn't.'

'Good.'

'I'm glad you have decided to visit Mother. Maybe we might go together now?'

'I suppose we can. But you'll not entice me into Whitby. Thank goodness the parish church was built on top of the east cliff and we can reach the churchyard without going into town.'

The following morning when John came into the dining room he informed Anna that he had told the groom to saddle her horse as well as his own. 'Yours will be ready as usual, Charles. Will you ride with us before going into Whitby?'

'After what Anna told me last night, I take it you will be visiting Mother?'

'Yes.'

'Then I'll ride with you. There is nothing in Whitby that can't wait until I get there.'

Neither Anna nor Charles commented when they left the stable yard and their father turned in the direction of the valley and the wood in which their mother had been killed. They followed, matching the gentle pace he set. When he drew to a halt close to the clearing in the wood, they too slipped from the saddles to accompany him the last few yards on foot. He stopped on the edge of the open space. The branches of the surrounding trees met overhead like a sheltering pall drawn across the scene to prevent the sun from committing sacrilege by brightening this place of tragedy and sorrow. Anna could sense a weight descend on her father. His head bowed, his shoulders slumped. Could she really know the agony he was going through? Tears welled in her eyes. She slipped a comforting hand in his and was thankful to sense a response. He still had feelings for those around him. He had not removed himself completely from the world.

They stood in silence for five minutes. Anna's thoughts embraced the mother she'd loved. Pictures of her came to mind, including those which had been conjured up the day before by Mrs Blenkinsop's mention of the parties at Hawkshead Manor.

John turned slowly away then stopped and surveyed the clearing. For the first time since his wife's death he saw it as the place that had robbed him of the woman he loved so deeply, somewhere that had left him with ache of hurt that would resist the cauterising effects of a new life. His eyes narrowed with hatred and that resounded in the words he uttered next. 'The trees shall be cut down, their stumps torn from the earth, and the whole ground will be turned by the plough so that it no longer resembles this place of tragedy and pain.' He strode to his horse.

Anna and Charles exchanged glances. Was this part of the exorcism their father must go through before he resumed his place in the world? They hoped so and that it would be one obstacle out of the way. Maybe the next would be removed beside the grave.

That possibility was cast from Anna's mind as they followed the trackway to the cliff top and turned in the direction of the ruined abbey, a silent sentinel to a life that once steeped these windswept heights in religious fervour. Today even the crumbling stones seemed to cast peace across the graveyard close to the parish church. At that moment the peace did not embrace Anna. This was the first time she had been back to her mother's grave since the funeral. That could not be taken as a sign of disrespect, nor lack of love, for her mother had been in her mind a great deal, but she had feared the emotional response of such a visit. Today she had been forced into facing such a reaction, for she would not have upset her father by refusing his invitation for her and Charles to accompany him.

They skirted the grounds of the old abbey and left their horses to champ the grass at the edge of the cemetery. John set off along a narrow path that ran beside a row of graves until he came to the wooden cross that marked the place where his beloved Elizabeth lay. That cross would remain the marker until the stone he had chosen had been suitably engraved and erected.

As Anna stood between her father and Charles she knew that her brother wept as she did with silent tears flowing down her cheeks. She glanced at her father and was momentarily shocked to see that he did not weep. Why didn't tears run down his cheeks too? Did he not feel any emotion? Then she realised what the expression on his face meant. He wept inside himself and the hurt was all the more severe since his sorrow did not find the outward relief of release. She clenched her fists tightly to control the compassion she felt for him lest it overwhelm her.

A few moments later her father turned and walked slowly towards his horse. Charles waited until Anna was ready. As they moved from the grave he stepped beside her and took her hand to comfort her, but also to draw some from her for himself.

'Are you all right?' he whispered.

She nodded as she dabbed her eyes with a lace-trimmed handkerchief. Charles brushed the tears from his cheeks and cleared the lump from his throat.

Their father was waiting for them when they reached the horses. 'Thank you for coming with me,' he said quietly.

Anna kissed him on the cheek and Charles placed a comforting hand on his shoulder. No word was needed to strengthen the family bond.

'Will you come into Whitby?' asked Charles tentatively, not knowing if it would cause an outburst from his father.

But all it brought was a shake of the head and the quietly spoken words, 'No, son. I don't want to meet people. The memories would be too painful. You see to things and prepare for that visit to Holland.' He patted his son reassuringly on the arm, then swung into the saddle.

Charles helped Anna to mount her horse and for a few moments watched the two people he loved most dearly ride away together before he climbed on to his mount and rode into Whitby.

Chapter Five

Later that week Charles took the mail coach to York where he stayed the night at the York Tavern in St Helen's Square and caught the diligence to Hull the following morning. By late afternoon he had booked a passage on the *Britannia* sailing to Amsterdam in two days' time. Before he returned to the Neptune Inn in Whitefriargate he made an appointment for the following morning to see Mr Heatherington, one of the leading traders in Hull with whom the Masons had done business on a number of previous occasions.

He had enjoyed an evening meal and was relaxing with a tankard of ale in the residents' room when a young man of about his own age approached him.

'Good evening, I'm sorry to intrude. You are Mr Charles Mason of Whitby?'

Charles was surprised but taken by the soft lilt in the stranger's voice. He had dressed with care. The dark blue of his jacket, cut away square at the waist, with knee-length tails at the back, was complemented by grey trousers and white shirt. A light blue cravat was neatly tied at his throat and his hair was well groomed. He gave the impression of a young man from a reasonably well-to-do background.

'I am,' replied Charles.

'May I have a few words with you?'

Charles gave him an enquiring glance.

'Business,' said the young man.

'Do sit down.'

'Thanks.' Before he did so he extended his hand and introduced himself. 'Julian Kirby.'

Charles nodded and felt a strong grip which did not indicate a domineering personality but a desire to be friendly. 'Pleased to meet you.' He knew of a comparatively new family firm trading in Hull. He had heard they had come from Scarborough in order to take advantage of the better facilities for expansion. His interest was roused. If Julian was of this family then maybe there was an opportunity of trading with them.

He saw a young man, touching six foot, with an open face and laughing eyes that would attract the attention of the opposite sex, young and old. They not only gave him an automatic charm but compelled attention. He held himself with a confidence which gave him the air of knowing what he wanted, something which would reassure anyone with whom he was doing business. Charles found himself liking Julian Kirby even before they started talking.

'Are you of the Kirby family who recently started trading in Hull?' he asked at once.

'Yes. Septimus Kirby, founder of the firm, is my father.'

'So you have a proposition to put to me on his account?'

'No, not on my father's account but on mine. He does not know I'm here.'

'Any undesirable reason for that?' Charles signalled the waiter and ordered a drink of

Julian's choice.

Julian gave a little smile at Charles's straight talking. 'You are a cautious man, Charles Mason.'

'You have to be in our business.'

'May I ask if you have the final responsibility for trading arrangements?'

'At the moment, yes. My father and I usually work closely together but, alas, he has chosen to become something of a recluse since my mother's recent death and has handed the responsibility of running the firm to me.'

'I'm sorry about your mother.' Julian's condolences came with a genuine sympathy that did not escape Charles's notice. 'It's a pity your father is taking his loss that way, but maybe it's fortunate for me.'

Piqued that this young man could see fortune in someone else's misfortune, Charles asked testily, 'How's that?'

'It means that I will have to deal with you, someone of about my own age. You'll understand better than the older generation when I tell you that I want more responsibility and my father won't give it to me.'

Charles pursed his lips, paused a moment, then, satisfied that Julian had meant no harm, said, 'So you want to do a deal with me which, if it brings you the profit you expect, you can present as proof of your abilities?'

'Precisely.'

Charles nodded. 'Before we discuss this matter any further, tell me how you knew who I was and how you found me?'

'Our firm has had dealings with Mr Heatherington so we knew that the firm that ships most of his goods into Hull from the Continent is yours. That fact was good enough for me. I went to ask him when he was likely to have contact with the Masons again. Fortune smiled on me. He has a meeting with you tomorrow. He told me where to find you and added that if I wanted to see you, I would have to look sharp as you are sailing to Holland the day after tomorrow.'

Satisfied with the explanation, Charles asked, 'So, what do you want from me?'

'To ship goods from the Continent for me, if the price is right.'

Charles admired the steely look and forthright statement delivered in a way that showed that Julian knew what he wanted. 'I think we could work on the same terms as we do with Heatherington's. But I would not want to be importing goods that might cut into their trade.'

Julian listened intently to Charles's terms, considered the proposition, then stuck out his hand. 'Agreed.'

Charles exchanged his grip and a bargain was sealed, one which, unknown to either, was to have far-reaching consequences. 'What sort of merchandise would you want me to handle?'

'I was thinking of wine. It's a commodity that my father has had little to do with but I believe we should make the most of what, in my opinion, is a growing demand.'

'I agree with you. We do ship some for Heatherington's but it is only a small amount of the very best wines for a specialist market.'

'Would you do the buying for me as well as shipping? I presume you have contacts on the Continent? I will pay extra for that service.'

Charles gave a wry smile and gave a little shake of his head. 'We would act merely as shipping agents for you. The purchase and arrangements for the goods to be at the quay would be your responsibility and that of the persons with whom you are dealing. That is the most amicable way for all concerned. There can then be no accusation that I have not made a good purchase for you. Besides, why pay extra for something you can do yourself?' He gave a momentary pause, his attention fixed on Julian. 'I see from your expression that you are disappointed. I take it that you have no contacts in the wine trade?'

'None. Can you make any suggestions?'

'I can give you the names of four reputable firms trading out of Amsterdam.' He smiled to himself when he saw relief come to Julian's face.

'That would be most helpful.'

'How will you get in touch with them?'

'By letter, I suppose. Maybe you could take one for me?'

'Personal contact would be best.' Charles snapped his fingers as a thought struck him. 'Rather than give you those names, why not come with me? I'll introduce you to one of the leading merchants in Amsterdam. His advice will be invaluable.'

'You would do that? But I'm a comparative stranger.' Julian showed amazement.

'We have shaken hands on a deal.'

'Yes, but introducing me to prospective

suppliers in Holland was not part of it.'

'Well, I'm making it part of it. I think we have got on well from the start and will continue to do so in the future.'

Julian smiled. 'I came here in some trepidation but as soon as I saw you that disappeared. And when you spoke, I felt I had found a friend.'

Charles returned the smile. 'I had the same feeling too. It was as if I'd known you for some years. You'll come then?'

'Yes.' There was no denying the enthusiasm in his voice.

'If your enterprise was supposed to be a secret from your father so you could impress him, how is he to condone your going?'

'I'll tell him a friend wants me to go with him to Holland. Father's always telling me to widen my experience of life before I take on more responsibility within the firm.'

'Good. I sail on the *Britannia*.'

'I'll book a passage immediately,' Julian said, excited by the luck that had come his way.

As the *Britannia* met the sea at the mouth of the Humber the two young men leaning on the rail, getting their last look at Spurn Point, breathed deeply on the sea air.

'Are you a good sailor?' asked Charles.

'Yes, and I like to be on deck. You won't see me in my cabin until it's dark.'

'Someone after my own heart.'

'Then we should enjoy the voyage. Have you any family, Charles?'

'There's my father and my sister Anna, two

years younger than me.'

'I can tell from the way you speak her name that you think a lot of her.'

'I do. We are very close. And you? Have you any brothers or sisters?'

'Two sisters – Rebecca, a year younger than me, and Caroline, a year younger still. You must meet them. You don't have to stay in an inn when you come to Hull in future, you must come to us. I know Father will enjoy talking business with you, Mother will fuss over you, and my sisters cannot help but be charmed by you.'

'You're a flatterer,' laughed Charles. 'And you must visit us. I hope by then my father will be over his desire to meet no one. You are a stranger and he might accept you, as you have no place in his past.'

'Maybe I would be of some help.'

'That could be possible.' Charles seized on this chance to hasten his father back into the world he once knew. 'We will make you an invitation soon.'

'Good. I look forward to it.' Julian straightened, turned and leaned with his back to the rail. 'Now, Charles, you had better acquaint me with the trading possibilities in Amsterdam.'

'Things have not been too good, with Napoleon's attempt to keep British trade out of the Continent. Thank goodness the Navy negated his attempt at a blockade, and now that his defeat appears to be near there is more chance for open trading. Napoleon is unpredictable but countries such as Holland see the necessity of trading for economic survival. It has

101

gone on clandestinely throughout the war. It was risky but worth it to keep trade flowing. You needed the right contacts, those who could be trusted. My father was adept at getting them. I hope I can keep up the good work he did.'

'I'm sure you will and I'm grateful for what you are doing for me,' replied Julian.

'You'll find what you want in Amsterdam. It's a very important commercial centre, trades with all corners of the globe. It's the place where things happen. It has an excellent system of canals. They're lined with buildings of all types, not just warehouses. In most cases there is a roadway alongside the canal often lined by trees, mainly elms. So you have a picturesque city. There are few squares or public buildings. The streets are narrow and, like anywhere else, various areas have developed differently.' Charles gave a little smile. 'It has a charm all its own. I suppose that has a lot to do with the architecture which is so different from ours.'

'I certainly look forward to seeing it after the picture you have painted, but I must not let it distract me from the main purpose of my visit.'

'Wise man.'

They both felt invigorated when they stepped ashore. Charles quickly hired a carriage to take them to a small exclusive hotel on the Singel. After a few gasps of amazement at the rich variety of the façades of the buildings with their distinctive Dutch style, Julian lapsed into silence. Charles kept quiet, allowing him to absorb his first impressions of this thriving city.

Stepping out of the carriage, Julian let his gaze run along the tree-lined canal then turned to stare at the elaborate entrance to the hotel. Its green door was divided into two panels each with its own individually carved surround, the upper and larger one featuring scrollwork of feathers and leaves across the top. Above the door was a matching plaster strip from which an imitation tree, in green, sprouted in front of a cut-glass window. The windows on either side of the door had an equally elaborately carved framework as had those on the two storeys above. The arched gable held a carved lion and eagle in protective pose beside a shield.

Charles opened the door with the highly polished handle. They stepped into a cool panelled hallway, sparsely but elegantly furnished. Immediately a middle-aged lady appeared from a door on the right. Her face broke into a beaming smile.

'Mr Charles!' Her English was good with only a trace of an accent. She held out her arms and embraced him. 'It is good to see you again.'

'And you, Frau Hein.' Charles was equally warm with his greeting. He had taken to this motherly lady on his first visit with his father two years ago. She was small and round, but he knew that behind the soft exterior there was a person always in control of the situation. Her hair was straight, drawn tightly from her head into a small bun nestling at the back of her neck. It gave her an air of severity that was unjustified. Her hazel-coloured eyes were alive with an alertness which was quick to size up strangers. They had already weighed Julian up and he would have had her approval even if he had not been with Charles.

'Let me introduce my friend, Julian Kirby. Julian, this is Frau Digna Hein, a delightful lady who with her husband Roel runs this exclusive establishment. They are very selective in their clientele. Make sure they like you and you will have a home in Amsterdam whenever you visit.'

'Don't make us sound such ogres, Mr Charles,' she said with a chuckle. 'But I can see already that Mr Julian will be welcome here any time. My eyes tell me that.'

'Frau Hein, you flatter me and do not know me.'

'Ah, but I do. Your bearing tells me that you have confidence. And I know Mr Charles must have been impressed by you otherwise he would not bring you here. He knew I would like you.'

Julian inclined his head in acknowledgement. 'Frau Hein, you are most kind.'

She turned to the door from which she had come and called, 'Roel.'

They heard a quick step and a man of medium height and build appeared. On seeing Charles his greeting was as effusive as his wife's. She quickly introduced Julian who felt a warm, friendly handshake and knew that some unnoticed signal must have passed between wife and husband which said she had approved of him.

When Herr Hein had made his greetings he turned to Charles. 'Your father not with you?'

'Alas, no. My mother was killed in a riding accident recently and he has taken it so badly that he is almost a recluse.'

The expression that came to their faces displayed their shock. 'Oh, my dear boy, how terrible for you all,' said Roel, almost choking on his words. There were tears in Digna's eyes as she embraced Charles in a sympathetic hug that said more than words could.

'Come.' Roel indicated a door on the right.

They entered a room that was tastefully furnished. To one side and at right angles to the ornate fireplace was a chaise-longue covered in deep red moquette. Opposite were two matching armchairs. The floor was covered with a patterned carpet, and a wallpaper of subdued colours had been chosen to complement it. Several high-quality Dutch landscapes betrayed Digna's and Roel's taste in art, chosen not only for the subject but also for the skill of the artists.

'Please be seated.' Roel indicated the chaise-longue.

His wife sat in one of the armchairs while he went to a rosewood sideboard and poured out three glasses of wine.

'Your father must not grieve too deeply nor too long,' offered Digna. 'Your lovely mother would not want him to. Sadly I met her only twice. She was so charming. We got on so well. Tell your father to get back to work as quickly as possible. I wish he had been with you. Maybe I could have helped.'

While she had been speaking, Roel had brought the wine. He stood with his back to the fireplace. His face was serious as he raised his glass. 'To the memory of a dear lady.'

A respectful silence hung in the room. They

drank, each with their own memories.

'I wish I had known her,' said Julian, half to himself, but the others caught the words.

'I wish you had, too,' said Charles. 'You must meet my sister, she is very much like Mother.'

'I will look forward to that.'

Digna straightened her back as she took charge of the situation before it became too melancholy. 'Now, Charles, I suppose you are here on business? How long will you be staying?'

'You suppose right. I'm not sure for how long. Must you know exactly?'

Frau Hein shook her head and with a smile of understanding on her lips, said, 'Of course not. The rooms are yours for as long as you want. I suppose you would like separate rooms?'

'It would be more convenient,' replied Charles, who shot Julian a querying glance and received a nod of agreement.

'Very well. When you have finished your wine I will show you your rooms.' While they did so the Heins directed the conversation. It made Julian feel at home, and at the same time they learned about him.

When they took him to his room he thanked them for their hospitality and indicated that he would see them again for he was sure that if he found the trade he wanted he would be paying Amsterdam many more visits.

'I'm sure you will. We have survived the ruthlessness of Napoleon, and I'm sure we'll emerge from the recent setbacks all the stronger,' said Roel reassuringly.

Julian was pleased to find that was also the view of Hendrick de Klerk when Charles took him to a house on Herengracht. Standing on the tree-lined bank of the canal, its façade was rich with bright colours. Red bricks and white sandstone had been mingled into pleasing patterns and adorned with scrolls, pillars, vases and balustrades. The stepped gable, typical of many of the houses they had passed on the way, was highly decorated and held a panel with the carved relief of a sailing ship and the letters H d K in flowing script.

'You must be taking me to meet someone of importance judging by the outside of this house,' commented Julian when Charles indicated the building to which they were going.

'Yes, Hendrick de Klerk is one of the leading merchants in Amsterdam, if not the leading one. You'll find him a charming man and a very shrewd one. If he gives you any advice, take it. He has two sons who are engaged in the business with him. They too know the trading world inside out so pay heed if they are there, and also to his daughter Magdalena. She's pretty, she's a charmer, but behind her easy-going manner is a sharp brain. Her father soon recognised this. He gave her a good education which enabled her to develop her particular interests: music, art, a love of books and Amsterdam's architecture. He also saw that she was interested in the trading world. It took a forward-looking man to introduce a young woman into a man's world, but he did and encouraged her so that she is now as knowledge-able as her brothers and he seeks her advice readily.'

'Do I detect more than a passing interest in this young lady?' asked Julian with a teasing grin.

Charles returned it with a serious expression. 'You do.'

'So that means I shouldn't get ideas that I...'

'You certainly shouldn't.'

'All's fair in love and war.' Julian sensed Charles bristle. He slapped him on the shoulder and grinned. 'Don't worry. I'll keep my mind on other things. I couldn't mar the friendship you have shown me.'

'Good. As long as you understand.'

'Do you think her father will allow her to marry an Englishman?'

'We'll see when the time is right to ask him.'

The door of the de Klerk house was opened by a manservant who, recognising Charles, led them to a door on the right of the hall. He knocked and opened it. 'Mr Charles Mason to see you, sir.' He stood to one side to allow Charles and Julian to enter the room and then closed the door.

The room was fitted out as a study from which Hendrick de Klerk and his family could work on their business of trading in commodities from all parts of the world. Even though it was a working room the furniture was of the best. Four mahogany desks were arranged in a small arc at one side of the room which was almost three times as long as it was wide. Charts, plans and maps were affixed to one wall. Another had a series of paintings which charted the voyage of a trading ship from leaving port to returning with a full cargo. A tall window gave light from the street while at the opposite end of the room the wall appeared to be almost all glass with windows abutting both sides of a glass door which gave on to a small paved courtyard.

As Charles led the way a slim man, who obviously looked after his figure, moved lithely from behind his desk. His face was long and thin and his Van Dyke beard seemed to add to its length. The grey hair at the temples gave him a distinguished look which also came from the fact that he held himself straight, a legacy of his military training as a young man. His warm smile despatched any untoward ceremony from the meeting.

'My dear Charles, it is good to see you.' He held his arms wide to embrace his visitor.

'And you too, sir,' replied Charles as he returned the embrace.

'I've told you before, no formality, please.' The rebuke, so mildly uttered, could cause no offence.

'May I introduce my friend, Julian Kirby? Julian, this is Herr Hendrick de Klerk.'

'I'm pleased to meet you, sir.' He offered his hand.

Hendrick took it and Julian knew that he was greeted as a friend even before Herr de Klerk spoke. 'Welcome to my home and my place of work. As I said to Charles, no formalities.' He must put these two young men on the same standing. If this stranger was a friend of Charles then that was good enough for him. 'New to your firm, Charles?'

'No. His father is a merchant in Hull. Julian is looking to expand their range of commodities and wants to trade through Amsterdam. I've brought him hoping you will give him some advice?'

Hendrick's eyes filled with curiosity. 'I will if I can.'

'Thank you, sir,' said Julian.

Herr de Klerk raised a finger.

Julian smiled apologetically. 'Sorry.'

'Now come, sit down.' Hendrick indicated two chairs in front of his desk. As he returned to his own, he enquired, 'Your father did not come this time?'

Charles was about to explain when the door opened. The two young men looked round and were immediately on their feet. Julian's heart almost missed a beat. He was under a spell immediately and knew now why Charles had warned him against any attempt to gain this girl's affection. She was beautiful, he could think of no other word to describe her. Her face was heart-shaped and held exquisitely formed limpid eyes, their colour light blue, their brightness enhanced by her flaxen hair which came to her shoulders. They were eyes which could be serious but would always have behind them a bubbling mischief. Her dress of shot silk fitted her to perfection, emphasising her small waist and well-proportioned body. There was a queenly dignity about her as she seemed to glide across the room to them.

'Charles.' There was warmth and pleasure in her voice, which was soft and rich.

'Magdalena.' He held out his hands to her and she took them with a smile that expressed delight at seeing him. 'This is my friend Julian Kirby. It is his first time in Amsterdam.'

'My welcome to you,' she said as she offered him her hand.

He took it and bowed. 'I am delighted to meet you.' Her touch was gentle and soft.

'I hope you will be impressed by our city and that you have a pleasant time here.'

'Julian is here on business,' explained her father.

'He can enjoy himself at the same time,' Magdalena reminded him.

Hendrick shrugged his shoulders. 'Charles was about to explain to me why his father has not come.'

Julian was already drawing up a chair for Magdalena to join them.

Charles explained his father's absence which elicited deep sympathy from father and daughter.

'You must bring your father to us. Let him stay here. A change of scene and of company will do him good, and maybe seeing what is going on around him here will ease him back into his own work. He must come. He is important to our trade.' Hendrick threw up his arms in horror at what he had just said. 'My dear boy, I do not imply that you are not capable but I...'

'I took no offence,' broke in Charles quickly. 'And I thank you for your kind offer. I will do my best to persuade Father. Like you, I think it would do him good.'

'And I think he must keep his interest in his art collection. Tell him I'm keeping my eyes open for anything which I think he would like.'

111

'Alas, he says that interest has gone. The things he bought were for Mother so now he sees no point in continuing the collection.'

Hendrick gave a resigned shrug of his shoulders. 'Please bring him and we shall see... Now to business. Ours we will discuss tomorrow. Today, this young man will have my attention.' He gave Julian a reassuring smile for he had detected a touch of nervousness come to the young man.

'Tell me of your interests, the stability of your company and the commodities in which you wish to trade?'

Before Julian could reply Magdalena spoke up. 'Father, though this will be of interest and some significance to me, I think a chat between you two without anyone else present would be appropriate and more comfortable for Julian. Charles and I will take a walk by the canal.' She was rising from her chair as she spoke, signifying that she had made a decision which could not be countered by anyone.

'Very well,' replied her father. He would not go against his daughter's wishes, for he knew from previous visits that she thought the young Englishman pleasant company.

As the door closed behind her and Charles, Herr de Klerk gave Julian a small smile. His piercing blue eyes concentrated on the young man, verifying the decision he had already come to. This was a person he liked and, if that impression was furthered by what he would hear in the next half-hour or so, he would help him in whatever way he could.

'Now, Julian, let us get down to business. The answers to my questions, please.'

Julian felt tense in front of this man who projected a formidable presence, not by any strong physical attribute, but by sheer force of personality. Julian could sense that this was not through a desire to dominate, though he reckoned it could be if Herr de Klerk did not take to the person whom he was confronting. Julian felt no sense of domination now and as soon as he started to speak and sensed Herr de Klerk's interest, his nervousness gradually faded.

'Well, sir, first of all...'

Hendrick held up his hand. 'I said, no formalities.'

Julian gestured his apology. 'My father founded his trading firm in Scarborough on the east coast of Yorkshire. He did well, trading in all manner of goods. He began to feel restricted in Scarborough and saw better opportunities for expansion if he moved to Hull.'

'I know Hull and Whitby but I've had no dealings with any merchant in Scarborough, therefore I judge your father to be a wise man by moving.'

'I agree. I think there are greater opportunities for us in Hull.'

'So, has your father any specific commodities in which he is interested? I presume you are here as his representative?' He saw Julian hesitate. 'You are, are you not?'

Julian straightened his shoulders and projected honesty and confidence. 'I must be frank with you, I do not represent my father.'

Hendrick raised an eyebrow in surprise. He leaned forward on his desk and met Julian's eyes with a piercing gaze which said, Be straight with me or I will have nothing more to do with you.

Julian read it correctly and plunged straight into his explanation. 'I want more responsibility in the firm but my father keeps a tight rein and vets every move I make.'

'That's his privilege,' de Klerk pointed out coldly, naturally taking the side of a parent whose authority might be challenged.

'I appreciate that,' replied Julian, 'but there comes a time in every parent's life when they must trust their children.'

Hendrick smiled to himself for that observation had reminded him of his former opposition to his father's caution. 'Very true,' he agreed, and his mind turned to his own tolerant dealings with his children, firm but understanding and allowing individual talents to blossom.

'Well, sir, I saw that I needed to prove myself and decided to instigate some enterprise of my own which would show my father my capabilities. There is a firm of traders in Hull by the name of Heatherington. I knew that the Masons of Whitby acted as shipping agents for them. I wanted to see if they would ship something for me into Hull. I discovered where Charles was staying and went immediately to contact him.'

'You had not met him until this week?'

'No. When I told him my reason for contacting him he was sympathetic and indicated he would help. It was he who suggested I come to Amsterdam with him.'

114

'And here you are.' Hendrick smiled benignly.

'Seeking your help and advice.' There was hope in Julian's voice and it did not go unnoticed. Hendrick admired enterprise and initiative. 'What had you in mind?'

'Charles is willing to ship goods for me but, as he has a contract with Mr Heatherington, he does not want to deal in anything that might injure their relationship.'

'Wise man. But where does that leave you? Doesn't your father already have someone he deals with in Holland?'

'He has. Carel Decker.'

'Why not go to him?'

'If I did my father might hear of my dealings before I want him to.'

'So you came to me.'

'I discussed a possible choice of commodities that would not upset Charles's agreement with Mr Heatherington. He recommended that I sought your advice.'

'And those products are?'

'I believe there is a growing demand for wine in England. My father doesn't agree, so I see this as the opportunity to show him that there is profit to be made from it and also to show him that I have the initiative and drive to take on more responsibility. Charles tells me that Heatherington's only deal in a small amount of very highclass wines so that if I were to avoid these I would not upset their relationship.'

Hendrick nodded and pondered this information for a moment. 'Charles would ship your goods?'

'Yes.'

'We have dealt with the Masons for many years and have found them most reliable and efficient. You can be sure of good service from them. I think turning to the wine trade would be good for you. Though we are general merchants we do have our specialities but wine isn't one of them.' He gave a little smile when he saw disappointment cloud Julian's face. 'Don't worry, I know of several wine merchants in Amsterdam, any of whom I could recommend.' He paused a moment considering the next step. 'The best thing is for you to return tomorrow with Charles. While I am conducting business with him I will get my son Reynier to take you to one of those merchants, Pieter Bremer.'

'That is very kind of you. I appreciate your help very much.'

'It is nothing.' Hendrick gave a dismissive wave of his hand. 'When you have proved yourself to your father, bring him over to meet me and my family. Maybe we could do more business together.'

'I will, sir. I know he would be delighted to meet you.'

'Now tell me more about him, and about trading in Hull? I don't suppose Magdalena and Charles will be back just yet.'

'It is good to see you again, Magdalena,' said Charles as they fell into step beside the canal.

'It is also my pleasure,' she returned. 'I am so sorry about your mother.' She wanted to make her compassion known to him privately. 'She was

116

a charming lady and I liked her from the moment I met her. I will miss her visits. My heart goes out to you, dear Charles.'

'Your words are kind and I will remember them always. I know that she liked you too.'

'How is Anna taking it?'

'Devastated, as we all are, but she and I see that life has to go on. She is worried about Father becoming a recluse but we are determined to see that he doesn't.'

'I hope you soon succeed. When it is possible, bring Anna to see us too.'

'She would like that.'

'And you are always welcome, whether it be for business or pleasure.'

'It is always both when I have such a charming and pretty business associate here.'

'And what business can she expect this time, or have you none for her?' Magdalena asked coyly.

He did not answer her question but teasingly said, 'I am here to verify the arrangements for the shipment of the Heatherington merchandise. And there'll be whatever Julian wants. The ship will not be full with that so I need to purchase for our own business in Whitby.'

'Those commodities will be bought through my father?'

'Yes. And shipped on the *Grace*.'

'So you don't want the usual shipment of spices from me?' She answered his teasing with pouting lips and a disappointed expression.

He inclined his head as he said, 'Oh, dear, I've cast a shadow over your beauty. I must remedy it.' He smiled. 'Of course I want the usual from you. If you can manage it, I'll take double the quantity of gin and lace this time.'

'I'll consider it,' she chaffed haughtily.

'If you feel like that, I'll go elsewhere,' he goaded.

She saw the twinkle in his eye as they enjoyed this exchange. It matched that in hers. She held up her hands. 'All right, I surrender.' Her face lightened. 'I'll see to that for you. Let me know the proposed date of arrival of the...' She paused for him to add the information.

'The *Hound*,' he said. 'But I am considering using the *Grace* and the *Gull* as well for bringing contraband along with our normal goods directly into Whitby.'

'Be careful, Charles. That could be more dangerous than using the *Hound* and the *Hunter* as you do.'

'It will mean bigger profits. I think I must make the best of the situation while I can. I can foresee the government reducing tax on many of the goods and that would make smuggling less worthwhile, so I say, make the profit while I can.'

'True, but be cautious.'

'I will.'

'Will Laven and Myers crew the *Hound?*'

'Yes.'

'Excellent. They are very reliable. The containers will be as usual.'

'Good. They are easy to stow, unload and dispose of.'

They strolled on. Their conversation left business matters behind. They paused now and then to watch the activity on the canal, enjoying

118

each other's company in a friendship that had a deep empathy forged by Charles's first visit and strengthened since.

'As much as I don't want to, I think it is time we returned,' said Magdalena eventually.

'Very well.' The reluctance in his voice was tempered by the desire to comply with her wishes.

'Julian and I have had a most interesting talk,' Herr de Klerk informed them when they reached the house on Herengracht.

'You have been able to help him?' asked Magdalena.

'Certainly. When have I ever refused help to anyone to whom I take a liking?'

'Rarely,' she agreed. 'And what this time?'

'I am going to get Reynier to take him to see Herr Bremer tomorrow while Charles and I discuss business.'

'A good choice, Father, if Julian wants to go into the wine trade.' She turned to him. 'Have you dealt in wine before?'

'No.'

'Herr Bremer is shrewd. He has been in the wine trade for many years. He is a fair man, but his son is a different sort. He'll try anything for a quick guilder. If he's around, exercise caution. But you'll have Reynier with you so you should be all right.'

The following morning Charles and Julian enjoyed a brisk walk in the sharp air on a day when the weather promised to hold fine. Boats were already moving lazily along the canals.

119

There was a jauntiness about Charles's step, a brightness about his attitude. He once again expressed his pleasure that Julian was pleased with his interview with Herr de Klerk. 'You'll be in good hands with Reynier. You'll like him.'

So it proved. Julian took to the young Dutchman immediately he saw him. Reynier's handshake reciprocated the feeling.

'Shall we go?' His immediate suggestion showed a man of quick but certain decision, a man who did not believe in wasting time. But as Julian was to find out he was a person who knew how to put business aside and relax and enjoy himself, too, especially with good food. He matched Julian in height but was a little broader of shoulder. His eyes were bright and sharp like his father's, his hair flaxen like his sister's and mother's.

As they started to make their way through the city Reynier kept up a constant stream of information, pointing out landmarks, stopping to allow Julian to admire the scenes from the many bridges they crossed, and informing him about the trade carried out from the variety of warehouses they passed. He was articulate about the view they would see as they approached the bridge across the Amstel, the river around which Amsterdam had grown. Julian was not disappointed as they walked on to the bridge. Barges and ships lined banks already alive with activity as goods were loaded and unloaded. The diverse façades of the buildings – warehouses, residences, offices – serving a multitude of purposes gave the whole scene the atmosphere of a painting lovingly accomplished. Downriver another bridge was backed by a slender church tower topped by a golden sphere shimmering in the morning sun.

Reynier made no comment but left Julian to take in the scene. For his part he could not help but compare it with some the drabber aspects of the Hull docks, where builders and architects had notably failed to combine aesthetics with practicality.

With the view etched on his mind, he said, 'I never expected Amsterdam to be like this.'

Reynier smiled. 'I think most visitors get a surprise when they first come here. But now we should get down to business. You will see more as we walk downriver, cut back to Warmoesstraat from where Herr Bremer trades.'

Once they reached the building they were quickly shown to the wine merchant's office. It was pleasantly furnished though not as tastefully as de Klerk's.

Herr Bremer came from behind his desk to greet them. He was a small man, dark-haired, with a slight olive tint to the skin that made Julian think there might be some Spanish blood in him. If so this could be the reason for his specialising in the wine trade. 'Reynier, it is good to see you. Your father is in prime health, I trust?'

'Never better, Herr Bremer. He asked me to bring this young Englishman to see you. May I introduce Julian Kirby. His father is a merchant in Hull.'

'I am pleased to meet you, Mr Kirby.' Bremer smiled benevolently and shook hands with a solid grip. 'I hope your stay in Amsterdam is proving pleasant.'

'I only arrived yesterday morning. This is my first visit. I'm finding it a charming city and now I am pleased to meet you, Herr Bremer.'

'No doubt Reynier's father had a purpose in sending you to meet me?'

'He did, sir. He thought you were a person with whom I could do business.'

'Though I do deal in a variety of merchandise it is only when convenient as an adjunct to my main business – the wine trade – so I assume, as Herr de Klerk has sent you, it is wine that interests you?' While he was speaking he indicated two chairs to the younger men.

'You assume correctly,' replied Julian as he made himself comfortable.

'Then let us get down to business. What is your particular interest?'

'First of all I must tell you that this is the first time we have gone into the wine trade. I am therefore very much in your hands. Herr de Klerk assured me that I would be dealing with a fair man and I trust his judgement.' Bremer spread his hands in embarrassed acceptance of the compliment, as Julian continued. 'The shipping arrangements will be in the hands of Mason and Son who operate out of Whitby.'

'Admirable firm,' said Herr Bremer.

'The son, Charles, is with me in Amsterdam. He told me that they already ship wines for Heatherington's of Hull.'

'That is correct. They purchase some high-quality wines from me.'

'I want to avoid those for I would not want to damage the good relationship we have with the Masons. Maybe come down in quality without reaching a poor wine that would damage the type of trade I visualise – that is, providing discerning palates with pleasant, acceptable wines.'

Herr Bremer nodded. 'We will be able to supply you to those stipulations.'

'I am in your hands, because I do not know wines.'

'I shall personally select a variety for you. You can get reactions from your customers and then order accordingly in the future.'

'That is very kind of you, Herr Bremer.' Julian gave a little smile. 'The future? Well, that will depend on English tastes.'

'I'm sure we can tempt them. Let me give you a taste of one of the wines I will choose.' He rose from his chair and went to a mahogany cupboard from which he took three glasses and a decanter. He poured, took two glasses to his visitors and returned for his own. When he reached his seat he raised his glass and the three of them savoured the wine. He watched the two young men intently for their immediate reaction.

Julian raised an eyebrow in approval of the taste and Reynier pursed his lips and nodded.

Herr Bremer cast him an enquiring look.

'An excellent choice, Herr Bremer. A pleasant fruity taste without being overpowering, and there is the touch of the Spanish sun.'

Herr Bremer turned his querying look on Julian.

'A very pleasing taste,' he said. 'As I told you, I

123

don't know wines so cannot analyse like Reynier but I am sure this one could prove popular.'

Herr Bremer smiled. 'It was because you said you had no knowledge of wines that I chose that one. It is a good wine for beginners yet also satisfies the habitual drinker. I will make that one the bulk of the consignment and the rest will suit a wide range of tastes. Now, quantity and price?'

As these aspects were discussed Julian relied heavily on Reynier's advice and the suggestions put forward by Herr Bremer. Throughout their dealings the wine merchant made a list and four columns on a sheet of paper. They were nearing the end of the negotiations when the door opened and a young man entered who could be no one but Herr Bremer's son, except that he was slightly taller and had a harsher expression to his face. His eyes were less friendly, charged with suspicion.

His father introduced him as Coenraad. He nodded with token cordiality to Reynier. The hand offered to Julian was limp. 'Mr Kirby is from England and we are about to conclude a deal for a shipment of wine,' his father told him.

Coenraad had gone to stand beside him. He picked up the paper on which his father had been writing, glanced quickly at the figures. 'Against each wine you've put quantity, cost price and selling price.' There was a note of disgust in his voice.

'Yes,' replied his father firmly.

Coenraad tossed the sheet of paper back in front of him. 'Those are stupid prices. You know very well that you can get a better return from our other customers.'

'That may be, Coenraad, but Julian is a new customer whose trade I believe will grow. I have given him to understand that this is a special price which will cover three shipments only and then we will have to revise our terms.'

'Three shipments! I don't believe it.' Coenraad's face had darkened. He glared at Reynier. 'I expect this is your doing, talking my father into a deal on which we'll make practically no profit? And no doubt Mr Kirby will go elsewhere when those three shipments have been made.'

Reynier matched glare for glare, Julian bristled at the inference, but before he could speak Herr Bremer said sharply, 'This had nothing to do with Reynier, and I trust Julian.'

'Well, I don't.' Coenraad swung round the desk and stormed from the room.

Herr Bremer looked crestfallen. He was embarrassed by his son's behaviour. 'I must apologise.' He spread his arms in a plea for forgiveness.

'Don't apologise, Herr Bremer,' said Reynier reassuringly. 'I warned Julian that your son had a different temperament from you.'

'Forgive him. He is a good businessman but I'm afraid he wants to extract the most from any deal and that sometimes blinds him to future possibilities. He's hot-headed. Gets that from his mother's side of the family. Her grandfather ... oh, what a temper.' He shot a look at the ceiling with an expression that said he had experienced that temper personally. Then he shrugged his shoulders and said, 'Are you happy with the deal?'

'More than happy, sir. You have been most generous. And you can be assured that I will never think of buying wine from anyone else but you.'

'And no doubt you'll show my son how right I was when we negotiate again after the third shipment?'

'I certainly will.'

When they left the offices of Herr Bremer, Reynier suggested that they celebrate Julian's venture into the wine trade and took him to a quiet inn on the outskirts of the Jordaan area of the city. With tall wooden partitions dividing the tables from each other they were able to enjoy a degree of privacy. Reynier ordered two beers. When the foaming tankards had been placed in front of them by a young attractive waitress who expressed pleasure in having Herr Reynier visit her father's establishment again, and they had taken their first drinks, he leaned forward on the table in a confidential attitude.

'Have you any interests other than wine?' he asked.

'My father looks to those.'

'What about spices, nutmeg, pepper, vanilla? Tea? Gin? Brandy?'

'Duty is heavy on those and my father...'

'Never mind your father. You said you want to prove yourself to him, and you will through the deal you have made with Herr Bremer, but what if you could make more through the commodities I have just mentioned?'

'How can I make more than my father is

already doing? The duty...' He stopped. Reynier's inference dawned on him. 'You mean, smuggle?'

'Exactly, but don't you English regard it as freetrading? I can obtain any of those goods for you.'

'Maybe, but I can't smuggle them on board Charles's ship. I haven't a vessel at my disposal and no means to hide and distribute the contraband in England.'

'You can set it up.'

'Does Charles do any of this?'

Reynier shrugged his shoulders. 'I don't know. People don't talk about it even in their own families. There's too much at stake and the fewer people who know of your personal activities, the less likelihood there is of betrayal, accidental or otherwise. There are risks, but there's money to be made at it as you must know.'

Julian nodded as he considered the seeds that had been sown.

'As I say, I haven't the necessary ship and couldn't finance that without my father's knowledge.'

'Right. Suppose we go into this together? I will supply a ship, a small sloop, and trustworthy crew. I'll buy the commodities at the best possible price. I have connections. What you will need to do is arrange for storage and disposal in England. We can come to some arrangement about sharing the profits.' He called for two more beers. He had seen a gleam of interest in Julian's eyes and another drink would give him time to digest the proposal.

But Julian did not need more time. He was

tempted by the idea of greater profits. After the girl had brought the tankards he raised his and said, 'To a profitable partnership.'

Chapter Six

Charles and Julian watched the low Dutch coastline become a mere pencil mark on the horizon and then disappear.

'I have much to thank you for,' said Julian, lifting his voice above the swish of the sea, the creak of the ropes and crack of the billowing canvas. He turned and leaned back against the rail.

'Do that after you've made your first profit. I hope for your sake that will be soon.'

'I'm sure it will, and through Herr Bremer's generosity it should be greater than I expected.' His mind flashed to the possibilities of even more profit from the arrangements with Reynier. It was on the tip of his tongue to tell Charles about it but he remembered Reynier's warning. Trust no one. Instead he said, 'No doubt your interest in Magdalena will take you back to Amsterdam soon?'

'Of course. In my father's absence I can arrange these visits to suit myself.'

'Maybe there will be times when we can travel together?'

'You are thinking of returning?'

'Certainly. I'm determined to conduct this wine trade so that Father will be in no doubt it should become part of our regular dealings. In fact, I would like to see the first consignment taken aboard in Amsterdam and to sail back with it.'

'Right. The *Grace* will be assigned for that voyage. I'll be on board. She'll put into Hull for you.'

'I'd appreciate that, and will see that we have goods to ship to Holland.'

'Excellent. This is the start not only of a friendship, but also of a commercial arrangement that can benefit us both.' Charles held out his hand. Julian took it and an understanding was sealed.

As their ship was manoeuvred into the quay in Hull, Charles noticed the *North Star* berthed nearby. He knew she plied her trade between London and Newcastle. Pointing her out to Julian he said, 'I'm going to see if she's heading north and calling at Whitby. I'd rather sail than suffer that uncomfortable coach journey.'

As soon as they had disembarked they made enquiries and, learning that the *North Star* would leave the next morning for Whitby and New-castle, Charles booked a passage. Immediately, Julian invited him to spend the night at his family home.

He led the way quickly from the dock to Albion Street with its row of three-storeyed town houses. He climbed five steps leading to a smart dark green-painted door with an arched fanlight above. It stood in a small recess, the front of which was surrounded by an elaborately corniced and pedimented doorcase. White paint had recently been applied to the house's tall sash windows and gave a light, uplifting appearance.

The sound of the brass knocker resounded through the hall and brought a maid who, on opening the door and seeing Julian, greeted him with a smile as she said, 'Welcome back, Mr Julian, I trust you had a pleasant time.'

'Indeed I did, Nellie. This is Mr Charles Mason from Whitby. He will be staying the night. Please see that the guest bedroom is ready.'

'Certainly, sir,' she returned. She smiled at Charles and closed the door. 'The family are in the drawing room.'

Julian nodded and, after depositing their valises and slipping off their coats, indicated to Charles to follow him. When they entered the room excitement broke out. There was pleasure in her voice when his mother called his name. His two sisters jumped up from the sofa and ran to him to give him a welcoming hug and start firing questions about Amsterdam. Their queries subsided and they looked abashed when they realised there was a stranger witnessing their enthusiastic welcome. Julian's father had risen from his armchair.

'Welcome home, son.' He gave Julian a fatherly tap on the shoulder. 'Is this the young man who persuaded you to go to Amsterdam?' His gaze passed to Charles.

'It is, Father. Charles Mason from Whitby.'

'The Whitby merchants?'

'Yes.'

'I'm pleased to meet you, young man.' Mr Kirby's handshake was welcoming. He glanced at his son. 'I didn't know he was a friend of yours. When did you meet?'

'The day I told you I had been invited to accompany a friend to Holland.'

'And you were that after one meeting?'

'Yes, sir,' put in Charles quickly. He must avert any questions that might indicate he had gone to Amsterdam on business. 'I was going to Amsterdam on a personal visit to friends. When I met Julian he showed interest in the city and told me he had never been, so I asked him if he would like to accompany me.'

'I'm pleased that he accepted. It would do him good. Now come and meet my wife and daughters.'

Julian's quick glance of thanks expressed his relief at Charles's intervention.

'I am pleased to meet you, Mrs Kirby.'

'And I you,' she returned with enthusiasm.

'Mother, Charles sails for Whitby tomorrow so I've invited him to stay the night with us.'

'Splendid. I must tell Nellie.' She started to rise from her chair.

'I've already done so.'

'Good.'

'My daughters, Rebecca and Caroline,' put in Septimus Kirby.

Charles turned to the two girls. He gave a small bow and knew from the light in their eyes that he was being closely scrutinised.

They were dressed in similar style. Their muslin dresses, with only the slightest flare from the high waist, came to their shoes in scalloped flounces. Rebecca's muslin was purple sprigged in pink while Caroline had chosen a light blue muslin with a small motif in a slightly darker blue.

132

Puffed at the shoulders and coming from a lowish neckline, the sleeves were elbow-length.

Caroline's had been the more penetrating gaze of one seeking to know who had become a friend of her brother. Charles suspected that there might be a touch of jealousy of anyone who tried to draw close to a brother she adored. Her sharp brown eyes met Charles's for a brief moment and she turned away to a chair beside her mother, blushing in the knowledge that her scrutiny had been observed.

Rebecca's study had been for her own interest. It would have been the same of any young man who might become involved in the family's life, and from the fact that her brother had invited him to stay the night, it seemed as if this one would. Charles realised that her observation was different from her younger sister's. He saw it in her hazel eyes. They were as soft as suede, gentle, but with a glow about them that spelt curiosity and a mind ready to absorb new experiences. It gave an added attraction to her heart-shaped face which dimpled when she smiled and revealed shining teeth. Her brown hair had been taken up from the neck and held on top of her head by a small bow.

'No doubt you two young men would like to refresh yourselves? Julian, please show Charles...' Mrs Kirby paused and inclined her head questioningly at him. 'May I call you Charles?'

'Of course, Mrs Kirby.' He assumed his most charming manner.

When he reached his room and the door closed behind him he realised he had presented himself well to Mrs Kirby but it had really been for Rebecca's benefit. He had been aware that he liked what he saw. He pulled his thoughts up sharply. There was Magdalena to consider. Why had he been so smitten by a new acquaintance? It was nothing really. He had detected an interest in him, had been flattered and had reciprocated. He raised an eyebrow as if to expunge further thoughts on the matter from his mind.

Charles spent a pleasant time with the Kirbys. Mrs Kirby was a calm, gentle woman who ruled her family and household with benign watchfulness. She was curious about Whitby for it was a place she had heard about but never visited. Caroline, jealous of anyone else occupying her brother's time, had little to say. Rebecca found she had a love of books in common with Charles and was not slow to air her knowledge as a way of displaying her charm and lively mind. Septimus, when the three men were enjoying a glass of port after an excellent evening meal, turned the conversation to the merchant world.

Charles took this opportunity to say, 'Mr Kirby, I will be sailing on one of our ships, the *Grace*, in five days' time, with a cargo for Amsterdam. There will be space available if you have anything that needs shipping? When I mentioned this to Julian he thought there might be.'

Septimus glanced at his son but did not question what he had in mind. Instead he looked back at Charles. 'Yes. There is some wool for which I was about to arrange shipment. If you will take it, it will save further bother.'

'Certainly, sir.' He put his terms to Septimus

134

who was surprised to find that they were lower than he had been paying. With business matters settled, Charles continued in a different vein, 'May I ask, sir, if Julian may accompany me again? I will have some spare time in Holland and would be grateful for his company?'

'Of course. It will be good for him to pay another visit. Besides,' he looked at his son, 'you could pick up some valuable trading tips from Charles that will stand you in good stead in the future.'

When everyone had retired for the night and the household had settled down, Charles heard a faint knock on his door. He opened it to see Julian.

'A word,' he whispered.

Charles opened the door wider and Julian slipped into the room. When the door clicked behind him, he said, 'I'm grateful for the way you worked my next visit to Amsterdam.'

'Think nothing of it. I'm pleased to have your company. I thought the suggestion might be more acceptable coming from me than from you.'

'You're right,' agreed Julian. He held out his hand and their friendship was given a further seal.

'See you in four days.' Charles hunched his shoulders against the wind blowing off the Humber as he stepped on to the gangway to board the *North Star*.

Julian surveyed the dark clouds scudding en

135

masse from the northeast. 'It's going to be a rough voyage. Wishing you'd gone by coach?'

'Not a bit of it. It'll be invigorating. I'll enjoy it.' Charles raised his hand in a gesture of farewell.

'I hope you do,' called Julian, acknowledging Charles's salute.

He waited while all around him bustled with activity to get the ship away. Orders were yelled, tow-lines were in place, sailors cursed when the gangway snagged and threw it to one side when it came free, ropes were cast off, the strain was taken by the boats as oarsmen bent their backs to take the *North Star* to the freedom of the open Humber. Sailors scrambled aloft to unfurl sails to catch the wind.

Julian moved away from the quayside after a final wave to Charles. He turned up the collar of his coat as the first drops of rain spattered the cobbles around him and quickened his step, eager to be out of the miserable weather that was settling over Hull.

He took little notice of the activity along the waterfront and around the warehouses as his mind dwelt on the problem of organising a smuggling operation. If he was to go through with it he would have to have something arranged before he returned to Amsterdam and another meeting with Reynier. He could still abandon the idea. Reynier had given him to understand he had that privilege, and if he chose to do so nothing more would be said. Doubts filled his mind as he hurried on, head bent against the wind and the rain. Where was he going to find the men to carry out the smuggling?

Reynier said he would provide the sloops and the sailors. It had all seemed easy when he was in Amsterdam but now, in Hull, the prospects seemed bleak. Where were the suitable places to land contraband along the Humber? Where could he store it until he could dispose of it? He had no doubt that he would find a ready market once word spread about what was on offer, but the other problems looked insurmountable. Besides, he would have to keep the operation a secret from his father for he knew Septimus would not condone such an activity.

But the thought of the likely profits was tempting. Who could he approach to help him recruit a gang of men willing to take part in an illegal operation?

His mind was grappling with this problem when he was startled by a deep voice. 'G'day to you, Mr Julian.'

The way 'Mr' was accentuated made the voice instantly recognisable. He pulled up sharp and raised his eyes to the tall, burly man who blocked his path. He stiffened and met the contemptuous grin resolutely. 'I couldn't mistake your voice, Bill Grimes, though it is six months since I heard it.'

'And how's the young master getting on?' Scorn tinged the enquiry.

'No better for seeing you.' Julian made to pass him but Grimes stepped in his way.

'Not so fast, Mr Julian, I ain't seen you since you got me the sack.' There was menace in Grimes's rasping voice. He cast a furtive look around him. No one was taking any notice of two

137

people seemingly deep in conversation. Everyone was too preoccupied with completing their own tasks before the weather got any fouler.

Julian was fully aware that he would be no match for this man's muscular strength, honed on heavy loads, if Grimes chose to force him into the narrow alley beside which they were standing. But he was determined to show no weakness. 'You got what you deserved for thieving. I saw you with my own eyes.'

'Aye, you did that. And it turned you into a sneak. You and your rich life had no time for the likes of me scratting a living to keep you in comfort.'

'You were better paid than some in your position as a foreman.'

'Mebbe so, but that weren't enough when I had sick kids. My plea for some help in the way of a rise fell on your father's deaf ears.'

'That did not give you the right to steal from us. And let me tell you, my father was merciful. He could have had you prosecuted and that would have meant jail or deportation. Your children saved you from that.'

'And a struggle it's been these last six months. No permanent work. Just picking up the odd job now and then.' With everything Grimes said he put menace behind his words. He leaned nearer Julian, adding to his threatening attitude. 'How about some coppers for an old friend?'

'I've no more to say to you, Bill Grimes. I wouldn't...' The words faded on his lips. The mention of money sparked off an idea. 'What if I put a proposition to you?' he added quickly as he sensed Grimes was about to take physical action. Robbery in an alley with no one else nearby to identify the perpetrator was a distinct possibility.

Grimes hesitated. He eyed Julian suspiciously. 'What proposition have you that would interest me?' There was contemptuous disbelief in his voice.

'Do you want to earn some money?' Even as he put the question, Julian was wondering if he was doing the right thing.

Bill Grimes had worked for his father in Scarborough and had come to Hull when the firm moved there. He had been hardworking, had risen to foreman, proved trustworthy until he fell in with a bad lot and let drink rule his head. Then, needing money for better food for his sick children, he had stolen. Though he regretted it after being caught it was too late to keep his job. Maybe the prospect of receiving more money than he had ever done would eliminate these undesirable traits.

'Aye. But what...'

'We can't talk in this downpour.'

'There's a hostelry down the road aways.'

'Lead on.'

Grimes hesitated a moment. Suspicion still lingered. This was not like Mr Julian. What sort of a proposition was it? Whatever it was it wouldn't be approved by Mr Julian's father so he was wasting his time. But he may as well see what was afoot. He might be able to use it to his own advantage. No need to puzzle his brain now, he'd know soon enough. He matched his step to Julian's and rubbed his broad hand across his heavy jowls, sweeping away the rain that was running from his unkempt hair.

Grimes's appearance had not gone unnoticed by Julian. He had been smart until he came under the influence of an undesirable crowd. Maybe that association was what Julian was looking for now.

When Grimes paused before a doorway Julian noted the hanging sign creaking in the wind. It announced that this was the Dagger Inn.

Grimes pushed the door open and Julian found himself in a gloomy place fitted out with a long counter along one wall. The large oblong mirror on the wall behind helped to give the room a more spacious appearance. There were only two customers in the bar, not unusual considering the time of day. Julian called for two tankards of ale.

'That's civil of you,' remarked Grimes as he took his tankard.

Julian looked around and then indicated a table in a corner, out of earshot of anyone else. He shrugged himself out of his wet coat. Grimes swept his hand across his soaked jacket and trousers but it only took the surface water away.

Julian eyed him over his tankard as he took a draught of ale. It was obvious the man had let himself go since he had fallen on ill times but Julian thought, given renewed responsibility, he could become once again the man who had been an asset in Scarborough. There he'd held the respect of the men under him, for he led by example and was always fair in his criticism. Julian realised that Grimes was bewildered, suspicious, cautious, and yet anxious to know what he had in mind.

'A few questions before I put a proposition to you,' said Julian, placing his tankard on the table and cradling his hands around it. He fixed Grimes with his eyes. 'Are you in employment now?'

'No.'

'Have any more crimes against your name?'

'Not that the law knows of,' growled Grimes.

'What's that mean?'

'I ain't been caught.'

Julian smiled to himself. Long may that go on if I go ahead with my plans, he thought. He made no comment, merely nodded.

'If you are willing to accept what I propose it will mean that you must steer clear of the law.' Julian sensed the irony of his words.

Grimes raised his hands. 'So help me, I can do that.' If this young man was giving him a chance to make a legitimate living then he'd welcome it. But he was still suspicious. After all, it was Julian who had been instrumental in getting him the sack and putting his family on the edge of poverty. Was he trying to make amends? Salve his conscience? Well, whatever, Grimes would hear what he had to say.

'And you'll have to be tight-lipped.'

This made Grimes even more curious. Was Mr Julian up to something he didn't want his father to know about? 'I know when to hold my tongue.'

'You were a good worker, Grimes, until temptation got in the way. You had authority and knew how to use it. Could you do that again?'

'Are you offering me a chance to come back to...'

His words were cut short, his hopes dashed, by Julian's shake of the head and curt, 'No.'

Grimes's face darkened and hostility flared in his eyes and in his voice as he snapped, 'Then what the hell is this all about?'

'Calm down, man,' hissed Julian in a no-nonsense manner. 'I'm not offering you your job back but I *am* offering you a job. First I must ask you something else. When you came to Hull with us you knew no one here and unfortunately got in with some rum characters. Are you still in touch with them?'

'Aye.'

'How far can you trust them?'

Grimes gave a contemptuous laugh. 'As far as I could throw a belaying-pin if I dropped it at my feet.'

'Could you control them?'

Grimes hesitated. What was this young fella getting at? 'I reckon so. They're just an unruly gang with no leader. I reckon I could whip them into shape.' He clenched his hand and held up one huge fist.

'Let's hope that won't be necessary. It could create disloyalty.'

'Aye, and it could show what would happen if they step out of line. But I don't think they will if the money is right.'

'It will be.'

'You sound sure.'

'I am, if what I propose runs smoothly. However there will be an element of risk, of danger, of working unusual hours.'

'Mr Julian,' Grimes's voice was firm. 'None of that will matter if the rewards are fair.' He was witnessing changes in Julian he would not have expected six months ago. He was more mature. Appeared to have thrown off the shackles that his father had unwittingly, in most cases, imposed upon him. He found he was beginning to respect this new Julian.

The young man nodded. He let the conversation drop while the two beers he called for were brought to them. Then he leaned forward on the table, his eyes fixed on Grimes. 'What we have said and what I am about to say is strictly between us. None of it must be relayed to anyone else. If ever it is referred to in the future, for any reason whatsoever, I will deny that it ever took place. This meeting never happened.'

Grimes nodded. Whatever was coming must be deadly serious.

Julian took a drink of his ale, still studying Grimes's reactions as he did so. He could tell the man was curious, but it was a curiosity laced with interest in monetary rewards. He also saw the desire to have a position of authority again, and that spelt loyalty if he was trusted in turn. Julian knew then that he had a dependable lieutenant.

'Certain things have happened over the past few days that I believe have been fortuitous, among them bumping into you this morning. In four days' time I sail to Amsterdam.'

'You intrigue me,' said Grimes, eyeing him with a steadfast gaze as he leaned back against the wall.

Julian noted that all hostility had gone. In its

place were some of the attributes he had known in the man in Scarborough and in their early days in Hull. He motioned Grimes to come nearer.

Grimes eyed him for a fraction of a moment and then hunched forward, his crossed arms resting on the table.

'I want a smuggling gang setting up.' The words came quietly but clearly so that there was no mistaking that Julian meant what he said.

They brought silence for a moment but then Bill Grimes realised that Julian was serious. He had heard it in his tone of voice and seen it in the expression in the young man's eyes. When the enormity of this proposal hit him he started a deep-throated chuckle that turned into laughter.

'I'm deadly serious,' snapped Julian, irritated by Grimes's reaction.

His guffaws subsided somewhat but he still smiled broadly and allowed himself to chuckle. 'You were the one who reported me to your father, and now it's you who are stepping outside the law and want my help. Well, if that ain't a turnabout. You think I can organise a gang to work for you in an illegal trade? Aye, likely I can, but first I want to ask a few questions. How can you be sure I won't go to the authorities?'

'I told you, I would deny this meeting ever took place. Who is more likely to be believed, me or you?'

Grimes nodded. 'Why shouldn't I go to your father?'

Julian gave a little laugh of derision that he should ever have thought of doing that. 'Do you think *he* would believe you?'

'Ah, so your father knows nothing about this proposal. It's all yours?'

'Yes. Well, the idea was put into my head in Amsterdam from where I returned yesterday.'

'And to where you are returning in four days. And you have to have an answer as to whether you can set up a smuggling gang around Hull by then.'

'Right. You catch on fast. Are you interested?'

'Aye, but tell me more and talk terms.'

Half an hour later terms had been agreed. Grimes assured Julian that he would have no difficulty recruiting men, among them two who knew the low-lying land of the Humber estuary with its multitude of shallows and twisting creeks, sandbanks and marshes, like the lines on the palms of their hands. Aware not only of these hazards but also of the presence of Customs Officers and Preventive Men, they would meet the Dutch boat when it was due and pilot it to the chosen destination.

'I need to know all this for certain before I leave for Amsterdam. Meet me here, at ten in the morning, in three days' time.'

As he made his way to Albion Street Julian's step was brisk, not only to get out of the rain as quickly as possible but because he was elated to find that fate had played its cards in his favour.

Charles was pleased that he had been able to take the ship from Hull. Approaching Whitby from the sea gave a better vista of the town than coming by road. The sight of the abbey high on the cliff, the cleft which split its face and through which the River Esk found its way to the sea, was

145

a unique view which never failed to stir him. Even today, the dark, glowering clouds could not detract from the scene. They brought an air of sombre mystery to the close-knit buildings clinging to the cliff above the river. When sunshine flamed the red roofs of those same buildings a lively air embraced the town.

When he left the *North Star* Charles hurried to the office on Church Street to impart the news of the impending collection of goods from de Klerk in Amsterdam.

'The *Grace* will be in tomorrow. Let Captain Wilson know that she'll sail three days later for Amsterdam.'

'Very good. I'll have the cargo of foodstuffs and wool ready for loading the day before sailing.'

'Good. And inform Wilson that we'll be putting into Hull on our way there. I made an agreement with Julian Kirby, son of Septimus, whom I met on this trip, to ship goods for them.'

'They used to trade out of Scarborough.'

'That's right. They are now settled in Hull and with a nicely established trading business. It could prove lucrative for us.'

'Your father will be pleased of the new business.'

Charles gave a sad smile. 'If he is interested.'

When he left the office he called on Edwin Bennet, informing him that the next run of contraband goods would take place in seven days' time. He knew there was no more to be said. Edwin's efficiency and attention to detail would have everything in place that night. He had every confidence in Nicholas and Ralph when he informed them of the same matter.

Satisfied that arrangements on both sides of the Mason business had been taken care of, he went to the White Horse where he hired a hack and rode home. His thoughts now dwelt on Anna's rehabilitation of their father. He hoped her news would be better than the weather, which had turned into driving rain.

He was disappointed with her reply to his questions as he shrugged himself out of his wet coat. 'Very little improvement. He refused to see Mr Blenkinsop who had made a special visit – a social call, so I'm sure Father wouldn't have been drawn into discussion about work and trade. I had to make some excuse but I'm sure Mr Blenkinsop thought it a very lame one.'

'I'm sorry about that. I was hoping for better news. Let me get out of these wet things and then you can tell me all about it and I'll tell you about my trip to Amsterdam.' He started for the stairs. 'Where is he?'

Anna pointed to the study door and Charles acknowledged this information with a nod.

'How were the de Klerks?' she called after him as he climbed the stairs.

'Very well,' he answered, and disappeared along the landing to his room.

Ten minutes later, refreshed and regaled in clean clothes, he looked in on his father. 'I'm back.'

'Good to see you, son.' John looked up from the book he had on his desk. 'Did everything go well?'

'Yes. Herr de Klerk had hoped you'd be with me.'

This information received a mere shrug of the shoulders.

'As I came downstairs I saw Mary taking some tea into the drawing room. Are you going to join us?'

'I've had mine served here.' He indicated a tray set for one.

'Very well,' replied Charles amiably. He did not want to antagonise his father by insisting that he come to the drawing room. 'I'll see you later.' He wore a frown when he joined his sister.

'You no doubt tried to get him to join us but he wouldn't,' she commented as she poured the tea. 'That's his usual pattern, though since you went away he has had breakfast and the midday and evening meals with me.'

'You've done well. How is he in himself?'

'Better. He's thrown off some of his lethargy but still insists that he doesn't want to see any people he knows.'

'What about strangers?'

'His attitude to that has not been tested yet.'

'Then we shall do so.'

Anna looked at him questioningly. 'How?'

'By inviting a stranger here.'

'But who? We can't invite just anyone.'

'It won't be just anyone. I met a young man in Hull on my way to Amsterdam, Julian Kirby, about my age. His father's a merchant.' He went on to tell her how the meeting came about and its result. 'I've already suggested that he visit us. He would be perfect. A stranger, young and likeable.'

'But his talk is bound to turn to trade.'

'I'd warn Julian to keep off the subject unless Father brought it up. You never know, he might with a stranger, but even if he doesn't, meeting someone new might help to put life into perspective again for him. It's worth a try.'

'Anything is if it will help Father.'

'Right. I'm going to Amsterdam again in four days' time with the *Grace*, and I've agreed to call at Hull for Julian. When we return I'll invite him to come back with me or sometime soon. In the meantime mention my visits to the de Klerks when we have our meal this evening.'

Though he had been away only a few days, Charles noticed a slight change in his father and hoped it was a sign that the battle to overcome his despondency was taking a turn for the better. John seemed brighter, more alert, and showed an interest in the conversation though that was of nothing of any consequence until Anna asked, 'Was your trip to Amsterdam satisfactory?'

'Yes. A good voyage both ways and business with the de Klerks was beneficial to both parties.' Charles was careful not to mention any detail. He hoped his father might ask and so show that his interest in the business was returning, but John made no query. Instead Charles detected a slight stiffening in his demeanour.

'Good. The de Klerks, were they well?'

'Yes. In very good spirits.' Charles turned his eyes on his father. 'Herr de Klerk told me to tell you that you would be welcome any time and suggested a change of scene might be beneficial to you.'

John's eyes glazed over. 'I think not,' he said quietly.

'Father, that's a very kind offer from Herr de

Klerk,' said Anna. 'I'm sure he would respect your desire not to talk business.'

'Maybe, but I don't want to go.'

'Why not? It would do you good. You could relax in a different environment and atmosphere. There would be new sights to see, new people to meet, and you could be in touch with the art world you cultivated in Holland.' Anna stopped, having realised she had let her tongue race away in her enthusiasm at the idea.

Her father looked coldly at her. 'Do I have to explain the situation again? Your mother and I shared happy times in Holland with the de Klerks. To visit them now would stir up many precious memories. That would hurt. A visit would not do me the good you think. I'm all right as I am. As for the art world, I've told you before, Anna, that part of my life is finished. It no longer has any meaning for me. Now, let us get on with our meal and talk of other things.'

Anna felt chastised and said nothing, deeming it wisest not to. At least her father had not left the table in anger and, though he had been hostile, she could regard his continued presence as a step forward. But she held her breath when Charles spoke.

'Very well, Father, if that's the way you want it. I won't mention Herr de Klerk's invitation again. You know it is there. However, before we leave the topic of my visit to Amsterdam, there is a request I would like to make.' He saw his father frown. He knew Anna was tense. 'I've made friends with a young man of my age, Julian Kirby, his father is a trader in Hull. He came to

Amsterdam with me. I like him and think he could be a good friend. I would like to invite him here on a social visit, if you approve.'

'Your friends are your friends. This is your home. If you wish to invite anyone here there is no need to seek my permission. Invite them, but let me know when they are coming.'

'I will. Thank you. I'm going to Amsterdam again in four days' time. I'll see him then and will make the invitation.'

His father made no further comment but picked up his spoon and started on his apple pie in a way that indicated that there was no more to be said on the matter.

Charles made one visit to Whitby in the next three days. Gideon assured him that the *Grace* would be ready for her voyage to Holland. Charles informed Edwin, Nicholas and Ralph that when he returned he would have further details of where the contraband could be picked up on the Dutch coast.

The rest of his time was spent with Anna and his father. He sensed they were coming together again as a family. He and Anna were pleased to see their father more relaxed than he had been since the loss of their mother, but still there was a barrier to his full recovery. Their determination to break it down and bring their father back to as normal a life as he could lead without his beloved wife drew Anna and Charles closer.

'I'm sorry to be going back to Amsterdam so soon, just when we seem to be strengthening family ties again,' he apologised to his sister.

151

'You have work to see to. It is no good winning round Father if there is nothing for him to come back to. The business must be there for him to resume his place in the world. If it isn't then our efforts would have been in vain.'

'You are doing wonderfully well with him.'

Anna gave a half-smile. 'I wish I could make more progress.'

'You will,' replied Charles with conviction.

'*We* will.' Anna emphasised, for she saw how vital her brother's role would be.

When, on the day before he was due to sail, Julian stepped into the Dagger Inn he found Bill Grimes already there, the only occupant. Grimes glanced at the door when it squeaked and, seeing Julian, called for another tankard of ale. He motioned Julian to the same corner seat they had occupied on their previous visit then picked up the two tankards and joined him.

'Well?' Julian was eager for news.

Grimes hesitated, revelling in the power of keeping the son of his former employer in suspense. He took a drink, wiped his hand across his mouth, gave a small knowing smile and in a low voice announced, 'Everything's arranged.'

'Good.' There was relief in Julian's voice and in the way he picked up his tankard and took a long drink. As he put the tankard down, he said, 'Tell me everything.'

'I've recruited eight men. We can get more if this 'ere smuggling grows. Also the two men I told you about who know the Humber.'

'They know how to hold their tongues too?'

'Aye. The money's too good for them to blab.'

'I sail to Amsterdam tomorrow. When I return I'll have information about the first run.'

'When will you be back?'

'I don't know.'

'Then how will you get word to me?'

'Look in here at this time, ten o'clock in the morning, every day. I'll be here at ten without fail the first day I am back.' Julian cast a glance at the barman. 'Can he be trusted?'

'The landlord? Aye. But I'll not make it obvious that I'm looking for someone. Now, you should meet your employees and then have a look at the sites along the river.'

'You've looked them over, haven't you?'

Grimes read that as an indication of trust, and though he liked it he wanted to make sure that young Mr Kirby was fully involved. 'Yes, but I think you should be aware of the complete operation and what it will involve. We have a sloop waiting to take us down the river.'

Julian drained his tankard and stood up. 'Let's go.' He did not want Grimes to think he was shirking any part of this enterprise. He started for the door and Grimes had hastily to finish his own drink. He was cramming a woollen cap on his head when he joined Julian outside. He maintained a brisk pace to Rottenherring Staithe close to the south end of the River Hull where a forty-ton sloop was tied up.

Julian followed him on board and was introduced to the Upton brothers. Greg was stocky, rugged, tough. His weather-beaten face spoke of hours at sea, ignoring wind and rain and treating the sun, as he did all other elements of nature, as friend or enemy according to the circumstances at the time. His eyes were sharp, those of a man who had gazed at sea distances most of his life. His brother Mike was less stocky but taller and Julian could sense power in his frame, honed by a hard life. His languid appearance was deceptive as Julian was to realise.

They were both dressed in thick jerseys and woollen caps similar to that worn by Grimes. They shook hands with strong grips and fingers that were broad and rough from handling ropes in all weathers.

'Grimes tells me you know the river,' said Julian.

'Aye, no one better,' said Mike.

'We'll show you,' said Greg. 'Better put these on, there'll be a blow out on the water.' He handed Julian a thick jersey and an equally thick cap.

'Thanks.' He changed into his new attire and, when they moved into the wide Humber, was glad of it. The wind was not strong but there was a bite to it.

The Upton brothers handled the sloop with easy skill. Julian knew the eyes of the three men were on him, assessing his attitude and to figure out if a well-bred young man had the stomach for the hazards of smuggling. He let them see he was enjoying the experience of sailing on the Humber and that he was assessing their ability as well as studying the shore-line, especially as they took the turn in the river and ran in towards the tiny village of Paull. Further downstream they took

154

the ship into a creek, manoeuvring it with a skill that caught Julian's imagination. No Revenue boat could follow them here and, when Mike pointed out the maze of creeks, he knew they had chosen this place for the variety of escape routes it offered.

'Are there more such waterways along this coast line?' he asked.

'Aye, and we know them all.'

'We have a brother, Luke, who farms out here. There's arable land beyond the creeks and marshes. He knows the way around this God-forsaken landscape as well as we know the waterways, and he knows where contraband can be stored awaiting distribution.'

'Have you asked him to join us?'

'Not yet.'

'I need men who know the Humber, its creeks and tides, and I need someone who knows the land.'

They left the ship.

'Keep on the path if you don't want to get wet,' warned Greg who led the way.

Julian saw the reason for his warning. On either side was ground, deceptive in its appearance, with tufted grasses that looked solid enough to take a man's weight. Closer scrutiny showed they were existing on sodden earth which would give no support. He was careful to keep in Greg's footsteps. After about a quarter of a mile the marshy ground gave way to arable land that had been worked as close to the marsh as possible.

Greg stopped. 'No need to take as much care now.'

Julian surveyed the prospect ahead of them. The land was flat as far as he could see but the bleakness near the river had given way to a more enticing landscape. This land supported a farming community but he knew the village far to his left also drew sustenance from the river and the sea. There was a scattering of buildings across the wide landscape.

'Yonder's where we want to be.' Greg indicated a group of four buildings about half a mile ahead. He set off in their direction at a brisk pace now that the path was less hazardous.

Julian noted that the land was well tilled and the farm buildings, with adjacent cottage, were cared for. There was a degree of prosperity here, not the sort of place one would associate with smuggling.

The sound of voices came from a building on the right. Greg immediately headed for the open door, which was wide enough for a cart to pass through. He stopped on entering the building and held up his hand, a signal for the others to halt and remain silent.

Two people were intent on fitting an iron hoop to a cart wheel. At such a moment they wanted no interruptions. It gave Julian a chance to study them. One was a youngster, hardly into his teens but holding the hoop with long-handled tongs and with the concentration of someone who had done this before. The older man gripped the opposite side of the hoop with similar tongs.

'Our Luke there,' whispered Greg close to Julian's ear. 'He was always one for the land, but he served his time with a carpenter and a

156

wheelwright and picked up the blacksmith's craft at the same time. Said it was necessary to know them all out here. The youngster's his son, Jim.'

The hoop, which had been heated to make it expand, was lowered carefully over the wheel.

'Right!'

Luke and Jim dropped their tongs, picked up two watering-cans and poured water over the hoop. With a hissing and sizzling, dense clouds of steam rose and billowed towards the open door. The wood squeaked and squealed under the contracting iron that firmly bedded the spokes into place.

Julian was fascinated and admired the concentration and skill of father and son working together as a team.

Jim took the empty cans away and scurried to recover both pairs of tongs and place them against the wall. He grinned at his uncles as he did so but did not speak, waiting for his father to acknowledge them first.

'Greg, Mike,' the man said almost before he had turned to face them so it was obvious that he had been aware of their arrival even as he was concentrating on his task. He wiped the sweat from his forehead and came to greet his brothers.

'Luke.' Greg exchanged a handshake with him and then punched him playfully on the chest. At the same time Mike gave him a friendly tap on the shoulder.

'Come to learn farming?' Luke's remark came as natural banter between brothers.

'You'll be back at sea before long,' chaffed Mike.

'Never,' returned Luke. His eyes turned to the newcomers.

'Luke, this here's Julian Kirby. Father's a merchant in Hull, originally in Scarborough.' Greg made the introduction.

Luke stuck out his hand and Julian felt a firm grip from a hand used to heavy work. Luke's dark eyes were making a judgement. 'Pleased to know you.'

'Julian, this is my brother. And this is his young brat, Jim.' Greg used the term with affection and tousled the youngster's hair.

'Hi, young Jim.' Mike stepped forward and gave his nephew a tap on the back with his clenched hand.

Jim swung round, a broad grin on his face as he grabbed his uncle's fist. 'When are you going to take me sailing again?' he queried with undeniable enthusiasm.

'You'll have to ask your pa.' Mike glanced at Luke. 'He's got the sea in his blood, Luke. You can't deny that, nor him.'

'More fool him,' commented Luke, but he took the matter no further. 'And who's this?' he asked, turning his eyes on Bill.

'Bill Grimes. Works for Julian.'

The two men exchanged greetings.

'And what's the nature of that work?' queried Luke. He caught the brief eye signal from Greg and turned to his son. 'Run on in, lad. Tell y'ma to make us a sup of tea.'

Jim ran off without another word. They heard him shouting before he reached the house, 'Uncle Greg and Uncle Mike are here!'

158

'Wanting Jim out of the way tells me something's in the wind. So out with it.' Luke's voice was sharp, brooking no nonsense from any of the four he eyed with suspicion.

'The old game, Luke,' replied Greg.

He slapped his thigh as he swung his back on them in a gesture of disgust. 'I knew it,' he snapped, and spun round again to face them. His gaze held his brothers' accusingly. 'I knew it. What the hell's got into you two?' His eyes flashed with anger. 'You know what happened last time. We were lucky to get out of a tricky situation with our lives, and you know it. We've settled down. I've got my farm, you've got fishing. What more do you want?'

Mike smarted under his brother's reminder but it did not prevent him from hissing one word primed by a powerful desire, 'Revenge!'

'Damn it, man. I thought we'd sworn to forget what happened?'

'Have you?' Mike laced his words carefully so that they would dig deep into Luke's mind and heart.

His lips tightened. His brother, with those two words, had recalled the tragedy that had blighted their lives. They reminded him of the moonlit night when their father had lost his life at the hands of a rival smuggling gang. Luke and his brothers had only just managed to escape the same fate. From that moment they had sworn never to engage in the illicit trade again. Now, even Luke had to admit that the desire to avenge their father's death had never left him. He looked at Greg, hoping that he would help him to make

159

Mike see reason, but he saw he would get no support there.

He shrugged his shoulders in a gesture of resignation. 'All right, let's hear what you have to say.'

Julian had been watching the brothers carefully and liked what he saw. They had a close bond and whatever they were talking about now seemed to draw them closer. He realised that if there was any doubt about them getting involved he must try to eliminate it immediately. He must assert his own position so that Luke had no doubt about it and would be able to appraise the situation fully.

'I think Luke should hear my proposition,' he interposed quickly. He saw Luke shoot him a glance as much as to say, What has this young whippersnapper got to do with it? 'I'm the reason your brothers and Bill are here.' He went on to explain how this had come about.

Luke listened intently, without giving away what he was thinking. He was silent for a few moments when Julian had finished. The others knew better than to speak. They hung on his decision.

He looked hard at Julian. 'I respect your reasons for wanting to do this, but do you know what you are getting into?' He held up his hand when he saw Julian about to speak 'Let me tell you.' He went on to detail the risks not only from Customs, the Revenue Men and the consequences if caught, but also that he might be ostracised by his family if they ever got to know what he was doing. 'You would not only be a sleeping partner, but whenever you were active there would be the possibility of being killed, by Customs or by rivals. That is what happened to our father.'

He went on to describe how they had been running contraband ashore along the Humber when they were surprised by a rival gang who, until then, had operated only on the sea coast of Holderness but were seeking to widen their activities. In the ensuing fight their father had been killed and they had barely escaped. It had made them decide to give it all up. 'Now you are wanting us to take it up again.' Luke shook his head doubtfully.

'Is this gang still operating along the Humber?' asked Julian.

'Aye.'

'From the exchange between you and Mike I take it that the thought of revenge has never left your minds. Here is your chance. I'm not advocating killing, but we can oust them from their territory and take their trade.'

'You talk big for someone who has never engaged in smuggling, but it shows a sharp and determined mind. It's a pity your father does not recognise it and use it in his legitimate business. That would have saved you from all this.' Luke glanced at his brothers. He saw they were eager to speak. 'Well?'

'We can soon set up the operation here,' enthused Greg. 'Mr Kirby has only to say the word in Holland and the first consignment can be on its way.'

'Play our cards right and we can get our territory

back and more,' put in Mike with equal passion. 'Then Father can rest easy in his grave.'

Luke turned to Julian. 'All right, young fella.' He held out his hand and in the exchanged grip was forged an understanding. 'One more question. Have you any idea where you are going to sell the contraband?'

'That's something I have to arrange.'

'I thought as much.' Luke glanced at his brothers. 'Do you think we can persuade our old customers to deal with us again?'

'Give them the right price and I'm sure of it,' said Greg.

'Then you need look no further,' Luke said to Julian. 'We'll set that up for you.'

'Thanks. I'm grateful. This is more than I expected. Once we are established we can look to expand.' His eyes moved swiftly across them all. 'I reckon we have a bright future.'

Chapter Seven

'Father, will you come to see me sail this morning?' asked Charles at breakfast. This query was not only a suggestion but also a plea for his father to throw off the apathy that still held him.

Realising the intention behind the words, John gave a rueful smile. 'I think not, son. The *Grace* is quite capable of leaving Whitby with you on board without me to see her off.'

'But Charles would like it,' put in Anna sharply.

'Of course I would,' he agreed.

'We can say our goodbyes here. They will be just as sincere,' replied John in a tone that brushed any further suggestion aside. 'You accompany your brother, Anna. You always did like watching ships leave the harbour. You can tell me all about it when you get back. Don't hurry on my account. I'll be all right. And while you are there, go and buy two dresses for yourself. I'll give you a note for Chapman's Bank. Get Cara Blenkinsop to help you choose. It'll give the girl a rest from that overbearing mother of hers.'

Anna had never left the house since her mother died, except to walk in the gardens, always being there when her father returned from his ride. Could she leave him now? But it might upset him, to refuse his generous offer. Besides she would enjoy a visit to Whitby and it might do her father good to be on his own. She sprang from her chair and hugged him. 'Thank you so much.'

As she moved away he grasped her hand. She stood still. His gaze fixed on her face, ablaze with the joy he had just brought her. 'Your eyes shine just like your mother's.'

She saw that his were damp, bent forward and kissed him gently on the cheek. 'Thank you, that means a lot to me.'

'Enjoy yourself. She would want you to.' He glanced towards Charles. 'You too, son. And if there is something in Amsterdam you would like, buy it.'

'Thank you.' He accepted his father's generosity, but what he would have liked more than anything was for them both to be working together again.

'Do you think Father is making progress? He's told us to enjoy life. I wish he would adopt that attitude too. Mother would want him to.' Anna made these observations as she and Charles rode to Whitby.

'I think so, but it is a slow process. At least he is showing interest in us. That must be a step forward when you think what he was like. Maybe his interest will gradually widen. We must just keep persisting. We'll have taken a big step when I can get him to talk business again.'

They rode straight to the White Horse in Church Street where they stabled their horses, Anna informing the ostler that she would be back for hers in the late afternoon. Charles knew his would have every care until he returned from Amsterdam.

'Father made a good choice when he had her built,' he commented with a nod in the direction of the *Grace*. She lay serenely beside the quay opposite the office.

'She's beautiful,' agreed Anna. 'Remember how proud he was to take Mother and us on that first voyage to Amsterdam?'

'It's one I'll never forget.'

'Nor me. I hope we'll do it again before long.'

'So do I.'

When they reached the office Gideon sprang to his feet. 'Miss Anna. How delightful to see you.' His pleasure was not forced, for he had always admired the vivacious child who had captured everyone's affection. He saw that the recent tragic event had thrust new responsibility on her and brought her more quickly to womanhood. Now she had the bearing of someone older than her years, but still a captivating charm.

'I am pleased to see you too, Mr Wells,' she said with a warm smile.

'You are here to see your brother off?'

'Yes, and then a shopping spree.'

'I'm sure you'll enjoy that.'

'I certainly will.'

Charles, who had been checking some papers on the desk, broke in. 'I see everything is in order and that you have given Captain Wilson sailing instructions.'

'Yes, sir. He knows there is a cargo to pick up in Hull.'

'Good. I'd better be getting on board.'

'Have a safe and successful voyage, Mr Charles. I look forward to your return. I have a likely cargo for the Baltic. Would you like the *Grace* to do that voyage when she gets back?'

'When is the *Gull* due?'

'Two days' time.'

'Is she needed then?'

'There's a cargo for Denmark but I can switch them round if I clinch the Baltic voyage.'

'Do that if possible and we'll send the *Grace* to Denmark, letting the *Gull* go to the Baltic. It will give Captain Walford valuable experience for the time when we expand our trade there.'

Gideon nodded his approval of Charles's reasoning and quick decision-making. It was something Anna admired too and in it she saw how the responsibility that had been thrust upon him had made him more mature.

Brother and sister left the office and went straight to the *Grace*. Seeing them coming, Captain Wilson came to the head of the gangway to greet them. He saluted smartly as they stepped on board.

'Good day to you both,' he said. 'And may I express my pleasure at seeing you again, Miss Anna?'

She smiled graciously. 'It is a delight for me to be part of all this activity once more. I wish I was sailing with you.'

'If it were so, you would enhance the enjoyment of our voyage.' Captain Wilson had a sparkle of merriment in his eyes as he gave a low bow.

'You know how to flatter a young lady.' Anna smiled. 'But then, with four daughters you've no doubt had plenty of practice.'

'I have indeed, miss. I have indeed.'

'We are all set to sail, Captain?' asked Charles.

'Five minutes and we should be underway.' He turned back to Anna. 'Remember me to your father. Tell him we miss him.'

'I certainly will, Captain. Thank you for those kind words.'

Captain Wilson saluted and turned to the last-minute tasks of getting the *Grace* under way.

Brother and sister made their goodbyes and Anna left the ship. As soon as she was on the quay the two sailors, who had been standing by, hauled the gangway on board. Ropes were cast off. The boats set to take the *Grace* downstream took the strain. Slowly the gap between the ship and the quay widened. Families of the crew, well-wishers and others, who broke off from their tasks ashore, shouted their good wishes for a safe voyage.

Anna watched and waved to her brother until the *Grace* had been successfully manoeuvred through the drawbridge and into the lower reaches of the river. She left the quay and by the time she reached the drawbridge to cross to the west side it had been lowered again. She paused in the middle to watch the *Grace* pass between the piers to reach the open sea.

Anna made her way to the Blenkinsop residence in Bagdale. The maid who answered the door recognised Cara's friend, invited her to step inside and went to the drawing room to announce that Miss Anna Mason had called to see Miss Cara.

'This is a pleasure,' cried Cara as the two friends exchanged greetings. 'Pray tell me what

167

brings you to Whitby?'

'I've just seen Charles leave for Amsterdam. Father suggested I should do so, and he also said that I should buy myself two dresses while I was in Whitby.'

Cara's eyes brightened. 'How exciting for you. Where are you going for them?'

'I want you to help me make my choice, so where should we go?'

'Wonderful,' cried Cara. She grabbed her friend by the arms and started for the door. 'Don't sit down. We'll leave at once. Mama is out but is expected back any time. If we don't get away she'll want to come along and, well-meaning though they may be, her suggestions will be nowhere near what we'll have in mind.' She hurried Anna into the hall. 'I won't be a moment.' She started across the hall, stopped and spun round. 'Anna, you will come back and have something to eat before you return home?'

She hesitated. Should she get back to her father? But maybe she shouldn't fuss so much. 'Thank you, that will be delightful.'

'Splendid.' Cara's step was brisk with the joy she felt as she hurried to the kitchen to inform the cook that there would be one more for the one o'clock meal. She told a maid to inform her mother of this and that she had gone shopping with Miss Mason.

'Let's start at Mrs Chadwick's in Baxtergate,' she suggested.

'Yes, but we won't be too keen even if we see a pattern and material that we like. We'll go on elsewhere.' Anna made this suggestion because she knew that Cara's mother always took her to her own dressmaker and Cara never got a chance to see what other dressmakers could offer.

'This is going to be fun,' she laughed. She took hold of Anna's hand and hurried down the garden path and into Baxtergate, anxious to be away before her mother returned.

They visited two dressmakers in Baxtergate before they crossed the river to call on two more in Church Street.

'Well, what do you think?' asked Anna as they left their last call.

'One more,' said Cara. 'Mrs Cassidy. She lives further along Church Street.'

'I haven't heard of her.'

'She only came to Whitby recently from Pickering. She's younger than any of those we have visited, but I have seen some dresses made by her and they are less conservative than what we have been seeing.'

'Good. Then let's go. I feel like something different.'

They were admitted to a parlour by a young maid, neatly attired in black frock and white apron. The two girls exchanged glances of approval at the uncluttered room with floral chintz covers on the two armchairs and sofa. The paper was a soft pastel shade with a small floral motif and helped to give a light atmosphere to the room.

The door opened and a lady of about thirty came in. Her smile was warm and friendly. Her pale blue eyes sparkled as they assessed the two young ladies who could become customers.

'Mrs Cassidy?' queried Anna, who was already

169

admiring the dressmaker's own dress. The cut was exquisite, the sewing so neat it was hardly noticeable, but it was the slight twist away from the conventional that caught her eye. It was as if the maker was anticipating a change in fashion. She liked it and immediately expected that there would be suggestions with a difference from Mrs Cassidy.

'I am.' Her voice had the soft tones of a gentle, considerate person. 'Are you here for a dress?'

'Yes.'

'Please do sit down while I get my patterns and material, though you may like me to design one especially for you.'

'This is exciting,' whispered Cara when Mrs Cassidy had left them. 'Isn't she elegant and pretty?'

Anna nodded. 'So different from some of the old battleaxes we've visited,' she said in a low voice.

When Mrs Cassidy returned the two girls were sitting primly with their hands folded on their laps, but, knowing that a relaxed client was more likely to be a buying client, she soon put them at ease with her pleasant chatter before showing them the patterns she had to offer.

Anna put her own ideas to Mrs Cassidy. Having gleaned this information the dressmaker made suggestions and explained her ideas about what she thought would suit Anna in the way of pattern and material. Within the next hour, leaning on Mrs Cassidy's advice and Cara's approval, she had decided on the day dress she would have.

'Your father said two,' Cara, who was enjoying

herself immensely, reminded her.

'I hadn't forgotten,' said Anna with a small smile.

'I would suggest something a little different for the second,' said Mrs Cassidy, who, apart from the fact that she had a new customer and another potential one, was enjoying the enthusiasm of the young women.

'What about a party dress?' cried Cara. 'Remember Mama's suggestion.'

Anna looked doubtful. 'I don't think Father would agree.'

'He's got to some time,' returned Cara. 'Besides, he's not going to stop you going to other parties, is he?'

'Of course not. He expects Charles and me to lead our lives as normally as possible.'

'Well, what are you waiting for?'

Anna was still unsure.

Mrs Cassidy wondered at the inference behind this exchange but she was not one to pry into customers' private affairs. If ever they did confide in her, and there were those who wanted a sympathetic ear, she assured them that nothing would be revealed by her lips.

'May I suggest, Miss Mason, that we think of something not too frivolous, maybe one that could serve as an evening dress *and* party dress?'

Anna was still hesitant.

'Let me show you,' Mrs Cassidy advocated.

'There's no harm in that,' prompted Cara.

'I suppose not,' Anna conceded.

Within the next half-hour the second dress had been ordered. Mrs Cassidy took measurements

171

and arranged for a fitting in a week's time.

'You'll look lovely in them both,' Cara enthused as they left the dressmaker's. 'That second one is divine. When your father sees you in that he cannot help but think of reviving the famous Hawkshead parties.'

'I wish it would make him do that.' Anna frowned. 'He's not as morose as he was, and sometimes is like his old self, but he still won't meet anyone who knew Mother.'

As she rode home she pondered the question of tearing down the barrier. Maybe meeting the young man from Hull, whom Charles had said he would invite, would help. She began to wonder what Julian Kirby was like.

Julian was quickly on board the *Grace* to greet his friend from Whitby, once she was tied up.

'Good to see you again, Charles,' he said with enthusiasm.

'And you. Did you get the wine dealt with?'

'Aye. Very quickly. The buyers were enthusiastic. Herr Bremer's choice had them smacking their lips as soon as they took a taste. They want more, and soon. Money from the first shipment is already in the bank. After three more I'll present my father with the evidence. Then he can't help but give me more responsibility.'

'Good for you, Julian,' Charles said, laughter in his voice at his friend's carefree enthusiasm. 'I see you have the cargo for Amsterdam ready.' He had noted that the foreman in charge had contacted Captain Wilson and the first bales of wool were being brought on board.

'We can't have the *Grace* held up. Time is money.'

Charles's laughter grew louder. 'Steady on, Julian, you've got to play sometimes.'

'Aye,' he agreed, 'but now's not the time.' He cast a critical eye over the operation. Satisfied, he turned back to Charles. 'How were your father and sister?'

'Father was a little better. Anna was – well, Anna. How about your family?'

'Very well. After you left there were a few questions about you, especially from Rebecca.'

Caught unawares by the last remark, Charles did not know how to respond. Julian smiled and gave him a playful dig in the ribs. 'Do I detect embarrassment?' he teased.

'I suppose you told her about Magdalena?'

'I did not! I wouldn't dash my sister's hopes.' His grin broadened at the sight of Charles's disbelieving expression. He picked up the bag he had dropped when he had greeted Charles. 'I'm going to stow my bag.'

Charles watched him cross the deck. He was glad that line of conversation had been broken. However, whether Julian's remarks had a foundation or not they had recalled Rebecca. She was still occupying his mind when he was rejoined by Julian, who knew it would be unwise to broach the subject again, even though what he had imparted was true.

Once the wool was safely stowed on board, Captain Wilson got the ship under way.

As they sailed towards the sea, Julian, leaning

173

on the larboard rail, studied the shore and the land downriver from Paull and wondered what part it would play in his future.

'That's serious study.' Charles joined his friend at the rail. 'Thinking you might not see it again?' he added jokingly as he nodded in the direction of the darkening sky.

'Just interested. I don't know this area downstream of Hull.'

'Doesn't look very inviting to me,' observed Charles. 'Could be treacherous with all those creeks and what looks like some marshland or saltflats. I should forget it. There could be some farmland beyond but that wouldn't interest you.'

Julian agreed, wondering what Charles would think if he knew the real reason behind his interest.

Though the sky brought rain and stronger winds, the sailors on the *Grace*, under Captain Wilson's skilful supervision, handled the conditions with ease and the ship made good time to Amsterdam.

With lodgings secured with Digna and Roel Hein, the two young men conducted their business dealings separately next day.

Charles's step was light with the thought of seeing Magdalena again. Reaching the house on Herengracht he was shown straight to Herr de Klerk who was working alone in his office.

'My dear Charles.' Hendrick rose from his chair and came from behind his desk with outstretched hand. 'It is good to see you again so soon. I hope the last consignment of goods was satisfactory?'

'Of course they were. As they always are from the House of de Klerk.'

Hendrick made a slight bow, acknowledging the compliment with a dismissive gesture of the hand. 'We pride ourselves on having the best as you know. I hope all went well for your friend.'

'Indeed it did. He is with me again but has gone immediately to see Herr Bremer. He will no doubt call on you later. I know he wants to thank you for your help in directing him to Herr Bremer.'

'It was nothing, just a use of my knowledge. Now what can I interest you in this time?'

The two men were discussing the trading prospects when, ten minutes later, the door was thrust open and Magdalena swept in, 'Good morning, Father!' The words faded when she became aware of Charles.

For the briefest of moments her smile, fresh as the morning dew, vanished. No one would have noticed its going if their attention had not been riveted on her. But Charles's was. He saw that momentary faltering and it struck a blow at his heart. The look he had captured was one that revealed not only feelings of surprise but also regret that this moment had come upon her now. It was as if his presence troubled her. It sent a chill through him.

'Charles, this is a surprise. I did not know you intended to return so soon.' Magdalena was in charge of her feelings again. She came forward, her hand extended.

Charles was on his feet. Though his thoughts were confused – had he really interpreted that swift change correctly? – he smiled pleasantly, took her hand and raised it towards his lips. He could not hide the adoration in his eyes. 'The last assignment was dealt with so quickly that I needed more of everything.' He knew she would realise that he was also referring to his illegal trade and foreseeing a meeting with her alone later. But that was pre-empted by her father.

'Magdalena, you know I have a meeting with Herr Jansz in half an hour, will you take over the completion of this deal with Charles? I have made some notes here,' he tapped a sheet of paper on his desk, 'please conclude the trans-action.' He came from behind his desk, shook Charles by the hand and left the room.

'Charles, do sit down,' she said politely as she went to her father's chair behind the desk. 'Have you dealt with all the items you want from Father?'

He felt she had said it a little too quickly, as if she was trying to put him off something she thought he would say.

'No, there are several others that I think he might be able to help me with. I have a market in Whitby for some glassware.'

She nodded, her eyes on the paper in front of her as if she was trying to avoid his gaze. 'I think we can do business in glass. Anything else?' Her tone was stiff, business-like.

Charles knew that she had a shrewd brain but she had never been cold while conducting business with him before. It bothered him. He had to say something. 'Magdalena, what is the matter? You have never adopted this attitude with

176

me before.'

'I don't know what you mean. I am myself.' She looked up only briefly on the last word and then returned her gaze to the paper.

'That is not so,' he said quietly. 'I saw a flash of alarm when you found me here unexpectedly. Why was it there, Magdalena?'

She did not answer but continued to gaze at the paper.

'Magdalena, please.'

She looked up slowly and met his enquiring eyes. He saw hers were damp and troubled.

'Have I done something to upset you?' he asked.

She swallowed and shook her head. 'My dear Charles, you could never offend me. But I have something to tell you, something that I would have preferred to say at a later date.' She paused and bit her lips. He waited. He saw a look come into her eyes that pleaded with him to understand what she was about to say. 'I am betrothed to someone in Amsterdam.'

The shock stunned him. The world became unreal. His mind reeled. Surely those words had not been said? He stared unbelievingly at her. She should be his and yet his deepest conscience told him that he had no hold over her. He had never approached the question of marriage even though it had been in his mind. It only needed the right moment but now that was gone, blown away by seven words. He felt his world crumbling around him. The future he had thought he would spend with Magdalena now lay in ruins.

'I'm sorry, Charles.' Her whispered words jolted

177

him back to the reality of the situation. She continued quickly before he could speak, 'I have always been fond of you since our first meeting. That fondness grew and was moving towards something even greater. My father must have noticed it because after your last visit he reminded me what he expected of me – marriage to the heir of an important trading house in Amsterdam.'

'But do you love him?' Charles's cry was a plea also for the truth and showed that, if he received the reply he wanted, he would fight for her hand in marriage.

'He is a fine young man whom I have known since childhood. Our two families have always been close and have long seen this union as something desirable.'

'Do you love him?' insisted Charles.

'No doubt I will do in time. He is a kind and gentle person whom I know very well.'

'Does he love you?'

'Yes.' The word came firmly, leaving Charles in no doubt that it was true. 'Father pointed out to me what this marriage would mean to both families.'

'The creation of a trading dynasty,' he said harshly.

'It's not just that,' cried Magdalena. 'Please try and understand. He is an only child. The business will come to him and to his children.'

'Yours!'

'It is important that his firm is not broken up and sold off. This way it will be preserved.'

'A convenient arrangement with your happiness at stake.'

Magdalena ignored the barb. 'I can be happy.'

'As happy as with me?'

'Who can tell? As Father pointed out, marrying you would mean living in a foreign land with ways very different to what I know. I would be a stranger, maybe not even accepted by some. Life there would be alien to me and the consequences might be disastrous.' She saw he was going to argue and went on quickly. 'If you have any regard for me, please accept this. Don't fight it. The answer would always be the one I have given you now. But I don't want to lose our friendship. That is important to me and always will be. Dear Charles, let us remain friends who can still meet in that spirit of friendship and continue to trade as we have done. Let our meetings be occasions in which we find pleasure in each other's company.'

Her plea came so much from the heart that Charles could not ignore it. As much as he felt hurt and viewed the future with a bleak outlook, he could not deny what she wanted. If he was to continue trading with the de Klerks, if he was to maintain his purchase of contraband goods through Magdalena, they were bound to meet.

His eyes looked on her with tenderness. 'I think too much of you to sully our relationship. I respect what you have said and wish you every happiness in the future.' He saw relief come to her eyes and with it a hope for the future. 'Magdalena,' he went on quietly, 'if ever you are in need of me in any way whatsoever, you have only to get word to me.'

She rose from her chair and Charles did

likewise. She came to him. 'Thank you,' she whispered, and kissed him on the cheek.

His arms came round her. He held her tight. 'Be happy,' he said.

'And you too. I know you will find someone worthy of your love.'

Their eyes locked on each other and their lips met in a kiss that sealed a new understanding but also expressed what might have been.

He released her and strode to the door. She watched him with tears in her eyes. She started to reach out and call him back. They had not completed the business left unfinished by her father. But that could wait. Charles would be back and it would be the beginning of a new relationship.

Julian's legitimate business with Herr Bremer was conducted smoothly to the satisfaction of both parties, though Herr Bremer's son, Coenraad, raised objections again. Over the next two days the goods were stored on the *Grace*, Coenraad unusually supervising the operation himself. The rest of the goods taken on board were noted by him, but he saw nothing untoward. If this Englishman, Kirby, was conducting any other business, and he had seemed thick with Reynier de Klerk, then it must be organised some other way.

Once Reynier received a note from Julian telling him that he was in Amsterdam, he immediately arranged a meeting.

'I see from the enthusiasm in your eyes that you

have managed to organise the reception on your shores,' said Reynier as they settled down with their glasses of wine.

'I have. The area we will use will be along the Humber. The dropping places will vary so we will have to devise a series of signals. One for your ship's arrival, one from us to signify that all is safe, and another as a warning. I have two men with intimate knowledge of the Humber and its waterways. Once we have your signal one of them will come out to your vessel to guide her to the unloading point.' He went on to enlighten Reynier about other aspects of the organisation.

'That all sounds highly satisfactory.' Reynier congratulated him. 'Now, down to details of the first run. I have some more items to purchase but they should be all clear to leave Amsterdam five days from now.'

'The eighth of September?'

'Yes. What time will be the most suitable?'

Julian thought for a moment. 'Arrive in the Humber at eleven at night. Your men should be looking to the starboard bow as they come in from the sea.'

'Good. I'll make sure that they are in full possession of our signal arrangements. If this goes smoothly and your distribution meets no problems then it could be the start of a very successful and profitable partnership.'

Chapter Eight

Sails captured the wind. The *Grace* cut purposefully through the waves, sending the foaming water singing along her sides. The two friends stood by the rail enjoying the motion and the sensation of the wind on their skin.

Julian breathed deeply, savouring the salt tang. He glanced at Charles. 'Out with it, man. Something's been troubling you since the day after our arrival. Business not go as well as you expected?' He well knew that aspect of the visit had in fact caused no problems but needed a lead in to what he surmised was the real reason for Charles's introspection.

'It was highly satisfactory.'

'So what's troubling you? Magdalena?'

Charles was silent. Julian read that as a sign that he was right. 'If it will help to talk, please do so, but I'll respect your desire to say nothing if you wish.'

Charles turned to his friend with a wan smile. 'Obvious, was it?'

Julian nodded. 'Yes. Even Frau Hein said you had a troubled heart. She hoped it would mend elsewhere.'

'Shrewd lady, but she's a mother and has probably had to deal with similar disappointments suffered by her own children.'

'And I've seen it in Rebecca. She had a beau,

Angus, whom she thought a lot of but he was killed last year at Salamanca.'

'I'm sorry. Has she recovered from the loss?'

'She is beginning to. It hit her hard but, with patience and persistence from all of us, she is beginning to believe there is still a life for her. What about you and Magdalena? Is there no hope?'

'No,' Charles shook his head sadly, 'but we remain very good friends and always will. Besides I will have to go on trading with the de Klerks, so I'm sure to see her. Under those circumstances we couldn't harbour bad feelings.' He went on to tell Julian of Magdalena's reasons for breaking up what he had hoped would become a permanent relationship.

'Better now than later, and better this way so that you remain friends,' pointed out Julian after he had offered his sympathies.

Charles tightened his lips, then, as if to shake off the disappointment, said brightly, 'There's still an exciting life ahead of me. I'm sure there's someone for me, somewhere.'

'Of course there is,' agreed Julian enthusiastically, thankful that his friend was throwing off his sadness. And it could be Rebecca, he thought to himself, remembering his sister's interest in Charles during his brief visit.

The voyage went well and the two young men were in a good mood as they sailed up the Humber heading for the Hull dock.

'Julian, why not come to Whitby with me? Meet Father and Anna? You've nothing to hold you here once you have seen your consignment

183

unloaded. I'll get Captain Wilson to delay sailing to give you time to visit your parents.'

'That's not possible immediately, but thank you for the idea. Remember, Father doesn't know about this shipment. I have storage and distribution settled but I must supervise them.' Julian was careful not to mention that there was also a smuggling enterprise to oversee.

'Of course. But the invitation is open for you to visit any time.'

'I would like to come. When we dock, let me check when the *North Star* is due to head north again. Would it be all right if I came to Whitby then?'

'Of course. Why not bring Rebecca with you, too? The change might do her good after her disappointment. I'm sure Anna would welcome some fresh company.'

'I think she would be delighted to come, and I can't see Mother or Father objecting when she'll have me to escort her.'

'Good, then that is settled.'

With arrangements made for Julian to arrive in Whitby in ten days' time the two friends made their goodbyes. Julian watched the *Grace* slip from her moorings then turned his attention to the storage of his consignment of wine. Satisfied with that, he called on two wine merchants with whom he had struck a deal before leaving for Amsterdam. All the bottles would be out of his hands by the end of the week. He was in a mood of elation as he walked home. Tomorrow would see a start to the implementation of his second venture.

Charles watched the cliffs of Whitby draw closer as the *Grace* altered course to run in towards land. His thoughts had wandered to Magdalena again and he regretted what had happened, but there was life still to live and who knew what lay ahead of him? That thought brought to mind his spontaneous suggestion that Rebecca should come to the Manor with Julian. Had some sub-conscious feeling for her coloured that invitation? He dismissed the idea, but, recalling his visit to the Kirbys, was reminded that he had been attracted to her. At that time a life with Magdalena had been foremost in his thoughts. But now ... what of the future? Such speculation was thrust from his mind as the ship passed between the piers into the bustle of the port that was so much a part of his life.

Gideon was at the quayside. Charles quickly acquainted him with the cargo and then listened as his manager informed him of the goods he had arranged for the *Grace* to ship out of Whitby in three days' time. Leaving Gideon at last, Charles sought out Edwin and told him that a cargo of contraband could be picked up by Nicholas and Ralph in two days' time.

After collecting his horse from the White Horse, he put it to a brisk pace, eager to be home.

Anna was pleased to see her brother, and warm in her greetings. She was also eager to impart information about their father.

'The day you left, I was in Whitby until supper-time. I was worried to leave him so long but I

185

needn't have been. He had been perfectly all right. Mrs Denston told me he had discussed some interior renovations to the house, and Jack Crane said Father had talked to him about purchasing two more horses. When I mentioned these matters to him he played them down, but there was definitely some enthusiasm there. I wish he would start meeting people again.'

'He's going to get the chance in ten days' time. I've invited Julian Kirby to visit and to bring his sister Rebecca.'

'Good. You've met her then?'

'Briefly, that time I stayed over with the Kirbys. She's nice. You'll like her.'

Anna raised an eyebrow and cast him a teasing look. 'Do I detect some interest? Ah, but there's Magdalena.' She saw anguish momentarily cloud his face. 'Something wrong, Charles?' she asked anxiously.

He told her what had happened.

'Oh, I'm so sorry,' she said. 'But, who knows? Maybe it's for the best. You'll get over it even though you are sad now.'

'I'm trying not to be too downcast. I know I can't reverse her decision. I did think of making a fight for her: go to see her father, put my case, explain how I could make her happy. But I realised from what she said that it would be useless and would only cause her more pain and anguish as well as probably destroying a friendship we both wish to keep.'

'I'm sure you are right.' Anna paused a moment before changing the subject. 'Now let me tell you about my day in Whitby after you left.' She told

186

him how she and Cara had enjoyed themselves after hurrying to escape from Mrs Blenkinsop.

'She'd be peeved when you got back and told her where you had been?'

'She certainly was.' Anna changed her voice to mimic Belinda's: 'My dears, you should have waited for me. My choice would have suited you admirably, Anna. Now you have no mother, you need an older woman's advice on such matters. Oh, what a pity I wasn't at home.' Anna threw up her hands in despair just as Mrs Blenkinsop would have done.

Charles had started to chuckle at her impersonation and now burst into laughter as did Anna, pleased to see her brother laughing after his gloom on telling her about Magdalena.

'So you got your two dresses?'

'Yes, but the second one is a party dress. Cara persuaded me.'

'Why not?' said Charles with enthusiastic approval.

'I wonder what Father will say?'

'Doesn't he know?'

'No. I merely told him that I had got two. I think I'll keep the second dress a secret until we can persuade him to revive the Hawkshead parties again.'

'You think we'll be able to do that?'

'We'll try when the time is right. When did you say Julian and Rebecca were coming?'

'Ten days' time. They're coming on the *North Star*.'

'I'll be able to wear my new dress for them. Not the party one, that will remain a secret until the

187

right time.'

'How are you going to keep that one from Father when he knows you've purchased two? He's sure to ask to see it.'

'I'll find a way.'

Mist hung low over the Humber, swirling eerily in almost imperceptible movement as the reluctant breeze started and stopped and moved again. Only the gentle lap of water and the occasional cry of an owl broke the pall of silence. Shadowy figures on the shore strained their eyes in the gathering dark.

'Curse this fog,' muttered Julian.

'Nay, lad. This is good. Shields us from the eyes of the Customs Officers and restricts the Revenue cutter,' said Greg.

'Maybe, but what about the Dutch sloop?'

'They'll be skilled enough to find the Humber even in this. Be patient and calm.'

Julian did not answer. Calm? How could he be? He desperately wanted everything to go right. He had been stiff with anxiety ever since he had left Hull with Greg, Mike and Bill. The tension had mounted in him since they had come to the water's edge and the time for the arrival of the sloop had drawn nearer. Now the hour was past. Where was the ship? Why wasn't it here? He rubbed his eyes as if to clear them, but could not dispel the mist. If anything he thought it was thickening. Imagination? He tried to pierce the gloom with his tired eyes. The signal? Where was it? The minutes were ticking away. He imagined Luke, waiting at the spot where they were to

188

unload the contraband, would be growing impatient; did not yet know the other man's capacity to await developments without undue anxiety.

'There!' Greg's whisper was close in his ear.

'Where?' Julian and Bill Grimes queried together. They saw nothing but fog and gloom.

'There!' Mike confirmed his brother's sighting and pointed in the direction of a flash of light, but it had disappeared again before Julian's eyes focused in the direction indicated.

Another flash.

'Got it!' His tone was filled with relief and excitement.

The four men watched intently. The light vanished, came again and then disappeared. Greg counted the seconds as they passed. Julian could feel the tension rising in the others. If this was the Dutch sloop they should see the prearranged signal after one minute.

'Fifty-five, fifty-six...'

Julian held his breath.

'...fifty-nine, sixty.'

The light reappeared steadily for several seconds. It was extinguished, came again, then disappeared and reappeared three times in quick succession.

'It's them!' Mike confirmed. He picked up a lantern which had been shielded in a metal box. He raised it, swung it once to the right and then to the left. There came a similar signal in reply. 'Away with you, Greg.'

He was already pushing a boat from the bankside with the help of Bill Grimes. Greg stepped over the gunwale and sat down on the centre thwart, unshipped the oars and started to row. In a few moments he was lost to the sight of those on shore. He rowed steadily with an occasional glance over his shoulder. The reappearance of the light now and then guided him towards the sloop. A ghostly outline gradually emerged from the fog and a few moments later took on more solid form. Then he was alongside. Willing hands helped him on board while others secured his boat. Few words were spoken, for every man knew the course of events now.

Greg went to the helmsman who allowed him to take over. Following the prearranged signals from Mike's lantern ashore, Greg took the sloop towards the creek they had chosen. Through the ship's captain he issued orders to the crew who brought it at a slow but steady progress to the landing point a quarter of a mile from the Humber. Mike, Julian and Bill had joined Luke there and they supplied willing hands to tie the sloop securely to firm ground. Not a moment was wasted and the contraband was quickly unloaded. With the final barrel ashore, Julian thanked the Dutch captain and told him to tell Reynier all was well.

Within a few minutes Greg was guiding the sloop back to the open water. Once there he took his leave and rowed back to shore while the sloop silently slipped away. Reaching land, Greg hid his boat among some reeds and rejoined the others. He found that the contraband was already being stored in the places Luke had chosen for this operation. It was hard toil and no word was spoken until they were finished.

Finally Julian leaned on a barrel of brandy, getting his breath back. His arms and legs were aching but he would not complain. The whole operation had gone smoothly. 'Satisfied?' he gasped.

'Aye.' Everyone muttered their agreement.

'This was only a small consignment to see how everything worked,' said Bill Grimes. 'I reckon we could do with more helpers next time. Mr Julian knows I can raise however many we want.'

'Aye, you're right,' agreed Luke. He eyed Bill seriously as he added, 'They must be able to carry out orders to the letter without question, and they've got to be one hundred per cent trustworthy.'

'They'll be that if the money is right.'

'And I said it would be,' Julian confirmed.

'Good. Now, do you want me to arrange the disposal of this lot?'

'Yes.'

Luke turned to Bill. 'Ten men at my place with two carts in three days' time to arrive between four and five in the afternoon, not all together. Watch they aren't followed and tell no one what they're about.'

Julian was impressed by the authority in Luke's voice and his obvious confidence stemming from previous experience. 'What do you want me to do?' he asked.

'Nothing, if you trust us to see to this side of the operation?'

'Of course I do.'

'Good. Then you play your part by organising

191

the incoming contraband. Good quality will always bring good prices and still be cheaper than the legitimate trade.'

'So when do you want the next delivery?'

'Word will get around that there's another freetrading gang operating in the area. We'll wait three weeks and let the curious think it's been a one-off operation. Then we'll do three runs in quick succession, each bigger than the last. That will get our rivals thinking, especially when I start disposing of some of our contraband in their territory.'

'This sounds as if you are using our smuggling as a means of smoking out your father's killers?' commented Julian.

'Aye, lad, it does.' Greg eyed him solemnly. 'If you can't abide that then say so now.'

Julian sensed the tension in the air as the other four awaited his answer. 'It's what I expected. I'll agree on one condition: no deliberate killing. I want no charge of murder hanging over me.'

Luke spread his hands. 'As if we would.' There was a small pause and he went on, 'We'll put them out of business instead. That will widen our territory along the sea coast, and then who knows how far north we can spread?' A determined expression hardened his eyes. His brothers recognised that the thrill of smuggling was back in Luke's blood and here was someone to be reckoned with. They liked what they had heard. This small beginning could turn into something big.

Luke's idea had spurred Julian. He now visualised running such a gang, and the wealth that could bring him. He recognised that through the Upton brothers, especially Luke, he had gained a foothold in the smuggling world he had never dreamed possible when Reynier had first put the suggestion to him. 'Three weeks before the next run, and then one every week for three more?'

'Yes, and by then we will be in a position to make a bigger run yet before Christmas.'

'I thought in the winter we'd have to stop?'

Greg laughed. 'Aye, the seas and the weather conditions can be rough then. But sometimes that's a help even though there's more risk. We'll probably ease up for a while after Christmas. Husbands will want to rein in their spending on their wives and mistresses for a month or two.'

'You do the organising in Holland. Leave this side of the water to us.' Luke gave his final word and with it was the inference that they had reached an understanding that could serve them all well.

As he sailed down the Humber on the *North Star*, Julian wondered what Rebecca, standing beside him, would think if she knew that last week he had run contraband ashore along this very coast. He felt deep satisfaction at an operation success-fully completed. Within five days he had been informed that the disposal of the contraband had gone well and that, at the prices they asked, there was strong demand for more. The temptation to forget the time-scale laid down by Luke had been strong but he insisted on a strict schedule and Julian knew better than to contradict his plan.

Julian was looking forward to visiting Charles

and seeing something of Whitby even though he knew his mind would be full of the impending visit to Holland when plans for future smuggling runs up to Christmas would be made with Reynier.

Rebecca was excited for different reasons. This was her first sea voyage, her first visit to Whitby, and she was looking forward to meeting again the handsome young man who was to be their host. As the ship sailed down the Humber she hoped she had good sea-legs.

She need not have worried. Even Julian had to admit surprise at how readily she took to the sea. Standing beside her brother when the *North Star* met the first waves, she removed her bonnet and shook her hair free. Exhilarated by the wind in her hair and the colour it brought to her cheeks, she slipped her arm under his and gave it a sisterly hug.

'Thank you for bringing me,' she said in a tone that was evidence of the pleasure she was feeling.

Julian was happy for her. He sensed that this break from the familiar surroundings of home and Hull was bringing a fresh perspective to her loss of Angus just over a year ago. Not that she would ever forget him but he would no longer be a dominant presence in her life.

Rebecca confirmed that when she added, 'I'm so looking forward to this visit, to meeting Charles again and becoming acquainted with his family.'

Rebecca had only experienced the genteel side of life in Scarborough and Hull. As they sailed into

Whitby she felt the hustle and bustle of the everyday life of the hardworking community. She marvelled at the picturesque ruined abbey and old parish church set high on the east cliff: all the red roofs clinging to the cliff-side down to the river. But it was the hubbub of activity that held her enthralled. Even amidst the creak of timbers, the squeak of ropes, the flap of canvas and the bellowed shouts of command, she heard the babble of voices rising from the staithes, quays and streets where the seething mass of Whitby people went about their daily lives.

'There's Charles!' Julian cried, and raised his arm in acknowledgement of his friend's wave.

Rebecca followed his direction and felt a tightening when her gaze alighted on the Whitby man. Beside him stood a young woman. Even from this distance Rebecca could sense her natural calmness and serenity. For a moment she suffered misgivings. She hoped Charles's sister was not going to be too prim and proper. If she were it would mar the excitement of these new experiences in Rebecca's life which she hoped to enjoy.

Julian too had turned his eyes on the girl on the quay and he felt immediately drawn to her. With that came impatience to be on the quay, face to face with her.

The *North Star* was manoeuvred to a berth on the east bank with all the skill of men who had visited this port many times. Once she was secure the gangway was run out and Rebecca and Julian left the ship followed by a sailor carrying their two valises.

Greetings and introductions were quickly made. Rebecca's worry was immediately dismissed. She found Anna to be neatly dressed, without any ostentation. The warmth of her smile made Rebecca feel truly welcome and her doubts were swiftly swept from her mind. She was further more reassured by the light in Anna's eyes which scotched any idea that she might be meeting a person who was prim. She saw that this was a naturally lively personality, one that would enjoy life.

Julian saw Anna differently. While he would have agreed with his sister's assessment, he was enthralled by her serene beauty, not classical but definitely attractive. She would always draw attention even if she did not set out to do so. Her skin was white and smooth over high cheekbones, lips perfectly shaped beneath a nose with a slight engaging upward tilt. Her eyes, perfectly set, were the colour of autumn leaves. Copper-tinted hair peeped from beneath her small bonnet and Julian imagined it released from its constraint, tumbling like a peat-coloured mountain stream.

He curbed his desire to walk with her to the carriage which Charles had left in the charge of two urchins who knew they would get a good tip from Mr Mason if they kept his horses under control. Julian picked up one of the bags as Charles took charge of the other, and Anna escorted Rebecca to their conveyance.

On the way to Hawkshead Manor she studied Charles's new friends. She had taken to Rebecca from the moment they had met on the quay but was experiencing misgivings about Julian. She felt a pang of jealousy at the evident closeness that existed between her brother and this stranger. Anna felt she was being pushed aside. She could see why her brother had taken to this man but was his charm merely a veneer? Was it being used to cloak some ulterior motive?

Though she had lived in large houses in the better parts of Scarborough and Hull, Rebecca had no experience of country manors.

'What a beautiful place,' she commented as the carriage approached the front of the house. 'And such an exquisite setting.' She glanced across the open ground sloping towards the woods where massive trees were proudly displaying their autumnal colours. 'You've lived here all your life?'

'Yes,' replied Anna.

'I shouldn't imagine either of you would ever want to leave?'

Anna gave a wistful smile. 'Maybe not, but who knows what life has in store for us?'

Charles brought the carriage to a halt and jumped down from his seat to help the others. The sound of wheels grinding on the gravel brought Jack Crane hurrying from the stable yard. He steadied the horses while the passengers climbed from the carriage.

Charles made a quick introduction and, turning to Rebecca, said, 'You do ride?'

'A little. Though Julian and I have not had the same opportunities as you, no doubt.'

Charles looked to the groom. 'We had better have two quiet mounts ready when they are needed, Jack.'

A man servant had appeared at the door and quickly took the valises to the rooms that had been allocated to the guests.

Anna led the way. As they entered the hall John appeared from his study. He came to greet them with the warm smile that had been missing from his face since the tragic accident. Anna felt joyous and full of hope that her father's full recovery would be sooner rather than later. She made the introductions quickly.

'I am pleased to meet you both,' he said. 'You are welcome to our home. Please make it yours.'

After the Kirbys had expressed their thanks and pleasantries had been exchanged, they were shown upstairs.

'This is such a lovely room with a beautiful view. It is so kind of you to have me, Anna,' said Rebecca when they were alone.

'It is a pleasure,' she replied. 'I know we are going to become good friends.'

'I hope so.'

'I know so. I sensed it when I watched you walk down the gangplank.'

'Then I believe you are right, for I felt it then too.'

'From what I hear it was the same when Charles and Julian first met?'

'I'm so glad they did.' Rebecca's expression turned serious. 'Can I say right away how sorry I was to hear about your mother?'

'Thank you,' returned Anna. 'May I ask you not to mention it to Father, though, unless he brings it up? Which I don't think he will.' She explained the difficulties she and Charles had had with him.

'I know only too well what he has experienced.' Anna showed her surprise so Rebecca explained her own loss. 'Talking about it helped to alleviate the pain. Mother and Father, Caroline and Julian, were a wonderful support, and gradually life became normal for me. Don't you think it would be better for your father to talk about it?'

'Yes, I do, but he was adamant right after the funeral that he wanted to sever any association that could only be painful to him.'

'But what about you and Charles, and this house?'

'We were exempt, thank goodness. But he is much better now than he used to be.' She described the changes she had seen and expressed her hope that John's acceptance of Rebecca and her brother, as guests in the house, would help him to overcome his attitude to the people who used to be his friends.

For a while after Anna had left her Rebecca sat looking out of the window, not really seeing anything for she was lost in her thoughts about what Anna had just told her. The sad story was never far from Rebecca's mind during the rest of her stay.

The week passed all too quickly for her. Her friendship with Anna deepened. They walked, rode and chattered until their tongues were tired. Anna took her to Whitby and there they called on Cara and Mrs Blenkinsop. When they found a common interest in the Hawkshead art collection, Anna explained why her father no longer added to it.

'You must try to revive his collecting, and follow up Mrs Blenkinsop's suggestion about the party. Both things might help him.' Rebecca's advice gave Anna cause for thought.

Julian was also delighted with his visit to Hawkshead Manor. He got on well with Mr Mason, and all four young people were pleased with the way John sought their company without ever intruding on the time they wanted to spend together. Both Anna and Charles were delighted with this as they were with the bright conversation he brought to the table at mealtimes, even rising to Julian's challenge to a game of chess.

The day before the Kirbys had to return to Hull was bright and mild for the time of the year. Charles and Julian had not returned from a visit to Whitby. Anna had some household arrangements to discuss with Mrs Denston, so Rebecca found herself with time on her hands. She went for a walk, enjoying her moments of quiet among such peaceful surroundings. She followed the path into the wood. Sunlight added glory to the golds, browns and reds as it filtered through the trees, bathing the leaf-covered ground in patches of light. She took the right-hand fork in the path and a few minutes later was aware that a little way ahead a patch of the wood had been ruthlessly cleared. She was surprised and curious because this act seemed alien to the carefully tended Hawkshead estate.

She stopped walking. Her body and mind tensed. She felt a presence. Someone was near. She glanced around her. She could see no one but felt someone was there. Rebecca stepped quietly to one side to avoid the trees that had obscured her view. Then she saw him. He was standing with his back to her, staring across the open clearing. Mr Mason! She perceived from his attitude and stance, the very set of his body, that he was confronting the same feelings she had before her tragic loss, but his were even more intense. She surmised this was the place where his wife had died. Rebecca's beau had been killed in a foreign field and she had no physical reminder of where the tragedy had happened. She turned away. She should leave John to his thoughts. If she interrupted he would have to give an explanation of what he was doing and that might cause a setback in his rehabilitation.

She paused and glanced back at the silent figure. And hesitated. Maybe she could help... She turned towards him and glided across the leaf-strewn ground, hoping that the rustle of the leaves did not disturb him until she was close.

'Mr Mason?' Her voice was soft and gentle. She saw him stiffen. His bowed head came up, alert to the intrusion. 'Mr Mason?' Rebecca repeated quietly.

He spun round. She saw annoyance in his eyes. This interruption on his private grief offended him. Then she saw him relax a little when he recognised the intruder, though there was still some lingering hostility. 'Rebecca, I did not hear you coming.'

'I'm sorry to have disturbed you.'

He waved his hand as if to brush aside her apology. 'It's nothing. I was lost in thought.'

'Wondering what to do with this space?'

'No. It's been done.' There was a snap to his voice.

'But it's so rough, so unlike the rest of your estate. I thought maybe you had plans for it?'

'No. It stays as it is. This ground is desecrated!'

'Why?' Rebecca knew she was treading where maybe she shouldn't, but something told her that Mr Mason, seething with recollections, would not hold back from answering her question.

'It is where my wife died.'

'And you had it cleared so you could no longer see it as it was? So that you could wipe out any reminder of your loss? But you haven't, have you? You still come here.' Her words came out sharp and cutting.

His eyes flared. 'What right have you to criticise, young lady? What right to pass judgement?'

'More right than you imagine, for I too have experienced the loss of someone very dear to me.' She saw the doubt in his eyes and went on before he had time to speak. 'Yes, I have. Angus, my beau, was killed in Spain serving in the Army. I can't visit the place where he was killed. You are lucky, Mr Mason, you can come here. That and visiting the places and people you and your wife shared together should help heal your loss and keep her close to you.'

'No, such actions only deepen the wound.'

'Only because you let them. You should look on them as gifts to her memory, and in that way you will still share your love with her and will feel hers for you still there.'

John was silent. His mind was crying out for

her to stop, yet the truth in what she was saying could not be denied.

'Think carefully, Mr Mason. If you continue to foster your reclusive attitude it will not only eventually destroy you, but harm those around you, too, those you love. Your wife would surely not want that? Be with her, let her be with you, and you will find a greater joy in life.'

A sharp reply sprang to his lips. What right had she to speak to him like this? But he knew nevertheless that there was much truth in what she said. How could one so young be so wise? Was it the result of the tragedy that had stalked her own life? He had to know.

'Rebecca, if what you say is true, you are wise beyond your years.'

'It is only what my mother and father taught me when I suffered. But I am young, tragedy might be more easily absorbed then. You have had a life with your wife to draw on to see you through. I had not. My thoughts were all of what might have been, of dreams unfulfilled. Yours can conjure up wonderful memories. You have shared experiences that can make your life still worth living.' She stopped, blushed, and gave a wan smile. 'I'm sorry, Mr Mason. I've rattled on, saying things I maybe shouldn't have said. I am sorry I intruded on your privacy. I hope you will not hold it against me and that we can still be friends.' She turned and walked away.

John stared after her, his mind in a whirl. So much came flooding in on him, but amid the confusion he heard himself call out, 'Rebecca, wait!' He stepped after her. She turned and waited for him.

'Thank you,' was all he said, but she could read in his eyes that there was a world of sincerity behind those two words and she knew she had triggered off thoughts she prayed would lead him to the right conclusions.

Chapter Nine

'Did you enjoy yourself?' Julian put the question to his sister on deck as the *North Star* was taken downstream towards the sea.

'Immensely,' she replied, giving one last wave to the two people on the quay who had made her visit to Hawkshead Manor one she would always remember. 'They are such a nice couple.'

'Especially Charles.' He looked seriously at his sister as he added, 'Could he take the place of Angus?'

'I liked him, but only time will tell.'

'We'll invite them to Hull before long.'

'I doubt if Anna will come until her father is fully recovered. She has a deep love and concern for him. When do you see Charles again?'

'Next week. We pay another visit to Amsterdam. That was a very fortuitous call I paid on him in Hull, on the off chance he could help.'

Two days after arriving home, Julian made his way to Luke's farm in the lonely countryside east of Paull, overlooking the wide estuary of the Humber.

After settling the proceeds from the first operation they decided on a date for the next run so that Julian could make arrangements on his visit to Amsterdam the following week.

'As we said, we'll do two more during the

succeeding weeks, so you can arrange those as well.'

'Have you had any reaction from your rivals?'

'Not directly, but there have been rumours apparently that a new gang has started operating along the Humber. Others will be waiting to see if it was an isolated run. After our next they'll know it wasn't.'

About the same time, Charles was discussing his next shipment of contraband with Edwin. A date was fixed, and the cargo of illegal goods decided, then Edwin said, 'There's a story going round that a while back contraband was run ashore along the Humber. I wonder if the Upton brothers have started smuggling again?'

'Any threat to us if so?'

'At the moment, no, but we had better keep an eye on further developments. If there's any encroachment on our area we'll have to do something.'

These thoughts were in Charles's mind when he picked up Julian in Hull the following week. He had a mind to ask his friend if he had heard anything, but decided not to in case it set Julian wondering why he should be interested. Awkward questions might be asked, and if Julian suspected him of smuggling it might lead to a severing of relationships, which would mean losing contact with Rebecca. Charles did not want that.

For a moment the thought disturbed him. But why should it? Now his relationship with Magdalena was severed he was free and so was

Rebecca. But were they both ready for a new relationship so soon after what they had gone through? Charles believed one should not let the past influence the future by holding back and losing the chance of further happiness. Rebecca came vividly to mind and he liked the recollection of her visit to Hawkshead Manor. Though she may still think of her lost love, he had seen a natural vivacity in her which would not allow her to hold back from enjoying life once more. He thought her stay had finally released her from her mourning and knew that, even in the short time she had been at the Manor, she had established a close relationship with Anna. If his sister liked her then that would help his own relationship, which he hoped might eventually blossom into love.

After Charles had placed his orders, including a double consignment shortly before Christmas, Magdalena suggested that they should take a walk by the canal. They discussed a date for the next cargo to be picked up. With business out of the way she said, 'I'm pleased that you have found someone else.'

'Is it that obvious?' he replied.

'A woman's intuition. I could tell when you looked at me that you were comparing me with someone else.'

He was shocked by the unmasking of what he thought he had kept disguised. He blushed and rushed to apologise.

She laughed. 'Don't be embarrassed, dear Charles. I am happy for you. I hope she thinks as highly of you?'

'I believe she might.' Because he had always found Magdalena easy to talk to, he went on to tell her about Rebecca.

'I think you have probably found your true love,' she commented when he had finished. 'I hope it will prosper.'

'And you, Magdalena? Are you happy?' He expressed his concern.

'Yes, Charles. I appreciate your thoughts for me. I am lucky indeed to have such a good friend.'

When Julian reported on the success of their first smuggling operation, Reynier was enthusiastic for the next one.

'You can count on a shipment each week for the next three weeks, and then a big one on November the eleventh to cope with the demand for Christmas,' Julian told him.

Reynier's enthusiasm became even stronger. 'For that one could you handle two sloops?'

'I'm sure we could. If it looks unlikely we can make alternative plans when we make the previous run.'

Two sloops: double the cargo, twice the profit for him. His mind drifted to what that could mean for the future. A home like Hawkshead Manor ... somewhere befitting Anna. He started. Was he letting his imagination run away with him? He found his thoughts turning more and more to her, remembering his visit to her home. It was not difficult for him to conjure up a picture of her. He could still see her enchanting smile which surely carried some special meaning when she caught his eye? Or was it just wishful thinking that he had brought out some special feeling in her? Was he colouring his memory with his growing feeling for her as she entered his thoughts more and more? He continually saw her vivid copper-coloured hair streaming in the wind, or dancing in the light of the sun when she released it while they were out riding. He could easily recall the way she walked ... no, he thought of it more as a graceful motion that enhanced her presence. Tantalising dreams. The future promised so much. He would seize it while he could.

Charles and Julian returned home enthusing about the boom in legitimate trading, but keeping to themselves their zeal for their illegal transactions. The dangers from this trade hardly tempered their eagerness. In the euphoria of their success both harboured prospects of widening their smuggling net. Julian knew he would have to rely on the Upton brothers, but he had faith in them. Charles, on the other hand, knew that if he wanted to expand this trade he had to be able to learn from and think like his father. He could only do that if John were back beside him, for he had so far refused to reveal the other contacts he had had in mind to extend their trade. Unless he returned to active duty the Masons' smuggling enterprise would stagnate and Charles did not want that. He hoped when he returned home he would find that the improvement he had detected in his father during the Kirbys' visit had continued.

'How's Father been?' was the first question he put to Anna when he reached Hawkshead Manor.

'I think he continues to improve, though he has become a little more introspective.'

'I thought he had thrown a lot of that off, especially during our visitors' stay?'

'So did I, but since they left he often seems lost in thought.'

'Dwelling on Mother again?'

Anna screwed her face up doubtfully. 'I'm not sure. It's as if he's reflecting on something of deep significance. I wonder...' She paused thoughtfully for a moment. 'On the last day of their visit, you and Julian were in Whitby and I was busy with household matters. I did not know what Rebecca was doing but when I had finished my discussion with Mrs Denston I could not find her. I sat on the terrace and later she and Father appeared from the direction of the wood. I attached no significance to it at the time, but I have come to wonder since if something passed between them.'

'What do you mean?'

'You know that Rebecca's beau was killed in Spain?'

'Yes.'

'I wonder if she spoke to Father of her loss and compared it with his?'

'If she did I doubt they would have returned in amiable conversation together. Besides, I know Julian asked her not to raise the matter of Mother's accident in front of Father.'

'That may be, but on meeting him could she

not have seen a reason to do so? If she did then he appeared to have accepted it very well.'

'And you think this present introspection might have something to do with Rebecca?'

'It could.'

'Did she discuss her circumstances with you?'

'She told me that she believed she got over her loss because her family talked to her about Angus. They never shut him out, but at the same time made sure her loss did not affect her outlook on the future.'

'Then maybe we should talk to Father about our lives.'

Anna made the first step during the evening meal when she asked, 'Father, a little while ago you talked to Mrs Denston about some renovations in the house. Have you thought any further about them?'

'You know what they were, do you think they are a good idea?'

'Yes.'

'Then let's get them done. The next time you are in Whitby make the arrangements.'

'Mother would have liked that.'

Both Anna and Charles held their breath, but the expected rebuff did not come. Instead they heard a quiet, 'Yes, I think she would.'

A quick exchange of glances showed not only Anna's and Charles's relief but also a belief that they had made a further advance in their father's rehabilitation.

'What colour would you like for the dining room?' asked Anna.

'I don't mind. You make the choice. Consult Mrs Denston if you wish. But get a good-quality wallpaper.' He paused then added, 'Why not get some new curtains and have the chairs in the dining room reupholstered too?'

'If that is what you wish,' she said quietly, delighted by his interest.

They received a further surprise when their father said, 'Get it done soon and then invite those two nice young people from Hull once more. I enjoyed their company.'

'We will,' replied Charles with enthusiasm. 'I know they would like to visit again.'

'Good, then that's settled.' There was the sound of heartfelt satisfaction in John Mason's voice.

'You must have worked hard on Father while I was away,' commented Charles when, later that evening, he was alone with Anna, John having retired to his study.

'I did nothing but lead as normal a life as possible.'

'Then normality must be having a beneficial effect on him.'

'That is so, but I still believe something happened between him and Rebecca.'

'I'm so pleased he suggested that they should come again. They will be good company for him.'

'You mean Rebecca will. Or rather for you.' He ignored her teasing smile and asked in all seriousness, 'You liked her?' He needed his sister's approval.

'Yes. We got on very well. I'm pleased for you, Charles.'

'What about you? Did I detect a liking for Julian?'

'Your friend is my friend,' she replied. He sensed coldness in her voice. 'But what do you really know of him? You only met him through business, after all. He sought you out.'

Charles was taken aback by his sister's implied criticism. His hackles were raised. 'Don't deny me my friends. I think I can be trusted to judge them adequately.'

'Maybe, but I'm concerned he might be using you.'

'Don't be ridiculous!' There was an irritated snap to Charles's voice.

'I might be wrong. I hope I am. But do be careful, you've a lot of responsibility to shoulder without Father's help.'

Charles jumped up from his chair and, without another word, hurried from the room.

Anna watched him go, sad to have quarrelled. The sooner their father was engaged in a full and active life again, the better it would be for all of them.

'Julian!' Septimus Kirby looked up from the ledger he had been studying. He frowned and asked in a puzzled tone, 'What are these entries for two shipments of wine from Holland and corresponding sales?'

Julian cleared his throat. He knew his father made a meticulous examination of the accounts every two months and had been preparing himself for this question.

'Exactly what it says, Father.'

'But we've never shipped wine from Holland in this quantity. Who authorised it? I certainly didn't.'

'I did.' The admission came out bold and clear.

'*You?*'

'Yes. That first visit to Amsterdam was not merely a pleasure-seeking visit by two young men.' He went on to explain why and how he had instigated it, and after the success of the first venture had followed it with a second. 'You were reluctant to give me more responsibility, but now I hope you will see my capabilities? I think you will recognise those when you look at the figures again and see the profit I made.'

His father had been silent throughout Julian's explanation. He glanced down at the ledger to verify that his first assessment of the figures had not been mistaken. When he looked up he fixed his gaze intently on his son. Julian waited anxiously. His father's words could dictate his future, make or mar his position, at least within the firm for he still kept his smuggling activities a secret.

'I could chastise you for involving the firm of Kirby and Son in a venture without consulting me, but I must admit I admire your initiative. The contacts you have made will be most useful. We will continue in the wine trade and that will be your sole responsibility. I will not interfere. I don't need to be supplied with details, only a word as to what is happening, and when.'

Julian was overjoyed and his thanks poured out. He felt a new aspect of his life taking shape. The added responsibility raised his status. His actions would help to direct the future of the firm which, one day, he would take over. In the meantime he would secure his own source of wealth from his smuggling.

The second run of contraband goods had also been accomplished successfully, but only after the Dutch vessel had almost run foul of the Revenue cutter patrolling the mouth of the Humber. With the sloop tied up safely in one of the creeks along the north bank, Julian once again noted the efficiency of the Upton brothers in dealing with the contraband. No one questioned Luke's orders which came fast and clear. He was everywhere, seemingly in six places at once. The men respected his knowledge and knew it was to their advantage to follow his instructions to the letter, for it would mean a quicker dispersal of the goods and more money in their pockets.

Though he took part in the landings, nominally as the man in charge, Julian knew it was in his best interest to allow the Upton brothers to deal with the contraband when it was landed. They had renewed contacts made during their previous smuggling ventures and everything looked set fair for the future. He decided that from now on he would let them deal with the receipt and distribution of the contraband while he remained responsible for the ordering and sailing arrangements, leaving Bill Grimes to recruit the necessary workforce on the ground when required.

When he put this proposal formally to the Upton brothers they immediately agreed. After their father had been killed they had lost their connection with the Continent, but now it was restored. They saw a partnership on the lines proposed by Julian as being advantageous to everyone. They also realised it would give them more freedom to act as they saw fit, and so enhance their opportunity to avenge their father, for Julian Kirby would henceforth have less of a presence in their activities.

'Julian, Father would like you and Rebecca to pay us another visit.' Charles put the invitation as they returned from their third visit to Holland.

'That is most kind of him, but I was about to invite you and Anna to Hull.'

'You would do me a great favour if you would come to Hawkshead instead. Father was much better after your last visit, and for him to extend another invitation is great progress. I feel sure if you come to us it will help him even more.'

'Put that way I cannot refuse you, my dear friend. And I'm sure Rebecca will only be too glad to accept.'

'Will you come north with me after your cargo is unloaded in Hull? I can delay sailing until you have brought Rebecca to the ship.'

Julian hesitated thoughtfully, considering what best to do. There was no longer any need for him to be present when the contraband was run to the Humber in three days' time. 'That would be most convenient, if a delayed sailing is acceptable?'

'Of course it is.'

As soon as he had made Charles's invitation known to the family, Julian left an excited

Rebecca and sought out Bill Grimes.

'I want you to tell Luke that the next delivery will be in three days' time. Contact should be made at the same time at the mouth of the Humber.'

'I'll be off right away.'

'I'll be in Whitby for the next ten days, but I'd like to know if the landing is successful.' Julian passed some money to Grimes. 'Get the coach to Whitby, come to Hawkshead Manor and ask for me. But keep this strictly to yourself. I don't want the Upton brothers to think I'm checking up on them, now that I've made them responsible for this part of the operation.'

As they returned down the Humber, Julian eyed the coast east of Paull and visualised the activity there three nights hence, with all its risks, excitement and sense of achievement. The seaway was quiet now but it took little imagination to foresee the risks the Dutch sloop might have to face. He half-wished he was going to share those risks, yet there was contentment too in knowing he was safe from them on this occasion since he would be seeing Anna.

'Rebecca, when you were here last time did you have a talk with my father about my mother's death?' asked Anna.

The impact of the unexpected question startled Rebecca and brought a halt to their walk.

They had left the house ten minutes ago on a morning when a bright sun struggled to counter the chill. Their steps had been brisk, their conversation easy. They experienced pleasure in each other's company – a rapport that was felt immediately on the Kirbys' arrival.

The query brought a moment of tension, for Rebecca immediately regarded it as hostile, a prying into what she regarded as private moments. Surely Mr Mason hadn't repeated what had passed between them? Though there was no reason for him not to, she conceded finally. He hadn't been under oath.

Rebecca was embarrassed. For a moment she avoided eye contact with Anna, but then, realising that the question must be faced, she met her friend's watchful gaze.

'Why do you ask?' she asked cautiously.

'There has been something different about him since you were here.'

'In what way?'

'He has been more introspective, as if grappling with a problem at the forefront of his mind.'

'He is not upset?'

'He does not appear to be, though we cannot know what his inmost thoughts are.'

'What passed between us was not meant to upset him. I hoped it would help.'

When Anna made no comment Rebecca knew she was waiting for an explanation, so she told her what she had said to John.

'Thank you for telling me. That explains his attitude.'

'I meant no harm.'

'I know you didn't. There is just a chance that it may have helped him face the future.'

'If I get another chance, do you want me to talk

with him again?'

'If he seems to want to.'

That opportunity came two days later when Rebecca, again without company mid-morning, walked into the wood and visited the clearing. As she stood there her mind was carried to what she visualised as the final resting place of Angus. She wished she had something as tangible as Mr Mason had. Melancholy began to press upon her. She had to take a firm grip on her feelings to eradicate it. She must not get into this sort of mood. Angus wouldn't want it. Besides her recognised period of mourning was over, and memories of him must not hold her back from life. Maybe a new one was being born here at Hawkshead Manor and in her relationship with the Masons, especially Charles whom she admired and felt sure was interested in her.

She turned to leave but was startled to see someone watching her from the edge of the clearing.

'Oh, Mr Mason!' She blushed. 'I did not hear you come. I'm sorry if I am intruding again in a place that must be private for you?'

'You are not, my dear,' he returned quietly. 'I think you were seeking comfort in your own sorrow. If this place has helped you then I am pleased.'

'It has. For a few moments I was almost overwhelmed with sorrow and pity for myself. Something or someone told me that was wrong. What passed through my mind in those private moments has made me see that Angus would not

219

want me to mourn. I believe he was warning me against letting my grief jeopardise my future happiness and that of those around me. I shouldn't let that happen.'

John nodded but did not answer.

Rebecca sensed he was reflecting on what she had said. She hoped his deliberation would lead him to the right course. She started to move away.

'Rebecca, wait. You think my mourning wrong?'

'I cannot be the judge of that. I can only guess at the power of your feelings for your late wife and how they could affect your outlook now. I know I am younger than you and my loss in many ways different, but like yours it was a terrible blow to me. But don't, I pray, let sorrow ruin your life and that of your family and friends.'

From the earnest look in her eyes he knew she was sincere. They held no criticism of his attitude, only a desire to help. He thought, If she is right, how much we can learn from the wisdom of the young.

'Walk with me awhile?' he asked.

'If that is what you would like.' She sensed that at this moment he wanted the comfort of company.

As they left the clearing their talk slipped away from the topic of mourning with a natural ease. By the time they returned to the house John had learned a great deal about the Kirby family. Rebecca had let her conversation flow, aware that this interest in external matters was something Anna and Charles had longed for him to show again.

Chapter Ten

From his bedroom window Charles gazed into the night. The strengthening wind caused stark branches to weave moonlit patterns across the landscape, until the whole was momentarily plunged into total darkness as clouds thickened across the moon. Not the ideal night for running contraband ashore but he knew Nicholas and Ralph were skilled sailors. If all had gone well, they should be approaching Sandsend about now. As much as he wanted to be there he knew it would be too dangerous for him to be absent while Julian and Rebecca were in the house. He eased his mind and curbed his desire in the knowledge that the operation was in Edwin's capable hands.

In the guest wing Julian was observing the same night sky from his bedroom with some misgivings. The rising wind and darkening sky were portents of difficulties along the Humber. He tried to console himself with the thought that the weather could vary along the Yorkshire coast and what prevailed in the vicinity of Whitby was not necessarily experienced further south. He pictured the lonely landscape along the river. Visualised the shadowy figures awaiting the Dutch sloop. Though he had arranged for the Uptons to be in charge there he had a growing desire to be with them, to experience again the excitement he had felt on previous occasions.

But the situation on the Humber was not as he visualised it.

Only Greg awaited the signal from the Dutch ship.

The day before it was due Luke Upton had called his brothers and Bill Grimes to a meeting.

'Greg, when you reach the sloop I want you to take her to a position two miles south of Owthorn on the sea coast. Bill, your gang must be in place there.'

Grimes eyed him suspiciously. 'Why the move?'

'In preparation for the run just before Christmas when two sloops will be involved. On that occasion we'll run one in along the Humber and the other near Owthorn. And, Bill, see that your men are armed.'

'Why? We've never needed...'

'Ask no questions, get no lies.' The words came with a force that left Grimes in no doubt he should not challenge the man in charge. But Bill Grimes had an idea what this was about. He knew Mr Julian would not like it, but could do nothing. Julian Kirby was in Whitby. He nodded in acknowledgement of Luke's authority.

'Bring no one who might turn chicken.'

Bill Grimes still said nothing but nodded a second time.

When he had gone Luke indicated to his brothers to sit down at the table. His wife came in, placed an apple pie and a jug of ale on the table, and ushered Jim, who had brought the three tankards, out of the room with her. She realised something was afoot and the less she and her son knew about it the better.

Greg poured the ale while Luke sliced the apple pie.

'You're after the Wharton gang,' said Greg. He did not disguise his approval.

'Why do you think I released some of the last consignment into their territory?'

'I heard that stung them, particularly as they couldn't find out who'd done it.'

'Aye, it did that,' chuckled Greg. 'But I reckon they drew the right conclusion when they heard we were operating again.'

'Exactly,' agreed Luke, leaning forward on the table, one hand cradling his tankard. He looked sharply at each of his brothers. 'And that's why I've let it slip that we might be running contraband ashore close to their territory.'

'That'll needle them.'

'Right. And I don't suppose they'll stand idly by and watch us.'

'A fight!' grinned Mike, slapping his right fist into his left palm, a sign that he was going to relish avenging his father, for he knew this was the real reason for Luke's decision to run this consignment ashore close to Owthorn.

'Aye, smashing the Wharton gang will not only please Father, it will give us mastery of that section of the coast. And who knows how far north we can go then?'

'Let the other gangs see our strength and we can rule the Yorkshire coast,' said Greg.

'But what about Kirby? He may not like it.'

'If he doesn't like what we are doing he can lump

it, but he won't be left to give evidence against us.'
Luke's words chilled with their meaning.

'We need him. He's got the contact in Amsterdam,' Greg pointed out.

'If he objects to our methods he might have to be persuaded we are right.'

'I don't think it will come to that,' commented Mike. 'Like everyone else he'll like the bigger purse.'

'Let's hope you're right.'

And they fell to discussing the final arrangements for the following night's work.

The winter pallor of the late afternoon had merged into darkness, alleviated by a pale moon only when the clouds relented. With darkness had come an extra chill in the air. Wraith-like figures moved silently in small groups, keeping close to the hedges in the flat landscape until they reached the undulating dunes. They drew their jackets tighter and pulled their caps further down their heads, for in this open ground there was nothing to stop the wind. Gentle though it was it still bit with a sharp edge. Soon they were gathered in a hollow among the dunes from which they could see the beach and hear the waves breaking and running up the sand. Apart from the cold there would be no menace from the elements tonight. The dark clouds to the north were being driven by a southwest wind which would keep them away from this low-lying coast.

Once he was certain that the full complement of men was around him, Luke issued his instructions quickly and deployed his gang to the best advantage. Some were sent to the edge of the dunes to watch for the arrival of the sloop. Others were posted to cover every possible approach that could be made by the Wharton gang should they be drawn into the trap he had set. He and Bill Grimes remained in the hollow, the central point Luke had chosen to conduct the operation from.

Time stood still. No word from the beach. No movement from the lookouts. Luke calmed his irritation. Beside him, Bill Grimes could sense the growing tension in the other man but made no comment as he settled further down in the sand.

'Where's the damned sloop? It should be here by now,' Luke muttered to himself, though Grimes caught the words.

Waiting was not easy. Grimes knew the men would be getting restless but had warned them to be patient, to do nothing until signalled by Luke Upton.

He sat up, stiffened and whispered, 'Someone's coming.'

Grimes had heard nothing but tensed beside Luke. Both men gripped their clubs tighter. A figure appeared. Grimes's recognition was immediate. The smallest man among his recruits. 'Shorty Wells,' he whispered. They scrambled to their feet.

'Ten men,' gasped Shorty.

'Where?' asked Luke.

'Two hundred yards in the direction of Owthorn. I spotted them moving in and tailed them.'

'Recognise any of them?'

'Aye. Jem Wharton.'

'The very man!' There was triumph in Luke's voice. 'We've got him.'

'They're holed up between two dunes. They've a view of the sea from there.'

'They'll not move on us until we're running the cargo ashore. We'll bring the other lookouts in and deploy them between the Whartons and our men on the beach. They're in for a big surprise when they move on us. Bill, pass the word.'

Grimes started to move away but was halted by a sharp whisper from Shorty, 'Wait!'

'There's more?' queried Luke.

'Aye. I was about to come here when ten more turned up. Instructions were given and these ten moved off. They're now on the other side of us.'

'Wharton's thinking a pincer movement will catch us out. Try to take us on two sides, would he?' Luke chuckled. 'He's in for a big shock then. Good work, Shorty. Bring the lookouts in.'

As Grimes and Shorty slipped away, Luke planned his strategy.

Jem Wharton must have located the fifteen men Luke had positioned on the beach at the foot of the dunes. He would wait and make his move from both sides as the contraband was being brought ashore. Luke decided he would wait for that moment and then release the men who were coming in from the lookout positions. He would then have the Wharton gang trapped between the dunes and the sea.

As soon as his outlying men were all assembled he briefed them on his strategy. They understood perfectly what was wanted. He sent Shorty off to explain the situation to Mike who was with the men on the beach. There was nothing to do now but await the arrival of the sloop.

The wind had risen a little, bringing with it an added chill, making the watchers shrug closer into their jackets, thankful that the flashes of lightning to the north held no threat to them.

Luke fixed his gaze relentlessly on the sea. Ten minutes of rising tension passed. 'There!' He wasn't the only one who had seen the flash of light. It brought a stirring among the men. 'Quiet,' he hissed. They settled. Nothing must give their presence away.

Another flash. Luke knew there would be three boats on the water laden with contraband goods, two belonging to the sloop and one used by Greg to reach the vessel when it had been sighted in the mouth of the Humber. He knew that after the next flash, Mike would return the signal and the three boats would head for shore. A few minutes later he saw shadowy figures rise and start towards the sea.

The boats came in, using the breaking waves to help their momentum. They grounded on the beach. Men eager to have the contraband ashore were already into the sea, positioned to steady and unload the boats. They hurried up the beach with boxes, bales and casks and dumped them close to the dunes, organised for easy dispersal. The boats, relieved of their cargo, headed back to the sloop for the next load.

Luke had expected Jem Wharton to make his move now but he hadn't. He sensed uneasiness creeping into his men, especially when the second batch of goods was landed without interruption. Now Luke guessed why Jem was waiting. 'Calm,' he whispered. 'He'll attack after the last load, expecting to get away with all the booty.' This reassured his men but heightened the tension as the moment they were waiting for drew nearer.

Mike and his men were strung out between dunes and the sea when figures raced from their right and left. Bales, boxes and casks were dropped. As planned they ran to close rank in order to confine the attack to a small area. Shrill cries from the attackers, meant to intimidate, rent the night but were countered by shouts of defiance. Club clashed on club. Men spun, ducked and counter-attacked. Wood crunched on bone. Figures tumbled to the ground, some in combat, others unconscious. Blood flowed, staining the sand. Cries of pain mingled with shouts of triumph as someone gained the upper hand. Then all was over, thanks to the yelling mob that emerged from the dunes and raced to engage the men on the beach. The Wharton gang's attack stuttered for a brief moment as this unexpected wave of fresh attackers charged them.

Luke was among them, his club slashing at a burly man wrestling with Mike. A blow to the neck felled him. Mike's yell of thanks was acknowledged by a slight raising of the hand as Luke let his gaze sweep swiftly across the antagonists.

'Jem Wharton!' he hissed triumphantly to

228

himself when he spotted the tall bulky figure he wanted. He started forward, thrusting a man out of his way as if he was a piece of paper. He found extra strength from his burning desire to avenge his father. He pushed through the swaying mass of fighters, oblivious to the blows that he parried with his left arm. Then he was there. His club whirled and caught Jem on the shoulder, sending him staggering from the man he was standing over, ready to deal a final blow. Bill Grimes rolled clear and scrambled to his feet.

Luke was oblivious to the yell of 'Thanks' as Grimes turned to ward off another attack from a stocky man.

Jem Wharton faced his attacker. 'Upton,' he hissed with contempt.

'Your time's up,' snarled Luke, his eyes fixed intently on Jem.

'None of it.' Jem's cry of defiance was accompanied by a swift movement that almost defied the eye. A pistol appeared in his hand, rising to be levelled at Luke. A club, flung by Greg, flew past Luke's head and took Jem between the eyes. He staggered back, tripped over an unconscious form and fell. Jem tried to struggle to his feet but Luke was upon him, driving him face down in the sand. Luke grabbed a handful of lank greasy hair and pulled Jem's head back, exposing his throat. 'For Father!' he yelled, and drew his knife with one swift stroke across Jem's throat. He released his hold on the man's hair and at the same time gave his head a contemptuous push. As he climbed to his feet he saw the fight subsiding, Wharton's men fleeing from the scene, his triumphant.

'All right, let 'em run,' he called when some of his men would have raced after the survivors. 'They'll do us no harm now Wharton's dead.'

He drew in deep breaths as if the tang of salt in the sea air would cleanse his mind and body of the carnage. Ten men lay dead, two of them his own, the rest from the Wharton gang, including Jem's brother. When he stood over that silent form, he said, 'That's the end of the Whartons. We can take over their territory now.' He glanced out to sea. The dark shape of the sloop still rode the waves. 'Any more contraband?' he asked Greg.

'The Dutchmen will be bringing the last two boatloads now. Mike had informed me of what was likely to happen so I told the Dutchmen to stay on board until I gave the signal for the last load. I've just done so.'

'Good. We have to get rid of this lot.' He indicated the corpses. 'We'll take 'em out to sea.'

When the two boats reached the shore Luke made arrangements for the bodies to be dumped as the sloop sailed for Holland.

As the ship slipped away into the darkness, he turned his attention to the contraband. 'The carts, Bill?'

'Should be arriving very soon.'

The words were hardly out of his mouth when they heard the creak of timber and the squeak of leather.

In half an hour the contraband had gone, the men had left, the beach lay silent and there was nothing to show of the turmoil that had disrupted the peace of this lonely strand of coast.

Anna came wide awake and sat up in bed, her pulse racing. She did not usually wake during the night. All sorts of possibilities pounded through her mind. Then, disgusted at her reaction, she told herself, 'Calm yourself, girl, it's only the window.'

She usually slept with it partially open but tonight, because of the storm, she had closed it. She thought she had made it secure after she had watched the lightning for a while, but she must have been careless. Though the storm with its driving rain had passed, the wind had not abated. It must have shaken the casement loose.

She slipped from the bed. She needed no light for she knew her room to the smallest detail. She moved unerringly across the floor to find the window rattling to the whim of the wind. She reached out but, with her hand on the fastening, stopped. Something unusual for this time of night had caught her eye – a light in the guest wing. In a brief moment of study she assessed it as Julian's room.

What was he doing awake at this hour? Curiosity prompted a variety of answers. Suspicious minds magnify possibilities and dismiss the obvious. Her earlier doubts about Julian reared themselves again and dominated her thinking.

A movement. The curtains were drawn back. Lamplight spilled on to the lawn below and then silhouetted the figure standing at the window. He stood for a few moments, peering into the night. She saw him raise his head as if reviewing the sky,

231

seeking information from it. He turned away and was lost to her sight but he had not redrawn the curtains. He passed in front of the window from left to right, returned right to left, left to right, right to left. It went on. He was pacing the room. The sign of a troubled mind? An indication he was wrestling with a problem? Hatching a plot? Anna raced through reason after reason, and not one of them favourable to Julian.

Ten minutes later he came to the window, paused to look out, then closed the curtains. Anna returned to her bed but sleep was long in coming as she still sought a reason for his behaviour.

When she entered the dining room for breakfast her father and Julian were already there. Breakfast was always an informal meal at Hawkshead Manor, taken whenever one wished between 8.30 and 9.30. Her father was tackling his boiled egg but Julian was just ladling some porridge from a dish on the oak sideboard.

'Good morning,' said Anna brightly, and went to kiss her father. 'I trust you both slept well?'

'I did, my dear,' replied John, patting her hand affectionately.

'So did I,' said Julian, coming to the table. 'Like a log from the moment my head touched the pillow, which was soon after we retired. I knew nothing until daylight woke me.'

Words of contradiction sprang to Anna's lips but she held them back. Better not to reveal what she had seen. Julian's words impinged on her mind. What was he up to? Why had he lied? She resolved to keep vigilant watch on this young man who had won her brother's confidence and to whom her father had taken.

With breakfast over, suggestions were made as to how they should occupy the day but none met with general approval.

'I think I'd rather like just to relax here and enjoy the sunshine on the terrace, maybe take a stroll around the garden. The sun is unusually warm for this time of the year. It's a good idea to take advantage of it, and I find it so peaceful here after the bustle of my life in Hull,' said Julian. 'But don't let me hold any of you back. I will be all right on my own.'

This was the first time the four of them had not done things together and immediately the suspicions lingering in Anna's mind were alerted again.

'Why don't we all do that?' she said quickly, before Charles or Rebecca could protest. 'The air is so fresh after the storm.'

'Very well,' agreed her brother, a little reluctantly. 'We can have a picnic on the terrace.'

Anna did not wait for further approval but hurried away to inform Mrs Denston of their plans.

The day passed well and the four young people had to admit by the end of the afternoon that they had enjoyed it. They had been joined by John Mason when he'd returned from his ride, and Anna and Charles were pleased to see the influence Rebecca and Julian had on his demeanour. They saw many of his fine attributes re-emerging and noticed that at one point, when

Julian made a reference to business, their father did not turn away from it, though he said little to pursue it in any depth. Julian was so amiable with them that Anna began to wonder if she had misjudged the young man from Hull. But her suspicions, now almost relegated from her mind, flared again when shortly before their evening meal, while she was looking out of the window beside the main door, she saw a rider approaching, his form dark against the evening sky. He pulled his horse to a halt at the steps, swung from the saddle and strode on to the terrace as if he was on an urgent mission. He reached for the bellpull but before he could make his presence generally known Anna had opened the door.

Light from the hall lamps flooded on to him. She saw he was well wrapped for an evening ride. His clothes were of coarse material, a cap crammed low on his head. He was tall and broad, giving the impression of strength. Anna almost recoiled from his heavy-jowled hard face and burning eyes, but mastered her response.

'Good evening to you,' she said, mustering an even tone to her voice.

'Good evening, miss,' he rasped, and saluted her with a finger to his forehead. 'Is this Hawkshead Manor?' The tone of his question told Anna that he hoped he had at last found the place he was looking for.

'It is.' She sensed relief come over the stranger.

'You have a Mr Julian Kirby staying here, I believe?'

Anna was immediately on her guard. She had a premonition that this stranger's arrival was

234

expected and that it was linked to Julian's behaviour last night and his desire not to be away from the house. 'We have.'

'It is important that I see him.'

There was nothing Anna could do but oblige this man. 'Very well, step inside. I will have him notified that you are here. Your name?'

'Grimes, miss, Bill Grimes.' He stepped into the hall behind her and gently closed the door.

Anna went to a bellpull and a few moments later a maid appeared. 'Please inform Mr Kirby that there is someone here to see him, a Mr Bill Grimes.'

The maid scurried away towards the library.

'You have ridden far, Mr Grimes?' Anna asked casually.

'Only from Whitby, miss.'

She was surprised but hid her reaction. 'You have the appearance of having come much further.'

'I have, miss. By coach from Hull.'

'Hull! Oh, my goodness. I trust it is not bad news for Mr Kirby?' Her hope that their conversation would lead to more information was scotched when Julian came hurrying into the hall.

'Ah, Grimes.'

'Good evening, sir.'

Sir. Anna noted the word. Was this man in Julian's employ then? Whether he was or not, why was he here and why had he arrived in such haste?

'I am sorry you have been disturbed, Anna. If you will excuse us we will walk on the terrace,' Julian said hastily.

She read it as an evasion of further questions. She could only reply with an inclination of her head. She waited while the two men stepped out of the door and then walked thoughtfully into the drawing room.

'Well, did everything go smoothly?' Julian asked eagerly.

'Luke moved the landing to the coast near Owthorn.'

'What?' Julian was incredulous. 'That was asking for trouble, moving in on Wharton territory.'

'Exactly what he wanted. And he got it.' Grimes went on to relate the whole affair in detail.

Julian was shocked by the killings but they had happened. There was nothing he could do about them now, and he realised he couldn't have done even if he had been involved in the actual operation. He had organised a smuggling venture, he had used men who knew the trade and its risks and were prepared to go to any lengths to make a profit. His lot was cast with theirs. He could opt out, but did he really want to? The money was good and would open new paths to him. Any doubt was immediately dismissed when he heard Grimes continue.

'The Uptons reckon that's the end of the Wharton gang. Now their territory will be ours. That will make us stronger and we could take over other areas along the Yorkshire coast. The Uptons figure there's a lot of money to be made. They've got the taste for smuggling again and now they have avenged their father's death they see nothing to stop them running a much bigger organisation.'

Julian nodded and said thoughtfully, 'And you and I will get our share. They need me as a figurehead, to smooth any trouble with authority and for my contacts in Amsterdam, and they need you to recruit the men. Good work, Bill. Did you fix a bed for the night in Whitby?'

'Aye. And a seat on the coach tomorrow.'

They parted and Julian watched Grimes ride away before returning inside. He went straight to the dining room where he found everyone had just been seated. He paused at his place and swept an apologetic gaze around them all. 'I am sorry for that interruption. Important business from Hull.'

Rebecca looked up in alarm. 'Something wrong?' she asked with a frown.

'No. Everything is perfectly all right. It was information that I needed, that is all.'

'Anna said it was Bill Grimes. I didn't know he was working for us again after what happened,' said Rebecca.

'He was a good man at his job, Rebecca,' her brother replied. 'I had something that needed doing and he was just the man for it, so I employed him.' He cursed himself for not instructing Grimes to use a false name when he came to Hawkshead Manor. Then Rebecca need never have known who had really come to see him. 'I want to surprise Father with it so I would be grateful if you did not mention this to him.' He received Rebecca's nod of agreement with relief. He knew she would keep her word.

Linking this exchange between brother and sister with the suspicions she already had regarding Julian, raised doubts about him once again in Anna's mind.

They were still with her when she and Charles watched the ship take their guests away from Whitby.

'That was a strange visit Julian had from that man Grimes,' commented Anna as she and her brother walked from the quay.

'Why? If Julian anticipated some urgent business then naturally he would leave word where he would be.'

'Did he mention it again?'

'No. There's no reason why he should. It was a private affair.'

'And something he had to keep from his father.'

'A surprise when he's ready with it.'

'And Rebecca was taken aback when I told her Julian's visitor was a man called Grimes. She told me he was sacked by Mr Kirby for wrongdoing. It seems strange that Julian should employ him.'

'It's your suspicious mind again, Anna. You really must stop thinking ill of Julian.' Charles was becoming irritated.

'I'm only thinking of you. I don't want you being let down or running into trouble through Julian, about whom you know very little.'

'I know he's a good friend,' Charles snapped.

'Very well, very well. Don't bite my head off,' retorted Anna.

'I'm away to see Gideon.' He was thankful to bring an end to this line of conversation.

'Then I'll visit Cara.'

'You can get all your chattering done with her. I'll see you in two hours at the White Horse. And don't be late. There's no point in spending more on the stabling of the horse and carriage than is necessary.' He headed off for the Masons' office.

Anna pulled a face at his back and then turned to the bridge to cross the Esk and visit her friend.

'Are we going to visit Mother?' asked Anna, as she sat down beside Charles on the box of the carriage.

'Certainly,' he replied, as if there should be any doubt about visiting the cemetery on their way home.

He flicked the reins and sent the horse forward, keeping it steady as they manoeuvred out of the White Horse yard and into Church Street. Their pace was slow through the press of people, some of whom were reluctant to get out of their way. They passed into the more open space beside the quays, along the east bank where the activity of a busy port teemed with life. They moved beyond it and turned into Green Lane which climbed to the top of the cliff. Charles let the horse continue at a walking pace to recover from the strain of pulling the carriage uphill.

As they neared the graveyard Anna saw a figure standing motionless beside a grave. She placed her hand on Charles's arm. 'Father!' she whispered.

Neither of them spoke as they stepped to the ground and walked quietly towards him. With his back to them and head bowed, his thoughts far away, John was not aware of them until they were

239

close and Anna said in a low voice, 'Father.'

He started and glanced round. 'Oh, hello.'

'You could have come with us.'

'No. They were your friends you were saying goodbye to.'

Anna knew this was a way of saying he did not want to go into Whitby where he was sure to meet someone who had been close when he'd shared life with his beloved wife.

'Do you ride here every day?' she asked.

'Yes.'

'Is that wise?' asked Charles.

His father gave a wistful smile. 'I've never thought it unwise.'

'But doesn't it keep your memories painful?'

'No. They are a joy. They keep your mother alive. Here I am close to her and she is with me.'

They fell silent. Both Charles and Anna knew there was no comment they could usefully make.

After a few minutes, with one last loving look at the words on the gravestone, John turned away, saying, 'Shall we ride back together?'

'That would be pleasant,' replied Anna.

Little was said on the journey. They shared a silence precious to a close family, but Anna and Charles realised that their empathy would not be complete until their father had returned to a life which involved other people, especially those who had been his friends and business acquaintances over a number of years.

After their midday meal they adjourned to the drawing room to have some coffee. When the maid had withdrawn, Anna said, 'You seemed to get on extremely well with Rebecca and Julian on this visit.'

'Yes,' replied her father. 'I like them very much. They are good conversationalists and sympathetic listeners. They do not push themselves and adapt very quickly to our way of life when they are here. I hope you will invite them again.'

'We'll do that,' put in Charles. 'But Julian said he would like Anna and me to visit them in Hull.'

'Then go. It will be good for you both. It could also be good for business, Charles. Anna, it's time you had a change. You've tied yourselves up here too much since your mother died. I'll be all right. You really will have to stop mollycoddling me. Besides you should get out among young people again. I've noticed you've been turning down invitations, Anna. You shouldn't do so for my sake. You've a whole future before you, and that should include young men like Julian.'

Anna wondered if her father's comment was meant as a seal of approval if Julian wanted to take their friendship further. If he approved of this young man, if he found him pleasant, was she misjudging him? Were her suspicions merely of her own making? These considerations were banished when she found herself saying, 'If you like meeting them, isn't it about time you started meeting your old friends again?'

'That's different.' A chill at what he viewed as implied criticism came into his voice.

'It is not,' she retorted. 'In fact I would have thought contact with old friends, people who knew you and Mother, would even be preferable to making new ones. And you've only made friends with Rebecca and Julian, no one else. How can you if you still lead the life that's mostly that of a recluse?'

'That's the way I choose it to be.'

'It's wrong. You say you want me to meet people of my own age, but if I invite them here it will be embarrassing to make excuses for your absence when they probably guess you are in the house. I'd rather not have them here, and because of that I'll turn down invitations to visit them. You will lose your friends, too, and that is not healthy. Do you think that is what Mother wants? You say you talk to her when you visit her grave.' She sprang to her feet, paused a moment, eyes fixed intently on her father. 'When you visit her tomorrow, ask her.' She swung on her heels and stormed from the room.

Embarrassed by her tirade Charles had remained quiet even though he supported what his sister had said. Now he looked up and met his father's hurt, enquiring expression. 'You know, she has a point,' he said quietly. 'Losing Mother was bound to change our lives. Someone who was so vibrant, so loving to all the family, was sure to leave a gap. But for the sake of her memory we should live our lives as near as we can to how we did when she was with us. Anna needs you to be as near as possible the father you were when Mother was alive.'

John had sunk his head into his hands. The words bit accusingly into his mind. What should he do? His world had collapsed and even though he had come to accept some aspects of it there were others he felt he would never come to terms with. But Anna? Would he be destroying her life if he carried on in the manner he was?

Receiving no response from his father Charles continued, 'I need you back in the business. Even more so after what I heard when I visited Edwin today.' He felt himself on a knife edge. His father had refused to discuss business but Charles felt that this was a time when the whole question of their relationship should be tackled after the things Anna had said. He waited.

His father looked up. 'What did you hear?'

Charles's heart leaped. Was his father really interested? There was only one way to find out.

'The night of our last run, which was successful, there was also contraband run ashore near Owthorn.'

'Whartons?'

'Aye, Wharton territory, but they didn't run the contraband.'

His father's gaze sharpened with the unspoken question, 'Who then?'

'The Upton brothers did.'

'What? They were asking for trouble.'

'The other way round. Word coming out of Hull has it that it was a trap and the Wharton gang fell into it. Jem Wharton was supposedly killed, though there's no proof. Everyone's tight-lipped, even the surviving members of his gang. They fear reprisals from the Uptons if they talk.'

'Revenge,' muttered John. 'Always something to be reckoned with.'

'And it means that the Uptons have extended their territory. Do you think they might try to move even further north?'

John pulled a thoughtful face. 'Bridlington ... Scarborough, maybe ... because the trade is not so well organised there. They wouldn't dare try to take over Robin Hood's Bay.'

'What about us?'

'I don't think they'd venture this far away from their real working ground, the Humber, but you never can tell what ambitions are sparked by gaining more territory as they have done through the elimination of the Whartons.'

'I wish you'd come back.'

'You can handle it. You've good men in Edwin, and Nicholas and Ralph.'

'Aye, but if we could widen our trade as you had planned, we could strengthen our position.'

'What I had in mind might have brought more danger than the Whartons. It involved operations out of Amsterdam.' John paused then added with a no-nonsense voice, 'Forget it, Charles. Leave things as they are.'

He knew it was no good pursuing the matter then, but at least his father had discussed the business and that was a significant advance.

Their father did not appear for the evening meal, and the following morning when Anna and Charles came down for breakfast they were surprised to find that he had already had his meal and had left the house. They both had the feeling that, after the exchanges of yesterday, he was avoiding them.

'I should have held my tongue,' Anna's regret was followed by tears. 'I was too critical, too hard on him.'

'Come now, Anna. You weren't. You mustn't think that. What you said needed pointing out to him. You may well have done some good.' Careful to avoid any mention of smuggling, Charles added so that his sister knew that she had his support, 'I told him a thing or two about the business and pleaded with him to come back to work. I told him I needed him.'

'What did he say?' There was a catch in her voice.

'He told me to leave things as they were.'

'Oh, what are we going to do? Where is he now? He's never left as early as this for his ride.'

'We'll just have to await his return. I'll stay at home with you today.'

'I would appreciate that, but you have work to do.'

'There is nothing that needs my immediate attention.'

'Thank you, Charles. You are a good brother.'

John rode at a steady pace on his usual route to the graveyard beside the parish church. It was a dour day, matching his mood. It hurt to have hostile words with his children. His mind toyed with them, and try as he would to banish them they kept returning. He swung near the cliff edge and reined his horse in. The gaunt ruins of the abbey lay a little way ahead, beyond it the parish church near which his beloved Elizabeth lay. He glanced across the sea, pewter today under a leaden sky. His eyes drifted down to the rocks far below. It would take but a step for him to end things and join the person who had filled his life with so much happiness. He would no longer be a hindrance. Anna and Charles could live their lives without the burden of his presence. He had arranged his affairs so that they would inherit everything. There would be no complications for them. There was nothing more for him to do in this world, so why not finish with it?

His eyes stared unseeingly yet he was aware of the sea splashing against the cliff face. Then, startled, he inclined his head, listening. A voice? Someone called. He glanced round, expecting to see a stranger but there was no one. Yet there had been something familiar in the voice, faint though it was as if it had come from far away. His contemplation was broken but still the feeling of depression hung over him like a pall. He turned his horse and rode on.

He slid from the saddle near the graveyard and walked slowly towards his wife's grave. He stood looking at the green mound, despair heavy on him. He cried out, 'What is it all about? What is the use of anything without you?' His heart was rent in two.

'*Look at the words, John.*' The voice again from far away. He moved his body uneasily. It couldn't be. '*Do it, John. Look at them.*'

He raised his eyes to the words 'Elizabeth Mason, Miss Me but Don't Mourn'. These words burnt into his mind. 'Miss Me but Don't Mourn'.

'I can do nothing else, my love.'

'*There's a life to live, John. Get on with it. Live it for me and for our children. They need you.*'

The voice faded. He looked round. He was the

only person in the graveyard. He knew he would be. That voice had been Elizabeth's. Imagination? The desire to hear her overwhelming his reason? No! It was her. Her soft lilt had been unmistakable.

He remained staring at the words carved on the stone. They were replaced by 'Live it for me'. He had a duty. She knew it. Now he did. 'Thank you, my love,' he said quietly. 'Be with me always.' There was no reply, but he knew she would be.

There was a moment when they were in silent unison, then he turned and walked slowly from the graveyard. He paused and looked back. He now knew that though there would be sadness in his future, visits here would also bring joy for they were together again as one.

Chapter Eleven

John felt a burden lifted from his heart and mind. As he put the horse into a trot he sensed new life flooding into him. He thought not only of himself and his beloved Elizabeth but of their children. They deserved better than the life he had been giving them lately. He urged his horse into a gallop.

The sound of hooves on the cobbled yard brought Jack hurrying from the stables.

John swung down from the saddle and tossed the reins to his groom. 'Take care of him, Jack.' He started towards the house, stopped and turned back. 'And, Jack, keep your eyes open for two more horses, presents for Anna and Charles.'

'Yes, sir,' he replied brightly, pleased to see the old energy in his employer.

John strode quickly into the house. As he entered the hall he shouted, 'Anna, Charles,' hoping that they would both be there though he knew there was a possibility that his son might have gone into Whitby. He was relieved when they appeared from the drawing room.

They exchanged glances. Hearing their father's shout had brought a mixture of alarm and surprise. Now, when they faced him, the change in his demeanour flabbergasted them and they were curious to know what had happened to rekindle the vibrant father they had once known and who had disappeared from their lives.

'Come, let us sit down.' John led the way back into the room.

Charles and Anna were wary as they followed him. Was this merely a passing phase or had he thrown off the mantle of gloom and despondency for good?

John stood in front of the fireplace and waited for them to be seated. He looked from one to the other.

'I want to apologise for my behaviour and attitude since your mother died. I had no right to subject you to my varying moods, some of which must have been very trying for you.'

'Father, there's no need to apologise,' said Anna. 'You went through a very harrowing time.'

'You did too, there was no need for me to add to your burden. I should have supported you as you supported me. For that I will ever be grateful. I don't know what I would have done if you had not been there. I will be ever grateful to you both.'

'Father, we only desire to see you enjoying life again as Mother would have wanted you to,' pressed Charles.

'I know she would,' replied John. He gave a thoughtful little nod, his mind drawn to his wife. 'I suppose deep down I've known it all along but, in my ignorance, chose to ignore it until today when she told me there's a life to live and I should live it for her and for you...' His voice choked as the memory of his graveside visit flooded his mind. With it came an undeniable presence in the room. The silence of his children told him they felt it too. He mouthed the word 'Elizabeth' to himself. Strength to face the future seeped into him. His world was held in suspense and then slowly resumed its reality. Elizabeth had slipped away but he knew she would be with him always. 'So,' he went on, 'we will resume our life as normally as possible.'

Anna sprang from her chair and rushed to him. She flung her arms round him and hugged him. 'Welcome back, Father! I have missed you.' There were tears of joy in her eyes as she looked up and met the pleasure in his.

'You are so like your mother.' His voice was soft and gentle.

Charles was beside them, taking his father's hand in a grip that expressed his feeling of exultation.

'I will come in to work with you tomorrow, Charles.'

'You couldn't give me a better present.'

'Good.' John smiled at his son and then turned to his daughter. 'Anna, you must no longer tie yourself to this house for my sake. Pick up your life again.'

'Does that mean we can think of a party?' she asked with enthusiasm, deeming it wise to make the suggestion while this mood of euphoria was on them all.

John hesitated. Anna tensed. His answer could mean so much.

He gave a small smile and a slight nod. 'Very well. You'll have to organise it with Mrs Denston.'

Relief swept over her. It meant the father they had once known was back again. She hugged him with delight. 'Thank you so much.' Her heartfelt gratitude was not only for him but also for her mother. She silently thanked Elizabeth for the influence she had exerted on her husband.

When she left the drawing room, overwhelmed by the surge of excited happiness Anna raced to her room. She flung open the door and ran to the rosewood wardrobe. She pulled the door wide, reached in and took out the second dress Mrs Cassidy had made for her. Her father had approved of their having a party again. Now she could wear this beautiful dress. She held it up against her, admired it in the full-length mirror, then swirled across the room in exultant dance. She tossed her head back in joyous laughter and did one more pirouette. Then she quickly replaced the dress in the wardrobe and ran from the room to break the news to Mrs Denston.

'Bring me up to date,' said John when Anna had gone.

'Our two ships are working to capacity at the moment. Captain Wilson is doing regular runs to Amsterdam in the *Grace*. Captain Walford, who took over the *Gull*, runs a tight ship but the men respect him. A different character from Wilson.'

'Where is he sailing to?'

'He did one voyage to the Baltic, taking advantage of a spell of mild weather before the winter freeze set in in that part of the world.'

'And now?'

'Portugal.'

John rubbed his chin thoughtfully. 'I hope the political scene remains stable.'

'We must keep a wary eye on developments.'

'I'm pleased to see you are thinking that way. Now how are the de Klerks?'

Charles told him of his dealings and the personal side of his relationship with the family. 'Herr de Klerk says you must visit him whenever you are ready.'

'I'm sorry about Magdalena,' John sympathised.

Charles's reply was a wistful smile and a shrug of his shoulders. 'What will be, will be. We are still friends.'

'Good. I'm pleased of that. Have you any plans to go to Amsterdam again?'

'We have one more smuggling run before Christmas. I haven't finally decided on the contents of the goods, so will probably go there to do so.'

'Very well. I will come with you.'

'Good. As regards the smuggling, I hope you will consider strengthening our operation even if only to deter the Upton brothers.'

'Do I detect worry in your tone?'

'Not so much worry as concern.'

'I'll give it some thought.'

'What about the plan you had in mind before Mother died?'

'That could be dangerous...'

'Tell me about it.'

'It's best for you not to know now. If I decide to go ahead I'll tell you, but it may not be until after we have been to Amsterdam.'

Though disappointed that his father would not reveal more, Charles was delighted that he was showing a keen interest again.

The following week was a busy one for the Masons. John discussed the trading situation with Charles and Gideon and made decisions on future enterprises, though he did not want to interfere with the trade Charles was conducting with the de Klerks. He saw the captains of his two ships, praising Captain Wilson for his efficiency and consideration for the firm of Mason and Son. He met Captain Walford and was cautious in his assessment of a man he had met for the first time, though he knew something of his reputation as a good seaman and hard taskmaster but one who was fair. John informed him what was expected of him.

After the appraisal of his legitimate trading, he turned his attention to his illegal enterprise and was satisfied with the way Charles, Edwin, Nicholas and Ralph had conducted the business in his absence. He paid particular attention to their concern about the Upton brothers.

'This could be purely revenge for Wharton killing their father,' Nicholas pointed out.

'Aye,' agreed John, 'but if there's territory for the taking, are they likely to let it slip out of their grasp? And might acquiring it make them think of expanding even more? However, what concerns me most comes from the fact that when they lost their father, they lost their contact with their suppliers and it seemed that there was no one else to take that role over. Now they've started smuggling again they must have found someone who has contacts on the Continent. If there's a new brain on the scene, who knows what his ambitions are? Keep your eyes and ears open. Any information could be valuable. Meanwhile let's be ready for the Christmas run at the beginning of December. After that, Charles, you and I will go to Amsterdam.'

'Father, Mrs Denston and I have decided on February the fourteenth for the party.' Anna greeted him with the news when they sat down for dinner that evening.

John gave a wry smile. 'You lost no time in getting that organised.'

'I saw no sense in delaying. After Mrs Denston and I had chosen a date we talked about what sort of a party it should be – a few hand-picked guests at a sit-down meal, or a wider guest list with a buffet. We decided on the former.'

'As you wish,' was her father's reply.

'A sensible one,' agreed Charles.

'If there is anything you want bringing from Amsterdam, Charles and I will be going at the beginning of the second week in December.'

'I'll consult Mrs Denston.'

Anna spent the following week planning the party and drawing up a guest list. Names flowed from her pen but she hesitated momentarily when she started to write 'Rebecca and Julian Kirby'. Of course they should be asked, she admonished herself. Besides it would give her another opportunity to observe Julian and prove herself right or wrong.

That opportunity came sooner than she expected, for ten days later an invitation came for her and Charles to visit the Kirbys for four nights in Hull.

Luke Upton opened the door of his cottage in answer to the knock that had disturbed his meal. 'G' day to you both,' he said as he stepped back and allowed Julian Kirby and Bill Grimes to cross the threshold. When he turned from the door after closing it he caught his wife's eye and gave a slight inclination of his head.

She rose from the table. 'Come, Jim, help me with your bed.'

The youngster realised it was wise not to comment on the excuse his mother was using to leave the men, though he knew she, being the meticulous woman she was, had made his bed shortly after he had left it.

'Don't let us disturb your meal, Mrs Upton,' said Julian by way of apology.

'You're not. Jim and I had finished. Luke was late, that's why he was still eating.' She slipped away followed by her son.

'Sit down.' Luke indicated the chairs vacated by his wife and son. He went to a cupboard, took out two tankards and placed them in front of the newcomers. 'Help yourselves.' He pushed a jug of ale across the table and sat down in the chair he had vacated. As he picked up his knife and fork he lifted his eyes to Julian. 'I expect Bill has told you what happened?'

'He has.'

'And you don't approve?' Luke prodded some meat and put it in his mouth.

'I've had time to think about it. Killing is never

far away from smuggling. Grimes assures me that the bodies will never be found.'

Luke gave a little chuckle. 'They lie far out to sea.'

'And none of the survivors will talk?'

'They know what'll happen if they do. Besides, with an expansion of our business we'll need more recruits. Employ the survivors and they won't talk about what happened on the beach at Owthorn.'

'Good. Then we carry on as usual.'

'The Christmas run will be the next one.'

'I'll be going to Amsterdam in two weeks to fix a date. Is there anything special we should run now we have more customers?'

Luke smiled. 'They all like the same. Plenty of brandy for the men, silks and lace for the ladies.' He gave a dismissive gesture with his fork. 'We'll get rid of anything you like to order.'

'Good day, miss.' Captain Wilson greeted Anna as she stepped on to the deck of the *Grace*. 'It is a pleasure to have you on board. I'm afraid we are in for a hard blow. It might be as well if you stayed below decks.'

Anna smiled her greeting and said, 'It may be a little while since I have been to sea, but I don't think I will have lost my sea-legs. A strong wind and a running sea will make the voyage all the more exhilarating.'

Captain Wilson returned her smile. He had uttered a caution, as was his duty, but he had known that to the vibrant and vivacious Miss Anna it would mean nothing. He had known her since girlhood, and how she had revelled in a rough sea whenever her father had taken her with him on one of his ships. She would enjoy it today.

So it proved. Anna took delight in the voyage. Standing at the rail with her brother, viewing the coast at Scarborough with its castle dominating the skyline, she drew a deep breath and in a joyous voice said, 'This is wonderful, and it's made all the better for knowing that Father has thrown off his dark mood.'

'And I am pleased to see my sister enjoying life again. I know how worried you were about Father, as I was, but I did have an escape in work. I hope you are going to enjoy these few days with the Kirbys and that you will realise that my friendship with Julian is a genuine one,' Charles told her.

She laid a hand on his arm. 'Believe me, I want to. I hope I'm proved over-suspicious. It was only concern for a brother I love dearly that prompted my doubts.'

'Then cast them away and enjoy yourself.'

Even across the space that separated them as the *Grace* was manoeuvred to the dockside, Anna could sense the pleasure and excitement in Rebecca and Julian who awaited them.

Julian's smile was broad as he greeted them. He took Anna's hand in his and raised it towards his lips as he made a slight bow. His eyes never left hers. She sensed a feeling of embarrassment, though it was hidden from anyone else. She was her own critic in the judging of her feelings towards this young man so courteous in his welcome. Charles was greeting Rebecca in a similar fashion, but he felt a spark of something deeper than respect as their eyes met. He had no necessity to doubt his growing feelings for Rebecca.

'A carriage awaits us.' Julian indicated the vehicle. He fussed over the comfort of his guests. Anna was polite in her thanks for his consideration. As they rode through the town she was fascinated by his knowledge of all its aspects. Facts were something she liked and her interest was sharpened by his willingness to impart them. He in turn was delighted to find someone who was not bored by the information and who readily posed questions.

'Here we are.' Julian was out of the carriage before the coachman could jump to the ground. He held out his hand to help Anna from the coach.

'Thank you for a most enlightening journey,' she said politely, and then stood to one side while he helped his sister. Anna surveyed the façade of the Kirbys' house and judged that, while this building did not share the proportions of Hawkshead Manor, it was equally well cared for by its owners. That judgement was endorsed when they went inside. The decoration showed an appreciation of colour, the fine furniture and curtains an awareness of taste.

Maids fussed over taking their coats and hats. Their luggage was whisked away unobtrusively. While this was happening Mr and Mrs Kirby with their younger daughter Caroline came into the hall to greet them. Their welcome was warm and genuine.

'It is a pleasure to meet Julian's friends,' said Mr Kirby, and added as he shook hands with Charles, 'We will be always grateful for the friendship you showed our son and for the introductions you gave him in Amsterdam.'

'It was my pleasure, sir,' he returned. 'I hope some day before too long you and my father will meet. I'm sure he would love to talk business with you.'

'I look forward to that.' Mr Kirby started towards the drawing room.

Mrs Kirby greeted Anna with a kiss on the cheek. 'I'm delighted to meet you. I've heard so much about you.'

'All good, I hope, Mrs Kirby?'

'There were times when your ears must have been burning.' She glanced at her daughter as they followed the men. 'See your father doesn't monopolise the young men with business talk. I want Anna and Charles to have a pleasant time, free from work.'

They had just entered the room when they were followed by two maids with trays set for tea.

'A little refreshment and then we will show you your rooms,' Mrs Kirby added.

Twenty minutes passed in pleasant conversation as Mr and Mrs Kirby got to know their guests better.

When Mrs Kirby saw that Anna and Charles had had enough she rose to her feet. 'Rebecca and I will show you to your rooms. Dinner this evening will be at six, until then please make yourself at home. Come and go as you like. I am

259

sure Rebecca and Julian with Caroline's help or interference,' she shot a teasing look at the youngest, 'will take care of you.'

So they did. Anna and Charles could never say they were neglected. Walks in the local countryside or around the town, a visit to the theatre, evenings playing cards or engaged in conversation, drew the four young people closer.

Charles and Rebecca felt the empathy between them strengthening. Glances were no longer of curiosity but held something much deeper, an interest that some day would require satisfying. They sensed that each was developing a thought process known to the other.

Anna, realising that there was an exchange of feelings between her brother and Rebecca, found that she wasn't jealous as she had been of the friendship between him and Julian. She liked Rebecca and did not resent her advent into Charles's life. With that came a softening of her own attitude to Julian. Had her suspicions been brought on purely by jealousy? Or was she now more susceptible to his attentions? Whenever she caught him glancing in her direction she saw admiration. It made her question her own feelings. Could she cast aside her previous caution and come to admire him in return? She had to admit that his visit had made her see him with different eyes. Now she realised, more than she had done at Hawkshead Manor, that he was an attractive young man whose laughing eyes, charm and upright six-foot frame drew attention, not purposefully sought, to himself. Had the worry over her father made her blind to Julian's attributes?

One of those, thoughtfulness, was evident on the day before Anna and Charles were to leave for home.

The four young people had gone into town to do some shopping and find a present for John. Over an hour had passed with no decision made when Julian made a suggestion.

'I admired many of the pieces of artwork I saw around your house but I did not mention them as I knew the reason behind the collection. Now you tell me that your father is taking a full interest in life again, might I suggest that you take him a piece of scrimshaw to add to the collection?' He gave a small shake of his head as if annoyed with himself. 'No, rather let me buy it for him as a thank you gift for his kindness to Rebecca and me when we visited your home.'

'But we couldn't let you do that,' protested Anna. 'You were welcome in any case.'

'That may be but I'm sure Rebecca joins me in saying that we would be delighted to do it. In fact, we insist.'

His sister added her voice to his suggestion.

'That is very kind of you.' Anna turned a questioning eye on her brother to seek his approval. 'Charles?'

'It's very generous, but if that's what Julian and Rebecca want, who are we to stand in the way?'

As the piece was chosen, Anna hoped that it would be the means of rekindling her father's interest in his collection, the one thing he had shown no inkling to resume as yet.

On hearing the sound of a horse's hooves and the rattle of wheels, John looked up from the book he was reading and through the window saw a carriage approaching. He jumped to his feet. Anna and Charles were home! He hurried on to the terrace to greet them.

He was eager to know how they had enjoyed their visit to Hull so, after they had shed their outdoor clothes and tidied themselves, he ushered them quickly into the drawing room and poured three glasses of Madeira from a decanter set on a small table beside the window.

'Now, tell me all about it,' he said as he settled himself in his chair to one side of the fireplace.

From a sofa opposite him Anna and Charles told him of their visit. He could tell from the readiness with which they imparted their information that they had enjoyed themselves.

'I'm so pleased for both of you,' he said when they had finished. 'The Kirbys sound a very good sort of family. You must add them to your guest list for the party, Anna.'

'I'll do that.' As she was speaking she was reaching into her bag. She withdrew a package. 'Rebecca and Julian have sent you this in appreciation of your kindness when they were here.'

'There was no need for them to do that, but it is a very kind thought.'

He took the package and unwrapped it carefully to reveal a piece of whalebone. A whaling scene had been etched on it. Though there was a certain crudeness in the execution of the etching because of the nature of the tools used – the squared off blade of a sailor's jack-knife, a sailmaker's needle, an awl or even a nail – there was an undeniably artistic quality about the picture of ship, boats and whale. John recognised, from the balance of these three, together with the depiction of the sea and icebergs, that the etcher had the eye of a natural observer.

'This is beautiful,' he said, half to himself. He sat looking at it, lost in his own world, his mind reaching out to Elizabeth, knowing how much she would have appreciated the object. In those few moments Charles and Anna remained silent. Then he looked up slowly. 'It is very generous of them to send me this.'

'Julian had noticed various pieces around the house,' explained Anna. 'I mentioned your collection. Maybe you'll start adding to it again?'

Her father shook his head. 'No. I think not.'

'Why not? You can't throw Julian's and Rebecca's kindness in their faces,' replied Anna testily, disappointed that her father had not seen this gift as an incentive to renew his interest in the collection.

'I appreciate their thought and their gift and it will be special, but not as part of the collection. That, as I've told you, was especially built up for your mother. Now there is no reason for me to continue with it.'

'But she would want you to,' Charles pointed out.

'It would be a memorial to her,' said Anna.

Again he gave a sad shake of his head. 'There would be no pleasure in choosing pieces to

263

enhance it when she is not here to share it.'

'What about me? What about Charles? Can't we share that pleasure?' Anna snapped.

He held up his hand as if to put a stop to any further discussion. 'Enough on the subject. You know my views and my reasons. Don't spoil your homecoming and the pleasure of this gift.'

Anna felt her temper rising and had to bite her tongue. She did not want to overstep the mark which might affect her father's rehabilitation. She had made her point. Maybe there would be another opportunity to drive it home in the future.

Charles's step was brisk along Church Street. He had no time to stop and friends and acquaintances were surprised as he passed with a mere nod of the head. He hurried into his father's office and let the door swing shut behind him. John looked up askance at the sudden intrusion.

'What ails you?' he asked, seeing the serious expression on his son's face.

'I've just seen a Preventive cutter putting into port and three more Riding Officers have been posted here.'

His father leaned back and rested his elbows on the arms of his chair. He steepled his fingers in front of his lips thoughtfully. Then he shrugged his shoulders in acquiescence. 'There's nothing we can do about it.'

'But Nicholas and Ralph are due tomorrow night with the Christmas contraband. We can't get word to them.'

'Then we'll have to trust them to outwit the cutter if they are spotted and we had better take extra precautions at Sandsend. Let Edwin know immediately.'

Charles left the building and hurried to Edwin's house in Tin Ghaut. He rapped hard on the door but it brought no result. Frustrated, he hurried to the White Horse where he waited impatiently while a horse was made ready for him. Maybe Edwin was at the cottage in Sandsend. Though he was anxious to leave Whitby as quickly as possible, Charles did not want to draw attention to himself so kept the animal to a walking pace. As he crossed the bridge he saw the cutter tied up on the west bank. He climbed the west cliff, and once clear of the houses put the horse into a trot and finally, when he deemed he was free from prying eyes, a gallop. He did not let up until he neared Edwin's cottage. Breathing heavily after the strenuous ride, he slipped from the saddle and knocked sharply on the cottage door.

'Thank goodness you are here,' he said to a surprised Edwin as he stepped past him into the cottage.

'Trouble?' queried Edwin.

'Aye.' He repeated the information he had imparted to his father.

Edwin was thoughtful for a moment. 'We'll have to rely on Nicholas and Ralph outsailing the cutter if it's active. We can't divert them to another place so we'll have to outwit any officials who are nosy enough to investigate activity onshore.'

'New riders will be extra keen to prove their worth.'

'Aye. And being strangers they'll not likely be

265

tempted by bribery. Maybe after they've been here a little while...' He left the possibility unexpressed. 'I'll post a watch on them tomorrow. If there are any signs of them moving in this direction, I'll set up a decoy. Leave it to me.'

Charles went away satisfied that the arrangements were in competent hands, but nevertheless could not deny the added risk of detection.

The following afternoon Edwin knocked on the door of a cottage situated in the cutting a hundred yards upstream from the one he used in Sandsend.

'Matt, a job for you and Clem,' he said when the door was opened by a stocky man whose dark hostile gaze softened on sight of him.

Matt made no reply but called over his shoulder to his brother who pushed himself out of a chair by the fire and came to join them. Matt was already taking a coat and cap from a peg beside the doorway. Clem did likewise and they followed Edwin to his cottage.

He indicated the chairs at the table and went through to a small room that acted as kitchen and scullery. He returned with three glasses and a bottle of brandy. He poured three measures and passed two of them to the brothers who had seated themselves at the table.

'Better let that warm you, you have a watching job.'

'For the cutter we hear tell is in Whitby?' asked Matt, pausing with his glass halfway to his mouth.

'No,' replied Edwin as he sat down. 'There's three more Preventive Men on station in Whitby. Newcomers can be a mite too keen. If there's any rumour of a run tonight, they'll be out. I want you on watch. If any of the Whitby riders head towards Sandsend, one of you's to let me know.'

'Usual signal?' asked Clem.

'Aye. I'll put Joseph on lookout for it and have a group standing by to lead any nosy officials a dance.' He refilled their glasses. 'Down these and then away with you.'

As they left the cottage Edwin handed them a small lantern.

'Are you coming to Sandsend tonight?' Charles asked his father as they strolled beside the quay on the east bank of the Esk. John was enjoying being back among the activity of the port again. Friends had greeted him warmly and were continuing to do so. No one questioned his absence. They knew how devastating the blow of losing his wife had been. Now they were glad he was back among them, and John was thankful to Elizabeth for guiding him to his rightful place among the merchants of Whitby.

'Yes. I told Anna we'd be late as there was a meeting in the Angel we had to attend.'

'Good.' Charles was pleased that his father would once again be overseeing the smuggling operation.

Father and son took a meal at the White Horse. Afterwards, wrapped up well against the chilly night, they mounted their horses and rode at a walking pace out of the town.

As they passed the building in which the Preventive Men were stationed they were observed by

Matt and Clem hiding in the shadows with a clear view of any movement to or from the building.

Once clear of the town, John quickened their pace. Halfway to Sandsend he led the way on to the beach and rode close to the sea for the rest of the way. It was the type of ride he enjoyed. The breeze was sufficiently strong to bring a running sea with whitecaps breaking on to the sand, marking it with a twisting latticework of foam before drawing them back into itself. Spray rose, misting the dark landscape. The clouds were high but there was no moon.

'Should be no difficulty tonight,' he called to Charles who was also enjoying the ride, though his mind did stray to the Revenue cutter and the new riders. He dismissed any doubts that the run would not be successful. He had implicit faith in Edwin and knew he would have made plans for any contingency.

'Glad to see you back with us, Mr Mason,' Edwin greeted them at the cottage.

'Good to be back,' he returned.

The glasses were out and the brandy poured while Edwin told them of his plans to deal with any interference should it occur.

They were discussing future operations and the increased demand for their contraband when an urgent knocking came on the door. Edwin was instantly on his feet. When he opened the door a breathless Joseph stepped over the threshold. He knew better than to say a word until the door was closed.

'Signal from Matt and Clem,' he panted.

'That means riders are heading this way,'

Edwin informed the Masons. 'Thanks, Joseph. Help yourself to some brandy and then back to your post. Keep a sharp eye out. You know the signal if the riders don't fall for our bait.' He took a warm coat from a peg and crammed a cap on his head.

John and Charles were on their feet too and the four men left the cottage. Joseph hurried away to be swallowed up in the darkness. Edwin led the way to the beach.

'Using the same signals?' John asked.

'Yes.'

'I'll watch for the sloop.'

Edwin nodded. He knew Mr Mason's sharp eyes would miss nothing. He turned to Charles. 'Joseph should be in position now. Could you concentrate on him in case he needs to signal us again?'

'Right.' Charles was tense. The next hour or so would see a successful run or a disaster. He did not want any failure to be laid at his door.

Edwin stiffened. A light along the coast had caught his attention. His watchers had seen the riders. He made his signal in return and knew that his plan to fool the Revenue men would be implemented. If that were successful there would be no unwanted observer of the contraband being brought ashore – provided Nick and Ralph had not run into trouble with the Revenue cutter. He knew it was on patrol for earlier in the day, when he had been in Whitby, he had seen it put out to sea.

Leaving Amsterdam, Nick and Ralph encountered the sort of weather they liked, enabling them to run before the wind, the bow cutting through the water and sending spray back across the deck. A full ship, a successful off-loading, and there would be more money in their pockets. They knew Mr Mason sold to the best advantage and in his absence his son had carried on in the same vein. But now Mr Mason was back with them they felt a certain sense of security, if such a term could be applied to the smuggler's lot. Their last three runs had been free from disruption but they knew it was unwise to allow their vigilance to slip, especially when they neared the Yorkshire coast. The night was dark, no moon or clouds to mar the starlight, but sailors' eyes were adapted to it.

The black mass of land was not yet visible when a shout from the lookout came sharp across the wind. 'Starboard bow!'

Nicholas focused his attention. Beside him, at the wheel, Ralph's grip tightened a little. There had been concern in that shout.

'Ship,' said Nick.

They held a steady course, eyes straining. They saw the unknown ship alter course to bring it heading in their direction.

'Cutter!' Nick's tone was sharp.

'Best avoid her,' advised Ralph.

'Aye,' agreed Nick.

As Ralph took the sloop to port, Nick called for more sail. The hands needed no second bidding. Contraband vessels wanted no truck with strangers.

'There were no reports of Revenue cutters in

the Whitby area before we left.'

'True, but who knows the reasoning of official minds?'

'Could be the Upton brothers' expansion has brought more attention to the Yorkshire coast.'

'Why the hell weren't they satisfied with their Humber trade?'

'Greed.'

'Aye, and vengeance.'

They had been keeping watchful eye on the other ship but if they needed any further confirmation of its intention they got it when a cannon boomed. The shot fell short but was clearly a signal to them to heave-to.

'Run out more canvas!' Nick knew this would be risky in the strengthening wind.

Edwin's signal had been quickly acted upon. Three boats, that had been hidden among the dunes, were run out promptly, down the beach and into the water. Speed was of the essence. Every man knew that the boats had to be launched before they were within sight of the riders. They were rowed away from the shore, the oarsmen keeping an eye on the direction from which they were expecting a signal. When it came they knew the riders would soon have them in their sight. They turned the boats quickly and rowed towards shore. They beached. Men scrambled out and quickly unloaded empty barrels and sacks and made their way up the dunes with them. Another signal. They knew that the riders had seen them and would soon be on their trail. They had no intention of lingering. It was essential that the riders were lured as far inland as possible to be lost in the labyrinth of small valleys and creeks that stretched towards the wild moors, before the sloop carrying the real contraband appeared.

Charles saw Joseph's signal. 'They've taken the bait!' he called.

'Good,' replied Edwin, thankful that his plan to draw off the riders had succeeded so far. They just needed Nicholas and Ralph to be here soon.

Time passed. The men on the beach became anxious. John's eyes strained to catch the flash of light he was expecting.

'They must have run into trouble,' commented Edwin. He slapped his arms to try to drive some warmth into them against the strengthening wind. Charles stamped his feet. John turned up the collar of his coat.

Edwin eyed the waves, lifting higher under the influence of the stiffening wind. 'It's going to be more difficult running the goods ashore,' he commented. 'Should we signal Nick to take them into Whitby?'

'That might be more risky if the Revenue Men suspect something is afoot this night, as they will when they realise they were drawn away on purpose. If they decide we couldn't bring contraband ashore here because of the sea conditions they might make a more intensive search in Whitby.'

'And what if we decide to take it here and the Revenue Men return?' asked Charles.

'There could be a few sore heads,' his father replied.

A quarter of an hour later, John was beginning to despair. His return to activity had brought bad luck to their smuggling. His lips tightened as he battled to overcome his fear that the sloop had been lost or taken. Still with his attention fixed on the sea he began to pace. Up and down. Fifty yards at a time. Up and down. He stopped in mid-stride, swivelling to face the sea and the breaking waves sending spray streaming over him. He rubbed his eyes. He was not mistaken. A light! He ran the few yards back to grab his lantern.

'A light!' he called. He raised the lantern and swung the cover to expose the light. Closed it. Opened it.

An answering signal came.

'Boats away!' called Edwin.

Activity broke out along the beach. Boats were launched. Men scrambled on board. Oars dipped into the water. Strong arms pulled. Bows cut into the first wave, rode high, then plunged into the trough. Backs bent and the boats were taken further from the beach. Men, strung out along the sand, watched for their return, ready to unload as quickly as possible.

The skill of the boatmen quickly brought them alongside the sloop. Contraband exchanged hands. Once a boat was loaded it was rowed back to the beach, dragged the last few yards by the breaking waves. Eager to have the contraband ashore and away before the possible return of the riders, the shore party wasted no time.

Word was brought to John Mason that Nick and Ralph had had a run in with a Revenue

273

cutter but had made their escape without any evil consequences to themselves. John knew they would have to wait until the next day to get the full story, for once the contraband was offloaded the sloop would be away to Whitby.

Every man knew his job and before too long the beach was deserted again. No one would have known the activity there had recently been across the sand.

Reaching Edwin's cottage, John and Charles were grateful for a glass of brandy to drive out the cold that had begun to settle on them again after the physical activity and the tension they had experienced on the shore. With one glass downed, Edwin offered them another and also some bread and cheese to stave off their hunger.

Feeling better for their sustenance, John and Charles bade him good night and mounted their horses.

They were riding at a steady pace and were halfway to Whitby when three riders broke from the cover of the dunes into their path, one settling his horse in front of the other two who barred the way to either side. John and Charles reined their horses in sharply.

'What's this?' called John with natural authority.

'Who may you be, sir?' queried the lead rider.

'John Mason and son Charles, of Hawkshead Manor. And might I ask you the same question?'

'Revenue Officers, sir.'

John peered in the gloom. 'I know the Revenue Officers in Whitby. I don't recognise you three.'

'Just been drafted in to stamp out the smuggling around here. Might I ask where you have been, sir?'

'Is that any of your business?' replied John indignantly.

'I'm afraid it is, sir. You see, we have reason to believe that contraband was run ashore along this beach this night.'

'We saw no sign of any activity when we came along.'

'And might I ask you again where you have been, sir.'

'We've been visiting friends in Mulgrave Castle.' John knew these men could easily check that statement, but he also knew that if they did Lord Mulgrave, like any of the district's gentry, would verify the Masons had visited him that evening. He would know why he was being asked and, as a customer of John's, would not want to be the means of cutting off a valuable source of brandy and tobacco for himself and silks and lace for his wife.

'Rather late to be returning, sir?'

'We had a splendid evening and time passed quicker than we thought.'

The Revenue Officer had no answer to this. Though he was not altogether satisfied, he could detain these gentlemen no longer. He turned his horse to one side and his companions followed suit. John and Charles spurred their animals forward.

'Goodnight,' John said amiably. 'I wish you every success in stamping out this infamous trade.'

The Revenue Officer made no reply that John

275

could hear but, as he eyed father and son he thought to himself, I wonder how much you two know of this evening's activity?

Chapter Twelve

'Where did you two get to last night?' asked Anna with a questioning glance at both father and brother.

'A business meeting, as we told you,' replied her father.

'In the Angel?'

'Yes.'

'Then how is it that there's evidence of sand at the back door? It wasn't there last night. I've no doubt you came in that way after you had settled the horses.'

The exchange of looks between the two men was only momentary but she caught it.

'Ah, well, after the meeting Sir Arthur Foston wanted us to see his new boat.'

'He has it housed at Sandsend.' Charles hoped he'd lent weight to his father's statement.

Anna made no comment. For some time she had wondered about the late meetings in Whitby that occurred from time to time. If she had any desire to challenge their facts now, she knew it would not alter their answer. Besides, should she really be doubting them? But she thought her father continued rather hastily, as if he wanted to evade any further questions.

'I've told my friends that I shall be recommencing our monthly meetings. I would like you to act as hostess at our dinner, Anna. I hope you won't mind the added responsibility?'

'Similar to those you held when Mother was alive?'

'Yes, it gives us an opportunity to talk business and discuss the development of Whitby in a relaxed atmosphere.'

She gave a slight inclination of her head, a sign of her acceptance. 'When will the first one be?'

'Next Wednesday.'

'Before you go to Amsterdam?'

'Yes.'

Anna considered wearing her best new dress for this occasion but eventually decided to keep it for the February party.

She had consulted Mrs Denston and Cook about the meal. They were both enthusiastic and delighted that something of the old days was coming back to Hawkshead Manor. Though they knew things would never be quite the same without their late mistress, they were sure Anna would prove a very capable hostess and were determined to give her every support that they could.

A quarter of an hour before the guests were due she cast an approving eye over the arrangements and then joined her father and brother in the drawing room.

'My dear, you look beautiful.' John's eyes were dampened by precious memories as he stood up and watched his daughter come to him. This last year she had grown up. She was no longer the child who had won his heart, now she was a young woman. But she still held his heart, and,

Oh, how very like her mother she was. He kissed her on the cheek. She gave him a warm, loving smile and thanked him for his observation.

'I've decided to greet your guests in the hall with warm mulled wine. Robert and James are standing by to see to that.'

'Excellent. Very thoughtful of you. I'm sure it will be appreciated on a sharp night like this.'

So it proved. Robert warned them of the arrival of the first guest and John, Charles and Anna went into the hall to greet him. Within a matter of ten minutes the other eight guests had arrived and all were enjoying the mulled wine, singing its praises after they had almost overwhelmed Anna with their effusive admiration for her. They had all known her as a little girl, petite and charming. Now they were enjoying the presence of a beautiful, sophisticated young woman who had a beguiling way of holding their attention.

Seated at one end of the table, opposite her father, she viewed the prospect before her: nine guests elegantly dressed in evening clothes. Three were about her father's age, the rest older. Here was authority, influence and money. She could have been overawed by the occasion but was determined not to be. It helped that she knew them all. Once they were all seated and talk flowed between them the initial qualms she had felt on their arrival disappeared and she relaxed in the convivial atmosphere. She kept up a lively conversation throughout a meal which satisfied all tastes and degrees of appetite.

She was aware that business talk was absent during the meal, so when she noted that everyone

279

had finished eating, she gave three sharp raps on the table. Immediately the flow of conversation stopped and all heads turned in her direction.

'Gentlemen, I think the time has come for me to take my leave...' Murmurs of dissent came from around the table. Anna smiled and held up her hand. Silence descended. 'Yes, it has,' she continued. 'It is time for your port and cigars and business talk. Therefore, gentlemen, you must excuse me.' She rose from her chair and, as one, every man stood and gazed with admiration at the young woman who had filled her first duties as hostess so successfully.

'Good night.'

'Good night, Miss Anna.'

'Thank you for the pleasure of your company.'

Compliments flowed as she walked from the room, pausing to kiss her father good night and receive his look of pride. She was enjoying their praise and her own sense of achievement. Her eyes were bright in the glow of attention and each man would have sworn that her smile was for him alone.

When the door closed behind her everyone was offering compliments as they resumed their seats.

'You've a beautiful daughter, John.'

'Charming, charming.'

'A great credit to you.'

'You're a lucky man, John.'

He acknowledged their praise with a gesture of his hands and a broad smile, filled with pride. Anna had orchestrated the evening well, even he had been surprised by her. He had not realised how much she had learned from her mother. And it had been no slavish copy of Elizabeth's routine, Anna had interposed her own touches.

'Thank you, gentlemen.'

They settled themselves comfortably in their chairs. Three decanters of port were brought to the table. John dismissed the servants. His friends relaxed in the murmur of conversation with their neighbours. Port was passed round. Cigars were accepted, religiously cut and lit with care. Everyone enjoyed the convivial atmosphere, none more so than John who was pleased that this return to society had passed off so well.

After a few minutes, Sir David Fielding stood up. He was a man of sixty whose slim figure, kept that way by daily walks along the cliff top, was just beginning to show signs of extra weight. He had a kindly face with alert eyes that hid a serious side beneath a light-hearted sparkle. He tapped the table. Silence came over the room. 'Gentlemen, I must say a few words.'

'Not too many, David.'

'Shorter than when you are on the Bench.'

Their banter was jocular.

Sir David smiled. 'I promise.' He made a brief pause and then went on. 'Seriously, I want to say, and I know that I am speaking for all of you, how delighted we are that John is with us again. He has been through a trying time, and I know how much he misses his beloved wife who filled these evenings with her own special charm, a role taken over tonight with such graciousness by Anna.'

Murmurs of agreement rippled around the room.

He looked hard at his host. 'John, we are

281

pleased to have you back in your roles of merchant, outstanding member of the Whitby community, and, dare I say it, leader of our fraternity of freetraders.' Again he gave a slight pause that added emphasis to the words he used as he looked at Charles. 'Not that we haven't been well served by young Charles, we have, and I mean no disrespect to him when I welcome his father back.'

Again, softly spoken words of assent flowed around the table.

'John, your good health.' Sir David raised his glass. The rest of the guests stood up, raised their glasses in turn and toasted their host.

As they sat down, John got to his feet. 'Thank you, David, for those kind words, and thank you all for echoing his sentiments. I must say that it is due in no small measure to the love of Elizabeth and my children that I have resumed a life as near normal as it can be under the circumstances.' He hesitated a moment, looked down at the table, his thoughts on the times he had shared with his wife. Then he looked up sharply and went on in a firm voice, 'I am pleased that Charles was able to carry on as in the past, and luckily we had no trouble on the last three runs. I thank you all for giving him your support and the usual facilities. Without those we would not be able to continue our operation.'

'John, there is no need for thanks. Apart from cheaper goods being made available to us, you are generous in paying for the hiding places we provide.'

He gave an inclination of his head and a gesture

of thanks with his hands. 'You also provide cover. Who would expect men of such integrity to be involved in what is basically smuggling, though we know it under a different name?'

There were murmurs and outbreaks of laughter around the table.

'I hope you are all satisfied with the goods from the Christmas run, which I must tell you was organised by Charles?'

Expressions of satisfaction came from everyone and appreciative remarks were made to Charles.

'I must intervene here.' Eyes turned to Abel Watson, a contemporary of John's whom they all knew was a hard rider at the hunt and not averse to taking risks. A man who could handle himself well in any circumstances. He had placed himself at John's disposal when it was thought Preventive Men might be about during a run, and had more than once led the officers on a wide ride into the moorland beyond Whitby. 'Yesterday I was offered goods at a price lower than we are getting.'

Surprised looks and murmurs were exchanged before everyone turned their eyes back to Abel as John asked, 'By whom?'

'The offer came to me in a strange way. I called in at the Angel for my usual and the landlord slipped me a sealed sheet of paper. It had my name on it. He said it had been left on the counter. He did not know by whom. I opened it and ... well, you can see for yourselves what it said.' He produced the sheet of paper and handed it to his neighbour who read it quickly, for it contained few words. It passed from one to the other until finally it came to John.

He read the words aloud to familiarise everyone again. '"If you are interested in purchasing brandy, gin, lace and tea cheaper than you can get it elsewhere, leave a note with the landlord".' John looked at Abel. 'Did the landlord know what this contained?'

'He swore he didn't, and also that he did not know who left it.'

'What do you make of it?' asked Sir David.

'I don't suppose that I'm the only one to be contacted,' said Abel.

'Is someone trying to take our business away by offering cheaper prices?'

'There is every possibility of that,' John said thoughtfully.

'I suppose you have all heard that the Uptons have started operating along the Humber again,' put in Charles. There were nods signifying that they had all heard this. 'And of the clash between them and the Whartons of Owthorn?'

'Rumours,' someone said.

'No,' replied Charles emphatically.

'Are you sure?'

'Yes. Jem Wharton was killed.'

'Revenge for the Whartons' killing of old man Upton?' suggested Jess Simpson, a horse trader with clients in Hull.

'That is the likely explanation,' continued Charles. 'But with Jem Wharton gone, along with others, I hear that their gang has broken up. Now, if that is so, couldn't the Uptons have taken over Wharton territory? And that might well give them ideas of expanding further and infiltrating our territory with cheaper goods.'

Everyone started to talk at once, agreeing or disagreeing with the theory expounded by Charles.

'Gentlemen, gentlemen.' John brought a halt to the speculation. 'Charles's ideas may be right or may be wrong, but I think we have to treat this offer to Abel seriously. Whether it has come from the Upton brothers, directly or indirectly, remains to be seen.'

'How can we find out?'

'That could be tricky.'

'I'll answer the note, showing interest,' said Abel. 'Then I'll keep watch to see who picks it up and follow him.'

'Any other suggestions, gentlemen?' asked John.

None was forthcoming.

'Then it is initially up to you, Abel.' John as leader stamped his authority on the suggestion. 'Report to me when you have any news. But one thing is certain, gentlemen, we cannot allow anyone to undermine our business with impunity.'

The following day Abel called at the Angel for his usual tot of rum and passed a sealed note to the landlord saying that it would be called for and would he make a note of who collected it? Abel, prepared to wait awhile, seated himself in one corner of the bar from which he could see the door and counter. Customers came and went but no one asked for the note. The bar became crowded and he rose to leave. As he moved from his table he was aware of a shabby urchin pushing through the throng of people towards the counter. Abel was drawn into exchanging a few words with an acquaintance. It was only when the door swung shut with a clatter, startling him, that he was aware that something had registered subconsciously on his mind. The boy had left the inn carrying a piece of paper!

He made a quick excuse to the person to whom he was talking and in a moment was out of the door. He looked round desperately to see the boy running along Baxtergate. Abel started after him but soon lost sight of him among the crush of people thronging the roadway going about their daily tasks. He hurried on, hoping to catch sight of him, but before long realised his task was hopeless. The boy had disappeared. He stopped, his lips tightening with frustration. He would never know to whom the urchin delivered his note saying he was interested in purchasing any goods on offer. He would have to wait for someone to contact him again. He turned to retrace his steps, unaware that he was being watched and had been ever since he had emerged from the Angel.

The watcher reported to a house in Bath House Yard where he found the urchin accepting a penny for his trouble. The watcher reported what he had seen and during the next day that information was conveyed to Luke Upton. He knew that Abel Watson was connected with the Whitby smugglers but knew no more about them than that. He had previously had no cause to find out. His father had ruled the gang along the Humber closely, but now Luke, with his taste for smuggling revived, desired to know more.

Especially if the Upton brothers, fronted by Julian Kirby, wanted to expand their territory. After their success against the Wharton gang he saw no reason for them not to contemplate further fields. From Abel's reaction he knew his note had been reported to the other men behind Whitby's smuggling and that they were suspicious. If it led to a physical clash then so be it.

Abel waited for a further approach but after a week reported to John that there had been none.

Over the next week there were reports of contraband from another source being sold in the territory that John Mason regarded as exclusively his. It worried him. If there was someone else trading, and it seemed that the Upton brothers were the likely intruders, then it could lead to action he would be reluctant to take. Such a prospect still concerned him when he and Charles left for Amsterdam.

Herr and Frau Hein were overjoyed to see John and made sure that he and Charles had every comfort for their stay.

John received an equally enthusiastic reception from Hendrick de Klerk and his wife, Katharina. With social niceties out of the way, John and Hendrick discussed business, strengthening their ties, while Charles and Magdalena enjoyed each other's company and settled the contents of the first contraband consignment to be picked up in the New Year.

Before the Masons left, Katharina insisted that they should dine with them the following evening.

John accepted, keeping his misgivings to himself. The last time he had dined with the de Klerks, Elizabeth had been with him. He knew he would miss her terribly. He would see her sitting opposite him, hear her soft voice in light-hearted banter or serious discussion, would catch her magical uplifting laughter. Even though she was no longer there. But he knew that, while she would want him to sense her presence, she would not want him to mar the occasion with sadness. Rather she would want him to enjoy it, and in doing so he would feel nearer to her.

After a delightful meal, enriched by friendly conversation, Katharina and Hendrick relaxed with their guests in front of a roaring fire.

'John,' Hendrick turned the conversation with a serious tone, 'knowing how you always liked me to keep my eyes open for any *objets d'art* that might interest you, and in the expectation you would visit us again, I have kept in touch with what has been going on. Two art auctions will take place in early January, one of which I think will be of interest to you.' John was about to raise a hand to stop Hendrick from going on, but as his friend continued speaking before he could do so, he knew it would be ill-mannered to interrupt at this stage. 'It is a collection of jewellery and miniatures that were in the possession of the de Root family. It is being sold for personal reasons. There are two paintings in particular that I think would interest you, but I think even more than those you should consider a unique necklace with matching ring. They are of silver and their motif is of two snakes exquisitely intertwined.

You might think that such a pattern would make for a heavy necklace, but it is not so. The great attraction is the delicacy of their workmanship and the fact that the eyes of the snakes are of diamonds. There is a provision of sale that the items should not be split up. Knowing something of your collection, I believe they would enhance it greatly, not only in value but in beauty. I know they will be much sought after but...' He let his pause imply that he thought John could outbid anyone else.

John seized the opportunity. He raised his hands, tightened his lips in a gesture of regret and said, 'Hendrick, I am grateful for this information, and for your keeping an eye on the market, but I am no longer interested in adding to the collection.'

'No?' Hendrick raised an eyebrow in surprise.

'No. You see, every piece in the collection was bought as a present for Elizabeth. Now...' John left the statement hanging in the air. He knew his friends would know what he had left unsaid.

'I understand,' replied Hendrick, 'but your collection was also an investment. One I have no doubt has grown in value. I think you should keep adding to it for that reason. I know the circumstances are different but don't you think you should keep enhancing its value?'

'That aspect never came into it for me and it doesn't now. The pieces were picked purely because I knew Elizabeth would like them.'

'But, John, wouldn't she want you to keep adding to it?' put in Katharina gently.

He gave a little shake of his head and sadness

touched his eyes. 'She is not there to see them, so what is the point in accumulating more?'

'There's Anna,' said Charles quietly. 'She treasured the collection as much as Mother, though it did not have the same significance for her. I know she will go on seeing in it all the love you gave to Mother. Maybe you should extend some of that to Anna now.'

'Charles is right,' said Katharina softly.

John looked thoughtful but made no reply. Sensing the sadness that had come over his guest, Hendrick quickly changed the subject. The evening soon resumed its agreeable and engaging atmosphere, for in deference to his host and hostess John threw off the melancholia that had threatened. But he had been given food for thought.

These particular exchanges kept him awake for an hour and were in his mind immediately he awoke. He banished them over breakfast and they were kept at bay as he said goodbye to Herr and Frau Hein and made a promise to visit them again before long. Once on board ship the memory of last night returned and was foremost in his thoughts as he watched the Dutch coastline recede until it was no longer visible. He turned from the rail and strolled towards the stern. Charles, recognising his father's intro-spective mood, though he did not know what occupied him, let him go. If his father wanted to share his thoughts he would do so, it was not up to Charles to enquire.

John stood for a while, gazing unseeingly over

the foaming wake. He was far away. Nothing, no sight, no sound, trespassed on his mind. Time passed. He started. The creak of timbers, the crack of the sails, the squeak of ropes, the swish of the sea ... he was back in reality. He steadied himself against the pitching and rolling of the deck. He heard commands rasped by the captain and first mate. Experienced the thrill of being at sea, part of a small enclosed world in which he was confined for the present. It brought him a feeling of well-being, though it was laced with memories of sharing this experience with Elizabeth. But so deep were those feelings they had shared in similar circumstances, when the small world of a ship drew them closer, he could not be sad for he knew she was beside him now, sharing them once again.

He paused a few moments longer and then walked briskly back to Charles who was still leaning on the rail. Hearing his steps, Charles glanced over his shoulder. He saw immediately that his father's introspective mood had left him.

'Charles, there are certain aspects of our trading with the de Klerks that I want to discuss with Hendrick. I also think that with the likelihood of the Upton brothers trying to infiltrate our outlets with their contraband, I need to make some new contacts in Holland.'

'The ones you spoke of before?'

'There is no need for you to know anything about them yet. I'll tell you all in good time, if I decide to proceed. So what I'm saying is that I will return to Amsterdam alone in January.'

There were lots of questions Charles wanted to

ask his father but he knew better than to press them on him now. He would hear more when John deemed it right to reveal his ideas and intentions.

Chapter Thirteen

Luke Upton, head bent against the chilling wind, made his way through the streets of Hull. He knew where he was likely to find Bill Grimes. Once contact was made at the Dagger Inn, he came straight to the point. 'I need to see Mr Julian on a matter of some urgency.'

'I'll go for him right away.' Bill rose to his feet, shrugged himself into his warm jacket and, leaving his ale unfinished, hurried from the inn. He could tell from Luke's attitude that he would not be put off. He was banking on Julian being at the Kirby offices but, as a dismissed employee, he could not risk coming face to face with Septimus. He sent a message to Julian via a small boy eager to earn a penny, waiting anxiously at the corner of the street. He was relieved when he saw the young man emerge and glance around him.

Seeing Grimes, Julian hurried over to him. 'Quick, man, what is it?' he asked irritably. 'We risk Father seeing us here.'

'Luke Upton's in the Dagger. Wants to see you urgently.'

'What for?'

'Didn't tell me.'

'I'll be with you in a minute.' Julian hurried back to his office. He grabbed his hat and coat and was shrugging himself into his attire as he re-emerged from the building.

Grimes fell into step beside him and it was not long before they reached the Dagger. Upton had his broad fingers cupped around a tankard when they joined him.

'What's so urgent?' asked Julian as he slid into a seat opposite Luke.

'I want another consignment early in the New Year – the sooner the better.' Luke sensed Julian bristle at the demanding tone of his voice. Alienate Kirby and his valuable contact with the supplier in Holland could be lost. Young Mr Kirby had set local smuggling in motion once again and regarded himself as the leader of the Humber gang. He had given Luke and his brothers a taste for the dangerous 'game' again. They had found it profitable under their father. It could be so again. Julian had been content to leave organisation along the Humber to them. With ideas of expanding their outlets Luke realised it was best not to assume too adversarial a stance.

He toned down his voice and expression as he continued, 'It would be advantageous to have a run early in January. I've made contacts in the Whitby area who will act as local agents for us. We've deliberately undercut the local gang and that has aroused interest. More goods will mean not only bigger profits but also greater oppor-tunities and the chance to outsmart the Whitby men and take over their territory.' Even before he had finished he knew he had won his point, for a gleam had come to Julian's eye at the mention of greater profit.

Even so, he was cautious. 'Won't the Whitby

smugglers retaliate?'

'It's likely. They had a lucrative trade which they won't want to give up.'

'That could mean clashes.'

'Aye. But we'll be ready for any such thing.'

Julian frowned doubtfully. 'I want no killing. I don't want to be charged with murder. I tolerated what happened at Owthorn because of your desire to avenge your father, and because you disposed of all evidence. This is a different matter.'

Luke nodded. 'I'll see to it.'

'Good. If that promise is not adhered to I'll see that the whole operation collapses and that will be the end of some useful profits for you.' Such determination rang in Julian's voice that Luke was left in no doubt that he meant what he said, in spite of the fact that he too would lose out. Julian saw that his point had struck home. 'I'll visit Amsterdam before Christmas and arrange for a delivery on the fourth of January.'

Life at Hawkshead Manor settled into a pattern as near to that of the past as it could be without Elizabeth. Charles and Anna expressed to each other their pleasure that their father had once again taken up his activities within the Whitby community, was enthusiastically rekindling his interest in the Hawkshead estate and seeing old friends.

Anna had thought of inviting a few friends for Christmas but with the February party pending she chose a family celebration and left it to others to call if they wished.

The season passed off pleasantly. Their servants made a special effort to make it as pleasurable as possible and the Masons made sure that their workers missed nothing of the festivities. Snow lay thick on the moorland heights beyond Whitby but a narrow strip along the coast escaped lightly and movement was little restricted. A few people called and John, accompanied by Anna and Charles, paid brief visits to special friends in Whitby. After the Christmas service in the parish church, John, with Anna and Charles beside him, stood silently beside the snow-sprinkled grave remembering Christmases past.

New Year meant little to them. It was merely a passage of time. John prepared to leave for Amsterdam, wondering if this visit would have any significance for the future.

John turned up the collar of his coat to help shelter him from the cold blast that swept along Herengracht, rippled the waters of the canal and sent people scurrying a little more quickly towards their destinations. John's was the de Klerks' house.

He had arrived in Amsterdam the day before, after a crossing from Hull that had kept him below deck for most of the voyage. After obtaining his room with the Heins he had made a brief visit to Hendrick to make an appointment for today.

Thankful to be out of the cold, he was ushered into his old friend's office. The Dutchman jumped to his feet when John walked in and greeted him with a broad smile and a firm handshake.

'Let me repeat what I said yesterday, I'm so pleased you changed your mind about the necklace and ring. I think it a wise decision to keep adding to your collection.'

John gave a resigned shrug of his shoulders. 'You, Katharina and Charles have persuasive powers. You made me see that maybe I was being selfish in not continuing to purchase more items. These pieces are for Anna. They are to be a surprise for her on her eighteenth birthday in June.'

An expression of amazement crossed Hendrick's face. 'You'll keep it a secret until then?'

'Yes. I had thought of presenting the pieces to her at a party we are having on Valentine's Day, which of course you know about.'

'Yes. We are all looking forward to coming. So why not give them to her then? An appropriate day, I would have thought.'

'She will have enough excitement that day. She will be the hostess. As I want her to have all her attention on the gift and what it means when I present it to her, I want to do so on her birthday. It will show her that part of my past life is re-established. It is highly appropriate that I do that on her birthday – a new beginning for the collection – for it was on Elizabeth's birthday that I presented her with the necklace that started it all off.'

Hendrick smiled. 'I'm glad you haven't lost your sentimental streak and that you are still a romantic at heart. So, my friend, we go to the auction in two days' time. You will be here at nine in the morning?'

John nodded. 'Now, Hendrick, there are two more things I must request. First, as I said, I don't want Anna to know about the necklace and ring, if I get them.'

'I'm sure you will if you have set your heart on it.'

'I might be outbid.' John pursed his lips then added, 'But in any case, I'd like you and your family to keep this strictly to yourselves.'

'No one in my household will reveal your transaction,' Hendrick reassured him. He gave a meaningful pause. 'And what is the second request?'

'This may seem odd to you seeing that Charles and Magdalena conduct a satisfactory trade in contraband and I am happy for Charles to continue it, but certain events have occurred on our side of the water that have made me realise we might have to expand into goods Magdalena does not supply.'

'Why is this?' queried Hendrick.

'Someone is selling contraband in my territory at cheaper prices, with the result that we have lost some customers. I believe if I can offer a wider range they'll come back to us.'

'I am sorry to hear this, my friend. A dangerous situation could arise. Have you any idea who it is?'

'No proof. But it might be a gang that operates mainly along the Humber. They recently took over territory along the Yorkshire coast just north of the river. If they are looking to expand further...' John left the implications unspoken.

'So what have you in mind?'

'Tobacco and porcelain, two items that Magdalena does not trade in.'

'Two commodities that are tricky because the Pawl brothers have a near monopoly on them, something they've maintained through their ruthlessness.'

'I know that because I made enquiries a while back before this trouble started. I shelved the idea of trading in these two items because of what I heard about the Pawls, but now I wonder if they may not be the answer to my problems.'

'They could be. I can tell you where to find them. They'll drive a hard bargain. They'll also want you to smuggle wool from England for them.' Hendrick looked hard at John. 'Think carefully on it, my friend, because that is something you have never done before. Apart from that they'll expect you to deal in those commodities exclusively with them, and woe betide you if they ever suspect you are not complying with their rules.'

'I would not do otherwise. But I see it as a way of counteracting the incursions at home, which I can see worsening if I do nothing about them.'

'Have you discussed this with Charles?'

'No. I have only hinted that I might be about to enter into a new deal but, because I knew there is danger from the ruthless men with whom I would have to trade, I have told him no more.'

'It is better kept that way. Allow him to continue with Magdalena, but for the time say nothing about this operation until you see it is going to work.'

'So, where will I find the Pawl brothers?'

'They are on the left bank of the Singel close to the Jan Roodenpoortstoren, the beautiful tower on the Tower Bridge, the Torensluis. You will see a brass plaque saying Pawl House. If you go there, don't be deceived. They will ooze charm but are hard men, ruthless if necessary, who always manage to escape enquiry by the law.'

'I'll be careful if I decide to pay them a visit.'

As he watched his friend leave Hendrick knew that John, though he had not voiced a definite decision, would be paying the Pawl brothers a visit.

John's request to see one of the brothers was taken by a clerk in an outer office. The thin man, stooped at the shoulders, entwined his fingers and peered at the stranger from rat-like eyes. 'Which one? They are both in,' he squeaked. There was irritation in his words, and when his eyes flicked back to a ledger on his desk John knew that he did not take kindly to being interrupted at his work even though to deal with callers was obviously part of his job.

'Either of them,' he replied.

The clerk tightened his lips in annoyance at not getting the answer he wanted. 'Who shall I say calls?' he asked tersely.

'John Mason of Whitby, England.'

'And the reason you want to see Herr Pawl?'

'Trade.'

'What sort of trade?'

John was getting annoyed at this cross-questioning. He glared at the clerk. 'That is between Herr Pawl and me. It is no concern of yours.' His voice was cutting. 'Now get along and find out which one will see me.'

The clerk met his stare but said nothing. John's piercing eyes were too much for him. He lowered his gaze and scurried away. He returned a few moments later and said grudgingly, 'Come this way. Herr Jacob will see you.'

John followed the clerk into a corridor where he stopped at the second door on the right, knocked and entered. 'Mr Mason from England,' he announced in a tone that showed his disapproval of the Englishman.

John stepped past him and found himself in a large spacious office beautifully furnished with desk, chairs, sideboard and cupboard, all in mahogany. They bore the hand of a craftsman and showed a buyer with taste. The man who rose from his chair behind the desk was of medium build, sharp-featured with probing eyes. John found them a little off-putting but suddenly realised that their searching had been quick and was replaced by a charm that would put most people at ease. But it only made John wary. Was it a case of the spider and the fly? He recalled what Hendrick had told him.

'Good day, Herr Mason.' Jacob Pawl extended a hand.

When John took it he felt a solid grip without any warmth in it.

'It is good of you to see me without an appointment.'

Herr Pawl made a little gesture with his hands as he said, 'Anyone who wants to talk trade is always welcome at Pawl House.' He indicated a chair to John.

'Your clerk did not think so.'

Herr Pawl gave a small laugh of amusement. 'He would rather all our visitors made an appointment first. So what is it we can do for you Herr Mason?'

John had made himself comfortable. 'Herr Pawl, I am interested in purchasing a large quantity of tobacco.'

'You have come to the right place.'

John fixed him with a firm gaze. 'At a special price.' The pause, though only slight, added meaning to the words that followed. 'You understand?'

The Dutchman met John's gaze with one of equal firmness. A tense moment passed before he replied, 'I think my brother ought to be with us.' He reached for a handbell placed beside a glass-lidded inkwell on his desk. He gave it one sharp shake. The bell had obviously been chosen with care and thought for the sound it produced, for it was not unpleasant in the room yet resounded clearly enough to reach beyond the closed door. A moment later the clerk came into the room but remained standing at the door, one hand on the knob. He raised an enquiring eyebrow at his employer.

'Lucas, tell my brother that I have a customer I would like him to meet.'

The clerk left without a word.

'I would also be...' John broke off as Herr Pawl raised a hand.

'Say no more until you have met my brother Max.'

John nodded and waited uneasily in his chair, though he hid his misgivings.

The door opened.

Jacob spoke. 'Ah, Max, I would like you to meet Herr Mason, a merchant from Whitby, England.'

John pushed himself from his chair and turned to meet the new arrival, 'I'm pleased to meet you, Herr Pawl.' He extended his hand and found it taken in a limp touch. Eyes surveyed him with interest but he thought he detected a touch of disdain in them, a look he suspected was reserved for foreigners even when they came as customers. It was also the look of a man very sure of his ground.

Max did not return his greeting but looked beyond him to his brother. With his back to Jacob, John had no means of assessing the glance that passed between the Dutchmen.

Max moved round John to take a seat at one end of the desk. 'Well, Herr Mason, what can we do for you?'

John realised that he must put on a firm front and show no weakness to these two men whose eyes were cold as they watched him. 'I'm interested in purchasing a large quantity of tobacco,' he replied.

'He expects special rates,' put in Jacob with a meaningful glance at his brother.

'Ah!' Max gave a moment's pause, his gaze speculative. When he spoke it seemed he had reached a conclusion and was prepared to test it out. His words were accompanied by a cynical smile. 'Herr Mason, why don't we be open about your request? You mean that you want us to supply you with tobacco that you can run as contraband.'

John smiled to counter Max's attitude. 'If that is what you wish, yes, by all means, let us call a spade a spade. I am interested in smuggling tobacco into England.'

'I presume that you mean your part of England, Whitby and the surrounding area?'

'Indeed. I would not want to usurp any trade you have with other smugglers along the Yorkshire coast. I hope you have none that would curtail the quantity I take.'

Max turned to his brother. 'Do we supply anyone else along the Yorkshire coast?'

'No.'

Max looked at John. 'It appears you will have the monopoly of purchasing tobacco from us for the Yorkshire market.'

'That is how I would like it to remain.'

'Ah, a man who would avoid conflict.'

'I do all in my power to make it so. Clashes are not good for trade.'

'What about officialdom?'

'I have managed so far to avoid any confrontations of significance with Customs and Revenue Men. I have my spies so we can counter any moves they make and divert prying eyes when we are making a run.'

'And you can go on doing that?'

John gave a short laugh. 'I sincerely hope so.' He eyed Max with curiosity. 'Aren't you being overly cautious? What concern is it of yours how things are conducted or turn out on my side of the water?'

Max spread his hands. 'It pays to be careful. Any mishap to you could have repercussions for us, apart from losing your trade.'

'My dear fellow,' replied John, 'I can see that this over-cautiousness of yours could hinder my operation. I will go elsewhere for my tobacco.' He started to rise from his chair.

'Sit down, Herr Mason.' Max's command was sharp. He fixed his eyes firmly on John. 'I was merely testing your attitude. Now, you want tobacco, we can supply it. But we want assurances. First, this must not be your only purchase. Trading must continue into the future. There must be further guaranteed orders. Secondly, as few people as possible must know from whom you purchased the tobacco.'

'My son is involved in the business and I will need to tell my smuggling lieutenant.' John thought it wise not to mention Magdalena or Hendrick.

Max's eyes became colder in their penetrating stare. 'All right but tell no one else or the deal is off. Thirdly, the contraband will be picked up by your designated vessel. That serves two purposes – no Dutchman will be at risk from English authority, and thanks to our arrangements here your men will not know where the tobacco comes from.'

'Agreed,' said John when Max cast a quizzical glance at him.

'Now, as to the question of price...'

John had come prepared for hard bargaining. It was only after half an hour that agreement was reached. It did not fully satisfy either side, for each wanted the advantage, but when they agreed on special purchases of porcelain also the deal was concluded.

'You saw the Pawls?' Hendrick put his query when John arrived back at the de Klerk dwelling the following morning.

'Yes,' replied John, 'but ask no more. They don't know that you directed me to them and I am sworn not to reveal with whom I am dealing. Please do not tell anyone of my arrangement.'

The urgency in his voice and the pleading in his eyes left Hendrick in no doubt that it would put John in danger if he did not comply.

'Very well,' he replied, 'but may I ask you one question, then this information will be a secret with me for ever?'

John hesitated only a moment and then agreed.

'Did they threaten you?'

'Not in a direct way. They were charming, as you said they would be, but their eyes were cold and at times the atmosphere was icy and threatening, as if they held me in contempt.'

Hendrick pursed his lips thoughtfully. 'I will say no more except that you must be careful.' He immediately banished his expression of concern and said brightly, 'Now, my friend, it is time we went to the auction.'

They left the house on Herengracht and after fifteen minutes' brisk walking were taking seats three rows from the front in the auction room. There were another fifteen minutes before the sale was due to start. After glancing through the catalogue and noting that the item Hendrick had told him about was number twenty, John studied the people filing into the room and speculated who might rival him for the necklace and ring.

When it came to it he was surprised that, after six people had dropped out of the bidding, his only opponent was a young man in his mid-twenties standing against the nearby wall. John could not but admire his appearance. His clothes spoke of quality and their cut indicated a meticulous tailor. John did not doubt he had money behind him. He held himself well, with an air of confidence. John expected to have a fight on his hands and knew he would have to pay dearly for the necklace and ring, but he was determined to have them. Anna deserved them.

A raised finger, an almost imperceptible nod sent the price continually upwards. In spite of the spiralling cost John displayed a sense of calm. It was something he had learned to do even though he might be churning inside with anxiety. Bluff your opponent and you had a better chance of victory. The upward trend continued. He smiled to himself when the young man showed irritation as he was forced to make another bid.

The contest was capturing the imagination of the rest of the auction goers, who, caught up in the escalating contest, whispered to their neighbours seeking identification of the bidders and speculating on who would eventually win.

To and fro, first to one then the other, the price went higher and higher.

John saw the young man's face cloud with momentary anger. If he had not been looking carefully he would have missed that expression and might well have dropped out of the bidding then. But that flash told him he had won. The next bid from the young man would be his last – one final attempt.

The price was called. The auctioneer looked in John's direction. He remained impassive. He had decided to have a little fun. The auctioneer called the price again. 'Once.' He raised an eyebrow at John, who did not respond. 'Twice.' Another glance at John. Again he did not react. He saw a look of satisfaction cross the young man's face. Victory was close. The auctioneer raised his gavel, but in the frozen moment of time before it started its downward path John called out a raised bid. A gasp ran round the room. Heads turned. He ignored them. His eyes were on his opponent. He saw frustration and anger boil over in a silent curse. The auctioneer called the offer and looked at the young man who grimly shook his head.

'Once. Twice. The third and last time.' A moment's pause. The gavel crashed on to the desk, signalling the sale of that particular item. Enormously satisfied, John sank back against his chair.

'Well done, John,' Hendrick congratulated him, 'but you had me on tenterhooks at the finish. I thought you were going to withdraw.'

He smiled. 'Just a little game I played with that young man. I hope he learned something from it. He should not let his real feelings be seen. I knew I had him when he showed anger and frustration. I knew he would go no further if I made one final bid. Naughty of me to tease him at the end.'

Hendrick chuckled at his friend's audacity.

They stayed until the auctioneer called a break halfway through the session. As they made for the door, they saw the young man had risen from his seat and was leaving ahead of them.

When they stepped into the outer room he turned to face them. He smiled warmly and said, 'May I shake hands with a worthy opponent and say congratulations, sir?'

John returned the smile and took the proffered hand. 'A fellow Englishman, and from your accent I would say you live not too far from me. John Mason of Whitby.'

'Well, I'm damned,' the young man cried, his eyes showing surprise. 'Lambert Finch of Langthorpe Hall in the East Riding. I'm pleased to know you, sir, and glad to hear it wasn't a Dutchman who outbid me. I'm delighted that the necklace and ring are going to a good home in Yorkshire.' He cast an embarrassed glance at Hendrick. 'My goodness, I hope you aren't one of them, sir?'

Hendrick laughed and shook his head. 'A Dutchman through and through.'

'My apologies,' said John hastily. 'Let me introduce my friend, Herr Hendrick de Klerk, a notable merchant in this city.'

'I'm more than pleased to meet you, sir.'

'Tell me, young man,' said Hendrick as they shook hands, 'how is it that you are in Amsterdam bidding for a necklace and ring of that quality?'

Lambert smiled. 'I think you would have said "one as young as you", but were too polite to do so. There is a story attached to it. There's a tavern across the way from here, would you two gentlemen allow me to buy you some refreshment?'

'That is most kind of you,' said John. He was impressed not only by Lambert's politeness and charm but also by his bearing and good looks. He was handsome with square chin, straight nose and deep blue eyes that caught the attention. His hair was well-groomed and shone with a dark lustre.

Lambert called for drinks and when they were seated said, 'Now allow me to satisfy your curiosity. How is it that I am bidding for a beautiful necklace and ring, worth every penny you paid for them? Well, I have a sister who is married to a Dutchman and lives in the Hague. I like to keep my eye on the art market, an interest I was born to and encouraged to develop by my late parents. So, when I visit my sister from time to time I study the market over here. I heard about the necklace and ring, went to view them, and had a great desire to add them to my collection for they resembled pieces that were once family possessions – my grandparents had them – but were stolen. I never saw them but they were described to me by my father. Whether this is the same set I cannot say but I felt that, even if it wasn't, I was restoring something to the collection started by my grandparents. Alas,' he glanced at John, 'you outbid me, sir. If you don't mind my asking, are the pieces of special significance to you?'

'I have a collection which was started by my purchase of a necklace for my late wife.' John found himself being open with this young man in a way he would not have been with any other stranger. It was as if Lambert's charm elicited information without his seeming to pry. 'Each piece that was added to it, whether it was jewellery, miniatures, porcelain or whatever, was for her. When she died I stopped collecting. Without going into my reasons, I have recently decided to start again. This was the first additional piece. It will be given to my daughter on her birthday in June. Herr de Klerk told me about it and I saw it not only as a gift to Anna, but as an appropriate piece to restart the collection.'

'It sounds as though you have a fascinating one?'

'I am pleased with it. You live nearby so why not come and see it? Better still, we are having a party on the fourteenth of February, you are welcome to come. The de Klerks will be staying with us. Please stay too.'

'That is most generous of you, sir. I would love to take up your offer.'

'Good. I'll get my daughter to send you an official invitation, then you will know I haven't forgotten. Oh, there is just one thing. Please make no mention of this purchase or that we met in an auction room. I want it to be a complete surprise to Anna. Only you and Herr de Klerk will know of it.'

'You have my word, sir. We should have the same story. We'll say we met in a tavern, two Englishmen in a foreign land.'

John smiled. 'Good idea.' He was grateful for

311

Lambert's astuteness.

The young man drained his glass and stood up. 'If you will excuse me, I must be on my way. Good day to you, Mr Mason, and to you, Herr de Klerk. I look forward to the fourteenth of February.'

The two men watched him leave.

'He carries himself well,' commented Hendrick. 'A most presentable young man.'

'Indeed,' agreed John. 'Most charming, and handsome too. So easy to talk to. He took his defeat well. I look forward to introducing him to Anna and Charles. I'm sure they'll get on well.'

John relaxed under the billowing canvas as the wind caught the sails and the ship met the sea at the Dutch coast. A sense of well-being and satisfaction permeated his whole being. The visit to Amsterdam had borne better fruit than he had expected. He had secured the necklace and ring, placed a large order with Hendrick at satisfactory terms, passed on Charles's requirements to Magdalena, and struck a deal with the Pawl brothers for tobacco and porcelain that he hoped would strengthen the Masons' smuggling activities and counter the incursions he presumed were being instigated by the Upton brothers. It was good to be back in active business again. He thanked Elizabeth for her words of encouragement, as he'd stood by her grave on the windblown Whitby cliff top.

The ship was one hour off the Dutch coast when the weather took a turn for the worse. Strong winds from the wrong quarter and heavy seas slowed the ship's progress. By the time the weather abated and became more friendly they were behind schedule. The delay cost John his onward journey by coach and meant an overnight stay in Hull. This did not worry him unduly except that he was not a man who enjoyed situations that could not be profitable in some form or other.

So, having booked a room for the night at the Cross Keys in the Market Place, he decided that a visit to the office of Kirby and Son might be useful. Besides, it would be nice to meet the father of the two young people whom he had taken to on their visits to Hawkshead Manor.

The clerk who took his request to see Mr Septimus Kirby was polite and friendly. In a few moments John was being warmly greeted. 'Mr Mason, I am so glad to meet you.' Septimus had come from behind his desk and his handshake left John in no doubt of the sincerity of his greeting. 'I have heard so much about you from Julian and Rebecca. I really must thank you for your kindness to them.'

John gave a dismissive wave of his hand. 'It was nothing. I was pleased to accommodate them, they seemed to get on so well with Charles and Anna.'

'A fortuitous meeting between our sons. I have to say that it has influenced Julian greatly. He speaks highly of your son, and of course your daughter. I must add that my wife and I were charmed by both of them when they came to stay with us.'

'I am so pleased. And you will never know what

the visits of your children meant to me after my wife's death. My rehabilitation was due in no small way to the wise words of your daughter.'

'Come, do sit down. Let me offer you a glass of Madeira.'

'Most kind.'

'Are you in Hull for long?' Septimus asked over his shoulder as he poured the wine.

John accepted the glass and explained how he came to be in Hull and was having to spend the night there.

'Then you must come to dinner tonight.'

'I don't want to put you to any trouble.'

'Nonsense! It will be no trouble. I'll send my clerk home to warn my wife that we will have a guest for dinner.'

He rang a bell and when the clerk appeared instructed him to deliver a message to the house on Albion Street and inform Julian that he was wanted in his father's office.

A few moments later the door opened and Julian strode in. 'You wanted to see me...' The words died on his lips as he gasped with surprise. 'Mr Mason! Sir, it's a pleasure to see you here.' He hurried forward to shake hands.

John offered a brief explanation for his visit.

'Mr Mason will be dining with us this evening. He is staying at the Cross Keys tonight and will catch a coach from there tomorrow,' explained Julian's father.

'No need for the coach, sir,' he said. 'I've just hired a ship to go to Whitby for a consignment of alum. You could sail on her. I'm sure you'd enjoy that better than a shaky coach ride.'

'Indeed I would,' replied John.

'She sails at ten in the morning.'

'I'll be on board.'

'Why don't you accompany Mr Mason?' said Septimus. 'You've been working hard lately. Have a little break. It will do you good to be at sea for a while.'

'Better than that,' put in John, 'why not accompany me all the way and have a few days at Hawkshead Manor? That is, with your father's permission?' He shot a glance at Septimus.

'I see no reason why not.'

'Thank you, Father, and thank you too, Mr Mason.'

'One of my ships will be sailing for Amsterdam in five days' time. You could return on her,' John suggested.

Julian glanced at his father for approval and got it.

'I look forward to it very much, sir. How is Anna?'

John smiled to himself. The young man's eyes had kindled. There was a different ring to his voice when he mentioned Anna's name. It was as John had suspected. Julian was more than a little interested in his daughter. 'Will Rebecca come with you?'

'Alas, she is with friends in Beverley for a few days,' put in Septimus. 'She will be disappointed when she learns she has missed a visit to Hawkshead Manor.'

'If I am to have a few days away, there are things I must see to before I leave. So if you will excuse me, Mr Mason?'

'Certainly.'

When he reached the door Julian hesitated a fraction while he said, 'See you tonight, sir.'

'A most enthusiastic young man,' commented John. 'A credit to you.'

'Those are kind words. I must reiterate the good influence your son exerted on mine with that initial invitation to accompany him to Amsterdam. Julian became much more capable after that and has assumed more responsibility within the firm.'

'Good, I'm pleased our sons get on so well.'

'Another glass of Madeira?'

John found Septimus an interesting and knowledgeable man. He discovered that he had left Scarborough and come to Hull because he was looking to expand his business and build it up to secure his children's future. As they discussed trading matters, John casually learned the names of several wool merchants from West Yorkshire who supplied merchants in Hull. Now he was in possession of sources from whom he might obtain wool for the Pawl brothers. This had certainly turned out a more profitable trip than he could ever have imagined.

As soon as the ship docked in Whitby John guided Julian through the flow of people to the Mason office on Church Street. He introduced Julian to Gideon and then informed his manager of the deals he had made with Hendrick and when the goods should be collected in Amsterdam.

'I have another call to make before we go to the Manor. I will leave Julian in your hands, Gideon, until I return. I shouldn't be long.'

Leaving the office immediately, he made his way quickly to Tin Ghaut and was thankful to find Edwin at home. He told him of the deal he had made with the Pawl brothers and of the arrangements made for the collection of the contraband tobacco and porcelain.

Edwin greeted the news favourably. 'This should strengthen our operation.'

'Have you any more news?'

'Nothing to indicate who's behind it but some of our customers have been approached by another source. I still think it's the Upton brothers. None of this started until after the incident at Owthorn and I'm sure they were behind that.'

'I'm inclined to agree with you. Putting tobacco and porcelain on the market would definitely rouse the Uptons to action. We must stay alert for any developments.'

'I'll forewarn Nick and Ralph when I arrange for them to pick up the first consignment from the Pawls.'

'And tell them that after the first voyage for tobacco they will be carrying wool to Amsterdam.'

John returned to his office and then, accompanied by Julian, made his way to the White Horse where he hired a horse and carriage. The drive was pleasant, though cold, and both men were glad when Hawkshead Manor came in sight.

'Anna is going to get a surprise when she sees who I have with me,' commented John, with a sideways glance at Julian. He caught that same brightening of his eyes he had seen in Hull when Anna was mentioned.

'I hope she's pleased,' replied Julian.

'I'm sure she will be.'

Julian took heart from that observation but it did nothing to stop his heart racing as they pulled to a halt at the front door of Hawkshead Manor.

John led the way, and as they entered the hall Anna appeared at the top of the stairs.

'Father!' she cried, delight in her voice. 'I was in my room, heard a carriage and wondered who was com...' Aware of someone behind her father her voice trailed away when she saw Julian. She quickly dismissed that moment of awkwardness. 'Julian, this is a surprise.'

'I hope a pleasant one, Miss Anna?'

She did not reply but, with a smile, came lightly down the stairs. 'How is it you are together?' she asked, and kissed her father on the cheek.

'Let us get out of our coats and we'll tell you.' He shrugged off his coat. 'Off with yours, my boy. Leave it on that chair. I think we deserve some chocolate after that cold drive.' He headed for the drawing room. Anna hesitated between following and waiting for Julian.

'Your father's ship was late into Hull yesterday. He missed his coach so stayed the night in Hull and had dinner with us. I had a ship chartered to come to Whitby for alum so I suggested he use it. He invited me to come here for a few days.' Julian explained his presence quickly as he escorted Anna across the hall.

'I see,' she acknowledged. 'I hope you enjoy

your stay.' She was polite. Not as effusive as he would have liked but did not seem displeased to see him.

Anna, for her part, had experienced a moment of concern when she had first seen Julian. She felt him to be an intruder. But that feeling only lasted for a moment. Julian must not be made aware of it. Besides, she did not really see him as such. She analysed the feeling as automatic to an unexpected arrival, even of a friend.

'I'm sure I shall,' replied Julian. 'It's always a pleasure to visit Hawkshead Manor. You make it so.'

Anna did not pick up on the compliment. Instead she asked, 'Rebecca did not come?'

'She is spending a few days with friends in Beverley. She will be disappointed.'

John was warming himself in front of the fire. 'I've rung for the maid.' At that moment a girl appeared and John ordered a pot of chocolate and told her to tell Mrs Denston that they had a guest for four nights. 'By the way, Anna, I met a young man in Amsterdam who lives at Langthorpe Hall in the East Riding – Lambert Finch. He's interested in art. When he expressed a desire to see our collection I invited him to the party next month. You'd better send him an official invitation.'

Anna was surprised that her father should welcome a stranger to the party. Invite him to see the collection by all means, but some other time would have been more appropriate. But what was done was done. If this stranger had stimulated her father's interest in his collection again then it

319

was a good thing. She made no objection.

Conversation flowed freely while they had their drink and it was not until Julian had been shown to his room that Anna was able to concentrate on her own feelings at seeing him again. Women's intuition told her that he had a special feeling for her, though she had not openly encouraged it. Her own attitude towards him was one of uncertainty. He was likeable, polite and considerate, but could she see him as more than a friend? Had her stand-offish attitude been caused purely by circumstances – her mother's death, her father's retreat into self-pity, her own desire to devote time to him and win him back to as near a normal life as possible without her mother? Now that had been achieved she had more time to think about herself and her own relationships. But was she ready for more than friendship with Julian? Did she want that? She knew her father liked him, otherwise he would not have invited him to come to Hawkshead Manor. If she showed the slightest inclination towards Julian, she had no doubt her father would approve. She could not analyse her own feelings with any degree of certainty. Maybe the next few days would help.

Chapter Fourteen

'Charles, will you be here to entertain Julian today?' asked Anna when she found him alone at breakfast the next morning.

'Sorry, Anna, I've already got appointments in Whitby that I must keep. Father will be here.'

'No, he won't. He informed me last night that he must see Sir Arthur Foston on a matter of some urgency.'

Charles nodded. He had known of this. His father had had a private word with him about setting up a trade in contraband tobacco and porcelain but he could not admit knowing of the necessity of his father's meeting with Sir Arthur. Word had to be passed to other members of the syndicate so that they would be prepared to give temporary storage space to this new contraband.

'Surely you don't mind being alone with Julian?' he teased.

'Of course not,' replied Anna indignantly, 'but it's a situation that could set the servants talking.'

'If you are concerned about that, why don't you come to Whitby with me? You can give Julian an interesting tour. Call on Cara. We could meet at the Angel for a meal between my appointments, say at twelve-thirty? I'm sorry I can't alter those, Julian's visit was unexpected, but I'll be with you tomorrow. Maybe we could have a morning ride and a walk in the afternoon, depending on the weather?'

'A good idea,' replied Anna brightly, relieved to be released from what might have been an embarrassing situation. Not that she couldn't have dealt with it, but she didn't want her feeling to be tested by the intimacy of being alone with Julian. Rather, she wanted her attitude to him clarified while in the company of other people.

Anna had seated herself at the table when Julian came in to breakfast. 'Good morning,' he said cheerfully.

Brother and sister returned his greeting.

'Did you sleep well?' asked Charles.

'I was so comfortable I barely woke once.'

'Help yourself to what's on the sideboard,' said Anna. 'You know our breakfast procedure.'

'Thank you,' replied Julian. He surveyed what was available and then chose to start with some porridge.

'I'm sorry I won't be able to spend much time with you today,' said Charles as their guest took his place at table.

'That's perfectly understandable,' returned Julian. 'I'll see you this evening.'

'I've suggested to Anna that you both come to Whitby with me and she can show you the town and maybe call on her friend Cara. We can meet at midday for a meal.'

'Sounds an excellent idea.'

'Good. Just one thing, Julian – beware of Cara's mother.' The corners of his lips twitched with amusement.

'Beware? What do you mean?' He saw look of

fun pass between brother and sister.

'Mrs Blenkinsop can be a little overpowering,' explained Anna. 'She's a nosy parker. She'll want to know all about you, and she'll read altogether too much into the fact that I arrive with a young man at her house unchaperoned. A lovely piece of gossip for her to pass on to her friends. But they all know her. They realise that the basic facts are generally right, but they also know she can draw the wildest conclusions from them.'

'So I must be guarded in both actions and words?' Julian asked seriously.

'Yes.'

'Or else we could have a bit of fun,' he added, with a twinkle in his eye.

'We could,' smiled Anna, 'but be careful how far you go.'

'Trust me, dear Anna.'

She realised she would have to and yet she was not alarmed by what he might do. She realised in her heart of hearts she did trust him. So why had she had her doubts about him? Why had she thought she did not know everything about Julian Kirby? What had first raised her suspicions? Here he sat at table with her, charming, polite, a good conversationalist, serious yet witty, and she could tell from the way he attended on her and the way he looked at her that he thought a great deal of her. Why did she hold back? Why was she not completely at ease with him?

As they rode in the trap to Whitby, the young men, after a brief exchange of business talk, diverted to other topics out of deference to Anna.

'I'll drive straight to the Angel. I can stable

there and bespeak a meal for twelve-thirty,' said Charles, slowing the horse to a walking pace as they approached the bridge to cross to the west side. He drove to the inn and left the horse and trap in the care of the ostler. Charles made the booking for four. 'Bring Cara with you,' he said to Anna and Julian as the landlord made a note of the time and numbers.

'What would you like to do first?' asked Anna when Charles left them to keep his appointments.

'I think I would like to meet the formidable Mrs Blenkinsop. And, from what you tell me, rescue Cara from her clutches for a while.'

Anna laughed at the light-hearted tone of Julian's voice. 'I'm sure she would welcome that.'

Whitby was alive with all the activities of a busy port as Anna guided him to Poplar Row behind Skinner Street.

'This area was once known as Farndale Fields and was acquired by the Skinner brothers who started this development,' she explained.

'They are making a good job of it,' he replied. 'Some handsome houses.'

'This is the Blenkinsop's.' She indicated a three-storeyed house, with basement, built in variegated bricks.

Julian had noticed that like other houses in this street each floor had a single window and a pair, the pair being under one lintel. Seven steps at right angles to the front of the building led to the front door, over which there was a semi-circular fanlight of delicate tracery, protected by a triangular canopy.

A maid opened the door in answer to the ringing bell. Julian saw that her face broke into a warm smile on seeing Anna. He realised that she was liked and respected everywhere, something that did not surprise him after his own observation of her.

'Is Miss Cara at home, Millie?' Anna asked.

'Please step inside, miss. I will tell her you are here.'

Anna, followed by Julian who gave Millie a friendly smile, stepped into the hall.

Millie had hardly closed the door when Mrs Blenkinsop flowed out of the drawing room as if she was making an entrance to an important function. 'Millie, have we visitors?' she enquired regally.

It was all Julian could do to suppress his mirth and he knew if he gave Anna a slight dig in the arm she would burst out laughing. He was sorely tempted to do so but restrained his impulse. It was obvious that Mrs Blenkinsop had heard voices in the hall and could not hold back her curiosity until they were announced, apart from the fact that it gave her the chance to make a grand entry.

Her words rolled on before anyone could speak. 'Ah, my dear Anna, what a pleasure it is to see you.' She swept forward and enfolded the girl in her arms without any thought that her full bosom was causing Anna embarrassment. Over the girl's shoulder Belinda's sharp eyes, full of curiosity, took in the stranger. She released Anna as she was saying, 'And who is this nice-looking person here?' She swept the girl aside and

325

extended a hand to Julian.

He responded by taking it gently and raising it towards his lips as he made a slight bow. 'A pleasure to meet you, Mrs Blenkinsop,' he said smoothly.

'This is Julian Kirby from Hull, Mrs Blenkinsop,' said Anna, straightening her dress after the over-exuberant contact with the lady of the house.

Mrs Blenkinsop cocked a telling eyebrow at her. 'Where have you been hiding such a handsome young man? It's not hard to see why you wanted to keep him a secret from the other eligible Whitby girls.'

'Mrs Blenkinsop, Julian is just a friend,' replied Anna, a little icily.

Belinda Blenkinsop nodded her head. 'Ah, that's what you tell me.'

Julian leaned a little closer to her and said conspiratorially, 'That's what she tells me too, but I think there is a little more to it.'

He was amused by the dagger-like look Anna gave him. He returned it with a wink and a little smile.

Anna was in a whirl of annoyance at his inference, and pleasure at the charm that had accompanied that teasing wink, as if they were close conspirators in this exchange with Mrs Blenkinsop.

At that moment their attention was drawn by footsteps on the stairs and they saw Cara coming down, followed by Millie.

'Anna.' Her friend's face was bright with pleasure. Then her gaze passed to Julian with interest.

'Cara.' Anna moved to the foot of the stairs and took the girl's hands in hers. As she turned she said, 'I'd like you to meet Julian Kirby from Hull.'

He bowed. 'I'm pleased to see you, Miss Blenkinsop. I've heard so much about you from Miss Anna.'

Cara blushed as she acknowledged his greeting. 'And I about you. I am sorry I was unable to meet you on your previous visits to Hawkshead Manor.'

'That is rectified now,' he replied. 'Anna is going to show me something of Whitby. I hope you will accompany us? And Charles has invited you to have lunch with us at the Angel.'

'That is most kind,' put in Mrs Blenkinsop quickly. 'Cara will be delighted to accept. Now, before you go, come into the drawing room and have a cup of chocolate to warm you on this cold day.' She was not going to miss the opportunity to find out more about this young man. First-hand information could be passed on triumphantly to her friends.

Before anyone could refuse she had tugged the bellpull that brought the immediate appearance of the parlour maid, who, anticipating such a request, had waited behind the door leading to the kitchen.

The young people could do nothing but follow Mrs Blenkinsop. 'Cara, you should find yourself a nice young man like Anna's Mr Kirby,' she said, oblivious to the embarrassment she caused her daughter and scowl that crossed Anna's face at the assumption that she and Julian were more than friends. 'Tell me about yourself, Mr Kirby,' she added as she sat down and indicated to the young people to do likewise.

'My father's a merchant in Hull. I have a mother and two sisters. We came to Hull from Scarborough originally because my father saw more chances there to expand our trade.' In the minute pause that followed he shot a glance at Anna.

Oh, no, she thought. What is he going to come out with now? Her concern, although touched with horror at what might be said, was also tinged with amusement.

'But *I* saw it as a chance to pursue my own rakish interests – cards, racing, wine, women and song. Have a good life, I say, it is all too short.' His words came in a voice that swept all normal convention aside. He saw a shocked look come over Mrs Blenkinsop's as face she drew herself up as if to ward off any undesirable contact. He saw that Cara's expression was blank, trying to reconcile these views with what she must have heard of him from her friend. He glimpsed Anna raise her eyes heavenwards.

'Mr Kirby!' The indignation in Mrs Blenkinsop's voice filled the room. 'I take back what I suggested to my daughter. Indeed I would *not* wish her to be associated with a man with such an outlook, and pursuits that can only lead to ruin.' She turned to Cara. 'My dear, I don't think you had better accompany Mr Kirby today. You should rather come with me to see old Miss Smurthwaite and do your good deed for the day by reading to her.'

'Oh, Mama!' Cara feigned disappointment, for

she had seen Anna wink at her.

'Certainly, you must.' Mrs Blenkinsop turned to Anna. 'I am surprised at you, consorting with such a person. And to bring him here ... well! I am even more surprised at your father for condoning an association with this ... this...' She spluttered to find the word.

'Rake, Mrs Blenkinsop?' Julian suggested mildly.

'Indeed!' She drew herself up. 'I must ask you to leave immediately, Mr Kirby.'

At that moment the door opened and two maids entered, bringing the chocolate and the necessary cups.

'Oh, dear, Mrs Blenkinsop, here is the chocolate. I was so looking forward to enjoying a cup with you in this beautiful room that shows such impeccable taste.'

Pride came in to her bearing.

'But sadly you have dismissed me,' went on Julian, 'so I must leave such fascinating company.' He allowed himself a moment's pause and added lightly, 'I hope the chocolate won't be wasted.'

It was too much for the young women. They could no longer suppress their mirth that was bursting to be out. They spluttered but could no longer hold back their laughter.

'Girls, don't be so rude!' cried Mrs Blenkinsop indignantly, glaring fiercely at the two young women.

'Oh, Mama, you don't think Anna would bring a real rake here?' The words came out amidst Cara's laughter.

'What do you mean?'

'From what Anna has told me, Mr Kirby is a very respectable person and not at all as he has portrayed himself to you.'

Mrs Blenkinsop's eyes narrowed as she glared at Julian, then, beguiled by his open smile, softened. 'Mr Kirby, have you been teasing?'

'My apologies, ma'am.' His mind was racing to find an excuse for his behaviour. He could not admit that it was as a direct result of his conversation with Anna about Mrs Blenkinsop herself. 'I have an awful habit of teasing people. Please forgive me and let us start afresh over the chocolate.' He cast a glance at Cara who immediately responded by starting to pour it, a signal to her mother to take no further offence.

'Very well, young man, I will forgive you.' Belinda put on a slightly hurt expression but that vanished when Julian politely handed her a cup of chocolate with charm and a winning smile. 'Mr Kirby, be careful, that habit might get you into trouble one day.' She then turned the incident to show herself in a good light. 'You may tease someone not so tolerant as I.'

'I will heed your words, ma'am. Now, you wanted to know about me?' He took a seat opposite her. 'I work with my father. I met Anna's brother in Hull. He introduced me to a merchant in Amsterdam and that has proved most lucrative, so much so that father has made me responsible for our trade with the merchants of that city.'

'There you are, Cara, what did I tell you? You should find a young man with the capabilities of Mr Kirby. It is a pity Anna already has her hands on him.'

'Mama!' Cara blushed.

Anna and Julian suppressed their smiles.

When they had finished their chocolate the young people wrapped themselves against the cold and left the house.

They had gone only a few yards when Cara could no longer restrain her laughter. It was a signal for the other two to join in. They had kept their own mirth in check in deference to her, but once she had started, her laughter was infectious.

'That was too bad of you,' scolded Anna, her eyes betraying her enjoyment of it nevertheless.

'Did you see Mother's face when she ordered you out of the house?' giggled Cara.

'You'd better not fall in love with a rake,' grinned Julian. 'If you do, she'll be apoplectic.'

Gaiety filled the rest of the morning as they walked through Whitby's narrow streets and along the west pier. They enjoyed the exhilarating feeling of the fresh breeze that brought a heavy running sea with white-capped waves beating into the shore, crashing against the pier and swirling where they met the river water.

Charles was awaiting them when they arrived for their appointment at the Angel Inn. Over a most enjoyable meal they amused him by recounting Julian's encounter with Cara's mother.

'What are your plans for this afternoon?' enquired Charles.

'Is there anything special you would like to do?' Anna asked Julian.

'If you young ladies feel up to it, I'd like to walk to the abbey.'

Anna glanced at Cara, who gave a little nod to indicate her agreement.

'Very well, the abbey it shall be,' agreed Anna. She looked at her brother. 'What time do you want to leave for home?'

'Whenever you are ready. I'll get here just after four.'

As they crossed the bridge Julian paused to admire the ships at their berths upstream. They turned into Church Street but did not pause at any of the shops. They passed the ends of alleys and yards climbing the cliff on one side and running down to the river on the other. Housewives sought out the necessary shops to fulfil their wants, sailors seized a respite at the inns, clerks hurried about their master's business, and boys ran in chase, teasingly mocking girls, checked by their mothers' experience. Anna, Cara and Julian, caught up in the ebb and flow of people, separated and came together again.

Anna reached the end of Church Street close to the bottom of the hundred and ninety-nine steps that climbed the cliff to the parish church and the abbey beyond. She turned to find Julian close behind her but there was no Cara. She looked beyond him trying to identify her friend among the mass of people. She strained to catch a glimpse of her. She saw her, but she was walking back the way they had come. What was she doing? She knew they were going to the abbey. Anna saw Cara stop and look in her direction. Anna waved. Cara responded. Then Anna realised she was indicating for her and Julian to go on without her and that she would go home. Anna knew that Cara thought she was playing gooseberry.

Julian had seen her too. 'It appears she is not coming,' he said quietly.

'Should we go after her?' Anna did not know what she wanted the answer to be. Did she want to be alone with him or not?

They saw Cara start to walk away from them.

'She seemed to indicate for us to go on. Will she be all right?' asked Julian.

Anna gave a small smile. 'Cara is not as innocent as her mother thinks. She can look after herself. I've seen her put leering drunks in their place when we have been out shopping.'

'If you are sure. Then I would still like to see the abbey.'

'Very well.'

They climbed the steps, pausing a couple of times to get their breath while admiring the view across the red roofs and the river. They strolled among the ruins, Anna telling him as much of the abbey's history as she knew.

'You recounted that with real enthusiasm and love of the place, as you did this morning about other aspects of Whitby,' said Julian when they left the abbey.

'Did I?' Anna smiled. 'I suppose I do love Whitby, it's an interesting place, but I wouldn't like to live here.'

'I didn't think you would. Your heart is at Hawkshead.'

'You are perceptive.'

'That is because you interest me.'

'An analyst?'

They had turned to stroll along the cliff top. It was something they had done automatically. When Anna thought back to these moments she realised that neither of them had suggested it. It was as if their minds were as one.

Julian smiled. 'Not at all. I didn't mean it to sound like that.'

'What should it have sounded like?' The words were out before Anna realised that they might sound as if she was leading him on. Did she really want to know the answer to her question? Deep down she knew she did. Was she falling under Julian's spell?

'It should have sounded as if I was interested in you as a person. That I would like to spend time in the company of Anna Mason, to get to know her better and hopefully for her to get to know me better too.' He stopped and turned her to him. 'Anna, I think I'm falling in love with you.' His eyes glazed. The world around him had disappeared. There was only the two of them. No one and nothing else mattered to him.

Her heart raced. Confused feelings rushed to her mind. They came and went so quickly she could not sort them out – aspects of him she admired, doubts she still had. His charm and wit were tainted by the air of mystery that surrounded him, as if she had not yet seen the whole person. Until she was able to penetrate that layer, could she ever be sure of her feelings?

His lips came to meet hers as his arms slid round her waist and drew her to him. They lingered there, expressing his feelings for her. She wanted to draw away, yet she didn't. She enjoyed the sensation of his lips on hers and the welling up of desire that came with his delicate touch.

When their lips parted, she stepped back. She felt his arms resist her movement for a brief moment and then let her go, but his hands took hers. He looked contrite. 'I'm sorry if I have offended you but...'

'Julian, you haven't. Please don't think that. But I'm not sure that I feel the way you do.'

'But there is hope for me?' he asked.

'If I want no more attention from you, I will tell you so.'

'Is there someone else?'

She shook her head. 'No. There is no one else.'

'Then you can expect me to go on trying to persuade you.' He kissed her gently on the cheek.

As he drew back she stopped him and returned his kiss. She gave a little laugh. 'I wonder what Mrs Blenkinsop would say if she could have seen us?'

'No doubt tut-tutted and looked disgusted. I wonder if Mr Blenkinsop still kisses her?'

She laughed at the thought. 'What will you think of next? Come on, it's time we were getting back.'

As they set off he slipped his fingers in hers and she did not draw her hand away.

'Father, what are we doing about the run of tobacco and porcelain tomorrow night?' Charles put the question when he went to John's study to say goodnight.

'I saw Sir Arthur yesterday. All the arrangements have been made for tomorrow night. You

335

and I? Well, we can't both be absent from the house when Julian is here. It will look better if you are at home, so I'll go and stay with Sir Arthur the night.'

'I was surprised that you invited Julian at this time.' Charles looked disappointed that he was not going to be actively involved even though there could be danger.

'I'm sorry, but it was an oversight on my part, an automatic reaction to the kindness the Kirbys showed me and Julian's offer of a passage by sea.'

Anna was surprised the following morning when her father told her that he would be visiting Sir Arthur Foston later that day and would be staying the night with him. She had thought he would not have absented himself when Julian was there. However, she realised that whatever the business was it must be important so she raised no objection.

John left shortly after midday and the young people walked in the gardens and in the woods, enjoying the peace and quiet and each other's company. After dinner they settled in the drawing room and relaxed with a glass of Madeira. After a while Anna noticed that Charles was becoming restless. Julian would not realise it, but she knew the signs – he wasn't comfortable in his chair, his conversation became a little stilted, he fiddled with the stem of his glass or ran his fingers along the chair-arms. She wondered about the reason. Had it something to do with their father? Did Charles know something about this business appointment that was going to keep John away from Hawkshead Manor for the night? She would have liked to question him, but she could not do so in front of Julian.

She knew what might calm her brother. She rose from her seat and went to the piano. The notes of Schubert's Piano Quintet in A major filled the room with their soothing sound. It was his favourite. Charles relaxed and his mind drifted away from the beach at Sandsend. He rested his head against the back of his chair and closed his eyes, letting his imagination roam in the idyll conjured up by the notes. The last of them faded but the silence that followed was still filled with magic. Anna started to idle with the keys. Charles pushed himself from his chair, smiled his thanks at his sister and walked thoughtfully from the room.

Anna drifted into some Mozart. As the notes flowed she sensed a special magic spread through the room, different from other times when she had played it, alone or for her father. This time there was only Julian.

The last note hung in the air. He stood up slowly as if any sudden movement would destroy the enchantment that surrounded him. Anna sat still, her eyes on the keys, her hands in her lap. Julian crossed the room, bent and kissed the top of her head. She half-turned and looked over her shoulder. He met her eyes and then leaned further forward to kiss her on her lips. She allowed the kiss to linger. When she moved he slid on to the piano stool into the space she had made for him.

'That was wonderful,' he said, taking her hands

in his. 'How did you know it was a piece special to me?'

'I didn't.'

'Then there must be a unique affinity between us. We must be closer than we thought. I love you, Anna Mason.'

She met his gaze which spoke of his deep feelings. She was racked by indecision. There was a lot to be admired in him but there was still doubt nagging at the back of her mind.

'Julian, I'm still not sure.' Her face creased with uncertainty.

'But you...'

'Please don't say any more.' She stood. 'I'm sorry, but at this moment I cannot say for sure how I feel.'

'If there is a chance...'

'Who knows what life may bring?'

Anna was thankful that, before any more could be said, Charles returned.

'Edwin, this contraband must be away as quickly as possible. Sir Arthur has arranged for a rapid onward despatch so that our customers can have these new goods without delay.' There was just a touch of worry in John's voice as he and Edwin, collars turned up against the wind, sought shelter close to the end of the cutting they would use to get the goods away from Sandsend.

'Everything is ready,' Edwin reassured him. 'When the ship is sighted you'll see a flood of men and women on the beach. I briefed them all yesterday as to what they had to do.'

'Good. If this is successful it will spike the

efforts of those who are trying to take some of our trade away. I can only think they must be the Upton brothers.'

'I'm sure you're right,' said Edwin, hoping that Nick and Ralph had had no trouble at Amsterdam. Dealing with a new supplier for the first time might prove tricky. He took a flask from his pocket and offered it to John who accepted it gratefully. The cold was beginning to bite into his bones. He took a swig and felt the brandy catch at this throat and then contest the chill that had threatened to drive him to seek shelter.

'Thanks,' he said as he handed the flask back. 'That's better. Sorry I forgot mine.'

Silence settled between them, each wrapped in his own thoughts as they awaited the signal. The night seemed exceptionally dark. The wind, though not strong, blew in from the sea and tempted the waves to break with a crash and unsettle pebbles and sand along the beach. Minutes seemed to stretch endlessly. John began to grow uneasy. This was a run that had to go right. He drew some measure of comfort from the fact that his spies had reported that there was no movement from the Preventive Men. They seemed content to sit around their fire this evening. But there were still risks: betrayal in Amsterdam, damage to the ship, seizure by a Revenue cutter. All sorts of possibilities leading to failure prowled his mind.

'There!' Edwin's sharp word broke into John's thoughts. They undermined his concentration and he missed the brief flash of the exposed light. He stiffened. His eyes strained against the darkness, willing the seconds to pass so he could see for himself the signal repeated.

It came. 'Get them away, Edwin.' Excitement had come to John's voice. Action was in the offing. The cold was forgotten.

Edwin ran down the beach towards the men clustered around three boats. 'Away!' he called as he neared them. 'Away!'

Hands on the bulwarks, men pushed the boats into the sea. Waves crashed against the bows. Ignoring the spray that soaked them, the men pushed harder, then, feeling the boats grow buoyant, scrambled on board, dipped the oars, and in unison set the boats towards the tiny light.

Men and women swarmed across the sand to be ready by the waterline for the return of the boats. Few words were spoken. Everyone knew exactly what they had to do.

The boats were lost to sight in the troughs of the undulating sea, to reappear again on the crest of the waves. Then distance took them from sight. Those on shore waited, eager to receive the contraband, anxious in case anything should go wrong.

A buzz went along the beach. The first boat was in sight on its return journey. It crested a wave, then was gone. Everyone was tense, urging it to appear on the next wave but it did not. There was nothing – only the dark sea. Anxiety gripped John. Where was it? What had happened? Then he saw it, upside down, held by a wave for a moment as if it was deliberately mocking their efforts. John cursed. Valuable contraband lost, the first time they had shipped tobacco and porcelain, but worse than that, men's lives were at risk. He ran to the boat he always had standing by for such an emergency. By the time he reached it the crew already had it in the water. He splashed through the waves, grabbed the bulwark and hauled himself aboard. The crew were already plunging their oars into the sea and then, as one, rowing as fast as they could, battling against the waves that would have driven them back and foiled a rescue.

John took over the tiller and, though the rowers needed no encouragement from him, exhorted them to greater effort. It seemed an eternity to everyone on board but in fact it took only a few minutes of hard rowing before they were alongside the overturned boat, thankful to see the whole crew clinging to it. As the boats bobbed on the water, eager hands hauled the stricken men to safety and the overturned boat was taken in tow. Reaching the shore, John ordered the men soaked by sea water to be taken to one of the cottages, given a change of clothing and a stiff drink of brandy.

There was still contraband to be dealt with. The operation could not stop. He delegated a new crew to take the boat to the ship lying offshore. The other two boats were nearing them. They ran aground. The beach became alive with people taking barrels and chests to safety, heading for prearranged storage places, each one knowing they would be well paid for their night's work. John and Edwin supervised the whole operation, encouraging here, cajoling there, eager to see this run to a quick and successful conclusion.

An hour later the beach lay quiet. Only the sea washed its way up the sand, came to a stop as if it could not find the strength to go further, then ran back to try again.

'You're just in time to say goodbye to Julian,' said Anna when her father returned to Hawkshead Manor the next morning.

'I had it in mind to see him before he left,' he replied as he took off his overcoat and handed to Elsie who had answered the doorbell. 'Where is he?'

'He'll be down in a moment. Charles and I are going to Whitby to see him off. We're to have some chocolate before we leave, come and join us.'

'Gladly. It's a bit sharp out there.' John followed his daughter into the drawing room.

'Did you get your business settled with Sir Arthur?'

'Oh, yes.'

'And no doubt had a pleasant evening afterwards?' she added with a smile, knowing that Sir Arthur's hospitality was second to none.

'We did,' replied her father, crossing the room to the fire. He held his hands towards the flames, then stood with his back to them. 'It was most relaxing.' Far from it, he thought as his mind returned to the hectic scene on the beach. If he had been coming straight home and not staying the night with Sir Arthur, he would have had some awkward questions to answer about the state of his clothes.

The door opened and Charles appeared.

'Ah, Father, did all go well?'

John knew the question really referred to the contraband run. 'Yes,' he replied.

'And your business was concluded successfully?'

'It certainly was.'

'Good.' Charles was visibly relieved.

'Father's just told me he had a relaxing time,' said Anna. 'You know how that would be with Sir Arthur.'

Charles smiled. 'I certainly do.'

'He was in good spirits,' said John. 'He and the family were asking after you both. I warned them about the party next month. You'll have to be getting the invitations out.'

'I have them all ready, Father. John will be delivering them during the next four days.'

'Good.'

There was a gentle knock on the door. It opened and two maids brought in the chocolate. As they were going out Julian appeared. 'Hello, sir,' he said, crossing the room to John. 'I am so glad you are back so that I can thank you for your hospitality.'

'Think nothing of it, my boy. It has been good to have you. I hope you have enjoyed it and feel better for the change, short though your stay has been?'

'I have enjoyed every minute of it.'

'Good. Then come again, and next time bring that charming sister of yours.'

Anna had poured the hot chocolate. Half an hour later Charles was taking the reins as, suitably wrapped against the chill, they settled

343

themselves in the carriage. The final goodbye was said to John and Charles set the horses at a brisk pace towards Whitby.

He brought them to a walking pace when they reached Green Lane and started the descent to the east side of the river where they knew Julian's ship would be berthed. As they drove along Church Street they saw a hive of activity on the vessel. Men heaved sacks on to their shoulders and hurried up one gangplank, to return empty-handed down the one nearby and repeat the operation. The stream of men at this work continued for another ten minutes by which time all the cargo had been loaded. Captain Walford was supervising the preparations for sailing, sending his men about their tasks with a sharp tongue.

As Charles pulled them to a halt a young urchin and his friend ran to the vehicle, brushing two others out of their way in their eagerness to be the ones to offer their services.

'Shall we look after your horses, mister?' they called.

'Aye.' Charles grinned and tossed the reins to them. They caught them with an aplomb that expressed their ability and thanks. He jumped to the ground, fished in his pocket and presented the boys with a penny each. 'Just hold them steady, we'll only be here while this ship sails.'

'Aye, aye, sir,' they cried in imitation of the many times they had heard such acknowledgement by Whitby sailors.

Charles turned to see Julian helping Anna to the ground. He took Julian's valise from the carriage and the three of them took up a position nearer the gangplank. Charles cast his eyes over the scene. There was bustle and rush all around the departing ship. This was nothing exceptional when a vessel was close to sailing. Further along the quay there was also much activity as two other vessels prepared to leave on the tide. Noise, rising and falling, pierced by raucous shouts of command, abuse and laughter, swirled around the ships, fled along the quay and ricocheted off buildings, while over all there floated the plaintive screech of seagulls weaving their invisible paths on the wind.

'Looks as though we'll have about ten minutes,' observed Charles who had watched many a ship leave from these quays.

'Thank you for a splendid time,' said Julian. 'And I would like to thank you both for your friendship. It means a great deal to me.'

'As yours does to us,' said Charles. He glanced around and then said, 'Excuse me, there's someone I want to see.' Without waiting for a word from them, he hurried off.

Surprised by the suddenness of this Anna watched him, wondering who he had seen. His step was quick, with an urgency about it. He weaved and twisted his way through the crowds. She saw him reach out and grasp someone by the arm. Recognition passed between the men and Anna saw them immediately fall into an earnest conversation. She did not recognise the other. Then her attention was drawn from the incident as Julian's voice penetrated her thoughts.

'Anna, this gives me the opportunity to say

345

once more that you have captured my heart and it pains me to have to return to Hull. I wish I did not have to do so, then I would have more time to persuade you that I do really mean it when I say I love you. It would give me the chance to break down the barrier that is holding you back from saying the same.'

She blushed and cast a quick glance around her, hoping there had been no one within earshot of his words. 'Dear Julian, I am honoured that you feel this way but, as much as I like you, I dare not commit myself in the way you would like.' Her expression was a mixture of sorrow and pain mingled with pleading for him to understand.

He gave a wan smile. 'I will think of you always and take heart from the fact that you said there was no one else. Please think of me sometimes.'

She laid her hand gently on his arm. 'I will.' She glanced in the direction of her brother and was pleased to see him turning away from the man to whom he had been speaking.

'Who was that?' she asked when Charles reached them.

'Just someone we employ from time to time,' he replied, casually dismissing the incident. He certainly wasn't going to tell his sister that the person to whom he had been speaking was Nicholas Laven, a vital cog in a smuggling venture run by their father. He was relieved when, as he gave her his answer, a shout came from the ship calling for the gangplanks to be hauled in. Julian made his last goodbyes. He was on the gangplank and then the deck before any more could be said. He dropped his valise beside him as he stood by the rail and waved to them.

Ropes were cast off. The ship was eased away from the quay by the rowing boats that would tow her carefully through the drawbridge which had been raised and then on towards the gap between the stone piers.

Julian kept his eyes on his friends and waved. They returned his gesture. He let his eyes rest on Anna, concentrated his gaze and waved again, gently but full of meaning for her. She read it and raised her hand in acknowledgement but let it contain no more expression than that.

Charles had noticed Julian's gaze on his sister. 'I believe he thinks a great deal of you,' he said quietly.

She made no comment but watched Julian's ship out of sight on its way to the sea.

Chapter Fifteen

'I don't like it.' Luke Upton's face was dark with anger as he eyed his brothers across the table in his farmhouse.

The wind blew across the Humber and howled round the chimney pots as if mocking his recent unsuccessful incursions into the smuggling trade around Whitby.

His brothers, also grim-faced, tightened their lips. The extra shipment of contraband called for by Luke had been arranged by Julian without any trouble. The Dutch vessel had reached the Yorkshire coast on time and, after outmanoeuvring the Revenue patrol at the mouth of the Humber, had been guided successfully by Greg and Mike to the chosen creek. Unloading had gone well, as had the storing of the goods in new places organised by Luke. It was after that that things had gone wrong. The agents he had set up in the Whitby area had reported that interest had waned among their customers. Enquiries surreptitiously made to find the reason had brought the disturbing news that the Whitby smugglers had countered the Uptons' plan by making available tobacco and porcelain at a good price to customers who purchased their other goods as well.

'Can't we go into the tobacco and porcelain trade?' Mike suggested.

'Talk sense, man.' Luke snorted in disgust. 'The Whitby men have never handled those commodities until now. It's obvious they've done so to try to keep us out of their territory. They'll have made sure we can't muscle in on that trade. Have the supplier tied up so those goods aren't available to anyone else.'

'Then we'll have to be content to stay as we are,' said Greg.

Luke cast a venomous look at his brother. 'You getting cold feet? Father will be turning in his grave, hearing you say that. What the hell do you think he would have done?'

'Gone after them,' muttered Mike.

'Aye, and that's what we'll do.'

'Not another Owthorn?'

'No. Not unless it's necessary. Get the top man, that's all. He must be the one who has the contacts for the porcelain and tobacco. We'll eliminate him.'

'But he may not be the only one who knows them.'

'True,' agreed Luke. 'But get rid of him and it will make the others think, make them wary. That's when we'll bring pressure to bear in other ways.'

'What about Julian?' asked Greg. 'Remember, he said no more killing?'

'He need never know what we've done. It was his idea to see to the Dutch side of our enterprise and, because of our previous connections, to let us organise things here.'

'Get rid of him and we'll do it all,' suggested Mike.

Luke gave a short derisive laugh. 'Think, man! Get rid of him and we've lost the valuable Dutch connection.'

'We could do it.'

'He's known to the supplier. If someone like us stepped in the supplier would be wary. Julian is important to us and, remember, he set all this up through Bill Grimes. If anything happened to him, Bill would be suspicious. There is no need for him to know what we do after the contraband is landed.'

'Do you know who the leader of the Whitby smugglers is?' asked Greg.

Luke shook his head and pulled a face. 'No. It's a well-kept secret. He must be someone in a powerful position or head of a syndicate of gentry who have a loyal following. But there are ways and means of finding out when you want to know something.'

'The thirtieth of January – we'll have the next business meeting then if that date is convenient to you?' John looked at his daughter as he made the proposal.

'Certainly,' replied Anna. 'You want me to be hostess again?'

'Of course, you were a success last time.'

'Thank you, Father.'

'It's not too near the party in February?'

'No. Everything is in hand for that.'

'Good.'

'Replies to the invitations are already coming in. By the way, I've had an acceptance from the young man you met in Holland.'

'Lambert Finch? I think you'll like him. And the Kirbys? De Klerks?'

'Yes.'

'Splendid. How many do you expect altogether?'

'Forty including us.'

'I am pleased you kept to this format for our first party.'

'As I told you when you approved the idea, Mrs Denston and I thought it best to keep the bigger celebration for my birthday.'

'A very sensible idea. You will have had the experience of arranging this one before then. Your mother made the Hawkshead parties special so people will be curious to see how you compare.'

'Don't make me more nervous than I am already!'

'You'll be wonderful. I have every faith in your abilities, Anna.'

The dinner in January went as well as the previous one, the guests more than delighted to have Anna as their hostess again. They all fell under her spell and expressed regret when she rose to leave them to their port and business talk.

She was halfway up the stairs when she realised that she had left her reticule on her chair in the dining room. It was an automatic reaction for her to retrieve it and she was down the stairs and across the hall almost before she realised it. Nearing the door, she faltered. She would be interrupting a business meeting. Or maybe they hadn't started yet. Could she hear if they had? She lightened her step, then realised that the

351

voices were louder than she had expected. She saw that the door had not fully closed when she had left the dining room. It stood only slightly ajar and nobody in the room would have noticed it.

She caught her father's voice. 'I'm pleased to report, gentlemen, that the new shipment of tobacco and porcelain was successfully disposed of and our customers were delighted. It also meant we won back those who had deserted us for the cheaper brandy and lace.'

'That was a smart move of yours, John.' The words of approval were met with murmurs of agreement.

'Are there to be any more such runs?' someone asked.

'Yes. I made an agreement with the Pawls that they should only supply us so that we have the monopoly of the tobacco and porcelain trade in Yorkshire. Those who are trying to infiltrate our trade here can't use those commodities.'

An exchange of further comments, all coming at the same time, was indistinguishable to Anna. Then a voice she recognised as Sir Arthur Foston's rose above the others. 'John, be careful, there are other and more dangerous ways rivals can hit back.'

Anna was riveted, but chilled, by the implications of what she was hearing. Her father a smuggler! Charles, too, for he was in the room. And all their friends, pillars of local society, people who were respected and looked up to, were similarly engaged in an illegal trade fraught with danger.

'You mean my life?' She heard her father

chuckle. 'Ah, but no one knows my involvement apart from you.'

'You overlook the fact that you play an active part on the beach. You are known to all our helpers.'

'You think, thirty pieces of silver ... I doubt it, gentlemen. We pay our people well in money and kind. Betray me? No. They would have too much to lose and ultimately their own lives would be forfeit.'

Murmurs of agreement to this did nothing to ease the horror of the knowledge Anna had gained.

'Charles, we are a decanter of port short, can you rectify it, please?'

Prey to doubt and distress, Anna was only half-conscious of the request. The scraping of a chair brought the realisation that her brother would soon be coming out of this door. Panic gripped her. She glanced round, seeking a place of concealment. The well of the stairs was cloaked in darkness. She moved quickly out of the light cast by the oil lamps in the hall and on the stairs. She held her breath, suddenly fearful to betray her presence. She pressed back against the wall as if that would further shield her.

The door opened. Charles appeared, closed the door behind him and headed for the kitchens and the wine cellar.

Anna was torn between escape up the stairs and the desire to hear more. Those moments of indecision solved her dilemma for she heard Charles returning. He couldn't have been to the cellar. She must stay where she was. She felt horribly exposed. Surely he must see her? He entered the hall. It appeared to her as if he was coming straight to her, but when he reached the door to the dining room she realised her imagination had played tricks. He disappeared and shut the door firmly.

The tension drained from her, though she was still caught up in the confusion of her unexpected discovery and what she had overheard. She glanced towards the door. It was tightly closed. She would hear nothing more.

Her legs felt leaden as she climbed the stairs, each step feeling as if she was climbing a mountain. She reached the landing. The door to her room seemed miles away. Then she was there, pushing it open, closing it behind her. She sank wearily back against it, her mind trying to make sense of these new developments.

Two oil lamps, placed strategically so that light penetrated as far as the corners of the room, burned steadily. Her dressing table was laid out neatly with brushes, comb, trinket box, hand mirror, pair of candlesticks. Armchairs stood on either side of the window across which heavy velvet curtains were drawn. The wardrobe which held her clothes and the inviting bed were silent witnesses to normality. But Anna knew that the knowledge she had just gained changed everything for her. The future would always be laced with fear. Whenever her father and brother said they would be returning late or staying away she would know what lay behind their seemingly innocent absence. And she would fear for their safety until they returned.

She pushed herself from the door, walked wearily to the bed and sat down, shoulders hunched in despair. She felt her eyes mist but forced herself to hold back the tears. She would not cry, that would not solve anything. With that first spark of determination she realised that she must face the future with the same firm resolution. Before morning she must resolve what she was going to do. Should she say nothing, keep what she had learned a secret, locked away in her own mind? Should she confront Charles? Her father? Both?

Larger questions occurred to her too. When had the smuggling started? Was it a recent innovation or had it been operating in her mother's time? If it had, did she know about it? If so, had she condoned it? If she had been against it, had Father overruled her? But that would have led to disagreement and Anna had never known a harsh or wrong word between them. Why was there any need for her father, or indeed any of those men to whom but a short while ago she had acted as hostess, to be involved in smuggling? Was it to line their pockets or did they experience a thrill in outwitting the law? And how did her father come to be the leader as it appeared he was from what she had heard? All these questions and more were overshadowed by the one vital question she continually put to herself. What am I going to do about it?

Anna awoke with a start, puzzled for a moment by the fact that she was still dressed. Her mind cleared and was immediately assailed by her problem again. She realised that weariness must have overtaken her and, not conscious of her action, she had slumped on the bed and fallen asleep.

She pushed herself to her feet, went to the ewer, poured some water into the bowl and splashed her face. She glanced at the clock and saw that it was five o'clock. She was in limbo. Her mind was too active for her to sleep any more and it was too early to get up. She slumped in one of the chairs and eventually brought order to her thoughts. By the time she set about her morning toilette she knew what she was going to do.

After exchanging greetings with her father and brother, who were already in the dining room, Anna asked, 'Did you have a good business meeting last night?'

'Yes, excellent,' her father replied. 'Thank you for your contribution to the meal beforehand. You charmed everyone, Anna, and that put them in a good mood later which is ideal for a business meeting. I don't think you really appreciate how much you contribute and I thank you again.'

She felt uneasy at this praise in the light of what she had overheard. It made her feel like an eavesdropper. She had to reassure herself that it had been an accident. With her father in such a mood of elation she could not break her shattering news now. Instead she said, 'What are you doing today?'

'I have some things to see to on the estate,' he replied. 'Depending on how I get on, I might go to Whitby this afternoon but I will be back for the evening meal.'

Anna nodded. 'And you, Charles?'

'I will be going to Whitby this morning.'

'I might come with you as far as the church-yard,' said Anna. 'It looks a fine morning for a ride.'

'Good. I'll be pleased of your company.'

Half an hour later, brother and sister were riding away from Hawkshead Manor, heading for the path that would take them along the cliffs, past the abbey to the parish church.

Anna toyed in her mind with how she should put her queries. The enormity of what the answers would reveal almost made her change her mind. Maybe it would be better for her not to know. Maybe it would be better to leave the questions unasked.

Her course was decided for her when Charles said, 'There's something on your mind, Anna. What is it?' She cast him a startled look that brought a further comment. 'Don't deny it. I know you too well. At breakfast your behaviour was forced, though I don't think Father noticed. And since we left home you have been quiet and withdrawn.' He halted his horse, causing her to do likewise. 'Tell me,' he said, his eyes fixed firmly on her. 'Let me help you if I can.'

She avoided his gaze.

'What was your business meeting about last night?' she asked eventually.

He was surprised at the question. She had never been curious about these meetings before. What had sparked this off? 'Trade. Why do you ask?'

'Don't try to put me off, Charles. I want the truth.' A hostile note had come into her voice.

'It was about trade,' he replied firmly.

'Yes, trade, but what sort?'

'What we trade in – goods.'

Her face took on a sterner look and she steadied her horse with a firmer hand. 'Don't play with me, Charles. I know more than you think. Last night when I left the dining room...' She went on to tell him what had happened and what she had overheard.

His heart sank as she made her revelations. He could not deny the smuggling now she knew, even though her knowledge was only partial. By the time she had finished speaking, his expression was one of embarrassment and concern. Like their father he had hoped that Anna would never find out. Now she had.

'Do you want to ask Father about this?' he asked tentatively.

'I'd like to hear it from you first, then we can face him together.'

The horses were growing restless.

'I'll explain while we ride.' Charles put his mount to a walking pace which Anna matched. 'Three years before Mother died the business got into difficulties. I don't know all the details and they don't matter now. Besides, it was before I was involved in it, but once I was Father thought it wisest for me to know everything. I think he thought it better for me to hear it from him rather than gossip or hearsay. I should say that Gideon knows nothing about the smuggling – he believes that some of Father's friends helped the legitimate business by making loans.'

'Why didn't Father seek help that way instead of turning to smuggling?' asked Anna.

'You know him, he's a proud man. Didn't want to beg from friends. Instead he put a new enterprise before them. They liked the idea and a smuggling syndicate was formed with Father as its head and organiser.'

'But the risks?'

'I'll not deny there are those but with members of the syndicate being men of authority in the community it was possible to escape severe punishment or have cases dismissed as not proven. It was an audacious move by Father but the money he made from it saved the family business.'

'Why didn't he give up once the trouble was over?'

'The organisation was running smoothly. They were all making money, and regarded themselves as doing a public service by providing cheap goods – they were freetraders.'

'Don't mince words with me, trying to justify what they were doing – they were smugglers,' said Anna indignantly.

'That's as may be, but you've lived off the proceeds too.'

'Did Mother know about it?'

Charles shook his head. 'No. Father did not want her or you to know.'

'Well, I do now. I'm glad she didn't.'

'Don't you think she would have supported him?' Seeing her hesitate over her answer, Charles went on, 'I'm sure she would. They loved each other so much, they supported each other in everything. She would have done so if he had told her that the best way to save a business in difficulties and preserve the life we lead was to go into the smuggling trade.' He gave a slight pause and then added with emphasis, 'Please support Father as she would have done.'

Anna remained silent. They had reached the churchyard. They walked to their mother's grave without speaking. They stood there a few minutes, each lost in their own thoughts. Charles turned to go, touching Anna lightly on the arm. She raised her hand without looking at him, a signal for him to leave her.

She continued to look down at the headstone. Slowly her eyes moved to the grass mound below which her mother lay at peace. 'Thank goodness you are ignorant of the turmoil that has entered my life,' she whispered.

Silence enveloped the scene. Even the breeze had stilled. Anna stood transfixed as she heard a familiar voice.

'Charles is right. Give your father all your support in what he does as I would have done. Give him your love and mine.'

The words seemed to float from nowhere. As they drifted away she looked round. She expected to see ... but that was nonsense. How could she? Her mother lay at her feet. But Anna was not mistaken – she *had* heard that voice. She started. The silence all around was broken. Seagulls gave their plaintive cry on the breeze that kept them airborne.

Anna said a silent thank you and walked slowly

to the gate. There she paused and looked back, feeling at one with the mother she loved dearly.

'I think Anna has something she would like to discuss with you.' Charles addressed his father as they sat down in the drawing room after their evening meal.

'Is she afraid to put the proposition herself?' asked John as he made himself comfortable in his chair and reached for the cigars that he kept in a box on the occasional table beside him.

'No, I'm not,' she replied curtly, annoyed that Charles had pre-empted her, causing her father to voice a suggestion he surely knew to be false. 'It's Charles who is afraid that I'm not going to mention something that has been troubling me. When he and I spoke this morning he thought that I should.' She looked at him. 'You needn't have worried. Since you left me I have decided that it is in the best interests of all of us that I reveal to Father I know of his smuggling activities.'

This revelation startled John who looked up sharply from the cigar he had been examining. He frowned at his daughter. 'How could you? It's a secret I withheld from you and your mother.'

Anna told him quickly how she had learned about it, how she had tackled Charles that morning and what he had told her.

Her father said nothing until she had finished. 'So now you know. What does it mean to you that your father and brother are smugglers? And, more to the point, what are you going to do about it?'

'I was shocked at what I heard, devastated

361

when I thought about it, but I eventually accepted it when Charles explained. What will be, will be. I can do nothing about it.'

'Well then, we are all happy and everything is as it was.'

'It is not. I know now, I didn't before.'

'But you just indicated that it makes no difference?'

'It makes a difference to me, and consequently it will to you.'

'What do you mean?'

'If you want my support and blessing for this smuggling, freetrading, call it what you will, then I want to be part of it.'

'I beg your pardon?' Her father sat up, his expression thunderstruck.

'You can't,' put in Charles. 'It's too dangerous.'

'But you implied that the danger was minimal.'

Charles looked to his father for help on this point.

'Anna, there is always danger in smuggling.' John's voice was sombre. 'I could not put you to the risk.' She started to protest but he raised his hand to stop her. 'Let me finish. Charles may have implied that the risk is minimal but I must tell you that we have had trouble with the authorities. I gave instructions that confrontation and violence should be avoided if at all possible but there have been a few bruised heads and broken limbs from time to time. There are other smuggling gangs along the Yorkshire coast but there has always been an unwritten under-standing that we do not infringe on each other's territory. That has changed recently. Another gang has been trying to release goods into our area.' He went on to tell her what had happened and how he hoped he had counteracted it.

When he paused, Anna interjected quickly, 'Do you know who it is?'

'Not with any certainty, but we have our suspicions that it is the Upton gang who work the Humber. Recently they've taken over the region formerly operated by the Wharton gang on the Holderness coast.' He went on to enlighten her on what he knew about the clash between the two rival gangs. 'So you see, if the Uptons have ideas to expand further, we could be facing deadlier encounters because we cannot afford to let them muscle in. The syndicate are agreed on that. I cannot let you be part of it. It's too dangerous. And no one must ever know that you know about our smuggling. Word could get to the Uptons and they might use you to get their way.'

'I understand your concern, Father, but I can be part of it without taking risks. You can tell me all about the organisation, how it operates and what is going on. There can be no harm in that, and then I would share more of your life. I know Mother would have wanted to share it with you if you had let her into your secret.'

John bowed his head. Silence stretched between them. He looked up slowly. 'I suppose if Elizabeth had known she would have insisted, just as you are now.'

'Then let me be part of it by knowing what is happening so that we three can talk openly about it between ourselves. Those discussions need no longer be held back until you two can contrive to be alone, without me.'

John lapsed into deep thought. Anna and Charles knew better than to break his contemplation. He looked up and eyed them both in turn for a moment before he spoke. 'Very well, you shall know what there is to know. You can enlighten her, Charles.' He replaced his unlit cigar in the box, rose from his chair and left them.

Two hours later Anna had full knowledge of how John Mason's smuggling operation came into being, of the formation of the syndicate, how it was run, who their contacts were in Holland, and how the contraband was run from there and disposed of in Yorkshire. 'This threat from the Uptons has pushed us into smuggling wool from England to Holland. The first consignment will be run this week,' her brother explained.

'Who are your suppliers?' asked Anna, who had been enthralled by his account.

'Farmers who run sheep on the moors beyond Whitby, and we shall eventually look to other sheep farmers in the west of Yorkshire.'

'So, unless the Uptons take further action, all is set for a reasonably steady future?'

'It should be. But a word of warning, Anna. Keep this knowledge strictly to yourself. Don't tell a soul, no matter how close you are to someone. Be on your guard not to let something slip inadvertently.'

Anna guessed he was referring to what he thought was her blossoming relationship with Julian. She made no comment but said, 'My lips will be sealed.'

'And don't pester Father to let you take an active part in a run. He'll never allow that.'

A week later, with the knowledge that Nick and Ralph would be running contraband into Sandsend that night, Anna watched from a window as her father and Charles rode away from Hawkshead Manor. She had keyed herself up for this moment ever since she had come into her knowledge of the smuggling, and in spite of her father's refusal she was determined to see an operation in practice.

She changed quickly into her riding habit and hurried to the stables. Though he thought it strange that Miss Anna should be riding when darkness was not far away, the groom made no comment. It was not up to him to do so. He did as he was bidden and soon had her favourite horse saddled.

She rode quickly, avoiding Whitby, and circled inland of Sandsend to swing towards a position on the cliff top overlooking the beach that ran in the direction of Whitby. Anna turned her horse from the path and guided it into a narrow gully lined by stunted trees. After a hundred yards the gully swung to the right. Rounding the bend, she halted her horse and surveyed the prospect as best she could in the gloom cast by the gully's rough slopes. Her horse would be safe here and out of sight of the path she had just left. She slid from the saddle and patted its neck with a comforting hand.

'Stay quiet,' she whispered, close to its ear.

The night was cool but still. A few thin clouds

drifted slowly across the moon to shade the world momentarily before leaving it bathed in pale moonlight. She pulled her cloak around her and drew up its hood to cover her head. She scrambled up the gully's side and was about to head for the edge of the cliff a hundred yards away when she heard voices in a low exchange of words. She froze. They were to her right and slightly behind her. She estimated they must be on the main path and was thankful she had abandoned it. Discovery would be embarrassing after her father's emphatic refusal to allow her to take an active part in the operation.

The voices were drawing nearer. She dropped to the ground and pressed herself close to the earth. Two shadowy figures came into view. Who were they? Would her father send two men up here as lookouts? She doubted it. So what were they doing here? Was their presence in fact connected with the smuggling that would soon be in full flow on the beach below? Perhaps they were Preventive Men. If so, they could spell a threat to her father, brother and the rest of the smugglers. Anna was tense. What could she do? She decided to do nothing until she could interpret the actions of these men.

'What's the plan, Jake?' one of them said.

'Learn as much as we can. The more information we get, the better the Uptons will pay. Especially if we find out who the leader is.'

A chill gripped Anna's heart. The Uptons! She recalled what Charles had told her about them, their deadly action at Owthorn and their attempt to move into her father's territory. Father! He was in danger. Should she warn him? But these men seemed only to be fact-finding, not on a mission to harm him. Maybe she had better try and learn more.

The men had moved out of earshot. She pushed herself slowly from the ground and moved quietly forward, ears tuned to catch the slightest sound that might indicate an alteration in the men's approach to the cliff edge. She sensed the ground in front of her give way to a slight depression. She moved into it and was thankful that it ran to the edge of the cliff. Here she would be hidden from them but near enough to catch the odd word. She sank down, hoping that the men would not come in her direction.

'This'll do, Ned.'

Visualising them settling, Anna breathed a little easier but that did not detract from her alertness.

'We'll see everything from here.'

'Thank goodness our vigil is over soon and we can get back to Hull.'

'Aye, but it will have been worth our while.'

Silence settled over the cliff.

Anna stared out to sea where the undulating waves licked at the trail of light cast by the moon. How long it was before she was startled by the sudden flicker of light she did not know, but immediately her attention was drawn by what was happening on the beach and at sea. Three boats were run out, another held back. They headed for the signal from a ship offshore. Figures swarmed on to the beach as the boats returned. Boxes, casks and bales were unloaded. The boats went back and forth until the final shipment was made and the ship sailed away.

There had been no sound from the two men on the cliff but now one of them spoke. 'Some of the contraband is being stored in the cottages below. Let's find out where exactly and maybe identify the leader of the operation at the same time.'

Anna knew that from their viewpoint they must have been able to see the cottages that bordered the stream forming the small hamlet of Sandsend – the very cottages that Charles had told her their syndicate used. She heard the men move away. Should she follow, try and find her father and warn him? But these men from Hull would take no direct action. They had been sent as spies to gain knowledge on which the Uptons could act. Unmask them now, if indeed they could be found, and the Uptons would be forewarned. Let them go and her father could be prepared for any action the Uptons might take.

Anna suddenly realised that if she told her father he would know she had gone against his wishes. But there was nothing she could do about that. She dare not, for the sake of the syndicate, hold back what she had learned. She cast a last glance at the beach. The remaining figures were leaving. Only the waves moved against the sand now. Her first instinct was to ride to the cottages and find her father or Charles or Edwin, but she might be seen coming from the cliff top by the two men from Hull and that would alert them.

Although she took a circuitous route home she was still there before her father and brother. She was sitting in a high-backed armchair in the drawing room when she heard them come into

368

the hall and towards the room. The door opened.

'We saw the light under the door. I thought you'd be in bed. There was no need...' her father said as he crossed the room, but his voice trailed off when he saw Anna in her riding habit. Guessing what this meant, his face darkened. 'What's this?' he snapped, indicating her clothes.

'I was at Sandsend.'

Before she could say any more, he cut in harshly. 'I told you the limitations of your involvement, and the first time we run contraband since then you choose to ignore me! You'll get no more information from me.' He swung round on Charles. 'Heed that. No more information for her!' He started towards the door.

'Father!' Anna's tone was so sharp that it brought him to a halt. 'Hear what I have to say. You'll be thankful then I did not stay at home.'

John, his face still dark with anger, turned back. 'Nothing can justify your going against my wishes.'

'It will.' Though her delivery was quiet the two words came with such conviction that John knew he had to listen. Anna saw she had his attention now. 'Sit down, Father. You too, Charles.'

They silently did as they were told, sitting so that they were both facing her, and waited for her to continue.

'I am sorry I disobeyed you, Father, but my curiosity got the better of me.' She went on to relate exactly what had happened and what she had overheard.

John sat silent and thoughtful, staring absently

at the carpet. He grimaced in exasperation. 'Why can't the Uptons be content with their lot? Now there could be the open hostility I've always tried to avoid. Anna, you did well – though I still say you shouldn't have run the risks you did. Those men would have been ruthless if they had seen you. However, they didn't and it was a stroke of luck for us that you did what you did and overheard what you overheard.'

'What are we going to do about them?' asked Charles. 'It seems to me that if they know where we have stored the contraband they'll likely try a raid, thinking no one will guard it with inhabited cottages nearby.'

'More than likely,' agreed his father.

'So we can be ready for them. Give them the surprise of their lives and scare them off our territory.'

John tightened his lips. 'It looks as though it will come to that.'

'Do you think those two men will have seen and identified you?' asked Anna, showing her concern.

Her father shrugged his shoulders. 'We can't tell. All of us will just have to be more cautious. Tomorrow you and I, Charles, will see Edwin, inform him of what Anna heard and plan accordingly.'

Chapter Sixteen

Edwin knew there was something seriously wrong when he opened the door of his Sandsend cottage to a grim-faced John and Charles Mason. He ushered them inside with a nod. Once the door was closed he shot a querying glance from one to the other.

'Trouble, Edwin,' said John as he sat down and leaned on the pine table in the centre of the sparsely furnished room. Edwin waited until Charles too was seated and then pulled out the third chair for himself. John quickly informed him of Anna's exploits the previous night.

Edwin gave a little shake of his head. 'I admire Miss Anna's spirit, but she shouldn't have been there, Mr Mason. Did she not realise the risk she would be running? Still, it's mighty fortunate for us that she was. No doubt the Uptons will try something, but with this knowledge we can outsmart them.'

'I reckon we ought to get the contraband out of these cottages as quickly as possible,' put in a concerned Charles.

'No, Mr Charles, we'll use it as bait and teach the Upton gang a lesson.' Edwin gave him a wicked smile and a knowing wink.

'But we run the risk...'

Charles's objection was cut short by his father. 'No, lad, Edwin's right if his idea is what I think

371

it is. Well, Edwin?'

'I think the Uptons will organise a raid. Knowing that some of these cottages are occupied, they won't expect a guard on the stores. They'll believe they can easily take care of the folk here and have the contraband for the taking.'

'And we'll be waiting for them?' said Charles a touch of excitement in his voice as he realised what Edwin was planning.

'Aye. We'll be well and truly out of sight so that they will think there's no extra men here. They're sure to come by sea because it makes the getaway with the goods easier. I think they'll send a couple of men ashore to scout the site, and finding no one but folk abed, they'll signal to the others to come. The cottages will be watched in case the occupants are disturbed, while the main party takes our goods.'

'And where will we be?' asked John.

'I'll have some of our best men in the occupied cottages. Once the men watching those believe there'll be no opposition forthcoming from that area, they'll relax their vigilance.'

'And that's when we strike?' said Charles.

Edwin nodded. 'Aye.'

'We'll have men elsewhere too?' asked John.

'Oh, yes, Mr Mason. They'll be handy, hidden on the land round about.'

'Good. Then I shall leave the recruitment and organisation to you?'

'Certainly. But there is one more thing. I don't think either you or Mr Charles should be here.'

'Why?' John was taken aback by Edwin's

comment. 'I can't let my men take risks I'm not prepared to take myself. That's one of the reasons I'm always present at a smuggling run.'

'I know that, sir. The men know it too and it's why they would never divulge their knowledge of you to the Revenue.'

'Then I should be here.'

'I will explain and they'll understand. Think, sir. No one apart from the syndicate and the men you employ knows who heads the Whitby gang. From what Miss Anna told you, one of the reasons those two men were here was to try to identify our leader. We don't know whether they did or not but must assume they didn't. We don't want to give them another chance to do so. That is why I think you and Mr Charles should stay away.'

John's lips tightened. Charles's face was a mask of disappointment.

'I appreciate your reasoning, Edwin, but...'

'Sir, excuse me for cutting in, I know you can overrule me but I ask you not to. It will make things easier for me if ... no, *when* the Uptons come. I shan't have to worry about trying to keep you out of sight. In fact, if you are here I know that would be impossible – you are one always to be in the thick of the action.'

John still hesitated to give his approval to Edwin's suggestion.

Charles, though downcast, saw the sense in the reasoning. 'I think Edwin's right, Father. The longer we keep your identity a secret the better.'

John studied his hands a moment then nodded. 'All right.' He saw relief on Edwin's face when he looked up and asked, 'Will you be organised for tonight? We can't be sure when they will come.'

'Everything will be in place by evening and will remain so until the Uptons come. I believe they will act in the next two nights.'

Two figures huddled over in their saddles, jackets buttoned tight around them, caps pulled down over their ears as they rode across the windswept flats that spread towards the Humber. They had not spoken for the last hour. After their time on the cliffs at Sandsend, followed by their cautious nosing around the cottages, the ride from Whitby had been bleak. Sleep tempted them, but to stop in the open could be fatal. Besides they knew Luke Upton would be waiting, and he was not a man to be crossed. As it was they knew they had only half the information he'd wanted, so he would be none too pleased. But they thrust that thought from their minds, anticipating a warm drink, food and sleep. The eastern sky was beginning to show the pale light of a new dawn.

Candlelight burned in an upstairs window at the back of Luke Upton's cottage. It was the signal they'd agreed on that it was safe for them to approach.

Their weariness eased a little when they knew they were within reach of some comfort and would soon be out of the unfamiliar saddles. Though they had both handled horses before they were more used to sailing vessels.

They pulled their mounts to a halt close to the back door and slipped from the saddles. They were stretching their shoulders and easing their backs when the door opened and light from the cottage flooded in one sharp stream across the yard.

'Ah, it's you.' Luke's voice was gruff.

The two men followed him into the house.

'Jim, boy! See to them horses!' Luke's bellow filled the house and brought young Jim scurrying into the kitchen and out through the door. 'Mind you tend 'em right!' his father yelled after him. He looked at the two men and saw how weary they were. 'Sit down, Ned, Jake.' He waved a hand in the direction of the chairs around the oak table. 'Mary,' he called, and when she appeared almost immediately from the scullery, wiping her hands on a hessian apron, he added, 'Food, lass, for these weary travellers.' She scurried away without a word, trying to bring some order to the hair that had escaped from a comb at the back of her head. 'Well, lads, what news?' Anticipating the information he wanted, Luke eyed his two men eagerly.

'Contraband was run ashore last night and most of it is stored in cottages at Sandsend.'

'Empty ones?'

'Aye. Several other cottages are occupied, but we believe that's an advantage. There's not likely to be such a strong guard, if any, on those where the contraband is stored.'

Luke nodded. 'And the other news?'

Jake shook his head. 'We were unable to find out who leads the Whitby gang.'

Luke banged the table in annoyance.

'It's a well-kept secret around Whitby,' put in Ned. 'Folk are loyal. The smugglers treat them

375

right for their loyalty and that means tight lips. If anyone knows, they're not talking.'

Luke cursed under his breath. 'Maybe a raid on those cottages at Sandsend will bring him into the open. Then we can strike at the very heart of his organisation.' He was talking half to himself and lapsed into thought, so much so that he hardly noticed his wife bring in some steaming frumenty, bread, butter and home-made jam.

The two other men muttered their thanks with an appreciative nod and started into the food with gusto.

After five minutes, Luke spoke again. 'I'm putting you two in charge of the raid on those cottages tomorrow night. You need to rest now but we don't want to delay any longer in case they move the contraband.'

'Aren't you going to take charge?' asked Jake.

Luke shook his head. 'No. I think it best if none of the Uptons are there, then there'll be no direct connection with us and the missing goods. You two are capable, I know that from the old days. You were always trusted and praised by the old man, God rest his soul.'

'Aye, God rest his soul,' both men muttered in unison, then waded into their food again.

'Take as many men as you want and go by sea, then the contraband can be run straight back here.'

Some minor details were discussed before Ned and Jake left for a cottage in nearby Paull.

The next day Julian saw a sloop leave Hull. He thought it strange that there were about twenty men lounging on deck, giving every appearance that they were passengers and not on board to work. He was also intrigued by the fact that apart from the usual small boats such a ship carried there were another three tied down on deck. A strange mission, he thought, and his curiosity was roused even further when he recognised two men whom he had seen working with some authority in the Upton gang. But that wasn't their only occupation; no smuggler could rely entirely on that trade for his livelihood.

He watched for a little while and then lost interest when the vessel appeared to be heading for the Lincolnshire coast. Had he taken note longer and not returned to the Kirby office he would have seen the ship alter course and head for the open sea. But seeing the two men had jolted his intention of contacting Luke about the next consignment of contraband to be run from Holland.

The cloud-covered sky brought added depth to the darkness and hid the sloop lying off Sandsend. Ned and Jake climbed down into the boat that had been lowered from the ship. They seated themselves on the thwarts; Jake pushed them away from the side. Ned dipped the oars and with powerful pulls sent the boat through the undulating sea towards the tiny hamlet. The men they had left on board had strict instructions to continue their silent vigil until they received the prearranged signal.

The two men guided the boat to the beach and let it run on to the sand. They were out of the boat in haste and dragged it a few more yards so that it would be beached until required. They made their way swiftly towards the buildings, silent in the cutting against the dark mass of land rising behind them. From their previous visit they knew which cottages contained the contraband, but first they made a quick examination of the others. No sounds came from within, so, satisfied that the occupants were asleep and unaware that intruders stalked around their dwellings, they reconnoitred the remaining buildings and were elated when they found them unguarded. Their supposition had been right.

'The signal, Ned,' Jake whispered. 'I'll stay by the first cottage to direct the men when they come ashore.'

They hurried towards the beach, Ned going to a position where he would be unseen from the cottages should one of the occupants awake. He lit the lantern he had been carrying. When the wick burned steadily he uncovered the glass three times in quick succession and then revealed the light for two longer bursts. He saw an answering flash from the direction of the sloop and knew his signal had been seen. He covered his light for a few minutes and then allowed it to show steadily as a guide to the raiders. He kept his eyes trained on the dark sea until he saw the five boats moving towards the shore. He doused his light and ran to the water's edge.

The boats nosed into the sand. Their occupants jumped out. Ned issued whispered instructions and indicated where Jake would be. Men hastened away, leaving one man in charge of each boat. Ned hurried up the beach with the last man ashore. When they reached Jake, he had already delegated men to watch the occupied cottages and had sent others to get the contraband. Locks were shattered, and doors broken down, with little noise.

Ned and Jake were congratulating themselves on the smoothness of the operation as they supervised the robbery, urging men towards the beach to load the boats with casks, bales and boxes, when there was uproar from the occupied cottages. Startled, they swung round to see men pouring from them, brandishing clubs and swinging them viciously at the thieves heading for the beach. As if their appearance was as a signal, more men appeared from the clefts and hollows beyond the cottages. They swept towards the intruders with heart-shaking yells. Contraband was dropped in their haste to defend themselves. Skirmishes broke out, individual battles ensued, but the element of surprise had given a distinct advantage to Edwin's group. Within a matter of a few minutes the Upton gang, some with blood streaming from their heads, others with bruised and broken limbs, were fleeing for the boats. Jake and Ned saw it was useless to try to rally them, they were outnumbered and would not leave with any contraband this night.

Following Edwin's instructions, his men took no prisoners. He did not want the embarrassment of having to deal with them. He had kept a sharp eye open and had recognised Ned and Jake as men he knew had worked for the old Upton gang. It was almost certain they would have been recruited by the Upton brothers when they decided to start smuggling again.

The Whitby men halted at the edge of the sea. They yelled obscenities and sent jeers resounding across the water at those hastily rowing towards the sloop. When the boats were hardly visible, Edwin called his men to restore what contraband had been removed and dropped in the heat of the attack and the haste to escape. With everything in order, he was generous when he paid them for their night's work. He knew Mr Mason wanted it that way for it cemented loyalty. He dismissed his men and chose to sleep the night in the cottage at Sandsend rather than return to his house in Whitby.

He was up early the next morning and rode to Hawkshead Manor, for he knew Mr Mason and his family would be anxious for news.

Following John's instructions, he was shown quickly to the dining room where the Masons were in the middle of breakfast. All three looked up anxiously when he was announced.

'Good morning, sirs, and you, miss,' said Edwin as he strode in. He could see the question in all their eyes so went straight on to say, 'The attack came last night and we sent 'em away with some aching heads.' He saw relief replace enquiry, and went on to tell them in detail what had occurred. As he did so Anna got him some tea, but he refused her suggestion of something to eat. 'And I can now be certain it was the Upton gang,' he concluded.

'You saw the Upton brothers?' asked John.

'No, sir. They weren't there, but I recognised

380

two men who used to work with their father.'

'It is good to know who we are up against if they continue to try to expand their territory north.'

'If I may say so, sir, there's something that has been puzzling me. Jem was the brains behind the old gang. He was the organiser, the man with whom suppliers dealt. He had the contacts. I doubt if any of his sons could fill that role. They're not well travelled or versed in business.'

'But surely one of them...' started Charles.

Edwin gave a slight shake of his head. 'I don't think so. There was something about the old man that was different. His sons were only good for handling, hiding and distributing the contraband.'

'So what are you saying?' said Anna. 'That there is someone else behind them, doing the buying and running the gang?'

'Well, look at it this way, miss. Their father was killed by the Wharton gang and no effort was made to take revenge then. The Upton gang broke up. Later they appear again. They meet with success, so somebody has been able to revive them and obtain supplies. Upon that success they see a chance of expanding their territory, and at the same time revenging the killing of Jem. But I don't believe any of that would have come about without another's involvement.'

'They won't be so keen on expansion now, after the way you dealt with them last night,' said Charles.

'That's as may be, but it doesn't mean we can abandon our vigilance. The Uptons can be unforgiving.'

'And if what you say is true,' said Anna, 'and there is someone behind them, he could still be bent on his ambition to control smuggling along this coast.'

'That could put you in considerable danger, Mr Mason.'

John started to brush away such fears but was interrupted by his daughter. 'Father, remember, I overheard those two men hoping they could identify the leader of the Whitby smugglers. You've got to be careful.'

'There's nothing to worry about. They don't know who I am.'

'We don't know that for certain, Father,' Charles pointed out.

'If they knew who I was, don't you think they'd have been here before now to make an attempt on my life? None of the servants has seen any strangers and neither have we seen anyone acting suspiciously.'

'Well, we've been fortunate but we can't be too careful,' cautioned Anna.

'Pa! Pa!' Jim's yells brought his father to the door of the cottage. The boy slipped and slithered on the muddy path that led from the waters of the Humber, running as fast as his legs would go. 'The ship, Pa, the ship!'

Luke spun back into the house, grabbed a jacket and was shrugging himself into it as he re-emerged into the open.

'Good, lad,' he praised his son when he reached Jim. He clapped a hand on his shoulder and they both headed for the shore. He knew it would

382

have been a cold wait but his son was a willing lad. He wished he could have done better by him. Well, maybe after the success of snatching the Whitby contraband he would be able to give him some reward.

They reached the water's edge.

'That's it, Pa, isn't it?' Jim knew it was, he had an eye for boats and ships, seeing them every day on the river, but, boy-like, he wanted adult verification.

'Aye, lad, it is, but you don't need me to tell you that,' came the reply to swell Jim's pride in his own ability.

As they watched the sloop draw nearer a sense of foreboding began to come over Luke. There was little activity on deck, apart from those handling the ship to bring her safely into the creek. He had expected men to be at the rail, expressing their elation at a job well done. But there were no joyous shouts, no waving. Instead a mantle of gloom hung over the sloop. Luke cursed to himself.

The sloop anchored. Men piled off her while the crew made her secure.

'Where's the contraband?' Luke demanded, seeing an empty deck.

'They were waiting for us,' replied a downcast Jake.

'Didn't you give 'em a fight or did you scurry like rabbits?' snapped Luke with contempt.

'We were outnumbered. Didn't stand a chance,' protested Ned.

'They must have known you were coming. How the hell did they manage that?'

Jake shrugged his shoulders, shamefaced. 'Don't know, but they were well organised to surprise and repel us so they must have known.'

'Someone talked,' snapped Luke. 'Must have.'

'Couldn't,' replied Jake testily. 'I told none of my men where we were bound until we were at sea.'

Luke grunted. 'Then it's a mystery. I hope you've brought me something to redeem this fiasco – were you at least able to identify their leader?'

'No. The confusion was too great and the night was very dark.'

Luke cursed loudly. 'Something's got to be done to retrieve this situation! I want that Whitby territory more than ever now.' New determination came into his voice as he went on, 'Jake, and you, Ned, see your men know there'll be the devil to pay and they'll have me to reckon with if word of this night's exploits ever gets out. Especially if Mr Julian or Bill Grimes gets to hear of it.'

After passing through Paull, Julian rode nearer the Humber. There was little activity on the river so his attention was drawn to a vessel emerging from one of the creeks a short distance ahead. He reined his horse in and held it steady so he could watch the ship sail into the more open water.

He tensed. He had seen this vessel before. He dredged his mind. Yes, only yesterday, leaving Hull. Men were lounging on the deck, Ned and Jake among them. Two men who had worked with the Uptons. The sloop had been heading for

384

the Lincolnshire coast. Now it was leaving a creek the Uptons used for smuggling. What was going on? Where had this ship been? He set his horse in the direction of Luke Upton's cottage.

Luke was doing some repair work to one of his walls. He turned when he heard the sound of a horse's hooves. Julian's immediate impression was that Luke was not in a good mood and that he tried to hide it quickly by altering his scowl to a more friendly expression.

'Good day,' Julian greeted him amiably.

He nodded. If his grunt was a greeting it couldn't readily be recognised as such. It expressed rather more annoyance at being disturbed.

'I thought we'd better discuss the next cargo from Holland and when we'd like delivery,' said Julian as he swung from the saddle.

'Aye, maybe we should,' agreed Luke. He laid down his tools. 'Let's walk.' He gave Julian no choice and he reckoned that Luke wanted to be out of earshot of the cottage.

They talked about the next smuggling run, came to a satisfactory agreement about the cargo and left the delivery date for Julian to fix when he went to Amsterdam.

During their conversation he detected a lightening of Luke's attitude. The annoyance and edginess Julian had believed to be gnawing at the man when he had arrived at the cottage had all but gone. It was as if the thought of new action had dispelled whatever had been troubling him.

As they turned back Julian remarked, 'On my way here I saw a sloop leaving yon creek. It

385

looked familiar and I remembered I'd seen it leaving Hull yesterday. It had more than its usual complement of men on board. I saw Ned and Jake among them.' He sensed tension return to Luke. 'Anything I should know about?'

'No.' It seemed to Julian that the snap in Luke's voice was a warning for him not to be nosy.

But Julian was curious. If he was to trust these men to work with him then he wanted to know what they were up to. He fished for information by saying, 'The last I saw of it, the sloop was heading for the Lincolnshire coast,' little knowing that he had given Luke the opportunity of an explanation.

He seized on the chance. 'Aye. Ned and Jake had some business of their own. Told me they were hiring a sloop for the job they had on that coast. When I said there were some farm materials I wanted, they offered to get them for me when they were in Lincolnshire. They'd just finished unloading when you saw them.'

Julian nodded his acceptance of the explanation, but felt it had come too glibly from Luke. He wasn't at all sure he had been hearing the truth.

Chapter Seventeen

After the successful repelling of the raiders John suspended all smuggling operations. The members of the syndicate had all accepted his invitation to the party. That would give him the opportunity to acquaint them with recent events and warn them to be on their guard against any attempt to find out more about the Whitby smugglers.

On the night of the party he sat in his chair in the drawing room, staring at the cheerfully burning fire. His thoughts dwelt sorrowfully on the times he had sat here on party nights awaiting his beloved Elizabeth's entrance, radiant in a new dress.

John's throat constricted. He still missed her terribly. He forced himself to hold back the tears. Anna and Charles must not see him like this. Nothing must mar or undermine Anna's confidence or put doubts in her mind about her ability to step into her mother's place this evening. He rose from his chair and straightened his frock coat, drawing himself up and thrusting his shoulders back. The door opened and Anna walked in. He directed a smile of pleasure at her.

'You look radiant, my dear.' He came to her with his arms outstretched and admiration in his eyes. 'That's a beautiful dress.'

She twirled round so he could view it. The

high-waisted dress of pale blue broche silk fitted her to perfection. It fell straight from the waist and was topped by a short bodice, square-cut with cross pleatings. The puff sleeves came tight to her arm just above the elbows. Her brown hair with its hint of copper was brought up from her neck and tied on top of her head by a blue ribbon.

Anna's smile in return was warm and loving. She took his hands and kissed him affectionately on the cheek. 'And you look so elegant.'

A hint of sadness came over him as he said, 'Your mother would have been so proud of you.'

'Thank you, Father. That's the nicest compliment you could give me.'

'A glass of Madeira? We've just time for one before our guests arrive.' He walked across to the sideboard on which there stood glasses and a decanter. He filled two glasses and held one out to her. She took it and waited for him to take his. He raised it. 'To you, my dear.'

She gave a little nod of acknowledgement and took a sip of the wine. She let it linger on her palate, enjoying the sweet taste and smooth flow of the liquid. She took another sip, then pursed her lips and nodded approvingly.

'Nervous?' asked her father tentatively as they sat down.

'A little. It's a big step to take Mother's place on such an occasion, the first party since she died.'

'I know, but I'm sure you'll carry things off in your own delightful way and everyone will be charmed by you.' John eyed his daughter thoughtfully. 'I'm pleased that you and your brother persuaded me to do this. It's not good for me to be lonely even though you and Charles are very much a part of my life.' He gave a start. 'I'm sorry, my dear, I shouldn't go on so.'

'Of course you should, if it helps. There's no harm in it. Both Charles and I feel the same. Where is he, by the way?'

John gave a little chuckle. 'You know your brother, always appearing at the last minute, then he'll walk in as if he had all the time in the world.'

A few moments later he did just that, and casually crossed the room to pour himself a glass of Madeira. 'Well,' he said as he sat down, 'I suppose we can call this our celebration for what happened at Sandsend the other night.' He raised his glass and all three drank to the pleasure of knowing they had outwitted the Upton brothers. But Anna had a lingering worry that if the Uptons found out her father was the leader of the Whitby smugglers his life could be in danger.

Five minutes later such thoughts were driven from her mind when there was a knock on the door and Robert opened it to tell them that the first coach was approaching.

Knowing that the local guests would not be here for another half hour, John remarked, 'This must be the de Klerks and Kirbys.'

'It was hospitable of the Kirbys to invite the de Klerks to stay over night with them in Hull,' commented Anna. 'I'm sure they would be well looked after there.'

They drained their glasses and went into the hall. Anna smoothed her dress as she went and made a resolve that her disturbing thoughts should not be resurrected again this evening. She had a quick word with Robert who left the hall and returned a few minutes later with Mrs Denston, two maids and two man servants.

As the coach rumbled to a stop, Robert opened the front door and hurried down the steps, ready to help the passengers to the ground. All was bustle and fuss as the Masons welcomed their house-guests.

'It's a pleasure to see you again.'

'We are delighted to be here.'

'So pleased to have you.'

'I trust your journey was comfortable?'

'You must be cold.'

While greetings and exchanges were made the servants saw to the baggage and the grooms took charge of the coachman and his coach.

Inside there was bustle. The guests were shown to their rooms and invited to join the Masons when they were ready.

'Julian had eyes only for you,' whispered Charles teasingly to Anna as they returned to the drawing room.

'In your imagination,' she retorted.

'Oh, no,' he contradicted her.

'Well, Rebecca was all blushes when she greeted *you*. What's more, Magdalena managed to tell me she was pleased that Rebecca thought so much of you. Apparently you made up most of their conversation when they were together last night in Hull.'

'You're making that up?'

'We'll see.'

Twenty minutes later Robert informed them

that the next coach, no doubt containing the first of the local guests, was approaching. The Masons returned to the hall.

A quick glance told Anna that everyone was in position to welcome their guests as she had prearranged. Maid and man servants stood by to take charge of coats, hats and other outdoor accoutrements. Others stood ready to serve a warming punch, designed to combat the chill of the evening air.

The first guests to arrive were Sir Arthur Foston and his wife, his daughter and two lusty sons. They were soon followed by Mr and Mrs Blenkinsop and Cara.

'John!' Belinda beamed as he took her hand and raised it to his lips. 'This is indeed an auspicious occasion and one long overdue. It is good to have the Hawkshead parties back and I hope this will not be the only one. I'm sure dear Anna will manage as well as dear, dear Elizabeth.'

Anna, standing beside her father, looked uncomfortable. She caught Cara raising her eyes heavenwards at her mother's lack of concern for other people's feelings. Mr Blenkinsop raised his eyebrows at John as much as to say, Take no notice and I'm sorry she's opening old wounds. He took his wife by the arm. 'Come, my dear, there are others waiting to be greeted.' He eased her away towards the punch but movement on the stairs caught her eye.

'Ah, here's that nice young Mr Kirby. You remember him, Cara, don't you? How are you, Mr Kirby?' Belinda held out her hand to Julian when he reached the last step.

'Very well, indeed, Mrs Blenkinsop, and I hope you are the same.'

'Indeed I am, thank you. Just one regret – you aren't free for my Cara. Or are you?'

'Mother!' Cara's rebuke was sharp with admonishment and embarrassment.

Julian smiled understandingly at her as she and her father eased Belinda away.

Guests continued to arrive. The de Klerks and Kirbys joined them, to mingle, introduce themselves to strangers and engage in conversation.

Anna was pleased with the way things were going at this early stage of the evening and saw that the guests were spreading themselves between the two drawing rooms and the hall. She heard the door open and turned to see that the new arrival was a stranger. The impact he made was immediate. Even though he had not looked in her direction, he demanded her attention. He was tall and handsome, with clear arresting eyes. He held himself straight, which accentuated his height, and with it came a presence that seemed to fill the room. She was aware that some other people, still in the hall, glanced in his direction, drawn by that very presence.

'Lambert Finch,' whispered her father. 'The young man I told you I met in Holland. I must instruct Robert to show him to his room. Excuse me.' He stepped quickly across the hall to greet the new arrival.

Anna was curious. Finch had shed his coat and she saw that his clothes were of the best stuffs, immaculately cut to enhance his athletic figure. She saw her father exchange a warm handshake with him. A quip passed between them, bringing broad smiles. Then her attention was drawn to another new arrival, but she was aware of Robert leading Lambert Finch upstairs and her father returning to continue welcoming his guests. When the last of these arrived the Masons were free to mingle.

Anna was talking to the Fostons when she saw Lambert reappear on the stairs. She excused herself and went to meet him.

'Mr Finch, I hope you find your room comfortable and to your liking.'

'It couldn't be better, Miss Mason. Thank you for your concern and for your hospitality. I deem it an honour that your father invited me, a stranger, to your party.'

'He spoke highly of you on his return from Holland. I believe that sprang from your mutual interest in art.'

'Yes, it did. I found your father most knowledgeable.'

'It is an interest he's cultivated over the years, mainly through sharing a common interest with my mother for whom he created a collection.'

'And, I understand, a fine one. But I think in the quest for beauty he had no need to look any further than you.'

Anna blushed. 'You flatter me, Mr Finch. But I am no work of art.'

'Indeed you are, Miss Mason. Do you not think that the human form is one of the most attractive and enduring works of art, especially the female form? Is that not why it appears on so many canvases?'

Anna blushed even more. 'Mr Finch, I don't think this is the time for us to get into such deep waters. It would take too much time and I have my other guests to see to. Please excuse me?'

A teasing smile sparkled in his eyes and curved his lips as he bowed graciously to her wishes.

She left him in order to go and seek out Cara. He watched her glide graciously among her guests, pausing for a word here, receiving congratulations there. The admiration in his eyes was visible when a voice broke into his thoughts.

'I am pleased you could come, Mr Finch,' said Charles. 'My father tells me you are a fellow connoisseur. Do have a drink.'

Lambert accepted a glass from the tray offered by one of the maids. 'Ah, he flatters me, but it's true I am interested in beautiful things.'

'From what he told me when he returned from Holland, I think your interest runs a little deeper than that and that you have real understanding of the fine arts.'

Lambert gave a shrug of his shoulders. 'Possibly. After all, I was brought up to appreciate items of beauty and artistic value by my mother and father, who were keen collectors.'

'I believe you met Herr de Klerk?'

'Yes, a charming man.'

'He is here with his wife and daughter. They must be in the other room.'

'I look forward to meeting him again and being introduced to his family.'

'Alas, his two married sons were unable to come, commitments at home.' Charles glanced round. 'Ah, here's my good friend Julian Kirby.'

He made the introductions.

'My fellow house-guest,' commented Julian as they shook hands.

'Indeed,' replied Lambert, 'but I feel I am a gatecrasher. Mr Mason invited me when we found we shared a mutual interest. I am very much looking forward to Miss Mason showing me the collection.'

Julian bristled a little. Surely John would be doing that, having issued the invitation? Maybe Mr Finch had merely made an assumption.

Lambert had noted Julian's reaction and judged that this fellow was interested in Anna. Ah, well, he thought to himself, all's fair in love and war.

As the evening progressed, Anna gave everyone her attention, making them feel welcome and that their presence was important to the success of the party. In their turn they had nothing to express but pleasure at being back at Hawkshead Manor on such an occasion. To each other they commented on how well Anna had stepped into her mother's shoes, and how attractive she was in the splendid dress so beautifully cut. The ladies were not long in finding out who had made it, and were determined to make a future visit to the dressmaker. Whitby men were pleased to meet the merchants from Hull and Holland, and soon small groups were having lively discussions on a variety of subjects. But Anna was careful to see that people mixed rather than getting set into one group or another.

When the meal was called, the guests found

that she had given the place settings around the five circular tables careful consideration. The eight people at each found their interests were compatible or diverse, so as to create enquiry and keep conversation flowing.

Unknown to anyone, Anna had made a last-minute adjustment to the settings at her table so that she would be in the company of Julian and Lambert. She had smiled to herself when she was doing it, for she was well aware of Lambert's interest in her even in this short time and of course Julian had expressed his love for her. It would be interesting to see their reactions to her and to each other.

The guests were sorting themselves out, looking for the places allocated to them. Anna, who had kept the settings a secret, glanced in her brother's direction. He had found his place and she received his approving nod when he saw that Rebecca had been placed next to him. Anna smiled teasingly at him when he fleetingly pulled a face on seeing Mrs Blenkinsop taking a chair at his table, too.

'Here I am.' Her exclamation of delight at finding her place was loud. She looked round. 'Have you found yours, Cara? Ah, there you are with those nice young men.'

'Thank you for that compliment, Mrs Blenkinsop,' said one of the Foston boys who, with his brother, had taken their places along with Magdalena de Klerk and Caroline Kirby at Anna's table.

Mrs Blenkinsop scowled, sat down and immediately broke into the conversation between

Sir Arthur Foston and Mrs de Klerk.

Once everyone was seated, soup was served and wine was poured. While this was being done Anna said to the guests at her table, 'In case some of you have not been introduced, I'll do so now.' She did it quickly and precisely, with a brief word about each person's background. When she came to Lambert, she introduced him stiffly as 'Mr Finch' then added, 'I'm afraid I know little about you except that you are from Langthorpe Hall in the East Riding, and that you are interested in art.'

'Indeed, that is so, Miss Mason. It's an interest that was cultivated in me from a very early age. I receive a deal of pleasure from acquiring beautiful objects.' His eyes were directly on her and the inference behind the words was not lost on her. She bristled at such audacity, but was undeniably pleased by the compliment, too. 'And, Miss Mason, you have introduced everyone by their Christian names so I suggest you all refer to me as Lambert.' He glanced round them all.

Julian intervened. 'What do you do at Langthorpe Hall? I presume you farm. Do you have much acreage?'

Anna was relieved by his quick-wittedness. There was something quite unsettling about Lambert Finch.

She heard him answer Julian. 'Yes, I do farm the land for income, though I'm no expert and leave that side of things to a competent manager. He was employed by my parents, who were consumed by other interests. I kept him on when they died. He's worth his weight in gold.'

'If you have little interest in farming, how do you occupy your time?' asked Cara.

'I enjoy the countryside, love riding and walking, but, my dear Cara, I thrive on my love of art. I buy and sell as well as searching for pieces to add to my own special collection.'

'Anna told me earlier that you met her father in my country. Were you seeking art objects then?' asked Magdalena.

'Yes.' Lambert was about to expand upon the meeting at the auction when he remembered his promise to John. 'I have a sister who lives in The Hague. I visit her several times during the year and keep my eyes open for pieces that might interest me. I met Mr Mason by accident in a tavern when I was spending the day in Amsterdam. Two Englishmen in a foreign land – we were both surprised at the coincidence of hearing another Yorkshire accent.'

'And that meeting brought you here?' asked one of the Foston boys.

'Yes. Another coincidence. In the course of our conversation Mr Mason and I found we shared an interest. He invited me to see his collection and included this party in his invitation. Most fortunate for me otherwise I would not be here this evening with all you charming people. And I'm looking forward to Anna giving me a conducted tour.'

She met his glance. 'Ah, it was my father who made the invitation and no doubt it will be he who shows you his collection, some of which is not displayed. I have no idea what he intends to show you.'

Anna turned the conversation to other matters.

'Jeremiah, I hope your trip to Cumbria was enjoyable as well as successful?'

'It was, though the journey was none too comfortable and there was snow over Stainmore.'

'Thank goodness we didn't get a bad fall here,' commented Julian, 'and the weather seems to be picking up.'

'Don't be too sure. March can have a sting.' Lambert poured ice on Julian's optimism and Anna thought he took delight in doing so.

She deviated the talk to other interests. Conversation flowed. The whole room filled with a jovial atmosphere.

John Mason was pleased. Anna had done a splendid job. He hadn't realised how much she had learned from her mother. The thought of Elizabeth dulled his attention momentarily and when Katharina de Klerk on his right and Alicia Foston on his left engaged in conversation with their other neighbours he lapsed into thoughtful silence as he surveyed the room. He felt loneliness cast its heavy cloak over him even though he was among so many friends.

'John, you must be proud of Anna this evening.' The words, softly spoken by Katharina, brought him back to the present moment.

He looked across the room at his daughter and for one brief instant it was Elizabeth who smiled back at him, but it was Anna who gave him a slight wave. 'Yes, I am,' he replied.

'She'll have all the young men at her feet.'

John gave a wan smile. 'I don't think about that.

I'll not stand in her way whatever life she wants, but I'll be here to offer advice and guidance if ever she wants it.'

'Sensible man,' praised Katharina. 'Do that and she'll always love you and regard this as home. I believe there are two young men here this evening who would like to see more of your daughter.'

John eyed her with curiosity.

She laughed. 'You men don't see what's happening under your own noses!'

'What is?' John looked a little bewildered.

'I've noticed that young Mr Kirby, whom I got to know last night and like very much, has been showing special attention to Anna. Mr Finch has also sought her attention. A comparative stranger, I believe, but so handsome.'

'But surely...'

'Surely nothing! When a beautiful young lady can stir the hearts of eligible young men, each of whom sees her as his own, jealousy kindles between them.'

'You mean, that's happening?'

Katharina smiled. 'As I said, you men can't see what is happening under your noses. But don't worry. From what I know of Anna, she can take care of herself and will know her own heart when the times comes.'

When the meal was finished and everyone was leaving the dining room in twos and threes, Anna noticed the members of the syndicate drifting casually into her father's study. Charles had no need to attend that brief meeting so he and Anna ushered the other guests into the drawing rooms, Charles making sure that he had Rebecca to help him in entertaining them with pleasant talk. He had found her throughout the meal the most pleasant and interesting of companions and had determined then that he would see more of her. He had the perfect excuse to visit Hull more often on trading missions, and she gave him every encouragement to do so when he mentioned the possibility.

The syndicate was pleased with John's news that the Upton gang had been outwitted but someone urged caution and told John to remain alert. After he had given them his assurance that he would take no risks, they drifted back among the other guests. The rest of the evening passed off pleasantly and when the guests took their leave they had nothing but praise for Anna in their thanks.

John offered the house-guests a final drink before they retired.

Lambert was the first to make a move. 'I hope you will excuse me? This has been a wonderful evening and I thank you for inviting me, a stranger, and making me so welcome in your home.' He turned from John to Anna. 'Miss Anna, what a splendid and beautiful hostess you made. You lit up the evening so much that it will remain for ever in my memory, wherever I am and whomever I am with.'

She blushed at the meaning behind his words. 'I thank you for your kindness.' Her gaze was fixed on his but it was carefully non-committal and Lambert was too shrewd to read into it the meaning he would have liked.

He bowed to her. 'Good night.' He straightened, stepped back and surveyed everyone with a general, 'Good night.'

When the door had closed firmly behind him, Herr de Klerk commented, 'Still the same charm as when we met him in Amsterdam, John.'

'Indeed.' He glanced at Katharina and read in the slight rising of her eyebrows the comment, 'Didn't I tell you so?'

He pursed his lips and she knew he had taken her meaning.

'A flatterer,' said Anna crisply, endeavouring to brush Lambert's words aside. She sensed that Julian was squirming at such praise and wanted him to get the impression she did not respond to Lambert's flattery, though if she was honest a part of her rather liked it.

When the Kirbys took their leave for the night, the de Klerks also made their goodnights.

As the door closed behind them, John smiled at his children. 'Thank you both for making this such a splendid evening.'

'Don't thank me, Father. Anna was the main instigator. I had little to do with it.'

'I had your support. You were there whenever I needed any help or advice before today, and that was important. And tonight you were vital in your contribution to entertaining the guests, and will remain so during the stay of our house-guests.'

'Father, is Lambert Finch staying as long as the others?' Anna asked.

'I shouldn't think so, though no time limit was

402

stipulated. He came primarily to see my collection. I shall show him that tomorrow morning. Maybe he will leave in the afternoon, though I can't press him to do so. I would think if he does not do so he will leave the next day. I don't think he's a young man to outstay his welcome.'

'If you are going to show him the collection, what are we to do with the Kirbys and de Klerks?'

'I am perfectly sure that they will look after themselves and be happy to relax.'

'Then, you and I, Charles, will take Julian, Rebecca, Magdalena and Caroline for a walk.'

'A splendid idea,' agreed Charles, reading his sister's intention to get out of viewing the collection with Lambert. 'I'm sure Julian and Rebecca will be agreeable to that.' He winked mischievously at her.

Chapter Eighteen

'Good morning, everybody.' Lambert greeted them cheerily as he came into the dining room, restored to its normal layout after yesterday's party. 'It looks like being a fine day.'

Among the returned felicitations, Anna seized a chance to make a point. 'A pity you and Father will be viewing our collection or you could have joined some of us in a walk around the estate.'

'Ah, my loss,' returned Lambert, knowing full well that Anna's remarks had spiked any suggestion he might make that she accompany him in viewing the art works. 'Maybe some other time I could enjoy your company on such an expedition.' His eyes challenged as he met her gaze.

She sensed Julian bristle at the hint but made no answering comment to Lambert.

Breakfast, an informal meal, passed pleasantly. During it Lambert remarked on two of the paintings displayed in the room. 'You have made a good investment in the Dutch artist Aelbert Cuyp. Those two and the one in my bedroom have been astute buys.'

John acknowledged this with an inclination of his head. He was pleased by Lambert's remark. It showed he was a fellow connoisseur. 'I purchased them at a small auction in Amsterdam a couple of years ago.'

'You were indeed fortunate to find them.'

'I have a good friend in Herr de Klerk.' He smiled at Hendrick. 'Apart from being a business acquaintance, he keeps a look out for pieces in which I might be interested.'

'I am no collector,' put in Hendrick, 'but I am interested in art and pride myself on knowing something worth having.'

'Then Mr Mason is doubly fortunate,' said Lambert. He cast his eyes on Julian. 'Are you interested in art, Julian?'

He sensed this was an attempt to try and belittle him but rose to the occasion. 'I will not deny I am ignorant where art is concerned, but through my friendship with Anna and Charles I will no doubt soon come to appreciate its worth.'

When everyone had almost finished their breakfast, John silenced conversation around the table by announcing, 'Friends, please do whatever you want today. Relax around the house, walk in the garden or further still if you wish. If anyone would like to go into Whitby, inform John and he will drive you there. There will be refreshments for a light lunch here in the dining room from twelve o'clock until two. Come and take it as you please. There will be afternoon tea at four for those who want it. We will dine formally at seven.' He rose from his chair. 'Lambert, I'll meet you in the hall in ten minutes.'

'Very good, sir.'

'And fifteen minutes for the walkers – in the hall.' Anna moved from the table.

Lambert, seeing that Julian was still eating, left his place and followed his hostess.

405

'Anna.' His voice halted her near the foot of the stairs. She turned, one hand on the banister. 'I'm sorry I will miss the walk this morning. Maybe this afternoon we can take a turn in the garden?'

'Alas, Lambert, I don't know how long we are going to be.'

He looked crestfallen for a moment. 'Are you trying to avoid my company, Anna? Should I take this as a rebuff? But I will nevertheless extend an invitation to your family to visit Langthorpe Hall. I think your father would welcome the opportunity to see my collection, and I am sure he would like you and Charles to accompany him.'

'That will depend on Father,' she replied. 'Now, if you will excuse me, I must get ready to take my friends on their walk.' She turned and started up the stairs, feeling him watching her.

The tone of her voice could be taken as neither an acceptance nor a refusal and Lambert drew hope from that. He would have to see that Mr Mason accepted the invitation. He turned to the front door and walked on to the terrace.

When he returned to the hall, John was coming down the stairs.

'Ah, Lambert, I'm looking forward to this. It is some time since I was able to show my collection to someone who can appreciate it.'

'You flatter my ability, sir.'

'Your comments on those paintings told me you have the eye of an expert and certainly know Dutch art. And of course,' John paused, glanced round and lowered his voice, 'there was that jewellery.'

Lambert smiled. 'A memorable meeting, sir.

You have the necklace and ring safe from Anna's eyes?'

'Oh, yes. No one knows about it but you and I and Hendrick. And that will remain so until her birthday. Now, where shall we start? Maybe in one of the drawing rooms.' He started to stroll towards one of the doors. 'You no doubt noticed the paintings last night, but probably hadn't time to devote to them. Now you and I can really study them.'

'Indeed, sir.'

They had almost reached the door when footsteps on the stairs drew their attention. They saw Anna, Charles, Rebecca and Magdalena coming down, their mood jovial, laughter in their eyes and on their lips.

'Have a pleasant walk,' Lambert called. He glanced up and saw Julian looking down at him from the landing. Lambert gave him a wave and let his gaze return to Anna. She was not looking in his direction but he emphasised his own look of admiration, from which Julian could make his own interpretation. He followed John into the room and closed the door.

By the time the walkers reached the woods they had paired off and were strung out, though within sight of each other. Anna led the way with Julian, Magdalena accompanied Caroline, while Charles and Rebecca brought up the rear.

'This is my first opportunity to have you to myself, and to say that my feelings for you are still the same,' said Julian, determined that with Lambert indicating his interest in Anna he

407

should reaffirm his own feelings for her. 'I hope that yours have come nearer mine.'

'Julian, I still think a lot of you. I had some reservations at first but I now count you among my dearest friends.'

'No more than that?' He looked glum.

'Who knows? Dearest friends can come to be more. Maybe I have not yet recognised the spark that will tell me it is so. Be patient, Julian.' He drew some hope from the gentle touch of her hand on his arm.

'I hope this fellow Lambert is not preventing that spark from bursting into the devouring flame of love.' His tone was light and joking, but she recognised the serious intent.

'I hardly know him. I had not met him before yesterday.'

'Nor he you, but it is obvious to me that he is hopeful of creating an impression.'

'Well, he is attractively self-assured and soooo handsome.' She drew the word out in a teasing expression of interest.

'I don't find him so. Self-assured?' There was a note of contempt in Julian's tone. 'Cocky, I would say. Thinks too much of himself.'

Anna smiled. 'Jealous?'

'Rubbish,' he snapped indignantly. 'I've nothing to be jealous of.'

Anna burst out laughing. 'You should see your face!' Her eyes twinkled with the delight of chafing him.

Julian grunted, annoyed with himself for being caught out by her teasing. 'All right, but you be careful. You are going to have a suitor there who'll be persistent, unless I'm very much mistaken. And what do you know of him?'

'Very little,' she admitted. 'But please don't worry about me. Now, let's talk of other things and enjoy the walk.'

Julian, realising that he should not be a wet blanket, brightened up and contributed much to the enjoyment of the rest of the walk.

At eleven Anna called a halt. 'If any of you want lunch at the Manor then you should turn back now. If not we'll go a little further, have our sandwiches and then go on.'

'I'm for doing that,' said Rebecca. 'It's too nice a day to stay indoors.'

Her observation formed the consensus of opinion and the walk continued. Anna, as a good hostess, now took Caroline as her walking partner. Magdalena fell into step beside Charles.

'Charles, I am so pleased that you and Rebecca enjoy each other's company. She thinks the world of you. I could tell from the way she spoke when we were with the Kirbys in Hull.'

'It's comforting to know that, Magdalena. I feared she might think of me primarily as a replacement for the young man she lost.'

'Far from it, Charles. She loves you for yourself. You should tell her you feel the same about her.' Before he could reply she called out, 'Julian, come and talk to me. You see enough of your sister.'

'My pleasure, Magdalena.' She led him off, leaving Charles to resume his walk with Rebecca.

'I hope you will enjoy my company, Charles,' she said as she joined him. She gave a little smile.

'I think Magdalena engineered this.'

'I believe you are right.' His eyes betrayed the pleasure he found in her company.

'I hope you enjoyed the paintings in those two rooms,' said John as he and Lambert returned to the hall.

'I did indeed, sir,' replied his guest in a tone that showed he was genuinely interested. 'I was aware of them yesterday but unable really to study and appreciate them with other people wanting to engage in conversation. It has been a pleasure to do so in a leisurely manner this morning.'

John had studied the young man while they were looking at the paintings. His demeanour and bearing bore out the opinion John had formed on their brief meeting in Amsterdam. Linked with the judgement he had made during the party, John was highly satisfied that a lasting friendship was being forged. He had also been impressed by Lambert's knowledge. His analysis and judgement were sound. He was not afraid to comment adversely on what he saw if he felt the comment could be usefully debated. John appreciated his words and found that he was drawn in to appreciating techniques and meanings he had not been aware of before.

'You will have noticed the paintings on the wall as you go upstairs?'

'I have,' replied Lambert, 'and was able to view them a little longer than the others. I appreciated the fact that, because of the restricted space, those you have displayed there do not need the viewer to stand far back. I would like to look at them again in your company.'

'Yes, I did choose them with the stairs in mind. We shall look at them again, but first come to my study.' John opened the door to the room.

Lambert stepped inside and stopped. 'What a wonderful room.' His sharp eyes had taken it all in in one sweeping look.

It was a large square room, its walls painted plain white so that no pattern or colour contested with the paintings. These were hung with considerable care so that none infringed on another. The viewer, though aware that there were other paintings present, was able to concentrate solely on the one that had his present attention. The light came from two tall windows on either side of large glass doors overlooking the garden and open landscape beyond. This being John's study, Lambert had expected bookshelves but there were none, allowing every wall to be used to display paintings. Through an arch the width of a door in one wall, he glimpsed books and realised that John had created a separate room for them, conveniently placed next to his study. A large oak desk with an upright chair behind stood across one corner, placed so that the light from three windows fell across it from the left. The only other furniture in the room was one armchair and a small table on which stood four wine glasses and a decanter.

John was pleased by the look of appreciation on Lambert's face. 'A glass of wine, young man?'

'Sir, I would love one. But the beauty of one should not mar my appreciation of the other, and

411

at the moment the beauty of your collection outweighs the pleasure of the wine.'

'Very well, we shall savour that later.' John stood back and watched Lambert take a quick look around the display from where he stood. Then he moved across the room to a framed pencil sketch that hung on the wall in such a position that John would be able to see it from his seat behind the desk.

'Sir, this is exquisite.' Lambert said over his shoulder. 'The delicate pencil strokes bring out so skilfully the beauty of the subject. Who is she, sir?'

'My late wife,' replied John quietly.

'I'm so taken by her and the aptitude of the artist. Who produced such a work?'

'I discovered an eighteen year old in Whitby who forever had a pencil in his hand. Immediately I saw his work, I commissioned him to do that portrait. Also I hoped to purchase more of his work after he had completed that.'

'It sounds as though you never did?'

'Alas, no. The young man was not encouraged by his family. They had no eye for art, did not recognise his gift and regarded drawing as no way for him to spend his time. His father and three brothers were whalers and regarded drawing and painting as unfit pursuits for man. They wore him down with their derision and uncomplimentary comments. He went whaling with them. After that first voyage he told me he hated the life and after one more was prepared to leave home to follow his heart's desire. I was ready, on his return, to buy all his work to date so that he would have some income to start with. I saw him as someone with a future, and worth collecting.' John paused.

'It didn't happen?' said Lambert.

He gave a sad shake of his head. 'No. He was lost in the Arctic. Slipped when he was moving on to a whale to start flensing, and was gone before anyone could pull him out of the sea. I went to his home, when I thought his family would have got over the shock of their loss, still prepared to buy all his work, only to find that his mother had destroyed it. She could not bear the reminder of him.'

'Oh, no! What a loss, in more ways than one. Thank goodness you have that sketch.'

'It is very precious to me.'

'I can understand that.' Lambert remained looking at the drawing for a few minutes longer and then turned his attention to the other paintings.

When he had made his tour of the room, John shepherded him into the library. Similar windows and glass doors as those in the study let the light into the room. Two walls were lined with books. On the third the shelves had been faced with six glass doors forming the whole into a display cabinet. Two armchairs were placed to catch the best light from the windows from which there were open views of the countryside. A small oak table stood between them.

Lambert paused as John closed the door. 'What a wonderful room. I'll bet you spend many a pleasant hour in here.'

'Yes, I do. After my wife died I thought this

room my hermit's cell, but thanks to Anna and Charles I've changed my view. It is once more the place where Elizabeth and I shared many happy hours. The paintings you have seen and this collection here were gathered over the years of our marriage, so each piece has a special significance.'

'And now you will be starting again when you present that necklace and ring to Anna on her birthday?'

'Yes.' John gave a little smile, anticipating what lay ahead.

'I know this will seem presumptuous of me, sir, but would it be possible for me to see them again? Their beauty has haunted me ever since the auction, and just a glimpse would lay a ghost.'

There was a humble sincerity in Lambert's request that persuaded John to comply. 'I won't be a moment.' John went back to his study.

Lambert heard a drawer being unlocked, opened and closed again. There was a moment's silence, then movement, and a few minutes later John appeared from the study. He was carrying a small hinged wooden box. He placed it on the table, opened the lid, took out a piece of velvet and laid it beside the box. With care he lifted the necklace from the box and placed it on the velvet.

Lambert's intake of breath expressed his wonder at the exquisite beauty of the necklace, caught in the light from the windows. He leaned closer to examine it in more detail than he had been able to in Holland. He longed to reach out and touch it but curbed his desire for he knew it would be improper to do so unless invited by his host.

But his eyes searched. They probed every facet for the verification he thought might be there. When he was in Amsterdam he was troubled by the fact that he could not remember something his father had told him about his grandmother's necklace that had been stolen. On reaching Langthorpe Hall again he had gone straight to his bedroom and studied the portrait of his grandmother that hung there, trying to jog his memory. It was a noble oil painting of a woman in her thirties, a three-quarter view, her head turned, her expression with a touch of haughtiness despite the smile on her lips and friendliness in her blue eyes – wanting to know and be known by the person looking at her. A necklace hung from her throat. It had been carefully painted so that the beauty of both subjects complemented each other. Lambert had stood there entranced yet irritated that he could not recall his father's words.

'Oh, Grandmother C, can't you help me?' he had whispered pleadingly. It was the term by which she had been known. 'Sadly we never met but I'm sure we would have loved each other and had a lot of fun together. Help me to remember, Grandmother C.'

Grandmother C! It struck him like a thunderbolt. C! His father had told him to look closely at the snake's eyes on the necklace. He recalled doing so. The diamonds that formed the eyes were not in a complete circle, as one would have expected, but both had been left C-shaped, the initial of his grandmother's Christian name, Catherine.

Now in this room in Hawkshead Manor he peered closely at the eyes of a snake, sparkling on velvet. His chest tightened. He had to keep a tight rein on the feelings that threatened to overwhelm him. The eyes had been carefully set with diamonds to form the letter C!

'Beautiful,' he said as he straightened. He gazed longingly at the piece and said quietly, 'I don't suppose you will sell it to me? I will give you a third more than you paid for it. It is so beautiful.'

'From that sort of offer it sounds as though you see more in it than mere beauty. I recall the reason behind your interest when we were in Amsterdam. Maybe now you are sure that this was your grandmother's?'

'I am, sir.' Lambert explained why.

John listened sympathetically but replied without any hesitation, 'I'm sorry, I couldn't. I understand why you would like it but it has come to mean a great deal to me too. I look at it every day and see it not only as a wonderful gift to my daughter to mark her birthday but as a symbol of a reawakening of my life, a resumption of the Mason art collection, and my thanks to Anna for all she has done for me in the trying times since my wife's death. I know you will think that I could find another piece of jewellery for her but something else would never have the same meaning. And surely you can see it belongs round a woman's neck – Anna's – rather than displayed in a collection? Please try and understand that. You can be assured that it will be well taken care of and treasured.'

Lambert looked crestfallen. He bit his lip.

Silence hung heavy for a moment then he said swiftly, 'Sir, forgive me. As a guest in your house I had no right to ask you to sell. I know Anna will love it, and it will match her beauty as it did my grandmother's. Thank you for letting me see it again. Now, should we continue our viewing of the rest of your collection?'

John returned the necklace to its safe place and rejoined Lambert whose thoughts were still on the jewellery. Maybe there was another way to obtain it... After all, Anna was an attractive girl, one who would adorn Langthorpe Hall. For the moment he let that thought drift to the back of his mind and concentrated on the collection. He became so engrossed in what was displayed that he had seen only half of the items when John suggested that they should have some lunch and resume in the afternoon.

Lambert had hoped that the walkers would return for lunch but instead of Anna he had to make do with Mr and Mrs Kirby and the de Klerks.

'Mr Mason tells me that none of you have seen his collection and that he is to show it to you tomorrow. I can tell you, you are in for a treat.' Lambert went on to praise it highly and during the lunch was charm itself, so that when he made his goodbyes the following morning his store was high with the other guests.

John was on the terrace having a last few words with him when Anna came out of the house. 'I must bring Charles to say goodbye.' He went into the hall.

Lambert's face lit up when he turned to Anna.

'I was hoping you would come to say goodbye.'

'I would not be a true hostess if I did not do that. I'm sorry I was delayed, I hope I have not held you up.'

'Not at all. I would have waited so that my goodbyes to you might sustain me on my journey.'

'A compliment indeed, Lambert, if I truly had that power.'

'You have, and you will be often in my thoughts until you come to Langthorpe Hall in two weeks' time.' He saw surprise come into Anna's expression. 'Of course, you won't know. I have just made that invitation to your father and he has accepted. I look forward to seeing you then.'

'That is very kind of you.'

Their conversation was halted by the appearance of Charles and his father.

Once Lambert had departed on horseback John hurried back into the house to show the de Klerks his collection. Anna and Charles watched Lambert riding away.

'He sits a horse well,' commented Charles, and smiled to himself when he saw Anna give a little shrug of indifference. 'Don't tell me you haven't fallen under his charm?' he commented. 'Everyone else has.' He gave a small laugh. 'Well, all except Julian. You've got a jealous suitor there, Anna.'

'And he won't like it when I tell him we are going to Langthorpe Hall in two weeks.'

As he rode through a countryside beginning to bloom with new life brought by the warming spring, Lambert's thoughts were on the girl to whom he had just said goodbye. He recalled the chance meeting in Holland brought about by the jewellery. If it hadn't been for those fine pieces he would not have met John Mason and subsequently his daughter. Though he still coveted necklace and ring he had no doubt he had found an equal treasure in Anna. He must make sure that they both came with her to Langthorpe Hall, permanently.

'Walk with me in the garden?' Julian made the invitation to Anna after lunch.

The older people were looking at John's collection. Magdalena and Caroline were in the drawing room reading, and Charles was showing Rebecca the Hawkshead stables.

'Very well,' she agreed. 'I'll just get a coat and shawl.'

When she returned a few minutes later Julian drew a sharp breath and felt his heart quicken. Anna had put on a crimson velvet pelisse with a wide Van Dyke collar. Instead of a bonnet she had draped a pale blue shawl around her head, allowing it to hang down her back and from one shoulder in the front. It framed her face to perfection, bringing out the beauty of her features and complexion. Strands of copper-coloured hair peeped enticingly from the edges of the shawl.

'Anna, you look so beautiful.' Julian just had to express his feelings.

She smiled. 'Beauty is in the eye of the beholder.'

'You would be in any beholder's eye.'

'Come, let us walk.' As much as she was flattered and liked receiving Julian's compliments, she wanted to keep a distance. She had to admit that her early doubts about him had all but vanished. But was any unease that still lingered because Lambert, with all his charm, had recently entered her life? He was attractive too but in a different way from Julian. Lambert's charm was smooth and, linked to his handsome features and his bearing, almost irresistible but she felt that he may not be as dependable as Julian. She saw in this young man someone who was truly considerate, ever ready to help without being overbearing. Though not as handsome as Lambert, there was an attractiveness about him that was hard to resist.

Julian escorted her outside, along the terrace and down on to the path that led along the front of the house beside the lawn. They turned a corner and strolled across the lawn to the walled garden.

'I think there is a love match between Charles and Rebecca,' observed Anna wanting to prevent any continuation of the conversation they had just had.

She immediately realised that could not be avoided when he said, 'I'm sure you are right, and I hope it may be so between you and I also.'

'Maybe it can, but I must have time to feel convinced.'

'Time? Time is a stranger, full of uncertainties, unless we make it otherwise. We can only do that by seizing time and making it our friend.'

'And we must be sure of our friends.'

He stopped and turned her to him. 'I am of you, Anna. You are more than a friend to me, you are my love.'

She could not mistake the sincerity and worship in his eyes. Could she want more? Yet the image of Lambert pushed itself into her mind. She pulled herself up sharp, chiding herself for entertaining such thoughts about a man who was almost a stranger when one whom she knew much better was telling her that he loved her.

Julian kissed her lightly on the lips. He would have pulled away but sensed from her touch that she did not want him to. Anna drew on that kiss to try to blot thoughts of Lambert from her mind. It became more passionate and as she responded thoughts of him were exorcised.

But five minutes later, as they walked round the walled garden, he became prominent in both their minds.

'Anna, I have to go to Amsterdam on business but I will be back in two weeks. Will you come then to Hull as my guest? I'm sure Mother and Father will be delighted to see you.'

She stopped, let her arm slip from his and looked at him with concern in her eyes. 'Julian, I'm sorry, I can't. Father has accepted an invitation from Lambert for us to visit Langthorpe Hall.'

His lips tightened. Disappointment mingled with annoyance in his expression. 'Anna, you can't!' was an immediate reaction even though he knew his protest would do no good. An invitation had been accepted and that was the end of it. It would have to be fulfilled.

'I'm sorry, Julian.' She saw he was hurt. 'Really I am.'

He shrugged his shoulders. 'It can't be helped. But don't forget me when you are there. I know Lambert will turn on the charm and try to make you see he is the only one. Don't fall for it, Anna. Remember, I love you.' He swept her into his arms and kissed her with a passion he hoped she would remember throughout her stay at Langthorpe Hall.

Chapter Nineteen

'I wish you hadn't arranged for a smuggling run while we are at Langthorpe Hall.' John voiced his doubt as their carriage trundled across the Yorkshire Wolds.

'Father, I took the opportunity to make all the arrangements with Magdalena when she was at the party. It seemed the sensible thing to do. I briefed Edwin, Nicholas and Ralph. With the date and consignment set, I knew they were capable of handling the operation.'

'Charles mentioned it to me,' put in Anna. 'I approved his plan, and we both thought that because of recent events it might be as well if you were out of the way. The visit to Langthorpe Hall gave us the perfect opportunity.'

'It's better if you keep a low profile for a while, until we see if the Upton brothers make any more moves against us,' said Charles.

'I'm grateful for your concern,' replied John, 'but I'd rather be involved in the action.'

'I know, Father, but we are worried about your safety.'

He nodded but made no comment. He did not want an argument to mar these three nights away at Lambert's house. He knew Anna and Charles meant well. He turned the conversation to the countryside through which they were passing.

It was a landscape of big fields and low rolling

hills, all showing signs of the retreat of winter. Anna was thankful that the day was bright, for she thought this vast landscape, without sunshine and merging with grey clouds, could be depressing. It did not offer the rugged contrasts which she loved in North Yorkshire and seemed far away from the precipitous coastline around Whitby.

The trackway on which they were travelling dipped into a shallow valley. John slowed the horse as they neared the bottom of the hill where he turned it through an ornamental iron gateway. Before them stretched a wide gravelled drive with broad borders of grass to either side and splendid oak trees set at regular intervals towards the Hall, where the drive looped back on itself to form a perfect circle in front of the building.

'What a wonderful approach,' Anna commented, almost overawed by the scene.

The house was imposing but not overwhelming, in size just right to fit the valley in which it stood. Its every proportion was pleasing to the eye.

Lambert appeared at the front door and Anna's heart missed a beat, though she had steeled herself against being impressed by him. But he did make an attractive figure as he awaited them, the steps up giving him that extra height which made him even more imposing.

John drew the carriage to a stop. Lambert was down the steps quickly to help Anna to the ground, while the man servant who had followed him was taking charge of the luggage, and the groom, who seemed to have materialised out of the ground, was at the head of the horse and would take charge of the carriage once the visitors had been ushered inside.

'Welcome to my humble home, my dear Anna.' Lambert had seen her safely to the ground and now raised her hand towards his lips. 'I hope your stay will be enjoyable.'

'Thank you,' was all she could find to say as she met the dazzling look he gave her.

'Welcome to you, sir.' He shook John's hand with a firm grip that spoke of sincerity in his words. 'And to you, Charles.' Again there was an exchange of handshakes. 'You have had a pleasant day for your drive,' he continued, addressing the three of them. 'But rather cold. I have warm punch awaiting you.'

They made their thanks and comments as he ushered them inside. There they were met by another man servant and two maids. The man took the outdoor coats from John and Charles and was joined by the servant who had collected the luggage from the coach. They started up the stairs and were followed by one of the maids who had taken Anna's outdoor garments.

'They will return to show you to your rooms,' Lambert informed them. 'But first, that warming drink.' He nodded to the remaining maid who hurried off to the kitchen. She was back almost before Lambert had escorted his guests to the drawing room.

The punch and brightly burning fire drove out the cold and added their own particular welcome to Langthorpe Hall.

Anna saw that the fine proportions she had noted as they approached the house were

425

continued inside. This room was big, but not so big as to detract from its cosy feeling. Three tall windows looked out on to the terrace and beyond that to the valley along which they had driven. A large landscape painting was displayed on each of the remaining three walls with nothing else to detract from them. A sofa was set at an angle to the fire with two armchairs to complete the semi-circle, arranged at a distance from the fire to obtain pleasant warmth. An oak sideboard was positioned against one wall and a matching table against another.

As they enjoyed their drinks, Lambert told them how pleased he was that they were able to accept his hospitality and, on enquiry from Anna, gave them a brief history of the house. How it had been built by his great-grandfather, the son of the village blacksmith who had gone to London, made a fortune trading from the capital, but had never forsaken his roots. He had returned, bought the Langthorpe estate, which had been allowed to run down, and set about reviving it. He had turned it into good workable land and that in turn had made the village of his childhood more prosperous through additional employment. The hall had passed down through successive generations until he inherited on the death of his parents.

'I am trying to keep up the good work of my great-grandfather,' he concluded, and then checked himself. 'You touched on a favourite topic,' he said with a half-smile. 'I run on so. I apologise. You must be wanting to settle in after your journey.' As he was speaking he went to a

426

bellpull beside the fire and a few moments later a maid appeared. 'Liza, will you see that these good people are shown to their rooms?'

'Yes, sir.' She left the room quickly.

A few moments later when Lambert led his guests into the hall they found the servants waiting at the bottom of the stairs.

'I hope you will be comfortable in here, miss,' said Liza, opening the bedroom door. 'If there is anything you want, ring for me. Mr Finch has especially asked me to see to your needs. Can I help you to unpack now?'

'Thank you, Liza, but I think for a little while I would just like to relax. I will ring as you suggested.'

When she had left, Anna took time to assimilate her surroundings. When she had first walked into the bedroom she had felt at home. The room was well proportioned with two windows looking from the front of the house and one that faced east and would allow the morning sun to stream across the bed, its head against the opposite wall. Lambert had certainly set aside a pleasing room for her. The windows were hung with curtains in a bright floral pattern, and small watercolours of coastal scenes were displayed artistically on the walls. She saw that the dressing table was laid out with all the accoutrements she might need, the handles of the brush, comb and hand-mirror all fashioned in silver.

She strolled across to one of the windows in front of which there was an armchair but did not sit down. Instead she stood gazing out of the window. Her mind drifted and she did not take in any of the view. She could feel the room cosseting her. She felt at ease with the house, as if it had taken on an extra mantle of friendliness especially for her. Was it her own imagination that was doing this or had Lambert imbued it with some magic only he could conjure up? Had she felt anything similar at the house in Albion Street, Hull? But how could she? That had borne the marks of Julian's mother and father, it was their home, and though Julian and his sisters lived there they could not make their own individual impressions on the house. Here, at Langthorpe Hall, there was only Lambert to mould the atmosphere of the house. Though it might retain some aspects from its past it was his influence that predominated and he had made it comfortable, comforting and welcoming. Part of him was everywhere. Anna could sense it.

She started. Julian's words rang loud in her mind: 'Lambert will turn on the charm.' Was he doing that through the house as well as his own personality? 'And will try to make you see he is the only one.' Could he be? Life here would be pleasant enough, but would that apply to life with Lambert? 'Remember, I love you.' Julian's words rang clear in memory and she recalled his passionate kiss, wondering now if she had done right to accompany her father to Langthorpe Hall.

Throughout her stay Lambert was attentive, considerate, entertaining and charming. He took pleasure in showing his guests his gardens and

428

estate. Displayed a seemly pride in his artistic collection, had culinary delights placed in front of them by his cook, and thanks to his house-keeper and staff made them feel welcome and comfortable throughout their stay. Looking back, Anna had to admit that she'd wanted for nothing, every care and attention had been showered upon them.

She was well aware that on their final morning Lambert engineered the situation so that they could be alone together. He picked up on the fact that her father had shown interest in the working of the land at Langthorpe, saying that he was on the look-out for ideas to make better use of the farm at Hawkshead.

'As I told you, I am no expert and leave all that to my manager. Come, I'll arrange for you to talk to him.'

When John expressed his thanks and added, 'Charles, you had better come too, the estate will be yours one day. You could find some useful ideas here,' Lambert seized his chance.

'I'm sure Anna will not want to be bored with such talk. And so, sir, with your permission, I'll take her for a ride to see my horses in Pasture Field. It's about two miles away.'

'Very good,' agreed John with a dismissive wave of his hand. 'Well,' he added quickly, 'if that is what Anna would like to do?'

She was caught between them. She did not want to listen to talk about crop rotation and acknow-ledged that left her to Lambert's company. She was confident she could cope with him. Really, why should she worry? His behaviour so far had been the height of politeness and discretion. Besides, she would rather like to see the horses. Those in the stables had been impressive. What would the ones in Pasture Field be like?

'I would be pleased to see them,' she agreed.

'Very well. I'll take your father and Charles to the manager's office, and order the gig to be got ready. I'll see you in the hall in fifteen minutes.'

She inclined her head in acknowledgement and smiled to herself as she went into the house and to her room to get her pelisse and shawl. What would Julian say if he knew she was about to embark on an expedition alone with Lambert?

Lambert saw her comfortably seated on the gig and then took up the reins. He set the horse forward at a steady pace.

Lambert broke the silence between them by extolling several features of the landscape and indicating the boundaries of his land. He pointed out a stand of oaks. 'Those are earmarked for a shipbuilder in Hull, he'll get a fine vessel from them.'

'Doesn't it disturb you to chop down such fine trees?' Anna asked.

'I suppose it does, but the revenue from them will be put to good use and I have an agreement with him that he will provide me with timber sufficient to repair the roofs of two cottages I own in the village, so my workers will benefit also.' He changed the subject, adding, 'Pasture Field is just at the top of the next rise.'

When they reached the top he reined his horse to a halt. 'I like the view from here,' he said with feeling. When Anna made no comment he allowed silence to settle. He sensed she was taking in the view and was moved by it. A few moments later she whispered, 'It is truly beautiful.'

The undulating Wolds dipped and rose, forming layer on layer to the final rise that was the horizon. Clumps of trees dotted the landscape but it was predominantly grassland supporting sheep. Their silent grazing seemed to add an air of tranquillity to the scene. There was no sign of human habitation and Anna guessed that people had sought shelter in the valleys.

Lambert turned the gig so that they could look back the way they had come. Anna gasped. Below was the valley along which she had ridden on their arrival but from here, with the house at the far end, it looked like a painting in miniature, the house perfectly sited to harmonise with the valley and hills among which it nestled.

'Your great-grandfather knew how to pick a truly wonderful position and to exploit it to the best advantage. Thank you for showing it to me.' She glanced at him with a little knowing smile. 'I think you brought me this way in the certain knowledge I would admire it.'

He smiled back. 'I did. And I knew it would enable me to say, why don't you come every day and see its many different aspects and moods?'

The earnest light in his eyes made her ask, 'Do I take that to be a proposal?'

'My dear Anna.' He reached out and took her hands in his. 'That is exactly what it is. Spend your life at Langthorpe Hall. Come up here every day and view what is yours. You would do me the

431

greatest honour if you would become my wife.' He leaned towards her and kissed her on the lips.

She did not draw away but allowed his mouth to linger. Her mind was racing with a mixture of thoughts but at the back of them all was expectancy, a waiting for more to be said. Their lips parted. He looked at her with eyes beseeching answer in his favour. She waited, pondering, expecting to have her mind made up for her. The moments seemed to stretch to eternity but still the words did not come. Another man had said them before she left Hawkshead Manor, and those three words meant so much when they were spoken aloud. Did Lambert think the financial inducements he had made said them for him? If so, he was mistaken. Anna felt uneasy. Was there an underlying aspect to this proposal of his of which she had no knowledge? She had to break the silent aura of expectancy he had cast around himself.

'I'm sorry, Lambert, I cannot accept your offer,' she said quietly. 'As much as I would like to come up here every day and admire this view, it would be you I was marrying, not the view, nor the house, nor the fields, nor any of your other assets.'

His face flooded with disappointment. 'There's someone else?'

She nodded.

'Julian?'

'Yes.'

His lips tightened. 'Damn,' he snapped. 'Why didn't I meet you first?'

'I'm sorry, Lambert. If your sole intention in inviting us to your home was to propose to me, I

432

regret it has ended in disappointment for you.'

Lambert took a grip on a sense of frustration that could easily spill over into anger. Then he might reveal the secret with which he had been entrusted. Betray that and John Mason would immediately disassociate himself and his family from Lambert. The secret he held might still give him the chance he wanted, but it meant he would have to act before Anna's birthday.

'I am sorry that you cannot see your way to become my wife, but I will keep hope alive in my heart.' He held up his hand to stem the words that were coming to her lips. 'Say no more on the matter, Anna. And let me assure you, apart from this disappointment, the time you and your father and Charles have spent here has been most enjoyable. I hope we can remain friends and that I will be welcome at Hawkshead Manor.'

'Of course we can still be friends, and you will always be welcome at my home.' She leaned across and kissed him lightly on the cheek. 'Thank you for being so understanding.'

He smiled. 'Now, let us look at the horses.'

In a few minutes he was helping her from the gig. They'd reached a field in which ten curious horses crowded at the hedge, awaiting their arrival.

Anna rested her hands on the gate and watched them with admiration in her eyes. 'They are magnificent. Did you breed them?'

'Yes. Horses are my passion. That is one aspect of the estate of which I am completely in charge. The grooms, undergrooms and stable boys are there to help and look after the animals but it is my domain, whereas the farm I leave to the manager.'

'They know you and love you,' Anna commented as he opened the gate. They both stepped into the field. The horses were enjoying the petting, and nuzzled them affectionately in return.

'They've taken to you.' Lambert smiled.

She was delighted to find that they had developed an immediate empathy with her.

'Which one?' he asked.

'Which one?' She was momentarily puzzled by his question.

'Yes, which one do you think is the best?'

She looked at them critically as she moved among them, having a word here, a whisper there, patting a neck, gently rubbing a nose. 'Oh, I don't know, they are all so beautiful.'

She let her eyes rove over them all again. One moved and nuzzled her. 'Oh, you want me to say you, do you? Well, for your information I was just about to tell your owner that I think you are the best.' She patted the mare's neck affectionately, and glanced at Lambert. 'Don't you think so?'

'I do, and she is yours.'

'Oh, no, I couldn't accept!' she gasped.

'You could and you will. It gives me great pleasure to present Stardust to you as a gift.'

'You can't!'

'My dear Anna, why not? And don't read anything into my gesture that I don't intend. I accept your answer to my proposal. I won't say I am not disappointed, but it is your prerogative to make the choice just as it is mine to decide that I should

434

give you a horse as a reminder of your visit to my home. Now, say no more about it. I will arrange for Stardust to be taken to Hawkshead Manor next week.'

Anna hugged the horse's neck. 'You're magnificent. I hope you'll like your new home. I'll look after you.' She turned to Lambert. 'I'm overwhelmed and truly thank you for your generosity, understanding and this wonderful present.' She kissed him lightly on the cheek.

He smiled. 'I will always remember your visit.' He took her hands in his. 'If ever there is a chance...'

She stopped him by withdrawing from his touch. 'I think we should be getting back.'

He did not reply but escorted her to the gig. She sensed that disappointment had come over him again.

As they drove away Anna looked back. All the horses except one were trotting away across the field. Only Stardust remained looking over the gate as if watching her new owner for some sign of affection. Anna waved. Stardust snorted, turned swiftly and galloped away, as if a feeling of joy had come over her.

'I hope you both enjoyed your visit,' said John as he turned the carriage from the Langthorpe drive on to the trackway that led north.

Anna and Charles assured him that they had.

'And I hope you did too and gave no thought to events in Whitby,' added Anna.

John gave a wry smile. 'They did cross my mind but I dismissed them, knowing you both wanted

435

me to relax and enjoy my time with Lambert.' He cast a sidelong glance at his daughter. 'That was a most generous gift he made you.'

'Yes, it was.' Anna offered no more.

'And ... er ... is there anything else I should know about?'

'No, it was just a gift.'

'But it...' John was interrupted by Anna's laughter.

There was amusement in her eyes as she said, 'All right, Father, I'll put you out of your misery. And you too, Charles, for I know you are just as inquisitive as Father. There was nothing more to it than that. No ulterior motive to giving me Stardust. In fact, he did that *after* he had proposed.' She let the information hang teasingly.

'He did!' John gasped and hauled on the reins to bring the gig to a halt. He turned to his daughter. 'And?' he pressed.

'I said no.'

'What! But he's such a catch ... charming, handsome, rich, a fine house, a well-run estate.'

'I wanted to marry a man who loves me and whom I love, not wealth and all its accoutrements.'

'But if Lambert loves you,' put in Charles.

'Ah, that's exactly the point.'

'Surely he must if he asked you to marry him?' her father pointed out.

'Oh, certainly he asked me to marry him, but he never once said he loved me. Someone else has.'

'Julian?' cried Charles.

'Yes.'

'Has he asked you to marry him?' queried John.

'No.'

He looked perplexed, trying to fathom his daughter's love-life. How he wished Elizabeth was here to deal with this. He gave a little shake of his head. 'Then what...?'

'He will,' interrupted Anna.

'How do you know?'

'Oh, I know. A woman's intuition.'

'I'll never understand, but I suppose you know your own heart and mind.'

Anna placed a reassuring hand on his arm. 'I do, Father. Don't worry.'

'Whatever brings you happiness.' He kissed her on the cheek, then gave a flick of the reins to send the horses on their way to Whitby.

He purposely followed a track that took them near the rugged coast south of Whitby. He drew the horses to a halt when they had a fine view from the cliff top towards Robin Hood's Bay.

There was a fast-running sea and the breakers were sending foam crashing up the cliffs. Waves stormed to the shore, one after the other, to crash and mingle in a white torrent which was overwhelmed by the next meeting of sea and wind.

'It's good to be home,' said John with feeling. 'Langthorpe Hall was very civilised, a beautiful setting, but there was no drama there. Not like this. This is our country.' He turned to his children. 'I hope it will always be yours. Let no usurper like the Uptons ever disrupt it.'

The following morning, Anna insisted on accompanying her father and brother to see Edwin. She wanted to be involved in the smuggling more than ever.

They found him at home in Tin Ghaut. He ushered them into his humble house. Embarrassed by its untidiness, he cast Anna an apologetic look.

She smiled. 'If I go away from here criticising what I have seen then I am not worthy to enter your home, Edwin.'

'You are kind, miss.'

'So, Edwin, how did the run go?' asked Charles, anxious to know that his arrangements had met no snags.

'Very well, Mr Charles. No trouble at all.'

'The Uptons didn't appear?' asked John.

'No sign of them.' Edwin gave a little nod of satisfaction. 'I think we taught them a lesson.'

'You are sure there was no one spying on you?' asked Anna, recalling the two men she had seen on the cliff.

'Well, miss, I can't be absolutely certain of that. I did place three men to counteract anything of that nature. They saw no one, but it's difficult to cover every inch.'

'The cargo?' queried John.

'As Mr Charles said it would be. It was a calm sea that night, so we had no trouble getting the goods ashore. I dispersed them right away so Sandsend is clear. I thought it wise to do that as Nick and Ralph reported that they had been challenged by a Revenue cutter south of the Humber, but they outran her and gave her the slip.'

John looked a little concerned. 'That was all?

438

Nothing else happened?'

'No.'

'We'll go and have a word with them. Are they in port?'

'Yes. They said they would wait until you returned. If there are plans to run more contraband soon they would postpone their fishing.'

'Right, let's go and see them.'

Within ten minutes they were boarding a sloop tied up at the quay.

After congratulating Nick and Ralph on their success, John put a question. 'Are you sure it was a Revenue cutter?'

'Well, sir, we didn't wait about to be absolutely sure,' replied Nick, 'but Ralph, who took more notice of it than me, thought it *could* have been a Dutchman.'

There was a query in John's eyes.

'Aye, sir, but I couldn't be sure. It might have been that I still had on my mind what had recently happened ashore.'

'What was that?' asked Anna sharply.

'Well, miss, a Dutchman got talking to me. Seemed to be a bit too interested in what we were loading. Naturally I didn't tell him the truth but made up some story. He asked if I knew or had any dealings with Reynier de Klerk whom he believed had contacts in England. I said I'd never heard of him. He said he thought it strange that neither I nor the man from Hull to whom he had been speaking, and he indicated a ship on the other side of the dock, knew him, for he felt sure that Herr de Klerk was trading with someone in Yorkshire.'

'And that was all?' asked John.

'Aye, sir.'

'Could he have been a government official suspicious about contraband? And if so, could the Hull ship he seemed to be interested in have a connection with the Uptons?' Anna suggested.

'There's always that possibility,' agreed her father. 'He gave no indication of what he was about?'

'No, sir, but I have seen him around the docks on other occasions. Seemed to be watching, but this is the first time he has spoken to any of us.'

'Can you describe him?' asked Charles, who had been trying to link the connection with the mention of the de Klerks.

'Tallish. Hard face. Swarthy complexion.'

'Not Dutch then?' Charles picked up on this latter point quickly.

'No. More like a Spaniard, but he could have lived in Amsterdam for some time. He seemed familiar with the area we were in.'

John nodded. 'Well, no harm seems to have been done, but if you encounter any further such incidents in the future report them as soon as you get back.'

'Very good, sir.'

'We'll arrange for another run in a fortnight, so enjoy a bit of fishing.'

'Charles, I suspect you might know of whom Ralph was speaking?' said John as they rode home.

'Of course I can't be certain, but the description could fit Coenraad Bremer. He's not a very likeable character and I know he doesn't like the de Klerks.'

'I think next time you visit Amsterdam you might make a few discreet enquiries.'

Anna's visit to Langthorpe Hall had so occupied Julian's mind that the following week he could not settle and announced to his parents that he was going to Hawkshead Manor, pleading the necessity to see Charles about some trading mission he had in mind as an excuse for an uninvited visit.

Pleasure all round was displayed by the Masons at his arrival and he was delighted to accept their invitation to stay a few days.

He made his curiosity about their visit to Langthorpe Hall appear casual, but Anna knew what lay behind his queries and remarks. She gave him no satisfaction about what had passed between her and Lambert. He was to learn that two days later when Lambert, as good as his word, sent his gift to Anna.

John and Charles had left after a pleasant lunch to conclude some business in Whitby and Anna and Julian were relaxing on the terrace. The rattle of an approaching wagon disturbed them. When it came in to view Anna immediately realised it was the arrival of Stardust.

'A new horse?' queried Julian as they rose to their feet.

'Yes,' she replied. 'Stardust. A present from Lambert.'

Julian tensed. Jealousy flooded into him, and heightened when she said, 'She's beautiful and so

441

placid. We took to each other straight away. Come and see her.' There was excitement in her voice. 'Come on,' she called over her shoulder as she made for the steps.

Julian jerked himself out of the gloom that had settled over him and followed. Such a present and its acceptance could mean only one thing. Giver and recipient were close, maybe too close for his liking. What had gone on at Langthorpe Hall?

Anna directed the wagon into the stable yard where the Hawkshead grooms were soon taking charge of the new arrival. They were all delighted by Stardust's beauty and demeanour. While recognising the horse's quality, Julian felt annoyed at all the attention it was getting, for he saw in it a reflection of the attention Lambert too must have received. He stood by without saying a word.

'I must ride her now,' cried Anna after watching Jack lead Stardust round the yard in order to let her limber up after the journey from Langthorpe Hall.

'Very well, miss,' he called. 'We'll give her a rub down and she'll be ready in half an hour.'

'I'll go and get ready. Riding with me, Julian?'

'Of course,' he said. It was the polite thing to do when so invited, though he saw the ride as being too much of a reminder of Lambert. It would only heighten his jealousy and imaginings of what had happened at Langthorpe.

Half an hour later they rode out of the stable yard. Anna chose one of the nearby fields in which to become familiar with the new arrival. As

442

she suspected, it did not take long. Horse and rider seemed meant for one other. She waxed enthusiastic about the horse and frequently expressed her gratitude to the absent Lambert.

'Don't look so glum, Julian. Enjoy the ride.' She sent Stardust heading for the track through the woods before he could reply, smiling to herself at his gloomy mood since the horse's arrival. She knew what was biting him.

The sudden increase in her pace jerked Julian out of his dejection. He should stop feeling sorry for himself. He should stop seeing Stardust as an emblem of love between Anna and Lambert. A new sense of purpose was born in him. He would no longer hold back. He urged his horse on, caught up with Anna. There was laughter in her eyes and a teasing smile on her lips. Her hat slipped from her head to hang from her neck by its ribbon. Her hair, torn loose by the speed of their gallop, streamed in tantalising disarray. Exhilaration in the joy of being one with Stardust filled her. Julian matched her pace. The intoxication of the ride swept through him. It charged his very being with determination.

Anna began to slow the ride and brought her horse to a halt when they rode into a clearing. Sun filtered through the trees, dappling the ground with a patchwork of light and shade. She straightened in the saddle and took a deep breath, easing down after the exhilaration of the ride. She turned to Julian who was steadying his horse beside her. Their eyes met. Hers shone with exultation, his with query and hope. Not a word was spoken. He slipped from the saddle and came to her. Held out his arms to help her to the ground. She slid into them. When her feet touched the soft earth he still held her. She made no attempt to draw away but looked up at him. Their eyes locked. His lips met hers and she immediately accepted the passion implied in them. They were lost in each other and both knew that nothing else in the world mattered.

Their lips parted.

'I love you, Anna. Marry me,' he whispered hoarsely.

'I will.' The two words came softly but with a strength that left no room for misunderstanding.

He leaned back from her and looked deep into her eyes. He saw sincerity to match her promise. This was not a teasing Anna, nor one treating life lightly. He knew those persons and liked them but here was one proclaiming that they had a future together, something he had wanted to hear but thought he had lost to Lambert.

'You will?' he gasped as if he couldn't believe it.

She laughed as she said, 'Don't look so surprised, Julian. I love you.'

His unuttered words were spoken in a kiss which she accepted and returned. Passion swept through them. Their hold on each other tightened as if each would never allow the other to escape.

They held hands, walking across the clearing and on to a path that led to a stream. Its water cascaded over rocks in harmony with their joy.

'You thought Stardust had dashed your hopes,' commented Anna.

Julian gave a half smile. 'I did.'

'You had no need to fear.'

'Then what was the horse about? Was she a bribe?'

'No. Lambert gave me Stardust after he'd proposed.'

Julian stopped in his tracks. 'He did?'

'Yes.'

'And you turned him down?'

'Of course. I wouldn't be saying yes to you if I hadn't.'

'And still he gave you Stardust?'

'Yes. He was a generous in his disappointment.'

'Why did you reject him?'

'I wouldn't marry a man who never said he loved me. He didn't, but you did.'

'I've loved you since the first day I saw you.'

'I cannot say the same,' replied Anna. 'I was a little suspicious of you. In fact, I feel there are still some things I don't know about you, but I do love you. And that was my main reason for refusing Lambert's proposal.'

Julian swept her into his arms again and met her lips with all the love he could muster, to try to make her forget the doubts she still harboured about the unexplained aspects of his life.

John Mason approved of their betrothal, asking only that they say nothing publicly before Anna's birthday. At the party, when he had a special surprise for her, he would announce their intention to marry.

Chapter Twenty

Over the next four weeks John was impressed by the interest his daughter took in both his trading ventures, legitimate and covert. Now she was involved in the smuggling her interest had become stronger and encompassed all aspects of the Mason empire, as he liked to think of it. It pleased him because, coupled to Charles's enthusiasm, he sensed a prosperous future was ensured.

Anna was accepted by the syndicate after John had explained her part in identifying the connection with the Upton brothers, and no one objected to her being present at their meetings.

Charles's first visit to Amsterdam after they had returned from Langthorpe Hall proved disappointing regarding his enquiries about Coenraad Bremer. He did not want to arouse suspicions in Holland, so, because Magdalena had smuggling connections, and he knew she could be discreet, he made his first enquiries with her. She discovered no underhand activities orchestrated by Coenraad but promised Charles that she would be alert for any information about him.

The sun soon dispersed the early-morning mists on the first of May and its rays were warming the terrace of Hawkshead Manor when John, accompanied by Anna and Charles, strolled out of the house after breakfast to enjoy the air and the view.

'Anna, I think it is time we gave more thought to your birthday party in June. Time will soon slip by. This is to be a big occasion with many guests. You must get the invitations out soon, and remember we have an important announcement to make about you and Julian. It will be a significant day for you both so I want everything to be just right. I want you to remember it as a special token of my thanks for all your support and love since your mother died. There will be a similar occasion for Charles when his birthday comes round in October. So give some thought to it. Discuss it with Mrs Denston. I have had a word with her and she will be expecting you to consult her. I told her, as I am telling you now, spare nothing. You are worth it.'

Anna was delighted at this generosity in which she read his love for her. She flung her arms round his neck and kissed him on the cheek. 'You are so wonderful, Father. Thank you so much, not only for this party but for everything else.' She slipped her arm through his as they turned to stroll along the terrace. 'If you are intending it to be a lavish party it is going to be expensive, so no present.'

Her father smiled. 'I already have that.'

'You have!' Anna gasped with a note of excitement in her voice. 'You shouldn't, but what is it?'

He laughed. 'Ah, that's my secret. You'll have to wait until your birthday.'

'Do you know, Charles?' she asked.

He shook his head and smiled at his sister's enthusiasm. Since a little girl she had always tried to cajole secrets out of him, and nearly always succeeded. 'I don't know, and if I did I wouldn't tell you.' She looked at him coyly. 'No,' he said, 'I really don't know.' The firmness in his voice convinced her. Now she would have to spend the next few weeks wondering, and growing more excited as the day drew nearer.

The men spent two weeks studying the movements of the inhabitants of Hawkshead Manor. No particular pattern emerged. The master would leave of a morning at various times, either for a ride where he might be accompanied by either or both of his children, or else for Whitby accompanied by his son. On one occasion his daughter went too. There was no pattern to their return but they were always back, never away for a night. The two men realised that their mission might prove difficult but it was one for which they would be well paid if they were successful.

They were discussing in low tones a possible plan to achieve their objective over a tankard of ale in the crowded Black Bull in Whitby's Church Street when a stranger came to sit beside them. Their line of talk ceased and in a moment or two they fell into conversation with him, introducing themselves as Eric and Carl. In a few minutes they realised that luck might have dealt them just the card they wanted when, by a chance remark, the stranger let it be known that he was Fred, a groom at Hawkshead Manor.

'I hear tell your master's good to work for?' said Eric.

'Aye, he is that.'

'Pays a decent wage?'

'Aye.'

'And you get time off to come to Whitby?' asked Carl.

'Sometimes. There's an opportunity with the master visiting friends and the young ones in Hull.'

'So you'll get the chance a few more times before they return then?'

'No. The master's only away for the night.' Fred eyed the two men. 'Where are you from then?'

'Lincolnshire. We've come hoping to find a job.'

Fred gave a little chuckle. 'If tha's thinking of getting one at the Manor, think again. All the jobs are filled and folks hereabout think so much of John Mason there's a waiting list.'

'Then it'll have to be fishing or whaling.'

'Whaling? Rough life that.' Fred pulled a face. 'But if tha's bent on it tha'll have to be getting signed on. They'll sail this month.'

'Aye, we know that but can't make up our minds.'

'Best of luck, whatever you decide.' Fred drained his tankard and stood up. He bade them farewell and left the Black Bull.

'Well, tonight seems to be the night,' commented Carl.

'Aye, we can get the job done and line our pockets as well. No one else need know about that,' agreed Eric. They gulped down the rest of their beer and left the inn.

The evening sun was sinking in the west and drawing daylight with it as they approached Hawkshead Manor with caution. On previous visits they had decided that their best method of entry would be via the study or library windows. They were well away from the domestic and servants quarters, and with the Masons away the house would be quiet.

They surveyed the building for a while and then, using the cover of a beech hedge, made their way swiftly towards the house. They had about ten yards of open ground to cross and, after making sure no one was about, they ran to the wall of the house. They paused, then moved towards the library. While Eric kept a look-out, Carl examined the windows.

'This one,' he whispered. He had noted that the inside security catch had not been slid fully home. He slipped a knife from his belt and inserted it between the joins in the sash window, then inched it carefully towards the metal fastener. With each minute upward movement the blade of the knife got greater purchase. Satisfied with its position he put pressure on the bar. He clenched his teeth. His fingers strained. The catch was moving. He tried harder. Then he felt it slip its holder. Relief flooded over him. He relaxed. The way was open.

Carl gripped the glazing bar on the window and gently exerted upward pressure. He breathed more easily when he found the window moved without a sound. As the gap widened Eric came to his side. Not a word was spoken as they climbed into the room. Eric lowered the window but left a slight gap at the bottom to make their escape more easy if they were disturbed.

The light was still sufficient for them to view the room. They ignored the shelves of books and went straight to the display cabinet.

'There's a fortune in here,' gasped Eric.

Carl's eyes widened.

They stared in disbelief for a few minutes.

'Mr Finch said what we had to get was in the study,' said Eric. He moved quickly but quietly to the door.

After twenty minutes' unfruitful searching a frustrated Carl snapped. 'Forget it. Let's feather our nest from you lot.' He inclined his head towards the library.

'Right,' Eric agreed. They had reached the room when they heard the front door open. There was a pause. A match scraped. They saw a light beneath the study door. It flared and then settled to a steady glow. They knew a lamp had been lit. They remained still, tense, waiting for the next movement from the hall, hoping it would not be in their direction. But footsteps crossed the hall towards the study. Eric tapped Carl on the arm and indicated to him that they should go to the side of the door where they would be hidden when it opened. They pressed back against the wall, nerves and muscles tensed for instant action.

The door swung back. Light spilled across the room. A figure appeared, came into the room and, unaware that he was not alone, placed the lamp on the desk. The men sprang. Carl brought a swift, hard chopping blow to the back of the

451

man's head. He stumbled forward. Eric hit him hard. The man spun round to meet another vicious blow from Carl. He pitched to the floor, hitting his head against the corner of the desk, and lay still.

'He's out,' said Carl, standing over his victim.

'Let's get a few things and be away from here before he recovers.'

They went through into the library and broke the glass in the cabinet with as little noise as possible. By the light of the lamp, which Eric had grabbed when they left the study, they quickly selected some items of jewellery that they knew they could dispose of through a fence in Hull. They stuffed their pockets and left by the way in which they had entered the building. They did not pause to look back as they hurried away from Hawkshead Manor, now deep in darkness.

Mrs Denston came into the hall with a brisk step, one that made little noise on the marble floor. She had trained herself to move quietly so as not to disturb her employers as she went about her duties. She was on her way to the dining room to check that the table had been laid correctly for Mr Mason's breakfast. He wasn't a fussy man but Mrs Denston liked things to be right.

With her mind on what she was about to do and considering the tasks for the rest of the day, she was halfway across the hall before she realised that she had been subconsciously aware something was different. It brought her to a halt. Her gaze was drawn to the left. Mr Mason's study door was open. He was always particular that all doors were closed at night. If he had had cause to go to his study when he returned the previous evening he most certainly would have shut the door behind him when he went to bed.

She must close it now, but even before she reached it a sense of foreboding seeped into her. Something was wrong. Her step slowed. She approached the door with apprehension. Hesitating, she listened. There was not a sound from inside the room.

'Mr Mason?' Her voice was low, tentative. 'Are you there, Mr Mason?' She gave a slight tap on the door but there was no response. She stepped into the room with some trepidation and was brought up by the sight of a figure sprawled on the carpet near the desk. Shock and disbelief momentarily drove all other feeling from her until alarm took their place. 'Mr Mason!' Even as she called his name she knew he would not hear. She turned and hurried from the room. Panic threatened but she held it at bay, knowing that she had to be strong and take control of this situation with a level head.

Within a few minutes all the staff knew of the tragedy. Keeping a tight grip on her own feelings she soothed the distress everyone felt. Immediate action was necessary. Jack Crane was despatched with all haste to Hull to break the news to Mr Charles and Miss Anna. Another groom was sent with equal speed to Whitby for the doctor and to inform the authorities.

The doctor's verdict was that John had been killed either from a blow to the back of his neck or from striking his head against the sharp corner

453

of the desk. After examination John's body was taken upstairs to his bedroom.

The constable sent from Whitby to investigate came to the conclusion that John had disturbed one or more intruders who were there, on the evidence of the smashed glass and disturbed jewellery, to commit robbery. Who they were was a mystery, for no one had seen them and the employees of the house had not noticed anyone hanging around during the previous few days. The culprits had vanished. Where, who could guess? The world was a big place.

When Jack Crane reached Hull his enquiries for the whereabouts of Albion Street soon brought him help from a barefooted urchin whose dirty face lit up with a beaming smile when Jack chose him for a guide. He tossed the lad a coin when they reached the house he sought. The child caught it with the dexterity of an expert, yelled his thanks and ran off. The groom smiled as he watched him run, but his sombre countenance returned as he knocked on the door. This was a mission he wished he did not have to carry out.

The door was opened by a maid who looked questioningly at Jack, dusty after his ride.

'Good day. You have a Miss Anna Mason and a Mr Charles Mason staying here. I am Jack Crane, groom at their home. I would like to have a word with them, on a matter of urgency.'

His tone, expression and knowledge convinced the maid of the genuineness of his request. 'Please come inside,' she said. 'I'll see if they are available.'

Jack stepped into the hall, removed his cap and stood to one side as the maid closed the door.

'I won't be a moment,' she said, and crossed the hall to a door on the right. She knocked and went into the room.

A few instants later the door opened and Anna and Charles appeared.

'Jack?' Concern mingled with curiosity in Charles's eyes and voice. Alarm wreathed Anna's face when she saw Jack's grave expression.

'Miss. Sir.' The words would hardly come. 'I've bad news.'

'Well, what is it?' urged Charles when Jack held back. It was only a momentary hesitation but it seemed a lifetime to Anna.

'It's the master, sir. Your father's had an accident.' Jack screwed up his face. This wasn't as he had rehearsed it on his way to Hull. These words did not tell the truth, they fudged the core of the matter. Annoyed and impatient with himself, he shook his head. 'No, that's not it. It's worse. Your father was killed some time last night.'

Though the words sounded unreal to brother and sister the truth was evident in the presence of Jack Crane. He would not be here unless events were of such enormity they demanded it.

Anna went cold, then numbness took over. Her body emptied of all feeling. She wasn't hearing right. This was some waking nightmare. She was not standing in the hall of a house in Hull hearing that her father was dead. This couldn't be true, and yet the evidence that it was stood before her. She felt life draining from her. She swayed. Someone touched her arm. She took a grip on herself and heard a voice she recognised as her brother's.

'What happened, Jack?'

'Mrs Denston found him this morning in his study. He went out yesterday evening to visit Sir Arthur Foston. Must have disturbed burglars on his return. The glass on the display cabinets had been smashed and there are several items missing.'

The words and the information they bore echoed in Anna's mind, then lodged there. They were unreal. They didn't make sense to her. There was something not right but, in her dazed state, she could not latch on to what was troubling her.

'All right, Jack, we'll come at once. Wait a moment.' Charles glanced round and saw that the maid had stayed near the door to the quarters at the back of the house in case she was needed. He signalled to her. She hurried forward. 'Stay with Miss Anna while I see Mr and Mrs Kirby.'

'Yes, sir.' As he took quick steps across the hall he heard her say with quiet compassion, 'Would you like to sit down, miss?'

When Charles broke the new to the Kirbys there was immediate shock and horror, followed quickly by concern for their two guests. They hurried into the hall. Mrs Kirby took the situation in hand as soon as she had offered condolences and comforting words to Anna.

'Caroline, take one of the maids and start to pack Anna's belongings.' She turned to the maid who had stood by. 'Evelyn, take Mr Charles's groom to the kitchen and see that Cook gives him something to eat. He must be sustained for the return to Hawkshead Manor.' She looked at Charles. 'Let him drive you back, you'll have too much on your mind to handle the horses competently. We'll see that his horse receives stabling until it can be collected. Septimus, a drop of brandy for Anna and Charles.' Her husband hurried away to do her bidding. 'Rebecca, when Anna has had her drink, take her upstairs and see that she is well wrapped up for the journey. We don't want shock to take hold.' Rebecca, kneeling beside Anna, nodded. Julian had taken Anna's hands in his, hoping that she would draw comfort from it.

Mrs Kirby took in this little cameo. She turned to Charles who was accepting the glass Mr Kirby had brought him. 'Charles, would it be of help and comfort if Julian and Rebecca came with you and stayed until after the funeral? I don't want to push them on you at a trying time but if they would be of use in any way then they may do so.'

'Mrs Kirby, that is most kind of you. What do you think, Anna?'

His sister, who had just shuddered at her first reviving sip of brandy, found that it had done more than that. It had driven away some of the daze that had enveloped her and had brought her back to her immediate surroundings and situation. She felt the need for someone to be with them in this tragedy. 'Oh, yes, please, I would love to have them.'

'Then that is settled,' said Mrs Kirby with a finality that would brook no countermand unless it came from the Masons.

Anna felt her hand squeezed and looked up to see a light in Julian's eyes that gave her confidence to face the future.

Forty minutes later two gigs, one behind the other, left Hull and headed for Whitby. For Anna it was a journey made with a heavy heart. Her beloved father would not be there to greet them. His enthusiasm to know all about what they had done and the pleasure he always derived from knowing that they had enjoyed themselves would be missing. The vibrant life, that had disappeared after her mother's death and for the return of which she had fought so hard, would now be missing for good.

Dread began to fill her as they neared the Manor but she drew comfort from the fact that Julian and Rebecca were with them. They would help to stop her dwelling on her loss, and she was sure that Rebecca would offer every support not only to her but to Charles too. The thought of all the arrangements that would have to be made almost overwhelmed her but, since leaving Hull, she had sensed that Charles was quietly ordering them in his mind. She vowed to help him. They were met on the steps by the housekeeper and the servants.

Once they had made their tearful commiserations to their new master and mistress, Mrs Denston despatched servants to the various jobs she had allocated them. Seeing Julian and Rebecca she organised the preparation of their rooms with a few words to one of the maids.

Before Mrs Denston could say any more, Anna took a firm grip on herself. 'Mrs Denston, I am grateful for everything you have done so far and I know Charles and I will lean heavily on your support through the trying days ahead, but before we go on to discuss the many aspects of what has happened and what has to be done, please take me to see my father.'

Mrs Denston made no comment but she was pleased to see the strength in this young woman she had watched over for many years.

'Very good, Miss Anna.' She led the way up the stairs. Anna and Charles followed.

They entered the darkened room. Mrs Denston waited just outside the door. Charles took hold of Anna's hand as they moved towards the bed. Each drew comfort and strength from the presence of the other. They heard the door close as Mrs Denston left them to their sorrow. They stood by the bed looking down at their father, peaceful in repose. He had been so cared for in death that he appeared to be merely sleeping. A tear trickled down Anna's cheek. She wiped it away, determined not to shed another until she was on her own, but knew she would cry inside. Five minutes passed then she released her hold on Charles's hand. She went to the windows across which the curtains had been drawn. She pulled them back with a determined swish.

'Father would not wish to be in the dark. He was a man who loved the light and that's as it will be.'

Charles offered no protest. Though it went against convention, he agreed with her.

When they left the room Mrs Denston was waiting on the landing near the head of the stairs.

'Mrs Denston,' said Anna firmly, 'I have opened the curtains in my father's room. He liked light. I know it will be dark soon, they can be drawn then, but we will have a lamp lit for him.'

'Very good, miss.' It was something she would have preferred but she'd thought it best for Miss Anna and Mr Charles to make the decision about not following the usual practice. 'When you have refreshed yourselves after your journey, may I see you both in the east drawing room?'

'Certainly, should we say in ten minutes?' Anna glanced at Charles who nodded his approval.

When Anna came down she glanced in the west drawing room and was pleased to see that her brother was attending to the comfort of their guests. 'We will be with you in a few minutes. Mrs Denston wants to see us,' she told them.

Julian and Rebecca told her they understood perfectly.

When the housekeeper arrived, Anna indicated a chair and asked her to tell them about what had happened.

She sat down and related the facts as she knew them. She passed on the opinion of the doctor about the cause of death and the constable about the motive behind it. 'I had the master laid out as you have seen and took the liberty of asking the undertaker to see you tomorrow, Mr Charles, so you can make all the necessary arrangements as you would like them.'

'Thank you, Mrs Denston, we are grateful,' he

replied. 'It must have been such an ordeal for you. Our most sincere thanks.'

'Mr Charles, Miss Anna, I have been with you so long that I feel part of the family. It saddens me deeply that you have lost both your parents so young, but you know that I will be here to help as long as you want me.'

'That is very reassuring, Mrs Denston. I know you were very dear to our parents and you are just as dear to us. Thank you for all you have done, not just today but through all the years.'

'May I say I am pleased to see the young people from Hull? I am sure they will be a great support to you over the next few days.'

So it proved. The Kirbys helped both Anna and Charles to cope with the stream of visitors who came to offer their sympathy. They took their minds off the ordeal of the funeral that lay ahead, and were ready to help in any way asked.

The night before the funeral, when they had all gone to bed, Anna knocked on the door of her brother's room.

When he opened the door, she said, 'Something's troubling me. I want to know what you think.'

He pulled the door wide and admitted her into a room lit by three oil lamps. She seated herself in one of the chairs facing him while he sat on the edge of his bed.

'What's bothering you, Anna? Is it tomorrow? I'm sure people would understand if you did not feel up to facing it.'

She shook her head. 'It's not that. I'll be there.

461

I must. And I'll cope.'

'What is it then?'

Anna frowned. 'It's a worry I can't get rid of. I'm not sure that this was a robbery gone wrong.'

'What on earth do you mean?' Charles was shocked by the implication.

'Father's killing could have been intentional.'

'But the evidence ... the forced entry, the broken display cabinet, the missing jewellery. Everything points to the motive as robbery.'

'But supposing that was done to mislead us?'

'You mean, the main purpose was to kill Father?'

'Yes.'

'But if that is what they wanted to do, why do it inside the house? They could have waylaid him on his return home.'

'If they had done that there would have been nothing to cover their sole intention. Waiting inside for him then taking the jewellery made it look as if robbery was their main purpose and that they were disturbed by him while carrying it out.'

Charles looked thoughtful. 'So what you are really saying is that this is linked to the smuggling, and that the Uptons are behind it?'

When her suspicions were voiced it brought a shadow of doubt to Anna's mind. She realised she had no concrete evidence for her idea, nothing that could be used to make a proper accusation. But a deep-rooted feeling that something else lay behind this tragedy remained, and she steeled herself against the doubts raised by her brother's tone.

'Yes.'

'Can you prove it?'

'No.'

'Then forget it. You are moving into dangerous waters here. I think you are wrong. Besides, I believe the Uptons learned their lesson when we clashed with them at Sandsend, and they would have no way of knowing that Father was the head of the Whitby smugglers. And even if they had, they must have realised that someone else would take his place.'

'And that will be you?' The fear of what this could mean in the light of her suppositions hit Anna forcibly.

Charles nodded. 'Father always intended it that way because I was familiar with the set-up, know what is needed to keep the smuggling going as a profitable concern and have the contacts in Holland. I know he mentioned it to Sir Arthur but it needs the syndicate's agreement.'

Concern showed on Anna's face. 'Oh, Charles, do be careful. I don't want to lose someone else.'

Chapter Twenty-one

The parish church on the cliff top was packed for John Mason's funeral. This kindly man was well known and well liked in Whitby and surrounding district. The parson kept his eulogy short but to the point in praising the man he was about to bury in the churchyard, among the greening gravestones that bore witness to Whitby's connection with the unrelenting sea. Anna and Charles were thankful for that consideration for it lessened the ordeal that faced them.

Tears trickled down their cheeks as they stood by the grave, touched by the gentle breeze on a bright morning, the type of day their father liked. It was as if he had ordered such a day to say his farewells in. With the coffin resting deep in the ground, mourners and sympathisers came forward to offer their condolences to brother and sister. Knowing that special friends would come to the house they were wishing this interlude at the graveside over, and were thankful when only one person remained in the line.

'Lambert!' Both expressed their surprise at the same time.

His face was grave as he took their hands in his. 'I am so sorry about this. Word only got to me late yesterday otherwise I would have been here before. I left early this morning but could not get into the church – so many people. But

464

that is understandable.'

'It was good of you to come all this way,' said Charles.

'It is the least I could do. Though I had known your father only a short duration, I felt closer to him than mere time would indicate. How have you both been?'

'We've managed under very trying circumstances,' replied Anna. 'We were in Hull with the Kirbys when the news reached us. We were most grateful for their support especially as Julian and Rebecca returned to Hawkshead with us.'

Lambert glanced round and saw them standing across the churchyard, their concern for Anna and Charles evident even from this distance.

'You cannot return home today,' said Anna, 'you must come and stay with us.' She did not want him to think their friendship had ceased because of her rejection of his proposal.

'That is most generous of you, but I don't want to impose at a time like this. I had intended to find a room at one of the inns in Whitby.'

'You must not do that. You are welcome to be with us,' pressed Anna.

'Do come,' Charles urged. 'You'll help to divert us.'

'Well, if you are sure?'

'Then that's settled.'

After the last of the sympathisers had left Hawkshead Manor the five friends settled down in the drawing room, Julian with the satisfaction that the man he had once thought of as a rival for Anna's affections was no longer a threat.

It was inevitable that at some point the talk should turn to the tragedy.

'What happened?' Lambert asked. 'I overheard someone at the funeral say it was robbery.'

'Yes,' replied Charles. 'Anna and I were in Hull. Father had gone to spend the evening with Sir Arthur Foston. It seems that he returned home early. Sir Arthur told me that Father had complained of not feeling well and asked to be excused. He must have disturbed the burglars, with tragic results.'

'Do I detect that you don't agree with that theory, Anna?' asked Lambert. He had noticed that, throughout Charles's statement, she repeatedly gave slight shakes of her head.

Startled, she looked up sharply. His query had brought all eyes on to her. A quick glance around them showed her that, apart from surprise and curiosity there was also a general desire to help her if that was possible. Only Charles was afraid of how she would answer Lambert. There were things that should not be divulged. But was it worth the risk? Almost before Anna had considered this she found herself speaking rapidly.

'I don't believe it happened by chance.'

'You mean, these men came here with the purpose of killing your father?' Lambert asked.

'Yes.'

'But why?' queried an astonished Rebecca.

Anna took a deep breath and swallowed hard. Her brother looked warningly at her, as if to impart: 'Be careful what you say and how you say it.' But she plunged in. 'What I am about to tell you must remain a secret between us. Nothing of

466

what I say must go beyond these four walls. I want your promise on this.' She glanced at each one in turn and received a promise that sealed them to secrecy. She had their whole attention now.

'Father was the head of a smuggling gang that operated in the Whitby area.'

This announcement, made boldly without any excuses, caused everyone to gasp and brought stares of incredulity, but everyone's thoughts were different.

Rebecca's were of disbelief. This pleasant family couldn't be involved in such illegal trade, surely? Yet there was no other reason for her friend to make this statement. She waited for further explanations.

Lambert was just as taken aback as Rebecca. He could not equate the nefarious trade with a man of such a forthright character as John Mason. He had heard that the gangs were often run by well-to-do folk, even gentry, however. What was behind Anna's revelation and why had she made it?

Julian was more shocked than any of them, for Anna's words made him wonder with alarm exactly what might have happened here. Had the Uptons, unknown to him and without his approval, attempted to move into new territory, with tragic consequences? He felt more than uncomfortable with the information Anna had just imparted.

'And you think that his death might be linked to his smuggling activities?' he asked, his heart sinking.

'Yes. There is a gang operating along the Humber, the Uptons, who extended their territory into the Yorkshire coast of Holderness by eliminating a rival gang there. There was also an attempt, we believe by the same gang, to take contraband we had run ashore the night before at Sandsend.'

'When?' Julian put the question automatically, and just as automatically Anna answered. Julian immediately connected it with the day he saw a ship carrying an unusual number of men on board sail out of Hull. He hated to dwell on the possibility that men he knew had been involved in action against John Mason's gang.

'Does that make any difference?' asked Lambert.

Julian gathered himself quickly. It had been an unwise question to ask, for it could have drawn suspicion on himself. 'I just wondered if it had taken place only a day or so before the murder.' He diverted their minds away from that query by posing another. 'Did they succeed at Sandsend?'

'No. Father was suspicious that something of that nature might happen so we were ready for them. All they got for their trouble was a few aching heads.'

'And you think your father's death might be in retaliation for their lack of success?'

'Partly, but I think it's more likely to be linked with their attempt to move in on our territory. Get rid of the leader and the operation might collapse and they could take over.'

'But if you can't prove it, what can you do about it?' asked Rebecca, still struggling in her own mind to accept that the man she'd respected and liked was involved in smuggling.

'That's exactly what I say,' said Charles. 'All the evidence points to robbery.'

In her brother's eyes Anna saw disapproval of what she had done. 'Charles, I'm sorry if you didn't want me to say anything, but I felt I needed to tell someone what I thought, especially as you don't agree with me.' She shrugged her shoulders. 'Maybe our friends can help in some way.'

'Whatever way I can,' Lambert offered.

'And, of course, you have my services,' put in Julian.

'You make journeys to Amsterdam. The Uptons may run contraband from there. There is just a possibility you could learn something.'

'If I can, I will.'

'I don't know that I can be of much help,' said Rebecca.

'You know your friendship and kindness will help Charles at this time.'

'Will the Whitby gang still operate?' Rebecca asked.

'Oh, yes, very much so,' returned Anna, new determination in her voice that dismissed any doubt. 'We'll let no one into our territory. Isn't that so, Charles?'

'It certainly is. That's what Father would want us to do.'

'Father appointed Charles as his successor. If his death is connected to the smuggling we must taken extra precautions for Charles's safety, for he will be in danger too.'

Charles saw alarm come into Rebecca's eyes,

but in that found reassurance. Her love for him could not have been shattered by Anna's revelations.

He sought confirmation of this when the gathering broke up and he invited Rebecca to walk on the terrace with him.

'I hope this will not affect things between us? I love you just the same.'

With equal candour she said, 'I love you too. You are just the same person: kind, considerate, good to be with. That I know a little more about you, though it did come with shock, does not mar that image of you.' She could sense his relief. 'Would you have told me?'

'Yes, some time. I would not want to keep any secrets from the girl I want to marry. The timing would have been dictated by events.'

'Is this a proposal?' Her eyes were shining with an eagerness that overwhelmed him. He swept her into his arms and kissed her passionately. As their lips parted she said, 'I take it that it is?'

He nodded. 'It may not be the most appropriate day but Father taught me never to hold back if there is something that you desperately want to do. And your answer?'

'I love you, Charles Mason, and I will marry you.'

'My love.' He kissed her again, revealing all the feelings he had for her. When they continued their stroll along the terrace, he said, 'I will let you into a secret. Julian proposed to Anna a few weeks ago and she accepted.'

Rebecca's little squeal of astonishment was

mingled with excitement. 'I didn't know. Why didn't someone tell me? Oh, I'm so pleased.'

'Your mother and father don't know yet. My father gave permission but wanted it to be a surprise announcement at Anna's birthday party. Naturally your mother and father would have been consulted and permission sought before-hand – probably two weeks before the party. I have a feeling that Father had something special in mind but I don't know what. Now we shall never know.'

'What about the party?'

'I'm afraid under the circumstances it will have to be cancelled. Naturally Anna hasn't given any thought to that yet.'

'Do we make our news known now?'

'Shouldn't I ask your father first?'

'Maybe. Why don't you and Anna come back with us? We could settle both proposals with Father and Mother and it would be a break from this trying time for you both.'

'We'll see how Anna feels.'

Lambert realised that Anna and Julian would have much to talk about so he followed Charles and Rebecca from the drawing room, wondering how the unexpected and shattering news would affect the relationship between them. He went to his room, for he also had much to think about.

Anna looked at Julian in embarrassment. 'Now you know the darker side of the Masons' life, I will understand if you wish to sever our relation-ship.'

Julian had been contending with a variety of thoughts and questions ever since Anna's announcement. Should he reveal his own involvement in smuggling? But to do so would disclose his connections with the Uptons whom he was beginning to believe could be behind John Mason's murder and that would make him an accessory and destroy the love Anna had for him. He deemed it wisest to keep quiet about his smuggling activities for he did not want to lose her. But how long could he keep this a secret from his family and those dear to him? Anna's words were giving him a way out. Should he take it? But that would mean he would lose her and that he did not want.

'Anna, as far as I am concerned it makes no difference to my feelings for you. I must admit that it was something of a shock, especially to know that you yourself were involved, but it is you I love and still wish to marry.' He put his hands around her waist and drew her to him. His eyes were intent on hers, trying to convey his deepest feelings and erase from her mind any thought that he might wish to break off their relationship.

She met that gaze with one of relief and thanks. Mingled with the intense love she felt for him, the combination was overpowering. He pulled her close and met her lips in a fervent exchange that drove all doubt from their minds.

Ten minutes later when Charles and Rebecca came into the drawing room and broke their news Anna and Julian were delighted.

'Father would have been pleased,' said Anna. 'He thought a great deal of you, Rebecca, and I know you brought comfort to him and helped to direct his outlook on life after Mother died. Charles and I will be ever grateful for what you did. Charles, take good care of her, she's a very special and precious person.'

The four young people discussed their situation and decided that, for the time being, it would be better not to tell anyone of their commitment to each other, not even Mr and Mrs Kirby. It could wait until a more appropriate time. The same thought coloured their outlook to the birthday party and the decision was reached that it should be cancelled and maybe held later in the year.

Anna politely refused the offer made by Rebecca for them to visit Hull, saying there were so many things to see to. In her heart she did not want to leave the house so soon after the funeral. She felt it would be a betrayal of her father. Here she still sensed his presence, something she did not want to relinquish, for she knew that in being here he would help her cope with her sadness and the life ahead.

Lambert left early the next morning after telling Anna and Charles to contact him if there was anything he could do to help them over what he saw would be a trying period ahead.

There was a mixture of emotions when Rebecca and Julian made their departure later in the morning. Joy was mixed with sorrow and each had their own thoughts about the future.

Rebecca was concerned for Charles's safety

after what had happened to his father. Julian knew he would have to face the Uptons with accusations. As the carriage drew away Charles experienced the loneliness of responsibility, and Anna planned a course that could shatter all their lives.

She voiced this in reply to Charles's observation that they now bore the full responsibility for all aspects of their father's trading, whether legal or illegal, and he hoped she would share this with him.

'You have my full support and I will be involved in any way you think best, but there is one thing I am determined on – that Father's killers should be found and convicted of his murder.'

'How do you hope to catch robbers? They could be far away by now.'

'You are still convinced that is what it was then, a robbery gone wrong?'

'Yes. The evidence...'

'Evidence! Evidence!' she cut in sharply. Her eyes flared with annoyance that her brother should parade this argument again. 'It was made to look like robbery. I feel it. My instinct tells me it was connected to smuggling.'

'I assume you mean the Upton brothers? You are treading in dangerous places. If you could find them, and there are no doubt some who would take payment for furnishing the information, and dared to visit them, you'd never return alive. You'd finish up in some bog or at the bottom of the Humber and there would be no one to contradict their story that you had never been there. They'd deny all knowledge of you.'

'I heed your warning, Charles, but there are other ways of coming face to face with them.'

'What scheme are you hatching now?'

'It would seem from their taking over from the Whartons along the Holderness coast and then making the raid on Sandsend that they are looking to control smuggling along the Yorkshire coast. Well, supposing we lure them on with that offer?'

'I still don't understand.'

'Amalgamation. Suggest that we join forces. It would tempt them. We would arrange a meeting here.'

'And then what? I've no doubt that offer would attract them but if you are to accuse them face to face, you'd need evidence of their crime.'

'I'm not suggesting that we do this immediately. It wouldn't work if we did. They will be waiting to see if someone else takes over as head of the Whitby smugglers so we've got to show them that we are still operating before we make our proposal. In the meantime we search for evidence.'

Though he could not see how this could be found, Charles realised that there was no deterring his sister so he gave her idea his cautious approval. That was good enough for Anna.

After an initial discussion about Anna's revelation Julian lapsed into silence until they neared Hull when Rebecca posed a question. 'You've been very quiet. Does it trouble you that Anna is involved in smuggling?' When an answer was not immediately forthcoming, she added, 'Don't let it influence your love for her.'

Julian gave a wan smile. 'It doesn't, but I am concerned for her and Charles's safety. Smuggling brings risks without the added enmity of the Uptons ... whoever they are.' His thoughts were jumbled. If his sister knew that he had really been thinking about confronting the Uptons and what his future relationship with them could hold, he wondered what she would say.

The following morning Julian left the house in Albion Street early saying that he had some wine business he should see to. That was in fact farthest from his mind as he rode out of Hull across the windswept land that bordered the Humber.

Approaching Luke's cottage he smiled to himself when he saw Jim leap to his feet and race to the house, no doubt to tell his father of the rider who was approaching their cottage. A few moments later Luke appeared in the doorway and leaned against the doorpost. It was a truculent pose. Did this man know something about the happenings at Hawkshead Manor? It was a natural query for Julian whose mind was occupied by recent events. His eyes narrowed. He must get to the bottom of the whole affair. Had his successful return to smuggling given Luke a secret ambition to take over? Julian firmed his resolve to tackle this man head-on.

When he pulled his horse to a halt, Luke straightened up and came over to him. Jim had already come to the horse's head. Taking it, he led it to the drinking trough.

'I'm pleased to see you,' said Luke. He fell into step beside Julian to move out of earshot of his son. 'I reckon it's time for some more contraband.'

'I know it is but other things have occupied my mind.' The snap in Julian's voice took Luke by surprise. Before he could say anything Julian plunged on. 'What do you know of John Mason's death?' The question came straight and sharp as an arrow.

Luke stopped and faced Julian angrily. 'That sounds like an accusation!'

'What do you know about it?'

'Who the devil's John Mason?'

Julian gave a grunt of derision. 'Don't come the innocent with me. You know full well who he is. Or rather was.'

Luke's lips tightened. His eyes narrowed. He glared at Julian. 'Get it into your head, I've never heard of him. Got that?'

'He lived at Hawkshead Manor just south of Whitby. He was murdered by someone, possibly two people. And I think you instigated the killing.'

'Damn you! Didn't you hear me? I don't know the man. Never heard of Hawkshead Manor. Now what the devil is this all about?'

'John Mason was the head of the Whitby smugglers.'

'What?' Luke gasped.

If the surprise on his face wasn't genuine then Julian realised he must be a good actor, and he didn't believe that was in Luke's capabilities. Yet one never knew the hidden depths or talents of another human being.

'He was head of the Whitby smugglers.' Julian repeated his statement, watching intently to try to discover the truth behind the man's denial.

'How do you know?' asked Luke suspiciously.

'Never mind. The thing is that I do know.'

'And you suspect, because I took revenge on the Wharton gang, that I instigated this murder to move in on Whitby?'

'Well, after your raid on Sandsend...'

Julian's knowledge of this took Luke by surprise and he interrupted with an automatic, 'You knew about it?'

'I heard about it at the same time as I learned of John Mason's death. When I was told the time of that raid, I realised it corresponded with the day I saw a sloop leaving Hull with more men on board than is usual, and among those men two who normally run with your smugglers.'

Luke's lips tightened. There was no use denying the raid. Julian seemed so certain of these facts. 'All right, I'll admit I planned that raid, but I know nothing of Mason's killing.' He emphasised this denial again.

Julian was still not sure about Luke's innocence in the affair. If he was aiming to take over the Whitby territory the killing seemed to follow naturally from the unsuccessful raid, but he had to take this denial at face value.

'All right, Luke, but let's get this straight. We have a good working partnership which would not have come into being but for me. I know you would never have taken up smuggling again if I hadn't proposed it. That makes me the head of the whole organisation. That I allowed you to

478

take charge of the receipt and disposal of the contraband does not mean you may do exactly as you want. I tolerated the events at Owthorn but I warned you then: no more killing. And that included no fighting to expand beyond the territory we already had.'

'You've done well enough out of it,' snapped Luke. 'And we can do better now that the Whitby smugglers have lost their leader.'

'No! You forget Whitby!' Luke was startled by the anger that flared in Julian. 'You forget that idea. Others will take Mason's place.'

'You seem very well informed,' said Luke suspiciously.

'I am,' rapped Julian. 'There must be no movement against the Whitby gang. That's an order, Luke, and don't you forget it. Step out of line on this and you lose me. That would cripple our operation because I'm vital to it. You need me just as I need you. I can destroy everything. I have connections on the Continent that you would never get.'

'Don't you be so sure.'

Julian gave a little laugh. 'Oh, I'm sure, Luke, I'm very sure. You see, you would have no credibility after I'd spread word you could not be trusted. So forget Whitby. Forget it!' He glared at Luke for a moment, imposing his will on the man. 'Now,' he added as he relaxed in the knowledge that he had made the situation clear and thereby eased any danger that might have threatened Anna and Charles, 'let us get down to business and what you require on the next run.'

Luke nodded. He had never expected Julian

Kirby to have the courage to stand up to him this way. But Julian was right: they had a good organisation. It would be a pity to undermine it. 'All right,' he said, 'but let's get this straight too. I know nothing about John Mason's killing!'

Julian had much to think about as he rode back to Hull. Could he be absolutely certain that Luke was telling the truth? He had admitted to the Sandsend raid. Did that stamp his denial of the murder with the truth? If so, Anna was wrong and the murder of her father was not connected to smuggling. Julian was puzzled. Who had killed John Mason? Had it been a robbery gone wrong as Charles thought, or was there another as yet unknown motive?

Chapter Twenty-two

Sir Arthur Foston tapped the table to bring the members of the syndicate to silence in the dining room of Hawkshead Manor. 'Miss Anna ... gentlemen. I asked our hostess if the start of our meal could be delayed a few minutes while I said a few words.' He glanced around him. 'That is why you see no servants at the moment.' He cleared his throat. 'I am pleased, as no doubt you all are, that Charles and Anna are retaining their father's interest in our venture. You have voiced to me a variety of opinions about the future. I said nothing in reply, knowing that Charles and Anna intended to hold this meeting and it was here that I should tell you what I know.

'John must have seen the danger to him intensifying or perhaps had a premonition because it was not long ago that he asked me to see that the syndicate kept intact and continued to operate if anything happened to him. Though we know that smuggling is an illegal trade, John, like the rest of us, saw the benefit in cheap goods and that it was important to the local economy.

'He also requested me to leave Charles in charge, in the same capacity as John was himself. I am perfectly happy for that to be the case. Charles has worked alongside his father ever since the inception of the Whitby gang and knows the operation inside out. So, gentlemen, I see no reason to alter the status quo.' He cast a swift glance of enquiry around the table.

There were murmurs of agreement from everyone.

Sir Arthur turned to Charles. 'We all hope you will take your father's place.'

He stood up. 'Gentlemen, I am honoured that you should approve the wishes of my father. I know that is what he wanted, but if you had thought otherwise I would have abided by your decision. I thank you for your confidence, one which no doubt extends through me to Anna.' There was an immediate outcry of agreement. Charles looked down the table at his sister and smiled.

When the voices, clapping and tapping on the table died down, Anna said, 'Thank you, gentlemen. I will see that I fill the role my father would have wished. So first let me assure you that these meetings will go on as before. Now, if there is nothing else to be said immediately I think we should leave the usual topics for discussion until later and enjoy our meal first.'

When everyone agreed, Anna rose from her chair and went to the door which gave on to a corridor leading to the kitchens. A few minutes later she returned followed by the maids and two man servants carrying large tureens. Dinner was soon underway.

Conversation flowed, banter was swift, laughter spontaneous. At one point Anna sat back in her chair and surveyed the company. She was pleased that they all seemed in a pleasant frame of mind and were enjoying themselves. When she and

Charles had talked of holding this meeting, knowing that they must do so, she had feared that in the light of her father's death it might be a gloomy gathering, but it seemed that everyone had realised that the atmosphere tonight should be as John would have wished it. She was suddenly overwhelmed with nostalgia and wished her father was with them. Her throat tightened. Tears rose to her eyes. She forced them back. She must not give way. That would be betraying her father. She straightened her back and reached for her glass of wine.

After the last of the syndicate had gone Anna and Charles took a few minutes of relaxation in the drawing room.

'That went very well, Anna,' said Charles. 'Thank you for all you did.'

She gave a smile. 'It was nothing. I merely kept in mind what Father would have wished.'

'He certainly would have approved.'

'In view of everyone's desire for more contraband, when will you go to Amsterdam?'

'Next week.'

'You remember Nick and Ralph reporting someone questioning them in Amsterdam, and that whoever it was referred to a Hull ship?'

Charles nodded. 'Yes.'

'Will you try and follow that up? There might be some connection with the Uptons. Information being passed that might link them to Father's murder.'

'I still think you are being fanciful.'

'You never know. The murder could have been

instigated in Amsterdam and the Uptons in someone's pay.'

'Who in Amsterdam would want Father dead? He had no enemies who...' Charles's words abruptly ceased. It looked as if he was remembering something.

Anna was quick to notice. 'What is it, Charles?' she demanded, eagerly anticipating some revelation that would prove she was right.

'Nothing.' He gave a slight shake of his head as if dismissing his own thoughts.

'Charles!'

'It was nothing.'

'We're partners, Charles. I want to know!'

He hesitated a moment longer, debating whether it was wise to tell her. Then he saw the determined look in her eyes and knew she would not be fobbed off. 'Father told me that Herr Hendrick put him in touch with the Pawl brothers for tobacco and porcelain in Amsterdam. They are not the most savoury of characters and he indicated they could be dangerous, if crossed.'

'Do you think he did?' asked Anna with some alarm.

Charles shrugged his shoulders. 'I've no reason to believe he did, but who can tell?'

'I still think his murder is linked to smuggling. You must see if you can find anything out when you are in Amsterdam.' She saw doubt in him. 'Charles, please?'

'All right, Anna, for you.'

As he sailed for Amsterdam the following week, Charles's thoughts were occupied by Anna's obsessional belief that their father had died thanks to his smuggling role. He expected the enquiries he would make for her would disprove her theory and that would be a good thing even though it would bring them no nearer to the true perpetrator of the crime. Common thieves would be hard to find.

Once he had settled in with the Heins, who were shattered by the disclosure of his father's murder, he made his way to the de Klerk home. Joy to see him turned to shock and sadness at his news. After a few minutes' explanation of what had happened, Hendrick decided that Charles's mind would be better occupied with business. When Katharina had left to inform the kitchen that there would be one more for the evening meal, Magdalena rose to leave the two men to their discussions but Charles stopped her.

'Please stay,' he said. 'There is something you might be able to help me with. Anna has an idea that Father's murder was due to his smuggling activities. Herr de Klerk, you put him in touch with the Pawl brothers.'

'I knew them as men who could supply him with what he wanted. I've had no personal dealings with them, they have an evil reputation if crossed. Have you any reason to think that your father did so?'

'None.'

'They can be ruthless,' put in Magdalena, 'but there was a rumour recently among the suppliers of contraband that the Pawls had made a very good deal. If they were satisfied they would have had no reason for wanting your father dead.'

Charles told them of the report brought back by Nick and Ralph. He described the man making enquiries of them and his interest in a ship from Hull that was there at the same time. Hendrick gave an amused laugh and exchanged a knowing glance with his daughter.

'Sounds like Coenraad Bremer.'

Magdalena's agreement was accompanied by a smile. 'Unpleasant man, nothing like his father. I don't see him as being behind any murder though, he hasn't brains to organise it from here and he certainly wouldn't do it himself. Besides he hasn't had any dealings with you or your father, has he?'

Charles shook his head. 'No. If he was the person, what could be his purpose?'

'Coenraad doesn't like the de Klerks,' explained Hendrick. 'My sons always outshone him at school, better academically, better at sailing, skating, oh – everything. He was jealous, and ever since then has tried to outwit Leonaaert and Reynier, especially Reynier. If there was anything he could do to get him into trouble, Coenraad would do it.'

'I know Reynier is now smuggling, a newish venture for him, but he never says who with,' said Magdalena. 'If Coenraad suspected this he'd nose around. If he found the slenderest thread to go on, he'd report it to the authorities hoping they'd follow it up and catch Reynier. But as for anything more than that, such as your father's murder, he wouldn't get involved.'

'I agree with Magdalena,' said Hendrick. 'When Coenraad was making those enquiries he'd be hoping to implicate Reynier in some illicit trading, nothing more.'

Charles had listened intently. He knew the de Klerks to be shrewd judges and he valued their opinion. He was satisfied now that his father's murder had not been instigated in Holland.

Anna's hopes that Charles would return with evidence that would implicate the Uptons were dashed. The fact that Herr de Klerk and Magdalena had promised to listen to talk among Amsterdam merchants, especially those known to supply contraband to English ships, did little to cheer her. The violence of her father's death shadowed her mind.

'Don't look so glum, Anna,' Charles commiserated. 'You are going to have to accept the fact that we are not likely to discover who killed Father. He would not want you to become obsessed with it. You can't let it dominate your life. Besides you have Julian to consider. You can't drag him into this sort of thing.'

Anna made no comment. Maybe Charles was right.

During the succeeding weeks there was much to occupy her. Apart from the domestic side of running Hawkshead Manor, with the capable help of Mrs Denston and the support of all the servants, she threw herself into helping her brother with the estate, the merchant business and the smuggling.

Life settled into a pattern. Her birthday came and passed quietly though it stirred deep memories of her parents. She wondered what surprise her father had had in store for her. It must have been a close-kept secret because Charles knew nothing about it. Now she would never know what it was.

With the help of the efficient and trusted Gideon, Charles involved Anna more and more in the trading enterprise built on solid foundations by their father. She became a familiar figure in Whitby especially on the east quays where the Mason ships tied up, and people were pleased to see that the daughter of John Mason had accepted her loss. They were not to know how much she ached inside and still nurtured the idea that one day she would avenge him.

Her active involvement in the business raised a few eyebrows. Most of the men soon got used to the idea and, seeing her shrewdness and ability, welcomed her into what was usually regarded as a male pursuit. Others proclaimed that it was not a woman's place and that she should remain at home doing the things a young lady was expected to do. Anna took no notice of their snide remarks made in her presence and put it down to ignorance, blinkered foresight and refusal to see that there were, and always had been, 'women before their time' who were willing to step outside convention and make their mark on the community.

She found involvement in the legitimate trading interesting but the smuggling activities were much more exciting. She delighted in outwitting the Preventive Men and seeing smuggling runs carried out successfully. On the three runs in the next month she and Charles were alert to any possible interference by the Uptons. When none was forthcoming they concluded that the rival gang, realising that the Whitby smugglers were still operating and remembering the opposition they had met at Sandsend, were no longer eyeing their territory. But Anna privately wondered if they were lying low because they were involved in her father's death. She still held on to the idea that one day she would find out.

This hope burned brighter when Julian, on a visit to Hawkshead Manor, asked her if she had managed to unearth any leads. Admitting that she hadn't disturbed her, and she saw that, as time went on, the chances of doing so would fade along with her own desire. She resolved to take the action she had suggested to Charles – lure the Uptons to Hawkshead and accuse them face to face. Knowing he would not approve this plan she realised she must time it for a period when he was in Amsterdam.

Leaning on the rail, Julian watched the English shoreline fade into the distance. His thoughts were on his recent visit to see Anna and he was pleased with her agreement that when he returned they would announce their love and desire for marriage to his parents. His mind turned to smuggling and the fact that he had almost disclosed his own involvement to her, but when she still voiced suspicions of the Uptons he had kept quiet. Though he had outwardly accepted Luke's statement, there was still a lingering doubt in him about the truth of the man's denial. He wished there was something he could do to solve the mystery and ease all their minds.

He took his room with the Heins. The following day he ordered a large shipment of wine from Herr Bremer and then called on the de Klerks. Hendrick welcomed him and, with Reynier expected to return to his desk in half an hour, offered him a glass of wine and settled down to hear the news from England.

With Anna's agreement that their engagement should be announced on his return, Julian saw no reason to withhold this news from the de Klerks, such good friends of the Masons.

Hendrick expressed his delight and added. 'It is a pity her father wasn't here to share in her happiness. By the way, did Anna get her necklace? I'd been meaning to ask Charles when he was here but something always got in the way and I never got around to asking him. Maybe you know, being close to her.'

'Necklace?' Julian looked mystified.

'Yes. John bought it for her at an auction in Amsterdam. A ring too. He was keeping them for her birthday when they were to be a special surprise for her.'

'I know nothing about it. I'm sure Anna would have mentioned it.'

Hendrick looked a little concerned. 'I know the gift had special significance for him. It was not only to be a sign of his appreciation for all she had done for him but also to indicate that he was resuming his interest in his collection, something he had cast aside on his wife's death. Could the gift have been stolen in the robbery?'

'If it were to be kept secret until Anna's birthday, he wouldn't have put it in the display

490

cabinets and nothing appears to have been taken from elsewhere.'

'I would suggest you pass this information on to Anna so that she can make a thorough search for it. Those are valuable pieces.'

'I certainly I will. Did you see them?'

'Oh, yes. I brought the sale to his notice and was at the auction with him. The necklace especially was a delicate work of fine craftsmanship. That's when John met that young fellow, Lambert Finch. He too wanted the necklace but John was a crafty old bird in the auction room and judged from Lambert's attitude when he was going to drop out and outbid him.'

'I knew Mr Mason had met Lambert in Holland. I didn't know that they had been rivals for the same jewellery. Of course not. If I had then I would have known about the necklace. John must have sworn everyone to secrecy.'

'He did. We were careful not to let anything slip when we were over for the party in February.'

'Did you speak to Lambert at the auction?' Julian's curiosity had been roused by this unexpected information.

'Oh, yes. He was waiting to have a word with us when we left the room. He was charm itself in defeat.'

'Had he a special interest in the necklace?'

'Yes. Apparently he was almost certain it was one which had been stolen when in the possession of one of his ancestors. He said he had never seen it and was only going by the description given by his grandparents and father whenever the story arose. He must have been pretty certain of its

491

authenticity, though, because he tried to buy it from Mr Mason but John had set his heart on it for Anna, so refused.'

'How did Lambert take that?'

'Like a gentleman. He was so understanding and charming, and when he revealed that he had an interest in art Mr Mason invited him to see the collection at Hawkshead and suggested he come to the party in February.'

Julian was becoming more and more intrigued.

On the return voyage he had much to think about. If Luke Upton was telling the truth, was it possible that, in his desire to have the necklace, Lambert could have arranged a robbery? If that was so, what about the murder? Surely he couldn't have intended that to happen? But how to prove Lambert's involvement, if indeed it was true? Julian tossed the possibilities over and over in his mind but could not come up with a solution. Maybe the only way was to confront him face to face, but would that elicit the truth? He was no nearer a decision about what to do when the ship docked in Hull.

With plenty of daylight still left he decided to ride out to see Luke Upton and inform him about the next shipment of contraband. Accordingly he hired a horse and was soon riding at a brisk pace alongside the Humber.

Luke had known when Julian would be returning from Amsterdam but had not expected a visit from him until the next day. 'I'm glad you saw fit to come straight here,' he said with some relief in his voice as Julian halted his horse in front of the cottage.

'Something troubling you?' Julian asked.

'I have a note here, addressed to me, but it's really for you.'

Julian was curious as he took the envelope from Luke. He pulled out a sheet of paper, unfolded it and gave the writing a quick glance. His mind reeled. He read the note more carefully.

Hawkshead Manor
Near Whitby

To the Upton Brothers.

You won't know me but you may have known of my father, Mr John Mason of Whitby, chief of the Whitby smugglers.

Since his recent death my brother and I have taken his place. We know of your interests along the Humber and of your taking over the Holderness coast. We think it would be advantageous if we amalgamated our organisations and ran one smuggling enterprise. We would control a large slice of smuggling along the Yorkshire coast and could become strong enough eventually to control it all.

If you are interested in this proposition I suggest a meeting with your leader at Hawkshead Manor three days after receiving this note at two o'clock in the afternoon.

Give your answer to the bearer of this note. He does not know its contents so a simple yes or no will suffice.

Anna Mason

Julian stared at the letter, his mind in turmoil, but he did manage to ask, 'Who brought this note?'

'A groom from Hawkshead.'

'How did he find you?'

'Seems he rode into Hull. His enquiries as to the whereabouts of the Uptons took him to Bill Grimes who brought him to me because you were away.'

Julian nodded. What was Anna up to? If she still harboured suspicions that the Uptons were connected with the murder did she not realise that she could be courting danger in soliciting such a meeting? She obviously had a plan to elicit information from them but if Luke were telling the truth she would learn nothing.

'What was your reply?'

'I said yes. It's an interesting proposition. I thought you'd want to go.'

'Do you favour an amalgamation?'

'First of all, I believe this offer proves I had nothing to do with John Mason's death. His daughter would not consider joining up with us if she harboured any suspicions we were concerned in her father's murder.'

Julian raised his hands in acceptance of Luke's reasoning and as an apology for suspecting him. 'So what do you really think of her proposal?'

'It could be a good idea. But you must see what her conditions are before deciding. We don't want to be at a disadvantage. We want equal shares in everything – the running of all smuggling activities and the profits.' Luke frowned. 'I'm not

494

sure about having a woman involved, especially if she wants to run the organisation. You'll have to tread carefully. If she has any charm, don't let her use it on you.'

She's already done that, thought Julian to himself with a half-smile, but what he said was, 'I'll not let that happen. Our operation is nicely established and I don't want anything to upset that.'

'See it doesn't.'

'When did you get this note?'

'Yesterday.'

'Then I shall have to be there the day after tomorrow.'

Chapter Twenty-three

Anna looked at the clock on the mantelpiece of the drawing room. Its ticking had beaten the passage of time into her mind for the last hour. With each stroke came a tightening of her chest. Her heart had throbbed a little harder as she reviewed the events since her mother's death. The distress that had followed the fatal riding accident, John's descent into near-oblivion, the shock of discovering that her father and brother were notorious smugglers and had the approval of many of the local gentry and men of influence, her initial jealously of Charles's association with Julian Kirby, that strange visit by Bill Grimes and his association with Julian which still remained a mystery, the conflict with the gang run by the Upton brothers, and last but by no means least her father's murder and her difference of opinion over it with Charles.

Now, with her brother in Amsterdam, she hoped she would solve the mystery of John's death and gain vindication of her own opinion. She knew her plan courted danger but would not be afraid to face that.

The clock said it was twenty minutes to two. Anna rose from her chair. She could see the approach to the house better from her bedroom and wanted to get a glimpse of Upton before she came face to face with him. A little of the disadvantage she was beginning to feel as a woman about to confront a notorious smuggler would be dispelled.

She left the room, crossed the hall and started up the stairs. Her legs felt leaden. Had she once run up these stairs in high spirits without a care in the world, with her future so bright in the care of her wonderful parents? All that had been snatched from her by tragedies, and these same stairs had seen the broken bodies of her parents carried up them only to return in coffins.

She reached the landing, paused with her hand on the oak railing and looked down into the hall. She was beginning to wish she had Charles here. But he would have vetoed this meeting. She had realised she would have to engineer this contact when her brother was in Amsterdam. Now the moment would soon be upon her when she would make accusations she hoped would cause Upton to betray his complicity in the murder. She took a deep breath, stiffened her posture, moved briskly to her room.

She took a seat by the open glass doors that led on to a balcony on the south side of her turret bedroom. From here she could see the driveway along which Upton would approach the house. The day had been exceptionally warm for the time of the year and Anna was thankful for the cool breeze.

Today the trees and the valley were at peace. Only the faintest of breezes rustled the tops of the trees. This was God's country. Days like this she had loved to share with her mother when the world seemed only theirs and there was nothing to shatter the tranquillity. She sighed. Within a few minutes this world would be churning with the turmoil of accusation, condemnation, maybe violence. The risks she was running began to weigh on her mind. She had not prepared herself adequately for violence. She had pushed that possibility to the back of her mind while concentrating on what she would say to Upton and how she would say it. Should she start off with the proposal of amalgamation, the false premise she had used to lure him here, or should she move boldly in with her accusation, hoping that the shock of it would bring an automatic reaction to betray him? Or should she... She pulled herself up sharply. This was no way to be thinking when a reckoning was near. Calm yourself. You must not let him see your anxiety, she told herself.

She stiffened and inclined her head, straining to hear what she thought was a telltale sound. Yes! A horse. She stood up and positioned herself so she could see without being seen. The trees at the curve of the drive hid the rider. The rhythmic sound became clearer. Her heart began to race. The rider came into view.

For a moment Anna felt no reaction, then a mixture of anger, despair and futility rose in her. What on earth was he doing here? No invitation had been issued. Why should he come un-expectedly, on this day of all days? At any other time she would have been delighted to see Julian, but not today. His presence could ruin every-thing. She had intimated in her letter that she expected the leader of the Upton gang to come to

Hawkshead Manor. He could legitimately expect that their meeting would be devoid of witnesses. Somehow she must get rid of Julian as quickly as possible. Upton would be arriving in a few minutes.

She watched him from her room. Any other time she would have been racing down the stairs to meet him but now her mind, while admiring him, was struggling to decide how to get him out of the way. She had not reached a decision when she left the room to meet him. She opened the front door as he was coming up the steps.

'Anna!' He held out his hands to take hers. As their fingers met he drew her to him and kissed her.

She felt this to be more than a greeting. It was as if he was here for a purpose and wanted to reassure her that his arrival meant her no harm nor brought bad news.

'This is unexpected,' she said, turning with him to enter the house.

As they crossed the hall he said, 'I hope you will forgive me for dropping in unexpectedly but I had business in the area and so decided to call on you.'

They entered the drawing room. 'It is good to see you, Julian, but it is a little inconvenient. I am expecting a visitor.'

He smiled to himself when he noted the agitation in her voice. 'I'll leave when she comes.'

Anna just stopped herself in time from revealing that the 'she' was in fact a he. That would have made Julian more than curious. 'I'd rather you called back when you have finished

499

your business. Will you stay the night or must you get back to Hull?' She glanced anxiously at the clock. Two minutes before two. Now she was beginning to hope that Upton would be late.

Julian also glanced at the clock. 'Oh, I have time, I haven't far to go. And, yes, I would love to stay the night. It will give us longer to talk.'

She nodded, only half hearing his words, yet wondering what lay behind the statement that it would give them longer to talk. She didn't want to ask him what he meant as an explanation would only delay his leaving.

'Very well, I'll expect you later.' She turned towards the door as if to escort him from the room. He did not move.

'Plenty of time. I haven't far to go,' he said casually. Anna was irritated. 'I shall have to ask you to leave.' The clock struck two.

'Two o'clock,' he remarked lightly.

'Please, Julian, I am expecting this person at two.'

'And *my* appointment is for two.'

'Then you will be late.'

'No. I'm exactly on time.'

'How can you be if you are here?'

'I said I hadn't far to go.'

'But I hadn't...'

'Your appointment was with one of the Uptons.'

Anna's eyes widened. 'How did you know?'

For the moment he offered no explanation but said, 'In fact you asked their leader to come here.'

His knowledge made her gasp.

'It's two o'clock, Anna. You asked me to be here

500

at two o'clock?'

'I didn't...'

Even as she was making the denial the words faded on her lips. The meaning behind his statement bit deep into her mind. She was dumbfounded. Then words came in an incredulous whisper: 'You, Julian? You are the leader of the Upton gang?'

Her eyes widened in astonishment then hatred.

'Then you planned everything, Holderness was not the Uptons' idea, but yours. The raid on Sandsend was *your* idea, trying to take over our territory. And when that didn't succeed you had my father murdered and made it look like a common robbery. And you accepted our hospitality! You played the pleasant young man to gain Father's confidence and mine, and made a friend of Charles, no doubt hoping all the time to gain information about our activities. You were planning to take over all that Father had built up. I always said the murder was smuggling-related and I was right, but I never expected to find that *you* were behind it. Well, now I know who to report to the authorities.'

With every word hatred burned brighter in her eyes. She felt nothing but loathing for him now. She chided herself for being so gullible and swore that she would bring him to justice.

Her words battered him. Her accusations hurt. The look in her eyes devastated him. He needed to retaliate, to make her know and believe the truth. 'Anna!' His voice was sharp and loud to storm the defences she had raised. 'Yes, I am the leader of the Upton gang, but the rest is not true.'

She swung away from him. 'Don't deny it. Don't disgust me any further.' Her whole being blazed with fury.

He met it with equal ferocity. 'It's only your imagination that linked the Uptons with your father's murder. You seized on a possibility as if it were the truth but you have no proof at all. I suppose you hoped that by confronting Luke Upton you would get an admission, or at least a reaction, that would confirm your theory? But you could never prove it because it is not true.'

'You are bound to deny it!' Her face had paled with the intensity of her feelings and it heightened the darkness that beset her eyes.

'I'll deny it because we had nothing to do with your father's killing.' Julian's lips were thin with fury. He could not bear to see such distrust.

'That stemmed from the Sandsend raid. And *you* instigated that.'

'I didn't. The Uptons acted without my knowledge. And your father's death did not stem from that raid, Luke Upton has assured me of that.'

'And you believe him?' Her laughter was charged with revulsion.

'Yes. Would I be here now admitting that I am the leader of the Upton gang if I were involved or didn't believe him?'

'Well, what are you here for?'

'I'm intrigued by your suggestion of amalgamation – or was that merely bait to orchestrate a meeting at which you would make your accusation? It might make sense as you and I have already planned a future.'

'A future together?' she sneered. 'You still think

that I...'

'Yes, if you will listen to the truth!' he interrupted harshly.

'The truth! How do I know you'll tell me that after the way you have deceived me?'

'Will you just listen?' His exasperation was on the point of boiling over and if that happened there was no telling what the consequences might be.

Anna strode to the window and stood with her back to him. 'Get on with it,' she snapped over her shoulder.

Julian glanced at the clock. 'I haven't time now. I have another appointment.'

'What?' She swung round, her eyes on fire. 'You tell me to listen, I say I will, and then you tell me you haven't time? What do you want? I'll tell you – you're making an excuse to wriggle out of the situation because you know I am right.'

'You are wrong and I have an appointment here and now.' He deliberately emphasised every word so she could not mistake their meaning.

'What? Here?' Anna was mystified. 'Who with?'

'You'll see at quarter past two. I arranged our meeting for that time.'

Anna paced the room, her thoughts in turmoil. The man she was supposed to be marrying was a self-confessed smuggler. He had kept that secret from her even after she had admitted that the Masons followed the same trade. Secretive Julian who, when he was a guest in this house, gave her no information about his mysterious caller, Bill Grimes. Had she sensed something then that made her suspect Julian Kirby was not all he

503

seemed? Did he know more about her father's murder than he was making out? Was he protecting the Uptons or had he been telling the truth when he said they had nothing to do with it? Would the man she was betrothed to lie to her?

A bell rang in the depths of the house. She started and glanced at Julian. Outwardly he seemed calm but she sensed the tension heighten in him. He met her eyes but said nothing. They heard a maid's footsteps cross the hall. A door opened. A voice spoke, but the words were not audible. Footsteps. A tap on the drawing room door. The maid stepped in.

'Mr Lambert Finch to see Mr Julian Kirby.'

Startled by the name of this unexpected visitor Anna hesitated and glanced at Julian who gave a little nod.

'Please show him in,' said Anna.

When the maid had gone, she looked askance at Julian.

'Patience, Anna,' he whispered.

The door opened and Lambert came in. A slight hesitation came into his step, as if he was confronted by the unexpected, then he moved in his usual easy stride towards them.

The momentary surprise in his eyes made Anna wonder if he had expected her not to be there. There was no sign of that as he addressed her. 'My dear Anna.' He took her proffered hand and raised it to his lips. His eyes met hers and he realised that she did not know what lay behind his summons by Julian to Hawkshead Manor.

He straightened and turned to Julian. 'My dear fellow.' He held out his hand and Julian took it.

Warnings sounded in Lambert's mind when there was no warmth in Julian's touch, and he sensed hostility. Why this unusual request to meet him at Hawkshead Manor? 'I was mystified by your note asking me to meet you here, especially as you stipulated a particular time most emphatically.'

'The timing was essential. I did not want you arriving before me as I wanted words with Anna before you came. And it had to be today because this was the day she had summoned me to Hawkshead Manor, though she did not know it would actually be me until I arrived and was able to explain why I had come instead of the person she expected. And as you probably realised from Anna's reaction when she saw you, you weren't expected either.'

'You talk in riddles, sir. Please be more specific in telling me the reason why you wanted me here.' Irritation laced Lambert's voice.

'I must indulge your patience a little longer,' Julian replied. 'You will remember that Anna suggested her father's murder was related to his smuggling activities?'

'I do indeed. Have you found something out?'

Julian ignored the question. 'She mentioned the Uptons.' Lambert nodded. 'Well, Anna took things into her own hands and with Charles away in Amsterdam made a tempting offer to the leader of the Uptons in order to lure him here. What she was going to do then I have no idea but she succeeded in getting him here.'

Lambert looked bewildered. 'Well, where is he?'

'He arrived at the appointed time, two o'clock. Fifteen minutes before you. As I said, I wanted time to explain a few things to her.'

Lambert's sharp mind was not slow to realise the implication behind these words. 'You!' he gasped. '*You* are the head of the Upton gang!'

'Yes.'

'Then you are responsible for Mr Mason's murder!' His words were accusing and obviously stemmed from a desire to protect Anna from the consequences of this discovery.

Julian shook his head slowly. 'You've got it wrong. The Uptons had nothing to do with Mr Mason's murder.'

'How the hell can you be so sure?' Lambert's temper was rising.

'I know them, and they know the consequences if I ever found out that they were,' replied Julian firmly. 'No, Lambert, it wasn't them.' He had known all along that he had no evidence against Lambert and was relying on shock tactics. He saw that the other man was getting more and more irritated. Now might be the time to strike. 'But what of the necklace?'

'Necklace?' Even though he manufactured a puzzled look, Julian could tell that Lambert knew what he meant.

'Don't play the innocent with me, Lambert. You know what I am talking about. A necklace and ring for sale in an auction in Holland where Mr Mason outbid you.'

'A necklace my father bought in Holland?' Anna's tone cast doubt on the veracity of Julian's statement. Her father had never told her of such objects, nor even talked of attending an auction. Besides he had shown no inclination to renew his interest in such things.

'Yes. Your father bought them especially for you.'

'He never mentioned it to me,' she pointed out.

'They were to be a special surprise for you on your birthday. Only three people knew this: your father, Herr de Klerk who was with him at the auction, and this rogue here, Lambert Finch.'

'If it was such a secret, how do you know all this?' demanded Anna.

'When I was last in Amsterdam Herr de Klerk asked me if you had ever received your necklace. I knew nothing about it. He could see I was mystified so told me the whole story. It seems to me that Lambert coveted the jewels so much he was prepared to murder for them.'

'Wrong again,' fumed Lambert, his face a mask of anger.

'I think not.' Julian's retort was sharp and dismissive of his protest.

Malevolence filled Lambert's eyes at Julian's remark for it accused him of being complicit in murder. 'If you won't hear me out, Anna will.'

'And you'll tell her another pack of lies.'

Lambert bristled. 'No one calls me a liar and gets away with it.' There was menace in his words and movement.

'Stop it, you two!' Anna snapped angrily. 'Arguing gets us nowhere.' She glared at Julian. 'You are by no means without fault. You have kept information from me. Now I need to hear what Lambert has to say.'

Julian's lips tightened. His eyes smouldered at the rebuke but he knew if he wanted to keep Anna's love he had to comply. He agreed reluctantly. 'Very well, but listen with caution.'

Lambert curbed his enmity towards Julian. He too knew that he could do nothing else but agree to speak. His mind toyed with the possibility of, lying his way out of his dilemma but he immediately dismissed this as futile. He must hold nothing back and rely on Anna's understanding and mercy. He took a grip on his feelings.

'Thank you, Anna.' He was gracious. He had to be. 'It is true that I coveted the necklace. I had a special reason for wanting it.'

She listened carefully to his explanation, ignoring the grunts of disbelief and derision that kept coming from Julian.

'The blow of not buying the necklace was too much. I had got on well with your father and admired him, so when he invited me to come to the February party I accepted out of interest in his collection. I also hoped to find out where he kept the necklace, but your father was keeping that a close secret.

'I admit to being obsessed with owning it, so I employed two men to commit robbery. That was all they were intended to do. They were to keep watch on this house and move at an opportune time. Believe me, I had no intention of having your father killed. But he must have disturbed them. The result you know.'

'Only too well.' Anna glared at him with disgust and loathing.

'It wasn't meant to happen. They did not know

508

they had killed him.'

'So where are they?' cut in Julian.

'I don't know. They have disappeared.'

'A likely story,' mocked Julian.

'It's the truth.'

'I believe him,' said Anna, heading off Julian's hostility.

He gave a little snort of disgust. 'I suppose there's no hope of finding them?'

'I don't know where they came from or where they have gone.' Lambert saw that neither of them believed him but there was no more he could tell them. They would have to let the matter rest there.

'In that case,' said Julian sharply, 'you will have to take the full blame and I'll make sure the authorities have no mercy.'

'Where is your evidence?' said Lambert. The calmness in his voice warned them that he knew he had the upper hand.

'You've admitted your involvement,' started Julian, only to be interrupted with harsh triumph by Lambert.

'You can't use that! You've admitted *your* involvement in smuggling – wouldn't the authorities like to get their hands on the leader of the Upton gang?'

'Julian,' cut in Anna, her tone sharp but with no real threat in it as she went on, 'Lambert is right. He knows about you and we have no evidence against him. Bring him before the law and he'll deny everything. He'll denounce you and you'll be arrested.'

'But...'

'There is nothing more to be said.' She turned to Lambert. 'I accept your explanation but I am shocked that you should ever have thought of robbing Father after the kindness he showed you. Tell me one thing, Lambert. Did you hope to get the necklace by marrying me?'

He did not reply. He turned and walked briskly from the room. Julian started after him but Anna placed a restraining hand on his arm.

'No, Julian. There is nothing to be gained by detaining him. Just think of all the upheaval if we bring him before the authorities without proof. And it won't bring Father back. We'll hear no more from him. Let him go.'

Resigned to her request, he turned to her. 'As you wish.' He held out his hands to her. 'What of us?' Anna saw his eyes pleading for their love to continue as it was. 'I'm sorry for all my harsh words.'

She took his hands in hers. 'So am I. Forgive me?'

'There is nothing to forgive. Your reactions were understandable.'

'So were yours.' She kissed him on the lips.

'I love you so much,' he said, looking deep into her eyes.

'And I you,' she said as she held his gaze with an equal love. 'We have one amalgamation arranged. I think we had better implement the other too.'

He took her in his arms and held her tight.

'What of the necklace?' he whispered.

'We'll find it together and I'll wear it as Father would have wished.'

The publishers hope that this book has given you enjoyable reading. Large Print Books are especially designed to be as easy to see and hold as possible. If you wish a complete list of our books please ask at your local library or write directly to:

Magna Large Print Books
Magna House, Long Preston,
Skipton, North Yorkshire.
BD23 4ND

This Large Print Book for the partially sighted, who cannot read normal print, is published under the auspices of

THE ULVERSCROFT FOUNDATION